Last Curtain Call

Linda Harris Sittig

Freedom Forge Press, LLC
www.FreedomForgePress.com

Last Curtain Call

by Linda Harris Sittig

Published by Freedom Forge Press, LLC

www.FreedomForgePress.com

ISBN: 978-1-940553-06-1

This book is dedicated to brave women everywhere who courageously wage battles against injustice, and to miners all over the world who put their lives in jeopardy bringing energy to mankind.

I also want to dedicate this book to the individual miners listed at the beginning of each chapter who died in the mines of Western Maryland in the late 1800s.

Praise for *Last Curtain Call*

"Linda Sittig once again shows her mastery of cultural details in 19th century mid-Atlantic America with unforgettable characters that lead the reader to discover the true meaning of charity."

~ Gregory A. Barnes
Philadelphia Quaker author

"I love stories set in coal company towns. Every emotion seems heightened. Good, evil, hate, and love flourished in spectacular fashion in those towns because of the hard and definite class, racial, and sexual divisions. Linda Harris Sittig is a master of coal company town writing. Her characters are so real, I feel as if I could sit down and have a conversation with them. *Last Curtain Call* is the tale of Annie Charbonneau who takes on coal company officials who are quite willing to destroy anyone who would dare oppose their dictatorship, especially a woman. One of the best of this special genre. Highly recommended."

~ Homer Hickam, New York Times
Best-Selling Author, *Rocket Boys/October Sky, Carrying Albert Home*

"Linda Sittig brings the late 1800s mining era back to life with her realistic portrayal of the 1894 coal miners' strike. This historical fiction vividly tells the story through the life of an idealistic young lady named Annie Charbonneau. For those of us who live in mining communities like Western Maryland, Last Curtain Call reconnects us back to our past. A thoroughly inspiring and great read."

~ Jeffrey A. Snyder
Geologist Lead, Maryland Bureau of Mines

Table of Contents

The "Threads of Courage" Series....6
A Short Primer on Coal....7
Last Curtain Call 9
Author's Notes....290
Acknowledgements....293
Glossary....297
About The Author....302

The Continuation of the "Threads of Courage" Series

The first book in the "Threads of Courage" series was *Cut From Strong Cloth*. Inspired by the life of Ellen Canavan, the story follows Ellen's quest to become a business woman in the cut-throat textile industry of 1861 Philadelphia. Just as she is about to succeed, the Civil War erupts, and an arsonist sets out to destroy her. Through Ellen's story, readers meet Cecilia Canavan, Ellen's mother; Patrick Canavan, Ellen's brother; James Nolan, Ellen's business sponsor; Michael Brady, a would-be suitor; and Magdalena Fox, her future sister-in-law.

In this second book in the series, *Last Curtain Call*, the Canavan line continues some thirty years later with Patrick and Magdalena's children, Jonathan and Josie. They find their lives thrust into the chaos of the 1894 Western Maryland coal mining wars and the influence of a young woman, Annie Charbonneau, who will ultimately change their destinies.

This book is a work of historical fiction. Many of the names, characters, places, and incidents are the product of the author's creativity. The 1894 Coal Mining Strike of Western Maryland, however, was true.

A Short Primer on Coal

Coal is the by-product of plant fermentation that has become compressed over thousands of years. In the United States, there are two predominant forms of coal: anthracite and bituminous.

Anthracite coal is only found in six distinct counties in eastern Pennsylvania. Bituminous coal is found in and west of the Appalachian Mountains, in the steep sections of Western Maryland, western Pennsylvania, West Virginia, Kentucky, and Ohio.

Where anthracite is black, hard, and burns relatively clean—bituminous is soft, muted black in color, and burns with a lot of soot. However, bituminous coal makes for an excellent energy source and was used to fuel the ships of the U.S. Navy, and ocean liners—including the Titanic.

In their heyday, the coal companies in Western Maryland were shipping out over 8,000 tons of bituminous coal per week. Amazing, considering that a miner could dig only 4-5 tons per day by hand. In 1894, the companies decided to lower the miners' pay to 40 cents per ton, thus increasing the company's profits at the expense of the miners' take-home pay.

The United Mine Workers, still a young union, called for a massive nationwide strike to oppose the reduced wages.

Only three small communities in Western Maryland fought to retain their independence and not participate in the strike. This led to unprecedented local violence where miners on strike fought against miners who continued to work. The violence was so pervasive that it spread to even the women becoming embroiled in the conflict.

CHAPTER 1 - 1892

John Callagan, killed by fall of roof coal,
American Coal Company.

Five blasts of the coal company's steam whistle shattered the early October morning and caused a small flock of Canada geese to bolt upward into the slate-blue sky. The commotion halted seventeen-year-old Annie Charbonneau, in conversation with her younger sister Marie.

The girls had started walking to school, but now peered up at the escaping geese.

Then, without saying a word, they ran down the trampled path of Coal Bank Lane.

"Careful," Annie admonished her sister, as they dashed across the wizened planks above Squirrel Creek. The girls only stopped to catch their breath when the lane turned into a dirt road.

Up ahead lay the village of Porters Glen, where the streets were embedded with bits of coal and a black grimy dust clung to every building. Only the riotous plumes of goldenrod, growing in abandoned clumps, broke the monotonous color of coal.

Winded, the girls strode past the dimly lit saloons of Beer Alley and reached the intersection where their father's modest bakery hugged the northeast corner. Not glancing at the other weather-beaten shops lining Store Hill, they walked double-time toward Miners Row.

"No!" A woman's scream erupted up ahead and hung in the air like steam from an over boiled tea kettle.

"Come on." Annie tugged at Marie and they ran until they stumbled to a stop in front of the small whitewashed stone cottages that lined Miners Row.

Breathing hard, the girls stood frozen while the mining company's henchmen dragged Widow Klausman kicking and screaming, as her shoes clacked against the uneven oak-board walkway.

Annie and Marie backed up a pace when the coal men, dressed in faded baggy pants and well-worn canvas jackets, shoved the widow out into the dirt. Annie's eyes blazed when the men threw the widow's thread-bare carpetbags, and dented pots and pans after her, into the road.

Neighbors gathered in small groups as Widow Klausman's two children ran out of the house; but no one made eye contact. The children, dressed in hand-me-down jackets with bits of newspaper falling from the holes in their shoes, never looked back at the neighbors or at the coal men who flicked their sweat-stained brimmed caps in a gesture of finality.

Annie knew the unwritten code of Porters Glen—not to interfere with the mining company's policies. Even without the men's telltale black armbands, they were obviously an eviction crew. She shook her head at the injustice.

"Diebinnen!" Mrs. Klausman shook an angry fist at the coal police thugs.

A flush of blood-red crept up Annie's neck. *Get a hold of yourself, Mrs. Klausman. For your children's sake if not your own.*

The widow, however, had slumped to her knees on the ground, rocking back and forth and wringing her hands. The frayed hem of her woolen coat dragged in the dirt. Annie swallowed the lump of pity in her throat, watching the children cling to their mother.

Marie darted over to the sad trio. Spying trails of dried snot on their upper lips, she bent down until she was eye to eye with the chil-

dren. “Here.” She opened her school satchel. “You can at least share my sandwich.”

In an instant, one of the coal thugs seized Marie by the shoulder, digging his fingers in until she let out a cry of pain.

“Get your hands off her!” Annie flew to her sister’s side and pulled Marie away. Spittle formed in the corners of her mouth. “Don’t come near us again.”

The brute turned on Annie, lifting the baseball bat he had dropped in the road. “Interfering, eh? Pretty feisty.” He looked back at his comrades.

The lead man shook his head, and spoke in a loud voice for everyone to hear. “You were warned, Mrs. Klausman. We nailed the eviction notice on your door five days ago. You cooperate, or you leave.” He tilted his head in an almost imperceptible nod of what could have been sympathy.

Annie turned to face the other men with their beefy arms and oiled mustaches. They smirked at her and their lips curled into sneers. She could smell their power.

“Porters Glen don’t need the likes of you here.” One of them turned and spit a black stream of tobacco juice on the ground, hitting a clump of dried-up leaves near the little Klausman girl.

“My husband gave his life to that mine!” Mrs. Klausman sobbed.

The men stalked off as bits of their nasty laughter billowed out on the breeze.

One of the neighbors turned to another and said, “She should’ve just gone to the mining office and gotten the damn shoes.”

Marie shivered and whispered to Annie. “What did she mean, Annie? About shoes?”

“I don’t know.”

The girls watched as the widow got to her feet and collected her meager possessions while each child gathered one or two of the battered pots. Mrs. Klausman, with head held high but face streaked with tears, whispered to her children. The three of them turned and walked down the Pike, away from the village.

"What will she do?" Marie looked as if she might cry.

"She'll ask for shelter over in Slag Town; she doesn't have any other choice."

"Do you mean they'll have to go to the poorhouse?"

Annie let out a sigh. "At least they'll get mush and a few nights on a straw mattress; better than sleeping in the woods. Hopefully, she'll be taken in by relatives."

"It's not fair. I don't see how she deserved this. What if she doesn't have any relatives?"

"Then I don't know what she'll do."

Marie lowered her voice to a whisper. "Annie, could the coal company ever come after us?"

"No, of course not. Papa would never let that happen." Annie put her arm around Marie's trembling shoulders. "You don't have to worry about the coal company. Our family isn't tied to them and as long as Papa's store stays independent…the company has no reason to come after us."

Marie's shoulders still trembled.

"Come, on. We need to get to school. We don't want to be late and break our attendance record."

The two sisters turned away from the village and continued walking silently up the Pike toward the next town of Mount Pleasant and the newly built high school.

Annie peered at Marie, then grabbed her hand and gave it a squeeze. "Papa will always take care of us." And I would rather die than let the coal company put us through an eviction.

A few minutes later, the girls neared the big fieldstone house on Barn Hill where the superintendent of the mines lived. Two stories high with a wide, prominent front porch, it appeared to sit in judgment of the three-room company cottages and the thinly white-washed clapboards in the village down below.

Marie looked at the house. "Did you realize that Mr. Meyers' house has twenty-four lace curtained windows?"

"I know. I guess if Papa was the mining superintendent, all our windows would be lace covered, too."

Hints of an early winter appeared with a sudden stiff breeze that whistled down from the mountains and wedged itself into the crisp air. The vivid colors of the scarlet oaks, sugar maples, and beech trees had disappeared last week. Although the village residents lived under a gray cloud of coal dust nine months of the year, the surrounding mountains changed their palette with the seasons.

But today, Annie saw none of the beauty the landscape offered. She pulled up the collar of her wool cape and made sure the ribbons holding her hat were secure enough to fend off the chilly October breeze. Tying her wool scarf in a knot to secure it, she marched on toward Mount Pleasant.

CHAPTER 2

Perry Fazenbaker, killed by fall of roof coal,
Koontz Mine, newlywed.

Louis Charbonneau had risen at four o'clock, as was his custom, to enjoy a cup of *café au lait* before heading off to his shop. He stretched his arms before placing his night-stocking feet on the multi-colored rag-wool rug next to his bed, and then stood to begin his day. His routine never varied.

He smiled to himself, knowing that his two daughters were still asleep.

With high cheek bones and bisque complexions, Louis Charbonneau loved how his girls bore a strong resemblance to their French ancestors, and their older brother Stephen. Two years apart in age, Louis often marveled that his daughters differed so much from each other, in both temperament and appearance.

Annie mirrored her mother with blue eyes and toffee-brown hair. In addition, she had a stubborn streak inherited from her mother. Slender like a tom-boy, she wore her hair pulled back in a loosely tied knot on the back of her neck, and dressed in simple outfits that did not call attention to her figure. Her choice of clothes reflected her practical nature.

Marie, just fifteen, looked more like Louis with dark chocolate brown eyes and a rampage of coffee-colored curls. She wore her hair tied back with a bright scarlet ribbon matching her devil-may-care attitude. Dimples graced both sides of her mouth, and her clothes reflected the current styles displayed in the store windows of Mount Pleasant.

He sipped his coffee. How could eighteen years have passed since he and his wife left France for America? The population of Porters Glen had numbered around 800 souls when he and Thérese had arrived in the village. Most of their neighbors had hailed from Germany, Ireland, and Wales, and almost every other man was a miner. Louis had established his place in the community by opening a bakery. He had a small, but steady clientele with the townspeople; including the residents from Miners Row.

At the time, he'd known that the miners and their families lived in cramped, diminutive cottages with steep-sloped roofs and thick stone walls. Outside they had a modest yard, a privy, a coal shed, and space for a small vegetable garden.

What he had not discerned was the nameless unease that permeated the miners' lives and crept like a shroud from the mining office over to the seventy cottages of Miners Row.

Right now, the strong coffee laced with hot steaming milk was a reassuring vestige of his French upbringing and would warm him sufficiently for the ten-minute trek up to Store Hill, and his bakery.

He took as much pride in his home as he did his store. The white clapboard house, built in the pattern of four rooms down and four up, represented security and he worked diligently to pay the rent on time for both the bakery and his house.

As usual, he left at 5:00 a.m. and walked toward the village proper, where most of the shops and saloons would open their doors by nine o'clock. As he approached the bakery's front door, he paused. He sighed as he thought of his wife Thérese. It had been ten years since her death. Not a man to brood about the past, he still missed her.

Their store, a building of sensible, plain clapboard, had weathered gray with the years. It did boast a humble front entrance with two glass windows flanking the front door, and a slightly faded sign proclaiming, *Charbonneau's Bakery and Store*. The sign, like the town, had seen better days. He had painted it years ago in blue, white, and red to honor the tri-colors of France.

While the baking was his love, his wife's practical nature had insisted that they carry groceries as well.

Louis proceeded to light the ovens and straightened the line of canned goods he had ordered from the warehouse on Commerce Street in Riverton.

At nine o'clock on the nose, his clerk Bill Thomas arrived and opened the front door to the public, saying a good morning to Mrs. Lancaster.

Louis smiled as Mrs. Lancaster approached him. "Good morning, Mr. Charbonneau. I need to be quick today, just want some of your wonderful *brioche* buns. My sister will be coming over for lunch."

"Of course. Here, how many do you want?"

"Half a dozen should suffice, thank you."

As soon as she left, Louis made a mental note to start a new batch of the small crowns of butter rich buns. They were indeed a draw for the customers.

Within the hour, miners' wives began trickling into the shop. Although these women were frugal, they often splurged by buying one single flaky *croissant*. His more well-to-do customers usually purchased a dozen *pain au lait* rolls for that night's supper or one of his special oval-shaped loaves of bread.

With all the baking that occurred daily, the shop exuded a heady aroma of warm yeast married to flour, water, and salt—and Louis wore that scent like a cologne.

By nine-thirty, Annie arrived to help with the inevitable Saturday morning rush.

The small shop filled with groups of customers chatting with one another as they milled around the store and filled baskets on their arms. The sugary atmosphere enticed the shoppers to purchase at least

one baked good, and the red and white checked curtains not only softened the bare windows, but also held the aroma of sweetness within the threads of the fabric.

The doorbell jingled, announcing a new customer.

Louis looked up to see Randall Meyers. "Good day, Mr. Meyers." Louis walked from behind the front counter to greet the mining superintendent. "What can we do for you?" He extended his hand in a gesture of welcome.

"Good morning, Louis. Actually, I came to see your daughter Anne."

Tall, with a finely chiseled jaw and piercing brown eyes, Meyers wore his wavy dark hair parted on the side and topped it with a proper black felt fedora. Both his erect posture and his presence commanded attention, and his custom-fit black wool coat bore testament to both his class and his upbringing.

Annie looked up from the tray of pastries and walked over to join her father.

"I've come to ask Anne for a favor."

Louis rubbed his eyebrow. *What would the mining superintendent be wanting from his daughter?*

"I need a recommendation for a tutor. This would be for my son Robby. He's seven, but seems to be struggling with learning to read. I've heard that Anne has a straight A average in high school, so I thought perhaps she might recommend a teacher who could tutor Robby."

Louis's faced relaxed into a smile. "Oh, I see."

"Hello, Anne." Randall Meyers' eyes softened when he faced her.

"Hello, Mr. Meyers. I overheard your conversation with my father. The only teachers I know usually teach older students."

"I'd like to be able to count on you for this favor." His eyes never wavered from her face.

"I can ask around. If I come up with a name, I'll have my father pass it on to you." Annie gave him a thin but polite smile. "Is there anything you would like to buy here today?"

Meyers looked around at the trays of bread, cakes, and oth-

er baked goods. “What might you suggest? I’ll get something for my sister.”

“We have some fresh *kugelhopf* this morning—both the regular size cake and also some smaller individual ones. The slices are perfect for dipping in your morning coffee. Here, let me show you.” Annie went to the side counter while Meyers followed. She pulled out a tray holding a Bundt cake studded with raisins and almonds. Smaller cakes of a similar recipe surrounded it.

“I’ll take the regular size cake. Between the three of us—Robby, my sister, and me, I’m sure we won’t have any trouble finishing it.”

Once Randall Meyers paid for the cake and left, Annie looked up at her father. “Papa, why would Mr. Meyers ask me for the names of tutors? He could easily inquire at the high school himself.”

“I’m not sure. You do have a reputation for excellent grades.”

“Yes, but…”

“But what?”

“I don’t know. It seemed strange.”

“Perhaps we should feel honored that he came to you.”

“Perhaps.”

“Let’s count it as a blessing. It can only mean well for our family to be in good graces with the Superintendent of the Cumberland Valley Mines.”

Marie arrived an hour before noon. More customers filtered in behind her, including Herman Schumn, Paymaster of the Cumberland Valley Coal Company.

Louis watched Schumn rifle his smoke-stained fingers through his thinning hair, dislodging flakes of dandruff onto the shoulders of his ill-fitting gray overcoat. Schumn tilted his head first one way, then the other, and his penetrating dark eyes, sharp beaked nose, and threadlike lips made Louis think of a bird of prey sizing up a tasty morsel.

*

As Schumn swaggered through the shop, Annie wrinkled her

nose at his presence, but had to stifle a chuckle at his funny gait—thrusting his pelvis forward and constantly hitching up his belt, as if to prevent his pants from dropping.

She couldn't spend time snickering at Schumn because with Thanksgiving only a few weeks away, the shop was more busy than usual, and Annie needed to take pre-orders for the special cakes and cookies that had gained the Charbonneau's a modest amount of fame in this hardscrabble area of coal country. The poorest of villagers would find a way to purchase a few small *Madeleines*, the scalloped edge cake-like cookies, as a holiday treat for their children. The wealthier clients were ordering pies and cakes.

A local farmer approached Schumn. "Good morning, Mr. Schumn." Then he tipped his fingers to the brim of his cap. Schumn looked at the man, but did not return the greeting.

Instead, Schumn licked his lips, unbuttoned his coat, and cleared his throat. Women who had been trading gossip and talking in small groups ceased their chatter almost on cue. A few women turned away from his gaze. The tantalizing scent of freshly- baked French pastries and breads now drenched a silent air.

He walked over and stood directly in front of Annie. She did not flinch.

"Good day, Mr. Schumn. Can I help you?" Her eyes narrowed.

No one had made any reference to Widow Klausman or her children, but the pall of yesterday's eviction hung over the village like the odor of soiled linen. Annie could still smell the widow's despair.

"Came to see the new oven. You know, of course, I arranged the loan. Got your father a lower rate than the bank." He ran his tongue out over his lips, revealing uneven, yellowed teeth.

"My father's in back." She motioned to the rear of the shop. Behind the half wall that separated the customers from the baking section, Louis was inspecting the new oven that had recently been installed. Customers and neighbors had been pouring into the bakery all week to gaze at the marvel of the huge galvanized Blodgett oven sent all the way from Pittsburgh. Sitting solidly as a statue, the massive silver-colored oven stood a good five feet high and featured four large in-

dustrial baking compartments. Annie knew this would help her father bake more, which would increase the meager profits of the bakery.

Schumn scuttled sideways like a puny crab around the front wooden counter. Annie watched his approach. Then he paused for a moment, peered down intently at Annie's shoes, but said nothing before heading to the back of the store.

Women who had previously lingered over their selections, quickly brought their activities to a close, paid for their goods, and left. Annie watched one woman in particular drop her selected goods onto a table and quickly leave the building without buying anything.

Annie resented Schumn's presence even though her father said, "Just be polite to Schumn and any other officers of the coal company."

She gritted her teeth, knowing she had to be civil to him. Annie still fumed inside about Mrs. Klausman's eviction and wondered who had more power; Randall Meyers or Herman Schumn.

Schumn did not tarry, but talked briefly to Louis before coming back to the front. Then as he passed Annie he whispered, "Heard that you and Marie tried to feed the Klausman runts. I've got my eye out for the two of you, Missy. You don't want to mess with me." Then the bang of the shop door announced his departure. Annie held her breath until he left.

A few minutes later the front bell jingled again. Annie looked up to see Mrs. Morelli enter the store. As usual, Mrs. Morelli was wearing a coat that had seen better days. Annie uttered the standard greeting she gave all the miners' wives. "Good morning."

"Morning, Miss Anne. Just here to look. Won't be buying nothin' yet. Just come to see the new oven."

Of course you're not buying. You're just another poor woman from Miners Row.

Aunt Hulda, the Charbonneau housekeeper and assistant baker during peak times, ambled up to the front shelves, wiping her large floured hands on the sturdy white baker's apron that barely covered her sizable girth. "Good morning, Mrs. Morelli. You go ahead and look all you want, dearie. When you're ready to buy something, today or tomorrow, just let us know."

As Mrs. Morelli wandered off to look at the new oven Annie shook her head. "She won't spend any money here today—or next week either."

Hulda nodded, wiping a few strands of gray hair off her forehead. "I know. She's got it tough. Heard her husband lost a couple of fingers when he got pinned by a mining car in the last accident. That means he digs less coal than before. Plus, they got three young children to feed, so she's got to count her pennies. She still has her pride though, and that counts for something."

"You're always too kind to them, Aunt Hulda."

"Them? Who do you mean?"

"You know who I mean. The miners' wives. They're annoyingly frugal, and hardly spend much money in our shop."

"Annie, we're one of the few stores in the area that accepts cash. The women can shop here without having to use their miners' script."

"We saw Widow Klausman get evicted yesterday. She sat on the ground and cried in front of everyone. Marie tried to offer her children a sandwich and the mining police practically threatened us."

Hulda's eyes became slits. "What do you mean the police threatened you?"

"I said, 'almost.' They got mad when Marie offered her sandwich." Annie paused. "We heard another woman saying that Mrs. Klausman should have gone for the shoes. What did that mean?"

Aunt Hulda averted her eyes. "Just mining chatter, I suspect."

Annie waited for more information, but it was not forthcoming. "Well, couldn't she have found some old widower to marry? That way she wouldn't have gotten evicted."

Hulda made a huffing sound. "Don't go judging people when you don't know their story."

Annie cocked her head at Aunt Hulda's sudden brusque attitude.

"Women like Erna Klausman can't help being poor, and marrying some old widower isn't always the answer. And she probably can't read or write, so there's no way she could get a job to support herself and her children. Your mama, God rest her soul, understood how tough life was for the miners' wives."

Annie hesitated a moment. "Well, you should have heard her screaming at the mining police. It was embarrassing."

"No *esprit de corps*?"

"What does that mean?"

"The spirit of all sticking together. Usually the miners' wives help each other. Maybe Mrs. Klausman had alienated herself. Or perhaps the other women were too afraid of speaking up."

"What do you mean?"

"You're still young, Annie. Antagonizing the mining company is a wasted effort that only gets you hurt in the long run." Hulda's eyes took on the look of a remembered sadness. "Your mama knew that, too."

Annie remained taciturn, as painful memories of her own resurfaced.

Hulda must have seen the veil of sadness cover Annie's eyes. "Are you thinking of the times when your mama left to tend sick women on Miners Row? I know you resented her spending hours with those families instead of being with you. Am I right?

Annie shrugged without commenting, while tears stubbornly formed at the corners of her eyes.

"Are you still so angry, then?"

"If she hadn't gone to help that miner's wife, Mama might still be alive." The words spewed out with vehemence.

"Oh, *ma chérie*. Your mama couldn't say no when someone was ill and didn't have money for the doctor. Your mama was the only hope that many of the poorer families had."

"I thought the coal company had a doctor on the payroll."

Aunt Hulda looked away. "Sometimes a sick woman wants another woman to tend her; especially after she realizes that a bottle of Red Flag Oil won't provide the cure."

Annie fought the obstinate tears sliding down her cheeks. "She missed my eighth birthday because of spending the whole night down on Miners Row. Then she got the sickness."

"Annie. Your mama died from pneumonia, not some disease she caught from a miner's wife."

"The coal company should've been taking care of that family,

not Mama."

Aunt Hulda shook her head.

Annie turned away. What did Aunt Hulda know? The company was at fault just like the miners' wives. Ten years had passed since Mama died, punished for tending the sick on Miners Row. Annie's remembered image of her mother struggling to breathe as violent coughs racked her body burned in Annie's memory.

Nothing Aunt Hulda said, or did, would change Annie's mind.

"Miss Anne? Maybe you didn't hear me. I asked if there's any way I can go on the book?"

Annie looked up. "Silly me, to get some bits of flour in my eyes." She wiped the inner corners of her eyes. "Now, what were you saying?"

"I asked if you could extend my credit, just till next week when my husband gets paid."

"I'm sorry, Mrs. Reid, but you still haven't paid what you owe us from last month."

The woman's eyes pleaded before she even spoke. "Please? I got four children at home and my husband's been sick."

Aunt Hulda looked as if she might intervene, but Annie abruptly ended the conversation. "We can't help you."

Hulda started to follow Mrs. Reid, but the miner's wife held herself erect and walked away.

Aunt Hulda looked at Annie. "I hope someday you'll see what your mama saw."

Hulda shuffled off toward the back of the store and Annie watched as she changed direction and headed over to a young woman standing alone. Annie thought it might be Sophie Petrova, one of the newer immigrant wives, and hardly more than a girl. Annie saw that she had been crying and now stood clutching the ends of her mustard-yellow head scarf. *I know her; she hardly speaks any English and brings me her pennies on an outstretched palm. She's probably crying to Aunt Hulda about needing food.*

But as Annie watched, Aunt Hulda offered the girl a handkerchief, and then enfolded her in a large hug, as the girl's thin body trembled against Hulda's shoulder. It was obvious that Hulda knew this girl.

Now what? Annie wondered impatiently. The young woman pulled her thin coat around her spindly frame. Annie rolled her eyes. This wasn't her problem and she did not intend on getting involved. *Please don't tell me Hulda's going to take on another charity case.*

CHAPTER 3

John Fraley, crushed by a runaway horse,
Kingsland Mine.

Louis remembered Father Kelley from St. Bridget's visiting him after Thérese's death. The priest had asked Louis to come back to the Church and be an active parishioner. But Louis refused. What good was faith when God allowed good people to die young? Louis stubbornly declined to attend Mass as his own form of retaliation.

But Louis did agree to bring his children to Mass on Christmas and Easter. And in spite of his boycott against the Church, he honored Thérese's holiday traditions at home, reminding himself it was for the sake of the children.

On the first Sunday of December, after a hearty breakfast, he gathered his bow saw for the annual excursion up Piney Ridge to gather greenery for holiday decorations.

"Everyone ready?"

Annie and Marie held up three burlap sacks, hands already ensconced in grey thick wool gloves, and scarves wrapped snug around the collars of their winter capes.

"Where's Stephen, Papa?"

"He went down to stack wood for Mr. and Mrs. Klosterman. They're getting old, and it looks like a heavy snow might be coming this week."

The warmly clad trio tromped out the door and proceeded along the frost-rimmed path toward the western slope of Piney Ridge. Their feet crunched against the frozen grasses of the lower area, and their breaths came out in steamy puffs as they began the ascent up into the pines.

For Louis, the mountain called Piney Ridge presented a refreshing alternative to the noisy coal operations down in the village. High up, the air became clean and clear—causing lungs to rejoice. Easily seen from his front porch, Louis loved the mountain standing guard over Porters Glen.

"Papa, why are you stopping?"

He smiled. "I want to inhale the fragrance of the evergreens and the earthy smell of the forest."

Further up the mountain, the girls found white pines with showy branches. Louis cut the ones they selected, and the girls gathered them in three neat piles. One pile would be given to Aunt Hulda, the second pile would go to decorate the shop, and the third pile would lend an air of festivity to the Charbonneau home.

Louis would come back alone during the last week of Advent and chop down a white pine for the family Christmas tree, just as he had done when Thérese was alive.

Once they had collected enough greens, the trio began the descent, commencing the search for the coveted orangey-red bittersweet that twisted its way up and around the bare branches of the hardwoods. It had always been a game to see who could find the bittersweet first.

"Bravo, Marie!" Louis clapped when Marie won by discovering the woody vines. They cut several bunches of bittersweet to add to their greenery.

With their sacks full, Marie started to sing the Christmas carol that had been their mother's favorite—*Les Anges dans nos Campagne*, which translated into "Angels We Have Heard on High." Louis and Annie joined in with the French lyrics.

Annie's eyes sparkled as she gazed around her. Then she turned to her father. "Papa, I always feel closer to Mama when we're on the mountain. It's as if she's still nearby, and nothing bad can ever happen to us up here."

Louis smiled at Annie and her child-like purity. "Come, *ma petite chou*. We need to be getting back home."

As the trio began the descent back down the mountain, winter blue jays perched in the pines jabbered loudly, bidding farewell to the invaders.

*

On the following Saturday, right before closing, Mrs. Morelli returned to look around the store. As predicted, the woman still did not make any purchases, but Annie spied Aunt Hulda quietly dropping a few day-old rolls into Mrs. Morelli's coat pockets. Hulda feigned innocence as she slipped on her own coat, waved to Annie, and left the shop.

I suppose it doesn't matter what happens to stale rolls, although we should still be able to sell them at a discount and make a profit.

Louis came over to the counter and picked up the ledger and thumbed through the morning's receipts. Annie watched as his eyebrows drew closer together as he scrutinized the accounts.

"You have a good eye for numbers, Annie. Your mama would be proud."

Annie smiled at the compliment, basking for a moment in the glow of his approval.

"Let's finish up, Papa, and then go home and see what Aunt Hulda is serving for dinner."

Half an hour later as they stepped outside the shop, a few earnest flakes of snow started to fall. "Papa, look! This might be the first real snow of winter!"

"Let's just hope, not too much. Stephen needs to be able to work on Monday."

As Louis spoke, a line of miners threaded its way into town

from Big Vein Street and their half-day Saturday shift. As they passed Engle's Butcher Shop and McKenzie's Dry Goods, several shoppers called out greetings to the men.

Annie couldn't help but rivet her attention on the men and boys who were completely covered by a layer of black coal dust from head to foot with only the whites of their eyes showing. It was an all too familiar scene, how the miners walked in pairs, reversing the exact path they had trod that morning. They all obeyed the decades old superstition that to vary from the established route would only bring them bad luck.

Somewhere in the line she knew her brother Stephen would be carrying his small bird cage with the canary he carried into the mines each day. In his other hand he would be holding his three-compartment tin dinner bucket. The bottom part of the bucket held his drinking water, the middle section had contained a sandwich, and the top one was for dessert. She shuddered remembering that the tight fitting lid kept out the rats.

The bobbing heads of the miners, linked in conversation, appeared to her as a flock of crows strutting up the road.

"Stephen!" Annie called out in delight as soon as she saw her brother. He broke rank and trotted over to her.

"How was it, today?"

He nodded to his father, and turned to her. "Same as yesterday, and will be again on Monday. But I managed to load two and a half tons. Not bad for a half day's work. I tallied $1.25."

She wanted to squeeze his hand, but it was coated with coal grime. Instead she flashed him a wide smile. "Too bad you don't get to keep it all."

"I know. The deductions for the tools and pick sharpening do cut into my pay. But at least it's not the end of the month when they take out an extra dollar for the doctor. I should be able to keep eighty cents from today."

"Once we get the loan paid off, you can decide if you want to come back and work in the store instead of the mines."

"Thanks, Papa."

Annie squinted up at her eighteen-year-old brother. At five foot

nine, he towered over both her and Marie. Annie smiled to think that with his good looks of wavy brown hair and liquid blue eyes he was sure to capture some girl's heart in Porters Glen.

Louis smiled at his son. He had made no bones to the family about hoping Stephen would eventually come back to work in the store. But Stephen had shared his dream with Annie of wanting to become a newspaper writer. Not sure how it would work out, she just wanted Stephen to be happy.

Stephen and her father lost themselves in conversation, leaving Annie to drift in her own thoughts. What if Stephen's goal of becoming a writer could possibly take him away from Porters Glen? But is it right for one person to set boundaries on another person's dream?

Louis interrupted her musings by clearing his throat. Aunt Hulda was waiting for them at home.

The Charbonneau house sat back a bit from the lane, with a sizable yard supporting a vegetable garden. A slightly sagging wooden porch stretched across the front of the white clapboard house, while a utilitarian back porch held the old wash tubs for clothes' laundering.

Victorian in style, the first floor hosted a modest parlor to receive guests, a dining room for special dinners, and a large kitchen sitting opposite a small utility room. Upstairs three tidy bedrooms provided sleeping space for the family, and a smaller room for an overnight guest. As yet, the Charbonneau's did not have indoor plumbing. The result meant chamber pots at night and the outside privy during the day.

Hulda greeted them by standing firmly at the entrance to the house with her arms crossed and pointing her index finger toward the back porch.

Stephen grinned. "I know the drill, Aunt Hulda."

Annie stifled a smirk as she watched Hulda lord over the process of Stephen's nightly routine. Cap, work jacket and overalls on the wall hooks and boots placed over at the edge of the porch to prevent any dirt from blowing back into the house.

"I keep a clean house and no coal dirt is permitted here."

Annie laughed to herself because although Aunt Hulda's voice

was still thick with her French accent and authoritarian lilt, she was a push-over for Stephen and everyone in the family knew it.

Stephen grinned. "I swear, Aunt Hulda, you could take over an army with your ability to order all of us around."

Although he often teased her, Stephen loved the older woman; they all did.

Annie remembered how Aunt Hulda had come to live with them after Annie's mother died. Through the years Hulda became much more than just a cook and housekeeper; she became family.

How old was she now? Nearing fifty, Annie calculated.

Annie knew that her father appreciated Hulda's cooking and the well-organized kitchen she ran. The open pine shelves held spotless dishes that peered out at everyone, while heavy cast iron pans sat on the coal-fired stove. A trusty assortment of pots sat on tiered wooden shelves near the sink, and Hulda's well-loved baking utensils stood clustered together in a small cream-colored repurposed stone crock.

In the center of the kitchen a rectangular wild cherry farm table anchored the room. Thérese's pride and joy, she had bartered for it as soon as they moved into Porters Glen. Here, Hulda rolled out the dough for the family's fluffy milk bread rolls, or pastry dough for a pie, or set the table for the next family meal.

Entering the kitchen, and struck by the mingled aromas of Hulda's cooking and baking, Annie felt a twinge in her chest about Stephen. Although she and Marie were close, Stephen had always been Annie's confidant. She wanted him to stay in Porters Glen. He could always write for the Mining Journal.

He dashed in now from the back porch, wearing only his grey long johns and a grin. Hulda had already brought in water from the rain barrel and heated big pots of it on the iron stove for his bath. She pulled the beige muslin screen out from the utility room and opened it in a corner of the kitchen, allowing him the privacy to undress.

Like other miners, Annie knew he would ease his body into the tub of warm water, and use a cake of Lava soap to lather up. Soon a film of coal grime would slither off his hands, neck, and face and onto the surface of the bath water where Hulda would scoop up much of the

dirty film, slip it into a bucket, and toss the scum outside next to the tree line of the woods. Thank goodness that the rest of them bathed in a different wash tub.

Annie smiled to herself when he uttered, "Ah, thanks, Aunt Hulda."

Hulda called back to him. "There's Unker Salve for your hands and fingers when you get out," she yelled back. "Don't forget to use it."

"If I didn't know better, I'd think you're trying to spoil me."

"Well, no girl wants to hold hands with a boy whose fingers are hard with calluses. I should know." Aunt Hulda's face flushed with happiness as she indulged in being the center of Stephen's attention.

"Just don't be giving me any of that special rose scented night cream you make for Annie and Marie. The other miners would laugh at me."

"Ha! I wouldn't dream of wasting it on you."

Hulda carried Stephen's heavy cotton long johns out back to soak in a laundry tub. Later, Annie would use a wire carpet beater to bang the coal dust out of his work jacket, because it only got washed once or twice a month. Come Monday morning, Aunt Hulda would scrub his dirty overalls on a washboard, along with his long johns, and shirts. The rest of the family's clothes were washed separately from his.

Annie hated the entire laundry process. Thank goodness her participation was only required in summer when school was out.

The monotonous chore started with scrubbing and wringing, then placing the clothes in a second tub with soap, and swirling them around. Then wring again and again, and lastly place the wet clothes in the third tub which held the clean rinse water. One final wring and, in decent weather, the clothes would be hung on the rope clothes line out in the yard. In the rain, the laundry would be brought into the kitchen to dry on a folding wooden rack by the coal stove.

The kettle on the stove rattled, indicating a pot of tea would soon be ready. The European custom of having a big meal at noon became impossible for many families in Porters Glen when the miners did not return home until dusk. The Charbonneau's followed the new American tradition and ate a large mid-day dinner only on Saturdays

and Sundays, and carried a simple mid-day meal with them on weekdays.

Louis sat down at the table, as the smell of hot milk bread rolls floated through the kitchen. "Smells great, Hulda." He never failed to compliment her on her culinary talents.

"So, tell me why I rush home to serve this *cassoulet* hot from the oven and Marie is nowhere to be seen. She should know better than to go off somewhere by herself so close to dinner time."

Annie rallied to her younger sister's defense. "She's shopping for ribbons with her friend Giselle. Don't worry, she'll be safe. Everyone in town knows her. She'll get here in time for dinner. She always does. And no one else but you can make such a delicious meal out of white beans, pork chunks, and sausage rounds."

Hulda softened. "Ah, but the true *cassoulet* should also have duck and lamb, but…" The older woman tilted her head, shrugged her shoulders, and lifted her hands in a manner possibly learned in childhood, as if to say, "But what can one do?"

"Well, we love it just the way you make it."

Marie got home in time to slide into her chair and join in the family in saying the blessing. *"Bénissez-nous, Seigneur, bénissez ce repas, ceux qui l'ont préparé, et procurez du pain à ceux qui n'en ont pas.* Amen.[1]"

After the meal, the three siblings headed over to the sink to do the dishes. Stephen filled a shallow tin dishpan with warm water from the stove. Then he turned toward Annie. "So, how about you wash, I dry, and Marie puts away? Now, how's school going?"

Brushing the food scraps into a small bucket, Annie plunked a scraped-off dish into the warmed water. "Good. I'm glad I have just one more semester. Then after I get my diploma I want to apply for enrollment at Mount Pleasant College." She reached for another dirty dish.

"Really? You aren't satisfied being one of the first girls from Porters Glen to attend the new high school in Mount Pleasant? You want to be the first girl from Porters Glen to go to college too?"

---

1 Bless us, O Lord, and bless this meal, those who prepared it, and provide bread to those who don't have any.

"Yes."

"So, do you actually want to teach? Because, I don't know what else they offer."

"I think I do. But I'll have to wait to enroll until Papa pays off the oven loan."

"Why?" quipped Marie.

"Because, there might not be enough money for tuition until the loan's paid. And that's assuming I get in. They have to accept my application first."

"Well, no tuition worries for me. I can't wait to be done with school and start work as a milliner." She plunked a dried plate on top of her stack.

Stephen reached for a rinsed plate and then turned to Marie. "I didn't know that. Where do you plan to work? As a milliner."

"I'll go wherever women buy hats. Maybe I could start at Stern's, or go to Diamond's in Riverton."

Stephen handed Marie the dried plate. "I'd still like to write for a newspaper. But that won't happen for a while either. I gave Papa my word I'd stay in the mines till the loan is paid off. But I'm working on some opinion pieces right now about the lack of safety features in the mines. Once they're finished, I'll show them to you both before I send them to the paper."

"You're serious, aren't you, about the dangers in the mines?"

He nodded.

"I predict you'll be a famous reporter one day, maybe even uncover some scandal about the mining company." Annie blew him a kiss. *Dear God, keep him close to home.* Then she drained the dishwater and tried not to think of Stephen ever leaving Porters Glen.

CHAPTER 4

Edward Kerns, crushed between coal cars,
Ocean Mine.

A cold December Monday morning with the promise of snow found Annie and Marie at school, while Stephen stepped off the man-trip in the Porter Mine and began walking with the other miners deeper into the pit.

He had already adjusted his teapot light and attached it to his cap brim. The small single flame helped in the stygian darkness, but he always felt cramped in the mine tunnels that made tall men stoop over. His assignment for the day was to work with two of the older miners, Pete Dougherty and Mike Sullivan.

Droplets of water fell on his cap and trickled down the back of his neck as he followed Pete and Mike deeper into the mine.

The two older men changed course and went into a side tunnel. Stephen followed and tried not to gag on the overwhelming smell of sulphur that permeated the air. He lowered his tools and by the flickering light of his teapot flame, he surveyed the massive wall of ebony coal in front of him. Christ, it could be thirty feet thick. How would they ever dig it all out?

He swung his pick-axe in a steady rhythm while trying to breathe even breaths so his lungs didn't feel compromised. He did not look at the coal ceiling above his head because it would only remind him of how hemmed-in he felt. Ten minutes later a wave of claustrophobia rolled over him and caused his heart to pound and sweat to drip from his temples to his chin. He peered around at the closeness of the rock walls and the ghostly sheen from the coal and felt his eyes grow larger with fear.

Just take a deep breath, get control of it. Forget you're half a mile back in the mine.

"Charbonneau? You all right, kid? You're awfully quiet."

He jerked his head back, giving them a shaky thumbs-up. He liked these two men; they were a bit outspoken, but fair in dealing with their fellow miners. If he talked, his voice would crack and he didn't want them to know his fear. The complete darkness scared him and made him want to bolt out of the mine, but he forced himself to take some additional deep breaths to calm his fear. The air around him was close and heavy and unforgiving, and his clothes suddenly felt tighter across his chest. After three months in the mines, he had still not learned to conquer the anxiety of being so far underground.

"Hey, kid. Glad you got assigned to work with us today. Just try and ignore this old tunnel. At least we get to stand up, and don't have to work on our knees."

Stephen nodded and mimed to Pete and Mike that he needed to go take a piss, but in reality he wanted to rest up against a wall, waving his arms over his head. This technique usually calmed him from the claustrophobia. He watched Pete nod back, giving the go-ahead sign.

Stephen put down his pick-axe and walked around the corner to where he could stand out of sight. A few feet away a rock ledge jutted out from the timber-supported wall where he had stashed his dinner pail. He longed to open the top compartment and nibble at the piece of pie he knew Aunt Hulda had packed. Remembering the old mining adage of "eat dessert first, in case today you die" made him feel jumpy. The claustrophobia was bad enough; he didn't need to be thinking

about any silly superstitions as well.

He took a few more deep breaths. The floor of the mine was slick with oily water puddles, and he shifted his feet. *God, it's horrible down here,* he thought miserably. *Probably a lot like hell.*

The darkness added to his desolation. The sole available light came from the teapot lamps fueled by bacon grease. He could hear the other two men talking, their pick-axes beating a rhythm against the thick coal seam. Flickers from their lamps punctuated the darkness like sparks from a fire.

Leaning up against the nearby wall, he heard an ominous sound; thousands of little feet scurrying off in the darkness.

Rats? Hate them buggers. At least this time they didn't get my food.

He stood still and listened a moment longer.

Then he realized with a cold sweat what the sound really meant—rats running away from this tunnel section.

In the next instant the sound of mine timbers beginning to crack froze his attention. Before he could even shout a warning to Pete and Mike, the ceiling of their section imploded down on top of the two men, burying them under a five-foot-high pile of rocks, broken timbers, and strewn rubble.

"Jesus-Christ!" He leaned against the cold unforgiving mine wall, dazed for a moment, and then called out, "Pete? Mike?" No response. "Bird?" The canary that lived in a small wooden cage and accompanied him into the mine every morning was silent, too. Stephen peered around, listening for any noise, but not noticing the flame of his teapot lamp growing dimmer.

Panic gripped his bowels with the realization that he was trapped without a way of escape. He breathed in the toxic fumes and tried hard not to choke, but the dust of the rubble filled his lungs.

Gasping for air, he defecated in his pants. His mind raced with thoughts of possible escape, but he was too paralyzed with fear to bang out the miners' code of three taps to signify his location. Instead, he sank to the ground and covered his face with his hands in a desperate attempt to breathe. His hearted pounded as his ultimate terror was

coming true...being buried alive.

*

Some minutes later the body tipped over and lay motionless on the unforgiving mine floor.

Blackdamp accomplished what the cave-in had not. The poisonous gas mixture snuffed out the life of Stephen Charbonneau.

*

Porters Glen became alerted to the disaster by three long blasts on the coal company's steam whistle.

Louis joined the throng in the street nearest the mine. Anxious families desperate to find out about their loved ones' safety jostled into one another. As miners poured out of the mine's opening, Louis strained to find Stephen. He heard women shrieking with joy when they found their miners and saw young wives run unabashedly up to their husbands, safe from the claws of death.

When all the circular I.D. tags were finally checked against the miners who had spilled out of the entrance, Stephen Charbonneau's tag lay untouched on the board, along with Pete Dougherty and Mike Sullivan's.

They had not made it out.

Louis ran to the foreman. "Is there a hope Stephen might be trapped, but still alive?"

The supervisor shook his head. "I'm sorry, Louis, but we doubt it. The tunnel where he was working completely imploded, according to the miners who escaped."

Louis sank to his knees in the street. Sobs wracked his body as neighbors and friends came to him with words of sympathy. Louis did not even hear the words, all he could think of was that his only son had been killed inside the mine, and he, the papa, had asked his son to go work there. Anguish tore his soul to shreds.

The distant shrill of the steam whistle would alert all of Mt.

Pleasant, and Louis realized that Annie and Marie could hear the news before he got to them. In a ghost-like trance he trudged up the mountain road to the high school, unaware that he was even walking.

Louis entered the school office, and the two secretaries immediately jumped up and went over to him, giving him their condolences. Mr. Conner, the principal, stood in front of Louis with sympathy. Louis stood with his hat in his hands and his eyes red-rimmed with tears. How could he even say the words, that Stephen was dead?

Annie and Marie were called to the office and Louis saw that Annie already knew; something deep and primal within her being had always been connected to Stephen.

"Your brother," began Louis. But he could not continue. He fell into the girls' open arms and the three of them sobbed until no more tears would come. Holding on to each other, they left the school and began a silent walk back to Porters Glen.

Louis knew that life would never be the same again.

It took the mining company almost two full days to retrieve the bodies. With their corpses so badly crushed, no viewing was held for Mike Sullivan or Pete Dougherty. Although Stephen's body was intact, Louis had the undertaker remove it and prepare it for burial; rather than subject his daughters to the sight of their dead brother laid out for viewing in the family parlor. Three days after the disaster, St. Bridget's Catholic Church held a funeral for the dead men. Every family in Porters Glen attended.

*

After Stephen's funeral, the days passed into weeks. A chasm of grief rendered the Charbonneau family incapable of polite conversation with each other. Deep snows blanketed the house in an isolation that no one cared to break. Together, they remained wrapped in sorrow, not even celebrating Christmas.

January alternated between spitting sleet and formidable snow, often accompanied by icy winds that howled like Irish banshees. The weather mirrored their desolation.

Louis sat tonight with Annie in the kitchen.

"I hate to have to bring this up, but once the weather clears Marie needs to get back to school." He paused. "But…. Annie, I need you to come work at the bakery. Without Stephen's income from the mines, I'll have to let Bill Thomas go because I can't afford to pay him."

Annie's shoulders slumped and she stared down at her hands.

"Of course, Papa, I understand."

"Perhaps one day…" Louis squeezed his eyes shut to prevent the tears that were forming.

The next week Louis filled out the paperwork to withdraw his oldest daughter from Mount Pleasant High School. Back at home no one spoke of the sacrifice Annie had to make.

Sorrow filled Louis' days. Death had struck again; first his wife, then Stephen, and his oldest daughter's education. The sadness of it all weighed heavy on his heart, and now without Stephen's paycheck, each day's sales could make the difference between some profit and the ever present fear of foreclosure.

Annie arrived at the shop every day and helped bake the French confections and wait on customers, but Louis knew there was no joy in her duties. As winter slowly melted in spring, America plummeted into an economic depression. Louis hardly paid attention. Without Stephen, the only son who would have carried on the family name, the woes of the rest of the country did not concern Louis.

For the outside population, Louis hung a mourning wreath on the front door and the family wore black bereavement clothes, but inside, all their spirits were hollow.

Each morning, Louis gazed at the photo on the mantle of Stephen taken on his first day in the mine. Standing tall and proud, and holding his dinner bucket while cradling the canary cage, Stephen had grinned just as the photographer took his identification picture. The dimples around his mouth seemed to be winking.

Louis wanted to remember his son that way.

There was, however, no grin for Annie. Too quickly, she had been thrust into adulthood.

CHAPTER 5

John Schell,
killed in a mining accident.

The loud banging of the shop's wooden screen door interrupted the tranquility of the serene May morning. Annie felt the May breeze, mingled with the heavy fragrance of pink honeysuckle, roll into the store with the customer. The over-used musk cologne in the air belonged to Herman Schumn.

Dressed in a cheap imitation suit of what the well-to-do wore, he did not look at any of the customers, but circumnavigated the shop in clockwise fashion. He started with scanning the selection of canned tomatoes, corn, and green beans. Then he moved to the pine table where spinach, Swiss chard, and lettuces lay in individual shallow woven baskets.

Barely glancing over at the small new potatoes, he maneuvered himself to the early strawberries and stuck his hand into the small bucket. Sampling a few, he allowed the bright pink juice to dribble down his chin. Then he pulled out a soiled and poorly monogrammed handkerchief with the initials HES and wiped his lower face and fingers. All the while, his beady black eyes darted back and forth.

Taking his time, and ignoring the bags of flour, sugar, and salt, he sauntered over to the side countertop where a small tray of freshly baked *brioches* sat next to flaky rolls. He picked up a roll and poked it, leaving traces of dirt in the indentations from his grimy fingers.

Annie's nose wrinkled in disgust. Schumn tossed the roll back onto the tray, turned, and looked directly at Annie. He let his gaze wander from her head to her toes.

She stared back at him with ice in her eyes, but felt her stomach churn. His presence always unnerved her.

"Good morning, Anne." Schumn almost snickered the greeting.

"Good day, Mr. Schumn. Are you here to shop?"

"What's a matter? Afraid I'm here to aggravate you?"

Annie refused to rise to his bait.

"Because you have no idea how much trouble I can cause when I want to."

His grin thinned out and Annie steeled herself not to react.

Chien miserable. She waited a moment. "Then, what can I help you with?"

"Help me? Oh no, it is I who can help you. I came to remind you that your father's loan is now two months overdue. One more month and we have the right to repossess the new oven he bought, and take over the deed to the store."

Annie forced herself not to react.

"You know your father put the shop up as collateral for the loan." Schumn turned and leaned in closer. With his rancid breath spewing in Annie's face, he muttered, "There is a way you can help your family. Come see me at the mining office and I'll explain."

She stared at him in rigid silence.

He rolled his tongue out and over his upper lip.

She wasn't exactly sure what he meant, but she wanted nothing to do with him. "We can take care of our debts, thank you."

"Pretty bold, aren't you? There's plenty of girls here in Porters Glen who have helped pay off family loans with my help."

"I don't need your help." She crossed her arms over her chest. "And you can't intimidate my family."

He tugged on the end of his grease-stained mustache. "That might change. I could always approach Marie instead."

Annie visibly paled. "Marie? If you so much as step in her shadow, I will report you."

"Report me! To who? The mining police? Hell, I write their paychecks. You can't report me." Then he waved a boney finger in her face. "Just remember, if you don't pay back the loan, or cooperate as I see fit, I'll come after the oven, the store…and more. I told you before; you don't want to mess with me."

Then he turned and swept out the door, leaving an aura of ugliness in his wake.

Annie held onto the counter. *Mon Dieu.* She glanced up at the wall clock, relieved that within the hour the normal flow of customers would begin.

Aunt Hulda approached from the back, a warm aroma of freshly baked bread swirling around her. "And just what did that weasel say to you? I saw him jabbing his finger back toward the ovens. He come to badger you about the loan?"

"I'm afraid so."

Aunt Hulda's normally warm brown eyes turned to flint, and had she been a dog her ears would have flattened back against her head. "Nothing but an *asticot.* Don't you worry about his comments. Your papa will figure out a way to get rid of that maggot."

"He hinted that I could help pay off the loan. I hate to think what that meant."

Hulda clenched her teeth. "If he says something like that again, you come see me right away." Her eyes hardened and her breathing accelerated. "Promise me."

"All right, I promise."

Hulda placed a wicker basket filled with the day's bread next to the front counter and then shuffled back to the baking area.

Annie went to the tray of dinner rolls, and using her apron skirt, picked up the one Schumn had soiled with his fingers, and dumped it in the garbage bin. Then she walked over to the sink, pumped the handle and compulsively scrubbed her hands with vigor.

I should be finishing my senior year and applying for a spot at Mount Pleasant, but I'm stuck here having to deal with miserable Herman Schumn. Her chin trembled ever so slightly.

Even though Schumn had left, a sense of apprehension stayed forefront in Annie's mind. She did not trust the man and certainly did not want him anywhere around Marie.

The once beautiful smell of honeysuckle now hung in the air as an ugly reminder of his obnoxious visit.

*

Annie and Marie had only six more weeks of wearing black mourning outfits. But the residual effects of Stephen's death lived everywhere. Without Stephen's salary, Louis had to let Bill Thomas, his shop clerk, go. This would save the bakery two and a half dollars a day. Annie and Aunt Hulda had taken over as the main workforce in the store while Marie came home after school to start supper.

The shop bell announced new customers arriving. Four women entered the store and Annie saw by their clothes that they were some of the newer immigrant wives. Each one dressed from head to toe in a dark dress, heavy black stockings, and jet-black high laced shoes. Their ragged fingernails testified to a life of grueling house work, but all of them smelled of cleanly laundered clothes and they held their heads high.

To an outsider, they may have looked similar, all wearing their hair pulled back in a bun at the nape of their neck. Each woman's claim to independence, however, was woven in the colored threads of the head scarf she wore. Their scarves ranged from deep purple to hickory brown to forest green. No two were the same.

Almost at once, they split up and went to different sections, each carrying an identical covered shallow round tin, the size of a dessert plate.

You are new here, please buy something.

When the women reconvened at the front counter, Annie's shoulders sagged and her face tightened. Each woman held a small

head of wilted cabbage and a few additional items from the bargain table. One woman carried a prize of wrinkled carrots, another cradled four shrunken potatoes, while the third held two musty onions. The last woman asked for two cups of flour.

Having worked in the shop since winter, Annie knew it was still several days away from payday, which meant food was scarce.

"Good morning." She offered the rote greeting and began to tally their purchases. She knew the cabbages would make spring cabbage soup—easily stretched with additional water to feed a hungry family for two dinners.

The other single ingredients meant the four women would work together to concoct a "miner's pie"— a conglomeration of cooked potatoes or turnips and reduced-priced vegetables mixed with a dense gravy flavored with blood from the butcher and ladled into a small pie crust. The small four pies would be baked in one woman's oven, to save fuel, and later each wife would go home with her single serving pie, thus insuring the husbands would have something for dinner the following day.

Other wives would only be offering their families *pon haus* sandwiches: two pieces of thick bread spread with a concoction made from cornmeal, cheap pork renderings, and water—mixed together in a loaf pan, sliced and fried. The poorest families would not even have *pon haus*. Their sandwiches would simply consist of butcher's lard smeared on bread.

By nightfall the entire village would be steeped in the fumes of spring cabbage soup and *pon haus*, smells that lodged in everyone's nostrils and lingered for days. The smell often made Annie gag.

Aunt Hulda appeared and thanked them for their business as the women doled out their pennies. Then Hulda surreptitiously slipped a stale roll and extra mealy potato into each woman's pocket.

The women left without Annie even offering them a good-bye. They murmured "*Danke*" to Hulda as they left.

"So where are they from?"

"They're German, I think. Why didn't you thank them for shopping here?" Aunt Hulda scolded. "Those women probably each bake an

average of twelve loaves of bread a week at home, but still find money to shop in our store."

Annie just shrugged.

"You're still angry, aren't you?" Then her voice softened. "It isn't their fault you had to quit school. Hopefully you'll be able to go back and finish someday."

It wasn't just the quitting of school that festered in Annie's mind. No one in the family really knew about the night Thérese died, when she had called Annie to her side as Louis momentarily left the room.

Annie still poignantly remembered her mother asking her to carry on the legacy of helping the miners' families.

"Annie, you could learn how to use herbs and become a healer. That would give me peace."

But Annie had been too stunned with grief to answer. She wiped tears from her face and turned to answer her mother, but Thérese had expelled one last breath and died.

Eight years old and frightened, Annie had fought hysteria. Why hadn't she answered her mother? Throwing herself over her mother's still warm, but lifeless body, Annie sobbed until Louis came back and tenderly pulled her away.

Now, the heady smell of carnations, reared back into her memory, as did the ticking of a clock. Her father had placed the large bouquet of the flowers by his wife's night table, and the damn clock had been so loud.

Annie had breathed in the scent of the carnations as her mother lie dying. Annie had never told anyone about the conversation, and she still hated the scent of carnations.

"Annie?"

She looked up at Aunt Hulda. "I know I have to help with the bank loan. Stephen's death was.... oh, why even talk about it? He's gone and nothing will bring him back. But your giving out free food doesn't help us either. The next thing I know, you'll be offering them food on the book."

"Don't speak to me like that. My giving a few stale rolls and some soft potatoes isn't going to make a difference in your papa paying

off the loan. But it might just feed a few hungry children."

"Those women…." Annie did not finish.

Compassion moved into Hulda's eyes. "*Cherie*, those women are just trying to survive. The mining company owns them and their families."

"I guess. I'm sorry I snapped at you." Annie exhaled a deep breath and remained silent for a few moments. "I'm thinking of sending Stephen's old letters to the editor that he never got the chance to mail. I know he wanted to make people aware of the accidents in the mines and how the miners' families are often left penniless. It will be one small move against the coal company and I'll sign the letters with a made-up name so Papa won't get in trouble."

"Coming from a girl who can barely stand to wait on the miners' wives…I'm surprised."

"I just want to hold the coal company accountable for Stephen's death. Otherwise his accident has no meaning."

"*Cherie*, do you think anyone will read those letters?"

"I hope so. I haven't forgotten Mrs. Klausman's eviction either. People in other towns should know how the Cumberland Valley Coal Company treats the workers' families. We didn't even get compensation from Stephen's accident. The mining company assigned him to work in that tunnel, and they had to know it was unsafe."

"Other people probably do feel the same way about the mining company. It's just that there's nothing anyone can do about it. And at a nickel a copy, lots of folks can't spare the change to buy a newspaper."

Annie hit her closed fist in her open palm. "There has to be a way. I'm going to send off Stephen's letters until the mining company responds."

Hulda sighed. "Annie, your papa still needs you here at the store. At least for a while."

"I know." She paused, but continued looking directly at the older woman. "Aunt Hulda, I would need your help."

"With what?"

"With mailing the letters."

"Why me?"

"Because you take the train down to Riverton twice a month to shop, and if the letters are mailed from there, people would suspect the writer lived in Riverton. Promise you'll help me. We're not doing anything wrong, and you're the only one I can trust. We'd be doing this for Stephen." She gently bit her lower lip, waiting for the response.

The older woman smiled. "All right, *ma cherie*, I'll help. But don't be disappointed if there is no response."

Hulda plodded back to her baking station, sampling bits of crumbled pastries on the way.

Annie looked around at the painted white walls of the shop softened by inexpensive paintings of French landscapes that she knew her mother had insisted they hang. The old oak floor boards were mopped daily in an attempt to wipe off the many scuff marks of customers' shoes, and the counters were wiped off from the presence of fingers counting out change. By nightfall the bakery smelled of a cleaning mixture of thyme, water, and vinegar. Once a month the old wooden counters were polished in the same manner Thérese had used, a few drops of lemon oil mixed with linseed oil.

In this way, the shop still held Thérese's spirit.

Annie still felt the memory of her mother's pride in the shop. Thank goodness Mama died before Stephen. Losing him would have crushed her.

Harassing the mining company would be Annie's first step in retaliation against Stephen's death. What she would do next, she had no idea. But she owed it to Stephen to make the mining company accountable for its negligence.

*

This morning as Annie had gone out back of the store to use the outhouse, she tripped over a large chunk of coal that had fallen from the delivery cart. God, when would Porters Glen get indoor plumbing like Mount Pleasant? She chafed at living in a village that slaved to provide wealth to owners of the coal companies, but could not afford indoor toilets for the common folk.

She, and everyone else, lived in the shadow of the sprawling Cumberland Valley Coal Company, generally referred to as the CVC. On weekdays, the CVC steam whistle awakened the miners with two short blasts at 5:00 a.m. and one additional one later at 7:00 a.m. signaling the beginning of the day shift. Ten hours later, a final blast saluted the dusk and the end of the shift.

The whistle bookended Annie's days in Porters Glen, and she had grown used to its shrillness. The squealing brakes of coal cars and the constant rattle of iron wheels along the tram road also added to the daily cacophony, as did the clacking of the hoisting engine bringing the cars up to the tipple where the coal would be weighed.

The noises had never bothered Annie as a child, but now they got on her nerves. They signaled a constant reminder of Stephen's death and how the village was virtually held hostage by the coal company. She had no intention of staying in Porters Glen for the rest of her life. Somehow, she would find a way to leave.

Accompanying her hate of the coal company was the beat of constant tedium in her life; the day to day drudgery of getting up, going to work, coming home for supper, and starting all over again tomorrow. Nothing special ever happened, and the people of Porters Glen all aged before their time. National events such as the opening of the Chicago World's Fair might as well have been half a world away.

Boredom and irritation threatened to suffocate Annie, and the days became long—as Aunt Hulda would say, like *un jour sans pain*, a day without bread; so Annie retyped Stephen's first letter to the editor on his old second-hand typewriter and prepared to send it out.

*

A few days later Randall Meyers stopped by the shop.

"Hello, Anne."

"Oh, good afternoon, Mr. Meyers. Can I help you?" Annie couldn't help but notice that he was wearing one of the new Cheviot tweed suits that the bankers in Mount Pleasant wore. Must be nice to be able to afford those kinds of clothes.

"I came to order one of your pies for my sister's birthday...and to see how your family is getting on."

The pie was a reasonable request. But how sincere was he, asking how their family was doing? "Do you have a preference for what type of pie? Strawberries and rhubarb have just started coming in season, and we can make a tasty strawberry-rhubarb cream pie."

"Strawberry-rhubarb? That sounds delicious." He waited. "But you didn't comment on my question. How are you doing?"

Annie lifted her chin. "My family and I are moving along. Thank you. It hasn't been easy, but we'll survive."

Did he really care?

Randall Meyers nodded and lowered his voice. "Anne, perhaps this is not my place to say, but I heard that Herman Schumn has been coming in here. I am somewhat new to Porters Glen, but I know your family runs an independent store. You should not feel accountable to any demands he might make. As superintendent, I have the last say."

Instinct sent hackles up Annie's spine. After all, Mr. Meyers was the head of the whole coal operation and probably knew all the demands Schumn made.

When Annie did not comment he said, "I'll return on Wednesday to pick up the pie right before noon." He paused and smiled at her. "Thank you." The door banged shut as he left, leaving the shop's faded sign to swing in the breeze like a tired French flag.

Annie wrote down the order in the customer ledger. They should be able to get enough strawberries and rhubarb from Mr. Denison's farm, but she would need to check and make sure they had enough *kirsch* left. Their use of the cherry flavored liqueur made the Charbonneau's' pies stand out from any others in the area.

Once the business day concluded and the late afternoon light bathed the village in a soft wash of blue and rose-streaked sky, Aunt Hulda left for home with a bag of milk bread rolls. Marie's job for tonight was to produce a simple *potage aux champignons* and a wilted lettuce salad, with bread pudding for dessert. The creamed mushroom soup would complement the taste of the warm salad. Annie looked out the shop window for the appearance of Marie, due to stop in from

school on her way home.

"Papa, you are looking so tired. There aren't any customers this late in the day. Perhaps you should close up and come home."

"No, I'll be fine. Go on ahead and enjoy what's left of the day."

Walking down the road, Annie glanced at the ground where pink clusters of wild garlic had sprouted. Up by the hillsides, redbud trees had come into their full fuchsia blooms and they softened the landscape. Spring added pastel colors to the Earth, and she welcomed the change from the drab winters.

May had always been her favorite time of the year. She had often accompanied her mother up on the fringes of the mountain searching for wild ginger and other tender plants that Thérese would later use for treating ills or fevers. As they picked their harvest, Thérese would sing French folk songs and encourage Annie to join in.

If she concentrated, Annie could almost hear her mother's voice still wrapped in the melody of the spring breeze. She looked back toward the village. *Don't worry, Mama. I'll continue to work to get the loan paid off, one way or another.*

Then she turned and started up the path that led to Coal Bank Lane, humming a tune under her breath and stopping next to Squirrel Creek to pick some wild dame's rocket to bring home. As she bent to snap the tall stems of the clustered lavender blooms, the droning of a solitary woodpecker heralded the hint of summer days to come.

Climbing the rise, she glanced east toward the top of Piney Ridge. Then a shadow darkened the sky and she looked up, spying a hawk. Without warning, it swooped down and pounced on some unfortunate prey.

Goosebumps prickled Annie's arms. It was almost as if the hawk had been coming for her.

CHAPTER 6

Hayden Bowden, killed when caught in bull wheel, Jackson Mine.

The next day Annie arrived at the bakery shortly after eight o'clock. Louis had already left hours earlier to heat the ovens and get a start on the day. Because the miners' wives baked their own bread on Wednesdays, it was the least busy day of the week at the shop. This gave Louis time to prepare specialty items, like custom ordered pies.

"*Bonjour,* Papa."

"Here so soon?"

"I came in to help with the pie for Mr. Meyers."

Ever since she'd begun working full-time in the shop, Louis had noticed that Annie had given up her school girl outfits. She now wore her hair up in a loosely fashioned Gibson Girl style and covered her clothes with a clean white apron for work. She was reminding him more and more of Thérese.

Rummaging through the box of his wife's recipes he found the one they needed. "Grab your mother's special French rolling pin while I assemble the ingredients.."

As he looked at the recipe for *Tarte à la Rhubarbe,*[1] he stopped to appreciate that it was written in Thérese's own hand. Then he methodically pulled out the ingredients: rhubarb stalks, superfine sugar, eggs, crème fraiche, and the components to make a Pâte Brisée, or pie shell. "Ready? Let's begin."

"I remember, Papa, how it's done."

Louis watched Annie proceed to wash the rhubarb and cut it into small slender stalks. Her hands were strong but feminine, just like her mother's. As Annie worked her way through the recipe it was almost as if Thérese was there beside him.

*

The tangy-sweet scent of the rhubarb pie still hung in the air when Mr. Meyers entered the shop exactly at noon. "Hello, Anne, I'm here for the pie."

"I'll go in back and wrap it for you." A few moments later she returned. "That will be twelve cents, and I'll mark you down in the book as having taken a pie pan on loan. When you're finished, just return the pan to us."

He paid his bill of fare, but lingered. "Anne, it's been some time, and I still have not found a tutor for my son."

"Oh? I'm surprised."

"Truthfully, I didn't find a tutor I liked. I want to discuss the idea of you becoming the tutor."

Annie's eyebrows shot up. "Me? But—why?"

Randall Meyers put the pie down on the counter. "Because I think you would be the perfect candidate."

Annie wondered what he saw in her that would indicate she would make a good tutor.

Randall Meyers walked to the back of the store. "Mr. Charbonneau, I would like to discuss the possibility of Anne becoming a tutor for my son."

Louis stopped cleaning the sink. "Oh? Well, please sit down."

---

1 The full recipe and American measurements are included at the end of the book.

Meyers pulled three chairs together. "Louis, I know your loan is overdue. If Annie became the tutor for Robby, I would pay her well. It would be a gesture on my part in honor of your son's memory."

Annie sat ramrod straight, and then heard herself say, "If the mining company had put new safety pillars in the old tunnels, my brother and the men who died with him might still be alive."

Louis sat in rigid silence.

Meyers did not comment right away. "I'm sorry for your family's loss, Anne. But the mining company did not cause the cave-in."

"By their neglect, they did."

Louis spoke up. "Annie, it seems that Mr. Meyers is offering a gift here. Why don't you listen to his details about the tutoring?"

"All right."

Meyers took a breath. "Look, Anne. I'm not here to argue, and I cannot address your concerns about Cumberland Coal's safety issues. What I can do is set up this arrangement to help both of us."

Annie furrowed her brow. "This would only involve tutoring?"

"Yes, just tutoring."

"You do know that I didn't graduate from high school? I should be getting my diploma next month, but after the mining accident, I had to leave; to help out here."

Annie scrutinized his face. Was that genuine compassion she detected?

"Anne, I don't need a certified teacher. Robby's teacher from last year wasn't able to help him much. I need someone new, someone young who would be patient with his difficulties."

"What kind of difficulties?"

"I honestly don't know. I only see how he mixes up words when he tries to read and then gets frustrated and stops trying."

"I've no training in that. There must be someone else that could help you."

"I want you to tutor Robby. In return, I will see to it that the Citizens Bank takes over your father's loan, at a lower rate and with a longer time in which to pay it back."

She tilted her head. "Why are you offering to help us?"

"Everyone in the village speaks highly of your family. I need someone to help my son, and I am in a position to help you. It would be a fair swap."

Louis tried hard not to grin. While this would be a wonderful way to add income, he did not want Annie to feel pressured into taking the job. "Let Annie and I talk this over. Would that be all right?"

"Certainly."

Louis stood up and went back to cleaning out the steel sink. Annie felt his steps were lighter than before.

Meyers lowered his voice. "Annie, there would be two additional conditions to the job."

"What would they be?"

"I have a small hunting cabin up on Piney Ridge. I've fixed it up as a classroom and you would tutor Robby there. I have set aside $15.00 for the pay. Just tutor Robby for the three months of summer, three times a week. I can deposit the money into your father's account at the bank, or give you the cash if you prefer. Just three months, then you can quit if you choose. The fifteen dollars should significantly help with the loan."

"Why can't I tutor him at our house?"

"Because I don't want nosey neighbors knowing about the lessons, or gossiping about Robby's difficulties learning to read."

"What's the second condition?"

"As you may know, I'm a widower. My sister lives with me and helps take care of Robby. I've not made many friends here in Porters Glen, so the second condition is that you will stay after each lesson and we talk. I would like to get to know you better."

"You mean that you'll pay me…just to talk to you?"

His face reddened. "Don't make it sound so crass. I would like to have the pleasure of your company for a few minutes each week. I don't think that's too much to ask."

"But…nothing more? Just talk?"

"That's right. Just talk."

It was only for three months, and talking couldn't hurt. She would have to put aside her feelings about the CVC if this could help

Papa pay off the loan. And maybe this would show her whether she really wanted to be a teacher.

"Let me discuss it with my father."

"Of course. But please do not talk about this with anyone else. Gossip flies fast in small communities and I wish for our arrangement to remain private. Two days should be sufficient for you to decide. Good day."

He picked up his pie and smiled at her.

Was this the answer to their prayers? Or was he another hawk, dressed in the disguise of a do-gooder? Annie wasn't sure and even though Randall Meyers appeared to be sincere, she trusted no one from the coal company.

*

The next day Annie and Louis left the shop after they had closed for the day. Other shopkeepers like Mr. Engle, the butcher, and Mr. Brode, the barber, were also locking up their stores. Both men waved over to Louis.

"Papa, what do you think about Mr. Meyers' proposal? He'll be expecting an answer tomorrow."

"Frankly, I don't understand why the tutoring can't take place here in the village. You'll be isolated up there on the mountain. If you really want the job, I'll agree—as long as you take a dog with you."

"But we don't have a dog."

"We will as of tomorrow. Joe Rafferty's selling me that young shepherd he found abandoned last year. He'll make a good guard dog and keep you safe."

"Papa, don't be silly. I don't need a dog watching over me."

"You'll be going up the mountain and into the woods. You take the dog, or you don't take the job. I'm not completely comfortable with the idea of you tutoring in a hunting cabin."

"I told you, Mr. Meyers fixed it into a school room for his son. If it makes you feel better, I'll take the dog. Don't be such a worrier. I'll be fine."

The next day, a weather-beaten farm wagon rambled up Store Hill and pulled up in front of Charbonneau's Bakery. Perched on the seat was Mr. Rafferty and lying down in the back was a healthy-looking shepherd mix. The dog scrambled to his feet as soon as the old pine buckboard came to a stop. Both Louis and Annie walked out front to greet them.

"Thanks for bringing the pup, Joe. Much obliged."

As Louis counted out his payment, Annie walked around to the back of the wagon. The animal appeared to be a mix of German shepherd and perhaps Labrador retriever with a coat of amber colored fur and muted patches of black-brown. The dog's tail thumped in rhythm as soon as Annie smiled at him. "Hi there, I'm Annie." She extended her hand and he cocked his head and then looked up at her with warm brown eyes that immediately stole her heart.

"What's his name, Mr. Rafferty?"

"We just call him Dog."

Annie laughed. "Well if he's going to become a part of the Charbonneau family, he needs a French name."

Louis smiled, coaxing the wrinkles at the corners of his eyes to stand out. "He'll be with you the most, so go ahead and name him."

"How about Napoleon Bonaparte?"

Joe Rafferty laughed and slapped his knee with his cap. "He's used to something short, like Dog. I think you'd better give him a simple name so he won't get confused."

"All right. I'll call him, Bon. That way his name is part Bonaparte and part Charbonneau."

"Suit yourself." He shrugged. "Dog, jump down. Go on now."

The dog tilted his head to the side, but then jumped down into the road.

Joe Rafferty climbed back in the wagon and rested his muck-stained boots on the old warped floor boards for just a moment. Then he snapped the reins and the ancient Belgian draft horse lumbered out into the road. The dog seemed ready to chase the farm wagon, so Annie bent down and scratched him between his ears.

"It'll be all right, Bon. You're safe with us." She fed him a small

scrap of a roll. "Papa, where will Bon stay while we're at work?"

"I can build him a small shelter behind the house and tether him when we're gone."

"Can he stay inside with us when we're home?"

"*Peut-etre*. One more thing about this job. I want you to carry bear bells when you and the dog go up the mountain."

"Papa, please—now you *are* being silly. I'll have Bon to protect me."

"I have a small leather strap with two bells sewn on. You'll carry it in your pocket and if you hear any rumblings in the forest as you climb the path, you shake the bells as loud as you can. Bears will shy away from the noise."

"But bears don't usually roam below the big glade." Annie saw genuine concern on her father's face. "All right, all right. I'll carry bells." She smiled. "Come on, Bon. You'll come home with us."

*

A lone figure standing near the mining office watched the entire encounter. Herman Schumn's razor sharp eyes did not miss a thing. "Girlie got herself a dog. Wonder why?" He spoke his thoughts aloud, though only he could hear the irritation resonating in his voice.

CHAPTER 7

Montgomery Brown, killed by fall of roof coal,
Georges Creek Mine.

Two weeks later, near Memorial Day, Randall Meyers pulled a newspaper clipping out of his desk and read the Letter to the Editor one more time.

> *Dear Editor,*
>
> *Are the people of Allegany County aware of the injustices that the coal companies heap upon their employees? Men and boys are injured in the mines because of a lack in safety precautions. Families of miners who are killed while working on the job are not provided with any death benefit. Widows are often evicted after the death of their husbands, when they can no longer pay the rent.*
>
> *These are issues that the coal companies should be brought to task for.*
>
> *Molly S.*
> *Riverton*

Who in the hell is this woman and why is she writing this? He hoped she was a one-time complainer and would not write any additional editorials.

But he couldn't quite get her out of his mind. She had to be a bit bold to write to the paper with the intention of harassing the coal companies. Young or old, blonde or brunette, plump or well proportioned? Was she seeking attention or trying for revenge?

Regardless of her intentions, if she wrote again he would have to have her stopped. He needed to make a trip to the Mt. Pleasant Post Office and ask Tom Dodds if he had any idea as to where this Letter to the Editor had been postmarked. Then perhaps he could tell if this Molly S. really was from Riverton or not.

Who was this Molly S.? Did she have a son? One she ridiculed through childhood? And what of her husband? Had he been a miner, or was he one of those milk-toast fathers that never intervened when his wife started her cruel taunting's of their son. Did Molly S. lash out in her rages, using one of her shoes as a weapon?

He shook his head to clear the painful memories of his own life.

Then a terrible image loomed in his mind, his mother's face became Molly S.

"God damn, her," he shouted aloud. Whether he was referring to his mother or Molly S., no one would know.

CHAPTER 8

Thomas Wells, killed by fall of roof coal,
Georges Creek Mine.

Today was Annie's first day of tutoring. Part of her was excited, but a bigger part was scared. What if she couldn't help this boy, or what if the kid was horribly behaved? Then, what would she do? As she walked home from the shop, several different scenarios flashed through her mind, most of them with a negative tinge. She stopped to cross Squirrel Creek, and the familiar sounds of flowing water and accompanying frog-songs of June seemed to be cheering her on.

I can do this.

She stopped at her house and called out for Bon. He came running with his tail pumping back and forth like a duster.

"Good boy. Come on, we're going up on the mountain." She grabbed the bear bells from the bowl by the back door, slipped them in her pocket, and headed out for the hunting cabin. In the open, Bon raced ahead of her, and then stopped and looked back as if to say, "Hurry up!"

They climbed the lower path of Piney Ridge, progressed up the steeper hill, and veered left at the fork. The hunting cabin soon came into view and Annie spied Randall Meyers playing catch with his son.

The moment was more tender than she would have imagined, and the young boy seemed to be happy playing with his father.

As soon as Meyers saw Annie, the game ended.

"Hello, Anne!" He waved her over.

Annie swallowed the lump in her throat. "Hello, Mr. Meyers. Wow, you must be Robby. I can tell because your hair is dark and wavy like your father's. But your dad isn't missing a front tooth like you are." She smiled at the boy with what she hoped would be taken for genuine friendliness.

"Robby, you need to say hello. Just like we practiced."

"Hello, Miss Anne." Small for his age, the boy wore a mantle of shyness around him like a protective shield.

"Can we shake hands, Robby? I know we're going to become good friends."

The young boy hesitated a moment, looked back at his father and then took her offered hand and shook it.

"My, you're strong." Annie's comment brought a lopsided smile to his face and a hint of a sparkle to his vivid blue eyes.

"Let's go in, Anne, and see the room." Randall Meyers opened the door with the formality of a school superintendent.

Once inside, Annie had to admit surprise and pleasure. What previously must have been an old hunting cabin had been transformed into a cozy room containing a child's oak desk with matching chair, a modest slate board mounted on the front wall, a large paper map of the world tacked to another wall, and a sturdy pine shelf for holding books.

At the front, a straight back wooden chair sat next to a rect-angular pine table piled with slates, chalk, pencils, and a teacher's cloth-covered day book. The smell of lemon polish wafted throughout the small cabin.

"My, I wasn't expecting all this."

Randall Meyers' quiet smile seemed to indicate his pleasure with Annie's reaction. "Good. Well, then. I'll leave the two of you alone and come back in an hour."

Once the door shut, Annie took a deep breath.

Mon Dieu, aidez-moi.

"So, Robby, let's take a book off the shelf and see if there is a story we'd like to read." To her shock, she saw his body stiffen and tears well up.

"Whoa. You don't have to read. How about if I read to you, instead?"

Instantly the boy's shoulders softened. He pretended to swat at an invisible bug and rub his eyes at the same time. The tears stopped.

Annie walked over to the shelf and saw two McGuffey books, both labeled Third Reader. She doubted he would be able to decipher either of them. Flipping through the pages she found a short story about a boy and a dog.

"Do you like dogs, Robby?"

He nodded.

"I do, too. How about we invite Bon to come in and listen to the story with us?"

The boy's eyes grew wide. "You're not supposed to have dogs in school."

"Maybe so, but this is our school, and since I'm the teacher I say it's all right for Bon to join us." She opened the door, put her index finger and her thumb to her lips and whistled. Bon came hurtling toward the cabin with a wide canine grin.

"Bon, this is Robby. He's our new friend. Come inside." She opened the door to its fullest extent and the dog bounded in. "Robby, why don't you sit over here on the floor?" The boy looked surprised but complied. "Come here, Bon." She motioned for the dog to sit right next to Robby. "Now, while I read, you can pet Bon. He loves that."

As Annie began the story, Robby's hesitant demeanor melted with the presence of Bon's warm body pushed up against his side. When Bon plopped his head in Robby's lap, any previous tension evaporated completely.

"The End." Annie finished and shut the book. "There is something special about having a dog, isn't there? Do you have a dog at home?" The boy shook his head and pushed a shock of errant bangs off his forehead. "No? Well then, I'll share Bon with you. Now, let's have

you climb back up in the chair and Bon can lie at your feet. I'll pull the other chair up next to you."

"Aren't you supposed to sit at the table?"

"Heavens, no. I can sit wherever I want, and I choose to sit next to you." She moved the straight back chair and sat down, opening the pages to the story of the boy and the dog. "Here, let's look at the title and you tell me if you recognize any of the words."

Robby's shoulders tensed and he remained silent.

"Well, the title isn't so important. Let's look instead at the individual letters in one of the words." She selected the word "fishing" and covered up all the letters except the first one.

"Do you know this letter?"

"Can I pick the book up and bring it closer?"

"Why of course. Here."

"It's an 'f.'"

"Great! How about this one?" She moved her index finger to the next letter.

"It's an 'i.'"

"So you do know the letters of the alphabet."

"Yes. But when they get pushed together, they get jumbled up. Plus, I need to see them up close, so they're clearer."

Annie lifted her head. "Did your teacher ever let you move the book up closer to your face?"

"No. She said the book had to stay on the desk. That was the rule for everyone."

"I see. But in here I'm the teacher, and I say you can move the book as close as you want. Now watch, I'm going to show you some magic."

Annie took the chalk and a small slate and wrote in large letters the two syllables of *fish + ing*. She covered up the first syllable. "This second part here, the letters 'ing' always say 'eeng'. Go ahead—you say it."

"Eeng."

"Great, so if I tell you that this first part of the word is 'fish', and then we add the 'ing', it will make a new word. Try it with me."

She coaxed him to repeat "fish" and add "ing". On the third try

he said the entire word— "fishing."

"You just read your first word! Congratulations!"

For the next thirty minutes Annie wrote out short, easy words that ended with "ing" and got Robby to figure them out. She ended the lesson with him practicing writing the word "fishing" on the slate.

The new-found experience of success made his eyes twinkle. "Wow, it's almost like magic!"

"There's a lot more magic I know about letters, and I'll teach it all to you this summer."

"Promise?"

"Cross my heart." She smiled. "Hey, you've worked hard today. Let's go outside and play catch. And why don't you start calling me Miss Annie?"

When Randall Meyers returned, Robby ran up to him. "Dad! Come inside, I want to show you something."

Randall Meyers' puzzled expression brought a pleased smile to Annie's face.

Robby grabbed the chalk and slate. "Watch this. This part says fish and this part says 'eeng' and if you put them together you get the word 'fishing'. How about that?"

Randall Meyers appeared stunned. "That's great." Then he turned to Annie. "But shouldn't you be starting him with his letters first?"

"Robby, why don't you go outside and play fetch with Bon while your father and I talk." Robby raced outside.

"Mr. Meyers, has Robby ever been seen by a doctor about his eyesight?"

"No, why?"

"I think that may be a part of his problem. He told me that in his school the book has to stay on the desk. But when I told him to hold it where he wanted, he brought it up quite close."

"I never saw him bring anything up close before."

"But you never saw him hold a book, did you?"

"Well, no. That's it then? He just needs glasses?"

"I'm not sure there isn't something else hampering him, but I

promised I'd work with him all summer. It will be my goal to help him find a way to make reading easier."

"Thank you. I'll take him to see Dr. Paige in Riverton as soon as possible. I'm embarrassed I never thought of him possibly needing glasses."

"Good. I have another request; can you get us a large rag rug, and the First Reader of the McGuffey's series?"

"Robby's almost eight. He should be in the Third Reader."

"Yes, but I suspect he never learned how to read the first or second book, so I should start him there."

"All right, I'll get that for you. What's the rug for?"

"I'll start each lesson by reading a story to Robby. He gets to sit on the floor and pet Bon while I read."

"You're letting your dog come inside?"

"Do you have a problem with that?"

"No, not really. It just doesn't seem like a school room, then."

"Exactly." She smiled.

Annie started cleaning up the room, getting ready to leave when Randall Meyers reached out and touched her arm. She reacted with a startle.

"Remember my other condition? We talk with each other at the end of the lessons."

"I thought we just did."

"No, I mean social talking between two adults."

Annie swallowed her feeling of nervousness. "But I'm so much younger than you, Mr. Meyers. I'm not even sure what we'd talk about."

"We can start talking on the way home today. You can tell me something about yourself." Mr. Meyers locked up the cabin. "Come on, Robby."

Robby and Bon raced each other down the path. The air was delightfully warm.

Annie looked up at Mr. Meyers and tried not to think of him as the mining superintendent. "There's nothing really interesting about me."

"Tell me about your family, then. Where did your parents come from?"

Annie relaxed. "They were born in Alsace, France, where my father's family ran a small bakery. After my parents married, my father decided he could make more money in Canada, so they moved to Quebec. Many bakers, however, already lived there. One day he said he read about the new mining villages in America and knew that miners would always need bread. So, they moved and settled here."

"Were you born here?"

"No, I was born back in Quebec. Marie here in America, and Stephen in France." She paused, surprised that talking with Mr. Meyers wasn't as daunting as she had assumed. "How about you?"

"I grew up in Pittsburgh. My mother insisted that I go into business, so I studied at the Western University of Pennsylvania. I met my wife in a nearby library. The year after we married, she gave birth to Robby. But, she died a few days later."

"I'm sorry about that, Mr. Meyers."

"Thank you."

They engaged in a bit more small talk as they retraced their steps back down the mountain path. At the fork, Annie paused. "I turn here to go home."

Randall Meyers reached out and gently placed his hand on her shoulder. "I know you do. Thank you for today, and I'll look forward to us getting to know each other better."

Annie nodded, but felt better once he removed his hand. He seemed genuine, and from his interactions with Robby it was obvious he loved his son. But, she still felt a bit awkward in his presence.

"Miss Annie, can Bon always come with you?"

"Yes, Robby, I'll always bring him." She turned to Meyers. "My father insists on it."

"Well, it's probably a good idea. Till next time, then. Good-bye Anne."

When they parted, the clicking of crickets meant that the late summer afternoon was drifting toward evening.

*

Hidden out of sight, two men stood at a slightly higher elevation on Piney Ridge, where they sat on a large rock ledge with a view to the cabin.

"Seems pretty stupid we just sat here and watched her," one of them said to the other.

"We were picked for this job and we're not supposed to question orders, just do what we're told."

"Well nothing happened. She stayed in the cabin with the boy and then they came out and tossed a ball. She had a dog with her."

"Yup."

"Did you see Meyers come to the cabin?"

"Yeah, I saw him. He didn't see us, though. Remember, we're not supposed to ask any questions, just report what we see her do."

"Yeah, I know."

*

"I have a surprise for you." Louis smiled with an air of mystery about him. "Anyone about to turn eighteen should be treated to a special occasion. After your birthday dinner tomorrow, I'm taking you to Moat's Opera House to see the Cleveland Minstrel Show."

He cleared his throat. "I know you should be graduating this month…and I'm so sorry that couldn't happen. I hope this makes up for it, even if only in a small way."

No night anywhere, no matter how special, could replace her desire for a high school diploma. But she hugged her father and stayed in the embrace a moment longer. "Thank you, Papa. It's a wonderful idea. And don't worry, somehow I plan to go back to school and graduate."

Annie rarely had a chance to go on any special adventures, so she concentrated on the gift itself and not about missing high school.

Moat's Opera House had only hosted a real opera once or twice, but now catered to traveling shows and performers. However, it was still considered to be a place of entertainment for the surrounding communities and Annie was finally getting to attend a performance.

Marie surprised Annie the next day by sewing a few marma-

lade-colored rosebuds onto the standup collar of Annie's best cream linen shirtwaist and presented it as part of Annie's birthday gift.

"Please let me make you a new hat, too!"

"Don't be silly, Marie. Last year's straw hat will work just fine. But I do like the rosebuds on my collar. Thank you."

"Well at least wear this light orange sash instead of that heavy belt." Marie thrust the more fashionable tie at Annie.

Annie smiled at her sister's uncanny sense of fashion, and took off the belt and tied on the sash.

After the early dinner, a neighbor, Mr. Eisner, arrived. He would be driving them in his buggy up the mile-long stretch of the Pike. Annie would travel in style. Louis helped Annie into the buggy, complimenting her on her choice of outfit. Once they arrived and saw other buggies jockeying for positions in front of the Opera House, Louis nudged Annie.

"I want this to be a memorable evening for you."

"Oh, I'm certain it will be, Papa."

Annie smiled to think of how many times she had walked past St. Bridget's Church, with this building next to it, and never stopped to appreciate the lovely architecture of the opera house.

The brick corniced building consisted of multiple sections, with the height of the middle segment three stories tall. Craning her head, she noticed how all the windows had been designed with identical curved lintels giving a graceful symmetry to the front façade. A tan canvas awning covered each window on the street level, which she supposed helped to keep the summer sun at bay.

"Ready? Let's go in. Give me a minute while I purchase the tickets. Tonight we splurge; I'm buying the thirty-cent seats."

As they entered the theater, Annie's gaze riveted on the hundreds of red cushioned seats and the drop curtain on stage with its colorful painted image.

"Papa, look at the curtain. What a lovely picture."

"That's the Normandy coast. It's located in the north of France."

"Did you ever go there?"

"No, but I've seen paintings of it. Now, stay here while I go get

us some punch."

Annie stood by herself admiring the glow from the dozen new electric wall sconces that illuminated the large room. Electricity was a new marvel in Mount Pleasant, but had not yet come to Porters Glen.

Without warning, an oyster-colored linen cap sailed down from the balcony and landed at Annie's feet. Looking up, she saw a young fellow smiling down at her and gesturing to the cap, now on the floor beside her. She knew him. He was Frankie Hennessey from Mount Pleasant. She smiled back. He disappeared and she stooped to pick up the missile.

When she stood up, she saw him walking down the aisle. "Thank you for capturing my cap." He smiled and looked at her directly.

"How did it get dropped? And how did you get down here so fast?"

"Why, I tossed it down on purpose. I took one look at you and sailed my cap so I would have an excuse to meet you."

"But we already know each other. You're Frank Hennessey. I met you once in your father's store."

"Oh, I'm sure I would have remembered you."

"I'm Annie Charbonneau, from Porters Glen, and I was a bit younger when we met."

Just then Louis returned with glasses of punch and carefully eyed the young man.

"Papa, this is Frank Hennessey from Mount Pleasant. Frank, this is my father."

"Pleased to meet you, sir."

"Hennessey? Your father owns Hennessey's Store?"

"Yes, sir."

Complete silence followed as Annie and Louis sipped punch. Louis looked at Frank, who was smiling at Annie. "Well, Frank, we need to be getting to our seats. Come along, Annie." So saying, he guided Annie down the center aisle.

She did not look back until they entered their row. Then she peeked and saw Frankie tip his cap at her and disappear into the crowd.

The house lights dimmed. Banks Winter, a prominent minstrel, appeared on stage and started to sing. Annie smiled, thinking about

how good looking Frankie Hennessey was. Having stood in front of him, she couldn't help but notice his trim physique, and the clean smell that rose from his close-cropped jacket. His sandy-brown hair matched his slim mustache, and his gray-green eyes definitely caught her attention. Their color reminded her of the river whose banks cradled the city of Riverton.

His build reminded her a bit of Stephen, and she found herself hoping she might see him again at the end of the show.

An hour later the performance ended and the lights came back on.

Louis turned toward her. "Did you enjoy the show?"

"It was terrific, but when he sang 'She Was a Soldier's Sweetheart,' it made me think of Stephen. I do think Mr. Banks gave an excellent performance. Did you and Mama ever come here to see any of the shows?"

"Yes, we did; usually for her birthday." He winked at Annie. "I'm glad you liked it." Louis put his arm around her and guided her up the aisle.

Annie craned her neck to see if she could spy Frankie Hennessey, but he had left.

Outside, while they waited for Mr. Eisner to return, Louis asked, "How well do you know the Hennessey boy?"

"I met him once before in his father's store."

"Did he ever finish his schooling?"

"Lots of boys quit school so they can go to work."

"Schooling is important."

"I know it is, that's why I will go back."

Louis hesitated. "I wouldn't be getting my hopes up for someone like the Hennessey boy. The father might own a store, but that doesn't make the son a well-to-do man."

Annie nodded, but she was smiling inside with the image of Frankie Hennessey sailing his cap down from the balcony to get her attention.

CHAPTER 9

Patrick Kenney, killed by fall of breast coal,
Ocean Mine.

A week later, with the Fourth of July only five days away, Frankie Hennessey walked into the bakery.

Annie looked up, surprised to see him, and doubly surprised that her voice caught in her throat as she went to speak. *Oh, my, he is good looking.*

"Frankie, what are you doing in Porters Glen?"

"I came to do some shopping for my mother."

"Aren't there enough bakeries in Mount Pleasant?"

"None that have pretty clerks like you." He grinned.

Annie blushed. "Well, what are you looking for?"

"I'm looking for a product that has grown up some and still holds its beauty.

Annie looked around to see if her father or Aunt Hulda were nearby. "Honestly, Frankie, that's pretty bold." Her eyebrows furrowed, but her lips widened into a smile.

"What?" He played the innocent. "Actually, I came to ask if you would like to go to the Fourth of July Parade and Fair with me."

"Oh. Why, yes, I'd love to. That would be fun."

"Don't we have to ask your father for permission?"

She gave a sly grin. "I'll take care of that."

"Great, then we can meet at my father's store?"

"I thought you were going to call on me?"

"Yes, but I'd have to walk a mile down here to get you and then we would walk the same mile back." His smile exuded boyish charm.

"If you want me to accompany you on Fourth of July, you need to come here first." She stood her ground, teasing him with her hands on her hips.

"Wow, are you always so demanding?"

"Are you always so lazy?"

"Ooh, and the young woman has a tongue on her, too. You win. I'll meet you here at the shop at half past eight in the morning. Then we'll walk back up to Mount Pleasant to watch the parade."

Annie smiled. "Good. I'll see you then. Now, are you going to buy something here?"

"Give me a roll."

"How about a *brioche*? They're better than just a plain roll."

He looked at her with his left eyebrow raised.

"Of course—if it's a roll you want, pick one out."

He plucked a roll from the basket, deposited two pennies on the counter, and sauntered out of the store.

She liked his bold attitude; it made him all the more appealing.

*

At the end of the day, as Annie stepped out into the crowded street, she spied Herman Schumn walking toward the mining office. Seeing him made her skin crawl, especially after his comment about Marie. Annie resolved to have a talk with Marie.

The opportunity presented itself after supper that same night while the two girls did the dishes.

"Marie, has Mr. Schumn ever approached you?"

"What do you mean—approached me?"

"Well, like suggesting you could help our family pay back the loan."

"Annie, are you talking about that place at the mining office?"

Annie stopped in mid-air with a soapy dish still clutched in her hand and water dripping back into the pan. "What place?"

"Giselle told me last week there's a room where the mining widows go for a loan, or to get new shoes for their children."

"Shoes?"

"Yes, I think so."

"What else has Giselle told you?"

Marie shrugged. "Nothing, really."

"If Mr. Schumn ever approaches you for any reason, I want to know about it."

Marie nodded. "I doubt that would ever happen, so you don't have to worry."

But Annie did worry. At barely sixteen, Marie was as impulsive as a young filly. Although she made wonderful trims with her bits of fabric and ribbons, she did not always make the best choices when it came to friends. Giselle had already been seen smoking the newly popular cigarettes. Annie hoped Giselle wasn't filling Marie with stories about what the widows did, or didn't do, at the mining offices.

One day, someone might take advantage of Marie's innocence, but Annie did not want that person to ever be Herman Schumn. As she got ready for bed, thoughts raced through her mind. Why had she never heard about the room at the mining office? If it was true, and the mining widows went there, did other women go there too? And what connection did children's shoes have to do with it?

That night, Annie tossed and turned. In her dreams she saw a huge pile of shoes cascade down on top of her.

*

The day before the Fourth of July, Annie arrived at the cabin with a surprise for Robby.

"Miss Annie, what's that?"

"A gift for you."

"But, it's not my birthday."

"Maybe not, but it is a gift to celebrate how well you're doing in reading. Go ahead, open it."

Robby's fingers tore off the paper. "It's a book about dogs! Is it mine to keep?"

"Absolutely. We can practice reading it today."

As Robby looked through the book, Randall Meyers approached Annie. "That was a sweet and generous gift. My son is smitten with you, as am I."

Annie looked away from his direct gaze. "Robby deserves the book."

Randall Meyers waited, it seemed, for her to say more.

"Ready, Robby? Let's get started. We'll see your father in an hour."

Without further comment, Randall Meyers left the cabin.

*

By nine in the morning on the Fourth of July, Frankie had still not shown up at the bakery. Annie told her father a group of friends would meet at the parade, so she would not have to go through the formality of "Frankie coming to call." Annie paced the floor and had determined to give Frankie only five more minutes before she would leave for the parade on her own.

She stepped outside the shop and spied him strolling up Beer Alley toward Store Hill. He wasn't in a hurry, and that irritated her even more.

"Why are you late?"

"Well, and a good day to you, too, Miss Annie Charbonneau."

"Really, Frankie, you're half an hour late. What happened?"

"I am? I only stopped by the ball field to talk to some of the guys about our game later today."

Annie bristled. Obviously, she wasn't as important as a silly ball game. "Let's get going. If we wait much longer, we'll miss the parade.

Everyone in Porters Glen has already left." Then she saw he carried a slightly bulging pillow case. "What's in there?"

"It's my clothes for the baseball game, and a towel. You know I play for the Mount Pleasant Miners, right? Maybe you've seen one of my games?"

"I work full time in the bakery, so I don't get to watch baseball games."

"Really? 'Cause we often play here in Porters Glen, up behind Mr. Burns' Store."

She shook her head no.

"Well, you'll get a chance to watch me today. There's a big game this afternoon between us and the Connellsville Canalers."

The two of them fell into stride and started the walk up to Mount Pleasant. Frankie's easy-going smile and his playful attitude had a way of diffusing Annie's anger. By the time they reached Union Street, his sincere flirting had her smiling. Her previous anger had blown over like a summer storm. Vivid blue skies smiled down on them and the early summer heat brought a healthy glow to her face.

The parade consisted of groups wearing red, white, and blue ribbons and marching with banners associated with their churches or other groups. Four fire brigades from the surrounding towns also had positions in the parade, each pulling their polished red racing reels. People cheered as each fire brigade passed by.

But it was the Leidenschaft Band that impressed Annie the most.

The group of men in their matching red uniforms with gold trim marched in step with one another while playing instruments of flute, oboe, trumpet, and single drums. The beat of the music matched the beating of Annie's heart.

She clapped as the band tromped past, but she was also looking at Frankie out of the corner of her eye. There was no denying the physical attraction she felt, especially when he smiled at her with his lively gray-green eyes. Did he find her as attractive as she found him?

The after-parade festivities were set up next to the town's baseball field. Temporary booths had been constructed and festooned with

patriotic streamers. Most of the booths sold food like fried oysters, fried chicken, sausage rolls, root beer, and ice cream. Other booths had games of chance like ring toss, and they drew a fair portion of the crowd trying out their luck.

Farther over from the booths, a makeshift wooden stage had been set up so the mayor of Mount Pleasant could make his customary Fourth of July speech, telling all the listeners how fortunate the town was that the Cumberland Valley Coal Company had adopted them. Annie and Frankie listened to the mayor's predictable ramblings about the good life in Mt. Pleasant. Good life? Annie couldn't help but think the good life didn't reach the miners in Porters Glen. What would Stephen have had to say about that?

Once the mayor finished his speech, Annie and Frankie headed over to the games of chance. On the way they met a small crowd of Frankie's friends. "Hey, Frankie, who's the new girl?"

"This is Annie Charbonneau. She's younger than us."

Annie wanted to throttle Frankie. She already felt out of place not knowing these older friends. *I'm the only Porters Glen girl in the group; he didn't need to announce my younger status as well.*

"Well hi, Annie Charbonneau," piped up a boy whose physique matched Frankie's and who had a smartly dressed blonde girl hanging on his arm. "We don't know what you see in Frankie, other than he's a great ball player."

A few of the boys chortled as Frankie blushed.

"Hey boys, thanks for the praise, but you could have also told Annie how good looking I am." He turned and winked at Annie.

Now it was her turn to blush. *Yes, you are good looking and when you smile like that at me, I feel a warmth all over my body.*

Later, after the games and some sausage rolls and root beer, their crowd wandered over to the ball diamond where the baseball game would soon begin. Frankie went with his team behind a large rigged canvas curtain and changed clothes. Annie watched as he ran out onto the field, noting how good he looked in the uniform. She waved to him, and forgave his earlier indiscretion.

A large crowd of spectators sat on blankets and rooted for their

favorite team. The nine innings took up the rest of the afternoon and Annie made sure her straw hat kept the sun off her face.

Near the end of the game, the Connellsville Canalers were ahead ten to eight. Two outs had been called when Frankie came to bat with runners on first and second. Annie watched and saw the pitcher glare at Frankie. Frankie gripped his bat and swung. The sound of the bat connecting to the ball brought the crowd to their feet. The hit was a homerun. Frankie rounded the bases and the three runs won the game. The crowd went wild.

All of Frankie's teammates rushed onto the field, clapping him on the back and shouting cheers. As the team moved back toward their bench, Frankie turned and waved his cap to the crowd.

Annie became swept up in the thrill of the win and couldn't help but feel special when he ran off the field and headed straight for her. She found she couldn't keep her eyes off his sweat-stained figure.

"You were great!"

"Yeah, I was."

"No modesty on your part?"

"Why? I played great, and everyone there saw it."

He draped his sweaty arm around her and she found that his boy-now-man-smell was slightly intoxicating.

"Wait here for me while I towel off some of this sweat and dirt, and change clothes. I won't be too long."

He trotted off, leaving an image of his muscular torso implanted in Annie's mind. Then she spied a booth where you could have your fortune told. On impulse, she walked over.

"Pretty girl wants to know her future?" crooned an older, dark-haired woman with a prominent silver streak through her hair, and large gold hoops in her ears. She clapped her hands, which made her bangle bracelets clink like musical chimes. Annie could tell the woman was a gypsy. Her bright red head scarf matched her painted lips, and over her shoulders she wore a series of larger scarves, bright oranges, yellows, and greens that accented her white muslin top.

Caught up in the excitement of the day, Annie smiled. "How much?"

"Two cents."

"All right." Annie plunked down two pennies and sat on a make-shift bench perched in front of a small wobbly table fashioned from a wooden grocery crate.

The woman produced a well-worn deck of cards and shuffled at lightning speed. Annie had never done anything like this before, and it seemed frivolous to be giving away two cents over something as silly as a fortune teller. But she stayed, fascinated with the designs on the back of the cards and wondering what the woman would tell her.

Four cards appeared: the three of clubs, the five of diamonds, the queen of hearts, and the eight of clubs. The gypsy smiled and Annie saw a gold-filled tooth.

"You are French, no? Three of clubs say a country with three colored flag. And your family, they are five persons, yes? The five of diamonds say so. You are Catholic, for the queen of hearts is like Mary, the Queen of Heaven. And you are eighteen, because of the eight of clubs. Did I get this right?" She grinned at Annie's surprised reaction.

"But how could you know all that?"

The woman shrugged. "I have been reading cards for most of my life." She turned over three more cards. This time it was the queen of spades, the jack of spades, and the eight of diamonds. The woman frowned.

"No mother anymore, am I right?"

Annie felt a lump in her throat and barely nodded.

"And a brother once, but no more. Yes?"

Annie could feel the blood rushing toward her face, causing her neck to flush. The first four cards could have been guesses, but not this information. Not being a local, there was no way this woman could know these things. Maybe Annie should tell her to stop.

"The eight of diamonds shows future wealth." The gypsy stated. "Wait, we will turn the cards again." She flipped up the jack of diamonds and the jack of hearts, plus the ten of spades and the ten of clubs. She moved her head forward.

"You will have two men in your life and two jobs as well."

That might be Papa, and perhaps Frankie? But two jobs? How

could that be?

"Are you sure?"

"Yes, the cards never lie. I will turn one last time."

The gypsy smiled as the ace of hearts flipped over. "One child; will be the love of your life."

Annie sat still, taking in all the information. "Is there more?"

"No, I only do twelve cards. Thirteen would be an unlucky number." The woman smiled with a touch of tenderness. "But remember what my cards have shown you."

"Thank you." Annie got up and walked back to where she had left Frankie and saw him moseying across the field toward her.

"Ready for more fun?"

She nodded, but did not mention where she had been or anything the gypsy woman had foretold.

Walking her home after the fireworks, Frankie put his arm around her shoulder and she felt a warm flush. When they got to Porters Glen, he insisted on walking her up Coal Bank Lane until they reached her house. Bon sat on the front porch and began growling.

"Bon, Frankie's a friend." The hair on the back of Bon's spine lay flat once more and his ears popped back up to the top of his head.

"I didn't know you had a watch dog."

"He's more than that. He's my companion. And it feels good knowing he's here to protect me."

"So if I try and kiss you, goodnight, is he going to attack me?"

"Let's see." She winked.

Frankie pulled her behind a large bush, far from neighbors' eyes, and took her in his arms. With one eye open to look over at the dog, he kissed her full on the lips. Bon stared straight at Frankie, but did not react. Frankie extended the kiss and wrapped Annie in his arms in a lusty embrace. One kiss led to another and another. Annie could feel her breath quicken and her heart race, but she slowly backed up.

"No need to rush, Frankie."

His shoulders drooped, and Annie thought he seemed a bit dismayed. "All right. Happy Fourth then, Annie. I'll collect on those kisses another time."

"And I'll hold you to that promise." She smiled. Then she untied Bon and led him inside. From behind the living room curtain she watched Frankie walk back down the lane and her heart skipped a beat with the sight of his jaunty hips. A burst of desire ignited a smile on her lips.

First love had baptized her.

CHAPTER 10

Fred Holtzsnyder, killed by a fall of breast coal, Eckhart Mine.

The sunny weather from the Fourth of July lasted through to July 14th, when the Charbonneaus celebrated Bastille Day. They started with raisin sweet *kugelhopf* slices dipped in their *café au lait* for breakfast and ended the day with Aunt Hulda fixing a traditional Alsatian summer meal of onion tart, asparagus with Hollandaise sauce, baked sliced potatoes, and raspberry ice cream for dessert. Everyone got a small glass of Louis' homemade elderberry wine from last year's batch, and he gave the toast for Liberty, Equality, and Brotherhood.

But after Bastille Day, summer drenched itself with serious heat and moved into the sultry dog days of August. Frankie managed to come calling twice a week, sometimes taking Annie on picnics out at Borden Lake with his friends, other times taking her to watch his baseball games. Louis acclimated to having Frankie around, although he did not encourage the relationship, and told Annie to be careful and stick to seeing Frankie with groups of friends.

By mid-August Hulda posted a second Letter to the Editor, but so far there had been no response printed in the editorials.

Tonight, Frankie and Annie sat on the Charbonneau's front porch swing watching the magic of fireflies flitting through the night air in an orchestrated search of mates. The two sat side by side with their bodies touching each other. Annie could feel the radiant heat, but not sure if it came from her own body, or his.

Frankie leaned forward. "Guess what? I quit my job at my father's store and signed up to work in the mines. I start on Monday."

Annie's breath stopped as she paled. "What in God's name would cause you to do such a thing?"

"Because I want to get out from under my father's thumb, and earn my own money. The mines pay twice what my father does. I could earn as much as $490.00 in a good year."

"And your parents agreed to this?"

"I'm twenty, Annie. I can do what I want."

"God, Frankie. You have no idea of how dangerous the mines can be. I would never want that kind of life for you. Plus, by the time the CVC takes out all your deductions, there won't be nearly as much money as you think. Stephen complained about that all the time."

"I'll be making my own money, and it's important to me that I strike out on my own. I don't always want to be known as just John Hennessey's son. Besides, with my own job, I should be able to buy you a ring one day." A devilish grin spread across his face.

"A ring? Frankie, are you proposing?" Her eyebrows shot up.

"Not yet, but maybe someday."

A thundering lightness beat in her chest, but, marriage? She hadn't really thought about the possibility of marriage yet, and certainly not a marriage to a coal miner.

Annie slipped her hand into his. "Frankie, shouldn't we first talk about what we want for the future?"

"I want you to become Mrs. Frank Hennessey one day." He beamed.

Annie paused. "What if I didn't want you to be a miner, would you still marry me?"

"Just because I would get dirty and have calluses on my hands?

Oh, you'd get used to being a miner's wife, Annie. Other girls do."

"But maybe, Frankie, I'm not like other girls. I plan to return to school, graduate, and hopefully go on to college."

"College? Why would you do that?"

"I want to be the first girl from Porters Glen to go to Mount Pleasant Normal. They have a two-year teacher program, so I could become qualified to teach."

"Two years is a long time. I don't know if I'd want to wait that long to get married. Why do you want to be a teacher anyway? They don't make much money."

"I want to be a teacher so I could help children. I've been tutoring a little boy this summer and really enjoying it."

"You're tutoring? You haven't mentioned it."

"Well, I'm mentioning it now."

"I guess there's coal miners who have married teachers." He draped his arm over her shoulder. "We can work it out." But he didn't even ask who her pupil was.

Annie's heart raced at the idea of being married to Frankie, but she cringed at the idea of living under the thumbs of the CVC.

Dear God, let him absolutely hate the mine.

*

When he came over the next Saturday afternoon, they went for a walk in the back meadow, now filled with a blanket of blooming purple asters. Frankie reached for her and they held hands.

"After a week, do you still want to be a miner?"

"'Course I do. I told you, the money's good. Other than the fact that it's kind of cool down there, the guys told me it's about fifty-seven, year-round, but I'm all right with it."

"It didn't bother you to be a half mile back from sunlight?"

"Not really. The whole operation's pretty amazing. Did your brother ever talk about it?"

"Being in the mine? Of course he did, but not about how it actually works."

"Let's sit in the shade under that tree and I can tell you all about it."

They meandered over to a shady sugar maple tree at the far edge of the meadow, and sat down with their backs against the smooth bark. "For starters, I hang one of my I.D. tags, mine are all numbered 129, on the shift board so they have a record of who's working. Then I climb on the mantrip car with a dozen other guys. My heart starts to race with excitement as we begin the descent into the mouth of the mine."

Annie chewed on her thumbnail. "Frankie, I'm not sure I want to hear all this. It might bring back the painful memories of Stephen's death. You have no idea of how much I hate the mine."

"We're not talking about Stephen, here. I do want to share with you about what I do at the mine."

"All right." Annie swallowed a lump of nostalgia.

"When the mantrip reaches the bottom and we all climb out into the main entrance, that's called the heading, we go to our assigned area for the day. So far I've worked with two other guys, John Harriman and Paul Delaney. The hard work begins once we start swinging our pick axes at the layered coal seam. Some of the seams are 30 inches deep into the wall and 10 feet wide."

"The coal falls out in big chunks, doesn't it? I remember Stephen telling me that." Annie tried to not think about the dangers involved.

"Yeah, it falls down after you've undercut the seam and used the wedge bar to start prying the coal loose. After the coal falls, you gotta shovel the chunks into the coal car, and that gets tiring pretty fast. Once the car's filled, it gets hitched to a mule that pulls it down the track and out of the mine. But you gotta hang another of your I.D. tags inside the car, so you get credit for the load. Then you go back to swinging your pick-axe again."

Annie stole a glance at his muscular arms and realized he had a body well suited to being a miner.

"Meanwhile, the mules pull the loaded carts out of the mine and toward the tipple where they get attached to the hoisting engine. Finally, the carts move up to be inspected by Tucker Fatkin. He's the

weigh master. He's more important than you might realize, because he gets your I.D. tags to determine if you've picked your full five tons or not. Then he turns the tags back to the foreman for me to use again tomorrow."

"Stephen did tell me about the mules. He said it's the mule hay that attracts the rats."

"Yeah, the rats. They all warned me about them."

"Have you seen any?"

"Not yet. Supposedly they grow hideously big and are always scratching to get into your dinner bucket. If you leave anything out, the rats will get it. Some of the older men claim that the rat colony has over 200 rats in it, with some as large as barn cats. 'Course I don't believe that, but just the same, I keep looking over my shoulder when I hear anything scratching."

Annie shivered. "Stephen also told me rats are actually good to have in a mine because they can smell gas long before a miner can, and they also can sense when a cave-in is about to happen." She grew quiet. "Of course, that didn't save him. It took the mining crew two days to dig through all the debris to get his body out. He didn't have a scratch on him; looked like he was asleep. That's how we knew the blackdamp got him."

"Don't worry about me, Annie." He leaned over and kissed her full on the mouth, then sat back. "I promise to keep myself safe, for you." He reached down and gave her hands a squeeze.

But Annie knew that Stephen had been a part of the coal operation too, and in return, the mine had killed him. Until the mining company made adequate safety improvements, there would be other accidents, and more women would become widows. She did not intend on becoming either a miner's wife or a mining widow. Somehow, she needed to convince Frankie to leave the mine.

*

As the August days moved toward the end of summer, Annie's tutoring would soon come to a close.

Robby had made excellent progress with his reading, due in part, Annie suspected, to the new glasses and new-found confidence. She wasn't sure which surprised her more, the fact that she had been able to bring Robby almost to his grade level in reading, or the fact that she would miss working with him once the school year started.

Tutoring wasn't the same as teaching a classroom full of children, but her success with Robby made her believe that she really did want to teach. Of course that would mean going back to finish high school, and get into college. The fly in the ointment was Frankie's reaction to her wanting to teach. She'd just have to work on him so that he understands how important this is to me.

*

Two days later at the hunting cabin, Randall Meyers announced, "I'm delighted with the progress Robby's made and I want you to know how much I appreciate you." He touched her elbow.

Annie moved so that his hand fell away from her. "Getting him glasses certainly helped."

Randall Meyers did not move any closer, but kept his gaze on her face. "Have you heard the village hired a new principal for the elementary school? He's coming all the way from Philadelphia. I intend to meet with him as soon as he arrives."

"Philadelphia? How did they get someone from Philadelphia to agree to a job in Porters Glen?" Annie relaxed with the small talk.

"He and his sister are both coming here to teach. I believe their name is Canavan. Miss Canavan will be one of the new English teachers up at Mount Pleasant High, which brings me to my surprise for you."

Annie looked up at him and bit her lips.

"You must realize by now that I had hoped we would become more than just friends."

Annie squirmed. "You said from the beginning…just tutoring and talking."

"I know, but you are a very attractive girl and I still hope that we

might develop some sort of relationship together."

Annie swallowed. "My family is grateful for the tutoring money, and I have grown very fond of Robby. But, I still think of this as just a business arrangement. Nothing more."

"In time, you might have feelings for me."

"I'm sorry, Mr. Meyers. I don't see that ever happening. I had hoped you'd realize we'll always be two people who are just friends." Annie squirmed.

"I'm sorely disappointed in your response, and I will still hold out hope."

Annie remained stoic.

"However, I am a man of my word and I want you to have the surprise I mentioned. It is a thank you for all you've done for Robby, and a sign of my affection for you. I went to Mount Pleasant High to meet with Mr. Connor, the principal. The school is allowing you to re-enroll in September and complete the requirements for getting your high school diploma."

Annie's eyebrows shot upwards. "You did that for me? Thank you. It's a wonderful gesture, but…I can't leave Papa alone with the store. He still needs me."

"I figured as much, so I asked for special permission for you to attend as a night student."

"A night student?"

"Yes. You would attend one night a week and then do the assignments on your own. Your teacher will be Miss Canavan."

"My goodness. Thank you. This is more than generous."

"You can still change your mind about me…."

Annie blushed. Even though she had never given him any encouragement, she had suspected from the beginning that he would act upon even the smallest amount of praise from her. But his gift thrilled her. "When do I get to meet Miss Canavan?"

"You're scheduled to fill out the necessary paperwork with her on Wednesday."

Annie smiled to think that she had once wondered if Randall Meyers might be another hawk. But today he had offered her an olive

branch.

From this day forward, her dream of going for a college education could once more be on track. This time nothing would stop her; not her family, not the coal company, not even Frankie.

CHAPTER 11

Edward Sonnenberg, died in crash of coal cars, Midlothian Mine.

"Papa, I'm nervous about tomorrow."

"About going back to school? I thought you'd be delighted."

"I am delighted, but I'm nervous about meeting the new teacher. She's from Philadelphia and I've heard that people from big cities are not very friendly."

Louis smiled. "That would be like saying all Frenchmen have bad manners."

"What if she's rich, and finds Mount Pleasant to be…too….?"

"Stop worrying. You'll impress her with your knowledge, regardless of where she was raised."

"I'm going back upstairs to check my outfit one more time. I already polished my shoes and inspected my stockings for any holes."

"Annie, you'd be pretty no matter what you wore."

"You say that because you're my father. I want to impress a female teacher."

"Just be yourself."

Annie climbed the stairs and checked over her oyster colored shirtwaist, making sure the blouse had no wrinkles. Its puffy leg-o-mutton sleeves had been a devil to iron, but she wanted to look in style.

She slept fitfully through the night while thoughts of the new teacher slid in and out of her dreams.

*

Annie took off her shop apron precisely at two the next afternoon and walked home as quickly as she could, barely paying any attention to the colorful display of late August chrysanthemums, or the subtle changes in the leaves of the maple trees. She changed clothes and checked her appearance in the bedroom mirror. Using her mother's tortoise hair comb, she piled her hair high in a chignon and arranged her summer straw hat to fit snugly over it. Then she made the sign of the cross for an extra ounce of luck.

She stepped out onto Coal Bank Lane, took the shortcut through the back meadow, and saluted the hill maples that in a month or so would start wearing their autumn colors. Above her the sky wore a mantle of aquamarine blue with billowy white clouds sketched across its expanse. She knew the grayness of winter would eventually return, but right now she hummed with the thrill of excited anticipation mixed with a dash of nervousness.

Once in Mount Pleasant, she saw a group of young girls playing in the church yard. They were jumping rope and singing, "Lizzie Borden took an axe, gave her mother forty whacks…" Annie breathed a shallow sigh, remembering the yearned-for friendships she had never quite cultivated as a girl—she had always been too busy studying.

When she arrived at the high school, her carefully coifed tresses now dampened with perspiration and left wisps of curls framing her face. She scrutinized the school building; it did not look any different from last year, but she felt different. The main arched doorway of the red brick structure seemed to be welcoming her back. She exhaled an excited breath, and walked into the main foyer. A few doors down the hall was the office.

"Why, Annie Charbonneau! How are you doing?"

"Hello, Mrs. Gallagher. I'm fine, thank you. I have an appointment at half-past three to meet the new English teacher."

"That would be Miss Canavan. Room eight."

Walking down the corridor, she realized the school felt smaller to her somehow. Where noisy groups of students usually formed, the empty hallways echoed her steps. She smelled the freshly oiled floors as she found room eight and pushed open the door.

A man stood at the head desk shuffling through a stack of papers. He looked up when Annie cleared her throat. He quickly replaced his slight expression of surprise with a smile.

"Excuse me, I thought this was Miss Canavan's room."

"It is. I'm just trying to find an important paper she left here."

Was this man supposed to be in Miss Canavan's room going through her papers? Should she go back to the office or wait?

"Ah, here it is." So saying, he picked up a paper, folded it and placed it inside his jacket pocket.

Annie stepped further into the room. "Are you a friend of Miss Canavan's?" She noted his tall height and fashionable attire of a three-button cutaway walking suit made of gray cassimere wool.

"Excuse me?"

"I'm sorry, but you just lifted a paper off Miss Canavan's desk. I don't want her to think that I took it. That's all."

The man's left eyebrow shot up and he laughed. "Well, yes, I do know her. And no, I'm not a thief. I'm Jonathan Canavan, her brother."

"Oh, I apologize. I didn't mean to sound so impertinent."

"Jonathan! What are you doing here?" The young woman who now waltzed into the classroom grinned at him.

Annie stared at them for a moment. They made a striking pair, both with matched chestnut brown hair flecked with strands of subtle auburn. Both of them had clear complexions and piercing blue eyes that drew a focus to their faces. Miss Canavan matched Annie in height, but her brother Jonathan reached almost six feet.

Annie also noticed right away Miss Canavan's current sense of fashion with an ivory silk blouse with leg-o-mutton sleeves and a wide

brimmed straw hat decorated with summer silk flowers and ribbons that she had just unpinned and set aside. *Wouldn't Marie love this!*

"Hello. You must be my night student."

"Yes, I am." Annie's face broke into a nervous smile. "I'm sorry; I only expected to be meeting you."

"So, you've met Jonathan, then. He's the new principal in Porters Glen." Josie Canavan turned back to her brother. "Did you get the paper for the bank?"

"Leaving right now." He turned to Annie. "It was nice meeting you, Miss…?"

"Charbonneau. Anne Charbonneau."

"All right then, Anne Charbonneau, I'm off to the bank." He winked, planted a kiss on his sister's cheek, and nodded to Annie as he walked out the door.

"Well, an unusual way for us to start, but we should get down to business. Please sit here. I do think it fair to inform you that this arrangement is rather unorthodox and the school principal, Mr. Connor, has informed me that you will need to complete an entire semester. That means in addition to English, I will tutor you in mathematics, history, and science."

"I was a straight A student before I had to leave school."

"Yes, I've seen your record. Quite impressive. But last year's grades only count for a percentage of what you'll need to do now in order to graduate. I'm afraid you will need to prove yourself all over again. But don't worry; I'll help you get ready for the exams. There will also be a senior project required. You'll have to choose a project that will in some way benefit the community."

"Oh, I didn't realize that."

"You'll have till the Christmas holidays to decide on the project. If everything goes well, you should be done by January." Then Josie Canavan paused and added, a good bit more softly, "I heard why you quit school. I'm sorry for your loss."

Annie looked up at the young woman whose steely blue eyes looked like they could hold the light of kindness, or inexplicably turn to ice. "Thank you. I help out now in my family's store. But I always

wanted to come back and earn my diploma."

"Classes officially start next week, and you'll have to sign a paper before you leave today, but let's not waste any time. We can begin a recap of your studies right now. How about Shakespeare? Remember him?"

"'Some are born great, some achieve greatness, and some have greatness thrust upon 'em.' *Twelfth Night*."

Josie Canavan smiled. "I see you do remember."

As they continued the lesson, Annie tried to bask in the moment and stretch out the time. But she restrained her enthusiasm, so she would appear as a serious student.

Walking home, however, she felt compelled to run through the meadow with joyful abandon. This had been one of the best days of her life and the meadow had somehow transformed itself since this morning. No longer just a field of wildflowers, it now seemed to be the pathway to endless possibilities.

*

The weeks of September flew by, and although she could only see Frankie on weekends now, she tried to share with him her excitement of going back to school. He listened politely, but never asked her to elaborate on any of it.

Annie found that Josie Canavan was not only an engaging teacher, but also appeared to take a genuine interest in Annie's success.

"Annie, we've worked together for a full month and you've turned out to be an impressive student. I hope you have plans for next year."

"I intend to apply to Mount Pleasant."

"Wonderful. You must want to become a teacher, then."

"I think so. I tutored a young boy all summer and loved it."

"Mr. Meyers explained to me that you deserved the opportunity to finish school. Where did you learn the teaching techniques you used with his son?"

"I didn't know they would be called techniques. My parents

spoke mostly French with each other at home, but used English in the shop. My mother taught herself how to read and write English, and then she taught us." Annie paused. "Where did you learn how to teach?"

"I went to Swarthmore, just outside Philadelphia."

"Is that a college?"

Josie nodded. "Yes, it's a very good college."

"And Philadelphia is where you grew up?"

"That's right. And I still love it."

"What made you decide to come to Mount Pleasant?"

"Jonathan thought we needed a change and that we should try teaching in a rural area. We're both very close; more than just being twins. Our father died before we were born and our mother never remarried. We've been each other's best friend since birth."

"I should have realized he was your twin." Annie grinned.

"We're like two halves of a whole."

"Are you enjoying teaching here?"

"Yes, and I think Jonathan is, too. We share stories with each other about our new experiences. But sometimes he's perplexed by his students' actions."

"How so?"

"He told me that during the first week of school he witnessed children taking off their shoes at the end of the day, and walking home barefoot. When he asked them why, one of the boys explained they did that to save wear and tear on the shoes. Is that true? Because neither of us ever saw anything like that in Philadelphia."

"It must have been some of the miners' children. Their families are very frugal, and shoes cost a lot of money. Half the population of Porters Glen are mining families."

"I never imagined shoes being so valuable that you carry them instead of wearing them." Josie's previous smile faded. "Especially if your mother had to sacrifice to get them." As soon as she had uttered the last statement, Josie turned from Annie and a blush spread up her neck.

"What do you mean by a sacrifice?"

"Paying for them."

Annie felt Josie Canavan had more to offer to the conversation, or knew something about the subject of the shoes.

Josie, however, turned the discussion to another point. "You'll need to read up more on your American history. I've heard that exam seems to be the most challenging for students."

The subject of the shoes was over.

After dinner that night, as Hulda prepared to go home to her own house, Annie found her alone and posed a question.

"Aunt Hulda, my teacher Miss Canavan, made the strangest comment today."

"What was that?"

"She said that children in Porters Glen should appreciate the sacrifice their mothers make in order to buy them shoes."

Hulda busied herself collecting her bag and shawl.

"What did she really mean?"

"Shoes cost a lot of money and perhaps the mothers have to sell some of their belongings in order to get the necessary funds. Don't you worry. It's of no concern to you."

So saying, Hulda hurried out the door, leaving Annie suspiciously perplexed.

*

Annie let a few days go by and decided to confront the issue head on. After class on a delightful fall afternoon, she faced Josie Canavan. "Do you remember the conversation we had about the children in Porters Glen carrying their shoes? You commented about their mothers' sacrifice to get them."

"Yes, I remember."

"What type of sacrifice did you mean?"

Josie stared at Annie for a moment and then replied, "Perhaps you should ask that question at home, instead of from me."

"I already did ask, and Aunt Hulda evaded the question. Does the answer have something to do with the coal company?"

Josie stared. "Where did you get that idea?"

"My sister's friend said something about a room at the mining office that widows often visit in order to get help in paying the rent, or for new shoes. I thought she was making it up, so I didn't pay much attention at the time."

Josie took a deep breath. "Annie, I'm not sure I should be the one to talk to you about this. You're still a student."

"I'm eighteen, which means I'm an adult."

"Yes, well, perhaps that's so." Josie hesitated. "But… has anyone talked to you about male and female relationships? I'm referring to the physical encounters between a man and a woman."

"Aunt Hulda explained to me how babies are born, and how a woman gets with child. Is that what you mean?"

"Yes, but there are times when a woman and a man lie together not just for the purpose of creating a child. Did your aunt also explain that to you?"

Annie was silent for a few moments. "You mean like when some girls lie with their intended husbands to prove their commitment to each other?"

"That's one example." Josie blew out a forceful breath. "Annie, have you ever heard of the room in the mining office referred to as the Curtain Room?"

"No."

"Apparently it is a small room upstairs with a curtain instead of a door." Josie waited a moment. "It's where a woman goes if she needs to get shoes for her children, or if her husband can't work and the rent is due, or if the family has a loan they got from the mining company and now can't pay back."

Annie couldn't quite see the connection between the shoes and the rent being due.

Josie stared at Annie. Silence hung between them like a deafening roar. Josie's steely blue eyes searched Annie's face to detect even a hint of understanding the truth.

Annie suddenly remembered Mrs. Klausman's eviction and how the one neighbor woman had said that Mrs. Klausman should have just gone

and gotten the shoes. An uncomfortable feeling churned in her stomach.

"Are you telling me that the women...barter themselves, their bodies...to get shoes?"

"I don't think anyone forces them, but it seems the mining company uses the women's poverty as leverage. So, yes, I think this is the sacrifice we're talking about."

"My God, that's horrible. How did you find out about it?"

"Never mind how I found out, but it fits with the story of Jonathan's students carrying their shoes. I'm surprised, though, that no one has reported this to the authorities."

"That's because the CVC has fancy lawyers from the city that can get the company out of any jam. But, what about the husbands? Surely they must be furious."

"I doubt the women tell them. In some cases, I think the husbands just turn their heads, realizing they haven't been able to provide for their families. In other cases, the woman is a widow and has nowhere else to turn."

"The CVC shouldn't be allowed to get away with this."

"I agree."

"It's beyond cruel, what the company is sanctioning. It's even worse than their negligence with mining safety."

"I think this scandal has most likely been going on for years. The miners' wives are probably too scared of the coal company to make any allegations. What they need to do, is band together and help each other so no one has to visit The Curtain Room."

"But, how would that solve their problem of getting shoes for their children?"

"I don't know. But there has to be a way."

Judging by the flame of color in Josie's cheeks, Annie felt that she might have found a kindred spirit who would help her fight against the CVC. The question was, what could two young women do against the formidable coal company?

*

Later that week, Annie looked up with surprise to see Jonathan Canavan walk into the bakery, a boyish smile spread across his face.

"Hello, I came to get an end-of-the-week treat for myself. Mrs. Eisner's boardinghouse food is good, but I'm hankering for an indulgence."

"It's nice to see you again, Mr. Canavan. Can I offer you a *petit-four* or a small tart?"

"A petit-four sounds good. My sister tells me you are progressing in your studies and she hopes to write a recommendation for you in your college application."

Annie beamed. "Thank you. Yes, it's a dream I've had for years."

"Well, I for one, think that's an admirable dream."

Before she could reply, the door opened and in walked Frankie, fresh off his shift from the mine. Each footstep left an imprint of coal dust and grime on the shop floor. Annie tried hard not to grimace.

"Hello, Frankie. I'll be with you in a moment."

But Frankie walked up to the counter and looked the stranger up and down.

"Frank, this is Mr. Jonathan Canavan. He's the new principal here in Porters Glen. His sister is my high school teacher."

"Hello." Jonathan spoke first.

"I'd offer to shake your hand, but I doubt you'd want to do that, dressed as nice as you are."

"Next time, then," Jonathan said, standing his ground.

Frankie did not make any move to step aside and allow Jonathan to continue the conversation with Annie.

"Frankie."

"That's all right. I was finished anyway. Perhaps another time, Miss Charbonneau." Jonathan tipped his cap, and left without buying anything.

"Frankie, that was uncalled for. You were rude. And we need all the paying customers we can get."

"Not really. He doesn't belong in Porters Glen with his fancy city suit. I doubt he'll last the year."

"What's wrong with you? He's the principal here and his sister is my teacher. Are you jealous?"

"Not me. I've got nothing to be jealous about. But you've become so busy studying these last few weeks, I haven't seen much of you. I stopped to invite you to a hayride tomorrow night."

"That would be fun. But I would still appreciate it if you would make an effort to be polite to the customers in our shop, and be more careful about tracking coal dust in here."

"I'll call for you at seven o'clock."

His abruptness caused the muscles in her jaw to tighten.

He turned and reached the door, where his fingers left grimy coal streaks on the handle. Annie retrieved the broom to sweep up the trail of dried mud and coal dirt he'd left behind, and then took a rag to clean the door handle. She scrubbed it in annoyance and wondered if he would really ever quit the mines. More importantly, how would she feel if he chose the mines over her?

When she returned to the front counter, a different thought crossed her mind. Might Jonathan Canavan become a regular customer? Their short conversation reassured her that she was on the right track, choosing to become a teacher, and she looked forward to discussing her chosen career.

That night after supper, Annie checked over her current editorial before handing it to Aunt Hulda to mail. "I'm getting a bit discouraged. I wonder if these are doing any good."

"Unless it's their family involved, very few people rally to a cause that isn't theirs."

"Do you remember when I asked you about the shoes?"

Hulda looked at Annie with scrutiny. "Yes."

"Well, I think I know the story now, and how it's connected to the CVC."

"And how would that be?"

"There's a room at the mining offices called the Curtain Room. Poor women from the village go there and give the use of their bodies in exchange for shoes for their children, don't they?"

Hulda's face took on a look of resignation. "*Ma cherie,* I wanted to shield you and Marie from this. But *oui,* it is true."

"Does Papa know?"

"We have never discussed it."

"Why has no one tried to fight the CVC on this?"

"Annie, you have no idea of how powerful the coal company is. And the Curtain Room has been in existence for years. Promise me right now you won't get involved in any way."

"I can't promise that. Somehow, some way, the company has to be made accountable."

"Your letters to the editor are enough."

"No, Aunt Hulda, they aren't."

CHAPTER 12

John Kirby, kicked by a mule,
Eckhart Mine.

On an early September morning, Randall Meyers sat at his desk, drumming his fingers. Molly S. had become the subject of intense scrutiny within the CVC. *Five damn letters already!*

He had cut out each of the Letters to the Editor and had scanned them meticulously for clues. *No way in hell this woman is from Riverton; she knows too many pertinent details about the accidents.*

He leaned back in his large wooden chair to think. *Should he involve Sheriff King at this point? No, better keep it in the family for now.* He snapped back to attention and started a list of suspected facts.

1. Her Letters to the Editor always appear the last week of the month, possibly to coincide with paydays.
2. That means the letters are posted during the early part of the last week.
3. Send a man down to Riverton to hang out at post office during last week of each month and see if he recognizes anyone local.

A smug smile spread across his face. “I’ll find out who you are, Molly S.” He was already daydreaming about the best way to punish her for her interference.

CHAPTER 13

Benjamin Wells, crushed by a coal trip,
Ocean Mine.

Juggling her two purchases of new pillow cases and dish towels from Rosen's Department Store, Hulda took a moment to relish shopping in Riverton.

The city, ten times the population of Porters Glen, was laid out in a grid pattern with Baltimore Street running north-south, dividing the main shopping district. Along Baltimore Street were hotels, saloons, restaurants, and department stores; and the streets were thronged with people. Two banks designed in Italianate architecture anchored adjacent corners with their resplendent red brick facades and everyone dressed up to come shopping in town.

Rosen's was sandwiched between other large stores. Built from a light colored brick that spanned three stories, Hulda found it easier to shop mainly on the first floor.

But, it was the smaller shops along Baltimore Street, like Bond Jewelers and Howard's Confectionary, that Hulda enjoyed the most because they had whimsical window displays that changed monthly and invited the shopper to peer in at the displayed merchandise.

She walked down the block and then turned the corner onto Liberty Street. Here stood the post office, frequented by everyone in the downtown area. Hulda figured no one would be paying attention to what she was mailing.

Once she finished her errand, she crossed back over Baltimore Street to head to her favorite lunch spot, Gus's Luncheonette. Shoulders back, she strutted a bit with the idea that they would expose the CVC after all.

She had not gone far, when she thought she heard footsteps behind her. Turning and looking over her shoulder, she saw at a distance, a lone man following in her wake. He boldly stared at her, and she felt unnerved. Picking up her speed, she turned back to see if he was still behind her. A sigh of relief escaped her lips when he was gone.

Food had always been a way of calming her nerves. Without hesitation, she popped into Gus's Luncheonette and ordered a meat loaf sandwich. The comfort taste of the beef relaxed her and so she ordered a second one.

After her meal, but before she left the restaurant, she peeked her head outside the door. Good, the man was nowhere in sight. Adjusting her packages, she set out once more.

Just as she approached an alley opening between two buildings, the man darted out, slapped his hand over her mouth, and dragged her into the alley—then threw her against a stack of greasy trash barrels. Before she could regain her balance, her assailant hit her across the small of her back with something hard and wooden; knocking her to the ground. Stunned, breathless, and in pain, she lay motionless, paralyzed by fear.

"This is a warning," the man growled. "We know you're either Molly S. or working for her. Either way, you won't be mailing anything again. If another letter appears in print, I'll come back for you, and I won't be aiming for your back—I'll break both your legs next time."

Just then a young store clerk carrying a barrel of refuse opened a back door into the alley. He looked at the scene before him. "Hey you!"

The thug scowled. "Shut up. You didn't see nothing. Tell anyone and it will be your legs I'll be breaking." The assailant fled back to the street.

"You all right?" The boy put down the barrel and ran over to Hulda, who lay in a crumpled heap.

She looked up. "Yes, I'll be fine. Please go back to your work. Don't tell anyone. I don't want to cause any trouble."

The boy emptied the trash into a larger barrel nearby, and then disappeared back into the shop.

Hulda sobbed. How could she have been so stupid not to realize the danger of taking on the mining company? Who did she think she was? She was a widow, for God's sake with no husband for protection. She couldn't let them get to her again.

After several minutes she managed to raise her large body to a kneeling position, and then held onto one of the rain barrels for support. Shaking, she managed to stand. A sense of shame descended; she had ruined her stockings and wet herself.

Her back throbbed where she'd been hit; slowly, she hobbled out toward the street. With trembling hands, she smoothed her short cape, and then glanced anxiously over her shoulder as she walked to the train station to catch the three o'clock back to Porters Glen. She could not get the smell of his rancid breath out of her nostrils, nor the image of his mouth full of broken, yellow teeth. His attack on her made her feel dirty. She prayed the man was not following her.

When the train pulled into the station, she gingerly climbed on board and took a seat alone; hoping no one would detect the smell of urine on her.

Later when she disembarked at the Mount Pleasant Depot, she huffed climbing up the hilly street and turned left into an alley that led to the meadow shortcut to Lower Porters Glen. Her eyes darted around, still terrified the man might be nearby.

She walked slower than usual, and tottered through the field path, thankful that the walk was downhill, and the Charbonneau's house was clearly in sight.

*

Annie had returned from work early and spied Hulda cautious-

ly walking near the front yard. *What is she doing?* When Annie went outside, she saw the tell-tale stain on Hulda's skirt. "Oh, my God! What happened?"

"Please, take me inside. I don't want the neighbors to see me like this."

Annie steered Hulda by the elbow and once inside, she helped Hulda to a chair. "Now tell me what happened in Riverton."

"I'm all right, but the letters to the editor have to stop. Right now, I just want to catch my breath and then get to my own house."

"You only live over the next rise. No going home until you tell me what happened."

Hulda trembled. "I was leaving the post office when a man followed me and pushed me into an alley. He accused me of being Molly S. or working for her, and he told me if the letters don't stop, he would come back for me and break my legs." She stifled a sob. "Oh God, Annie, I was terrified. What if he does come back?"

Great wracking sobs shook her hefty body.

Annie threw her arms over Hulda's shoulders. "Oh, Aunt Hulda, I'm so sorry. I never meant to put you in harm's way. God damn the mining company! I'll stop the letters. But I swear I won't let them get away with this. I'll find a different way to get to them."

"Don't! I don't want any more trouble. The coal company is more sinister than you realize."

Annie brought Hulda a hankie. "Let me brew you some tea. I think you should rest here for the remainder of the day. Then I'll walk you home."

"I'll take the tea, but I want to go home. My clothes reek. And I don't want either your father or Marie to see me like this."

Later that night Annie lay in bed mulling over Hulda's attack. The CVC had obviously been following the Letters to the Editor after all. And they sent someone to Riverton, so they must think Molly S. really did live there.

What else can I do to get even with the CVC? I can't send any more letters. But, I refuse to let them beat me down. Somehow, in some way, I will make them accountable.

The fact that Annie had put Hulda in danger did not outweigh her fierce determination to set the wheels of retribution in motion.

*

A few days later Frankie strode into the bakery on his way home from the mine. "Annie, you know tomorrow is All Hallows Eve. I'd like to take you somewhere special."

"Where?"

"It'll be a surprise. Just be ready by seven o'clock." He doffed his miners' cap and opened the door to the shop, then turned back. "Wear something warm."

"Why?"

No answer came, just the echo of his whistling as he walked off down the street. None of his abruptness from the previous weeks was evident in his manner, and Annie wondered if he often changed moods.

She wanted to talk to him about Hulda's attack, but a deeper instinct told her to keep the information to herself—at least for now.

The next day turned out to be unseasonably mild for the end of October.

Annie came home from the bakery and smelled the wonderful aroma of Hulda's fresh applesauce cookies.

"Annie, will you be staying to join in the traditions of storytelling and fiddle music?"

"Not this year, Aunt Hulda. Frankie and I are going to be with some of his friends."

Aunt Hulda cast her eyes to the side. "Just be careful."

Frankie arrived later and knocked on the door, just as Annie opened it.

"Happy All Hallows Eve." She grinned. "Come in."

They walked into the parlor, and Louis stood up. "Welcome, Frank."

"Hello, Mr. Charbonneau. I plan on taking Annie to meet up with some of my friends and celebrate the evening."

"Here in Porters Glen?"

"Near-by."

"She needs to come home at a reasonable time. Have you gotten yourself a pocket watch yet?"

"No sir, not yet."

"Then how will you know the time?"

"Papa! Please. Frankie always brings me home before it gets too late."

"All right, but I prefer it if you would stick to Porters Glen. There are bound to be pranksters out tonight."

"I'll take care of her, Mr. Charbonneau. I promise."

Frankie waited till they were outside and then he put his arm around her shoulders as he led her down the walk. Stooping, he scooped up a blanket lying on the ground.

"Where did you get a blanket, or should I ask, why do you have a blanket?"

"I said it would be a surprise. We're going to watch the stars from up on Piney Ridge. That's why I asked you to dress warm."

"Piney Ridge in the dark? Surely you're joking. My father has seen bears up there."

"Not at night. They'll all be asleep."

"Frankie, we told my father we were going to be with your friends."

"Just a small white lie. Look, even if we saw a bear, all you have to do is make a lot of noise. That usually sends them back off into the forest. And we're not stupid enough to try and antagonize one."

"I don't like the white lie, but I do like the idea of you protecting me." She grinned, and then tied her hat ribbon under her chin to secure it, thankful she was wearing one of her newer ankle-length skirts that wouldn't drag on the ground.

"There's a full moon out tonight and I already marked the red and yellow sassafras trees along the path, so I know the way. Come on, it'll be great. There's enough light for us to see."

They held hands as they walked north up Coal Bank Lane and then turned east to climb the leaf-trodden path up Piney Ridge. They

climbed higher and when they forked off to the left and headed in the direction of Mr. Meyers' hunting cabin, Annie said nothing.

When the cabin came into view, Frankie announced, "Here we are."

"What do you mean, here we are?"

"I found this cabin a few weeks ago and decided it would be the perfect place to watch the stars on All Hallows Eve. Come over here."

Annie wondered if he knew she had tutored Robby Meyers in the cabin. She followed Frankie to a fallen log.

"Sit down. I'll wrap the blanket around us in case you get cold."

They sat side by side, with his arm around her and lover's heat seeping through both their bodies.

Annie remained quiet a while as she stared up into the ebony night dotted with the brilliance of stars and listened to the night noises of animals scuttling through the forest.

"Frankie, you do know I'm serious about wanting to teach, don't you?"

"Yeah, I guess so. If it's important to you, then it will be all right with me. I hope you feel the same way about me being a miner. I've decided it's what I want to do with my life, even though it will have its risks. I'm young and strong, Annie. I can beat the mine."

Annie winced. "It's a dangerous way to live."

"But it is an honorable way to live, and independent from my father."

A few minutes later a shooting star ran across the heavens and trailed out of sight.

"You know what that means, don't you?"

Annie shook her head.

"It's a sign from heaven that an angel's watching over us."

"Oh come on, Frankie. Don't be silly. Is that an Irish superstition or something?"

"No, really, it's true."

"Just who might this angel be?"

"Maybe it's Stephen trying to tell you that we're meant for each other."

She shivered in spite of herself, whether from the idea of Stephen watching them or from the night air. Perhaps both.

"Are you cold? Come on, I know where we can get warm." He led her over to the cabin, pulled a key out from under a rock, and opened the door.

"Frankie, this cabin doesn't belong to you."

"I know. I overheard Mr. Meyers telling my father about the cabin. So I decided to come see it for myself." Holding her hand, he led her inside.

She saw in an instant that the sanctuary of the summer school room had changed. The books and slates had disappeared and the two chairs now stood in opposite corners with boxes piled on them. The student desk, as well as the teacher desk had vanished. The only recognizable item left from summer was the rag rug. With no heat and only moonlight peeking in the two windows, the cabin seemed to have reverted to its original function of a hunting hut.

Frankie spread the blanket on top of the rug. "Come on, we can sit here and get warm."

She wanted to say that they shouldn't be there, but she also looked forward to him kissing her, and the dimples that framed Frankie's mouth melted her reserve. She sat down.

He lowered his body next to hers. "Annie, you know I love you, don't you? And that someday I want to marry you. I think you love me too. So tonight's the night I think we should commit ourselves to each other."

She held her breath. She wasn't expecting this. Not tonight.

He lightly brushed his fingers up and down her neck, and then kissed her passionately on the lips. Her body reacted with a hot flush she could not stop, nor did she want to. They continued kissing, each kiss more passionate than the last. He pulled her to standing. "I'm glad you're mine."

He untied the strings to her hat and then her cape, and laid both aside. Weeks ago he had slid his hand under her shirtwaist blouse, but her corset had prevented him from touching her breasts. At the time, she was flushed with innocent desire, but they were interrupted

by one of Frankie's friends coming into the room.

"Frankie..."

"Shh. Don't be afraid."

"But I don't think I'm ready."

"Why not? This is what people do when they love each other. You do love me?"

"Yes, but..."

"But, what?" A look of concern shadowed his face. "I promise I won't hurt you."

"I do love you. But I'm not ready for this."

"Why not?"

"Because it doesn't feel right, doing this up here, and trespassing. The first time is supposed to be special."

He paused, stroking the back of her neck. "I can make it special."

Annie stared at him without responding.

"Then can I at least touch you? I mean really touch you without all your layers of clothes. I won't make you do anything you don't want to."

Her thumb went up to her lips and she unconsciously chewed the nail—but she did not refuse.

Slowly he began to undo the small buttons at the front of her shirtwaist. "God, these are tiny." When she did not object, he finished and then gently pulled it off and tenderly gazed at her. "Gosh, how many layers do you have? Can I unbutton this covering next? Or do you want to do it?"

With fingers shaking, Annie unbuttoned the front of her white muslin corset cover and let it drop to the floor. She turned to face him, her heart racing.

"You've got buttons on the corset, too."

She nodded.

This time, Frankie's fingers trembled. Once he unbuttoned the simple corset and laid it aside, Annie only had a muslin chemise covering the top half of her body.

Frankie leaned over and pulled the chemise up and off.

Annie looked down to see the nipples on her breasts were erect

from the chill in the cabin, and possibly, from nerves.

Frankie bent forward and gently touched each breast, cupping them in his hands. Softly, he kissed one breast, then the other.

In spite of herself, she found her breath quickening and a pulsating sensation start between her legs. His kissing her breasts moved to him sucking on her nipples. *My God. What is this?* She moaned with surprised pleasure but also with a bit of fear. What would happen next? Then she panicked. "Stop, Frankie. Please?"

He groaned. "I want you Annie, you have to know that." He leaned in and kissed her hard on her mouth, darting his tongue inside.

Annie realized his manhood had swollen up against her. "Frankie!" She put both her hands firmly against his chest.

He pulled back; his cheeks flushed with both anger and desire. "I don't understand why not."

She put up her arms to cover her breasts. "Because when it does happen, I want it to be wonderful. Right now, I feel too scared to make it special."

He looked away, hands clenched.

"Please don't be angry with me."

"Angry? No. Disappointed? Yes. I thought you'd be ready for this." He dropped his arms in resignation.

"I'm sorry."

"Not as much as I am."

Annie reached down for her clothes, as conflicting thoughts raced through her mind. She loved Frankie, but she didn't want their physical commitment to each other to start in Meyers' cabin.

Frankie waited for her to finish dressing, and then took her in his arms. "It's all right, I can wait. I had no idea you'd be this beautiful." He kissed her again. "But I don't want to wait forever."

Struggling to find the right words to say back, she finally just nodded.

"I guess I'd better get you home, before your father begins to wonder where we are."

As Frankie held her hand and they walked toward the cabin's door, Annie noticed a bright piece of fabric thrown in a heap in the

corner. She stopped a moment because its color of perky mustard-yellow seemed somehow familiar.

"Is something wrong?"

"No, I just saw that cloth over there." She pointed to the corner. "It seems out of place in here."

"I doubt it belongs to any hunter. Men don't wear yellow."

Annie squinted at the cloth again as Frankie led her outside and locked up. With the moonlight to guide them, they walked back down the path as dried-up leaves crinkled under their feet. Annie felt conflicted. The feel of his hands on her breasts had excited her, and her nipples still tingled from where he had suckled. But, she also felt anxiety. Was this how married couples acted together in privacy? Was she right in stopping him? She did not want to turn him away, but how far could they go?

They soon arrived at Coal Bank Lane.

Frankie walked her to the door and kissed her in a long embrace. Then he turned up his collar and walked off down the hill whistling a tune.

Annie went inside and closed the front door, leaning against it to compose herself. Every nerve fiber still felt raw with a type of electricity that both delighted and frightened her. She had to admit that the feel of Frankie's hands on her naked breasts had been riveting. Even though tonight had not been the right time, she thought ahead to the day when they would prove their love for each other.

Then she thought of the Curtain Room and silently thanked God that she was safe from that evil, but quickly uttered a prayer for the vulnerable women who were not.

CHAPTER 14

Frank Shea, fell on a pick,
Allegany Mine.

By mid-November, Katharina Messerschmidt had become a widow.

Sitting in the small kitchen of her stone cottage, and dressed in her one good outfit, she contemplated her future. Henry had put aside the rent money for this month, so she was safe for a while. Next month would be a different story.

Her sister lived several states away, and she hadn't heard from her older brother in years, so family help did not look promising. The most logical plan would be to remarry—after all, her looks were her best asset, and she knew it. There had to be an eligible man who would want her and be willing to take her three children as well. What she needed was a list of either single or widowed miners. She would also need a reprieve for December's rent. No choice remained; she had to go to the Curtain Room.

Katharina had heard the stories other women whispered, so she had a good idea of what to expect. Whether anyone would gossip about her, she did not care. Her paramount concern was for survival.

Walking back to her dressing area, she took pains to fix her hair with the lovely bone hair comb Henry had given her as a wedding gift. Tying a scarf over her head in a gesture of modesty, she then buttoned up her mackintosh.

Outside, the early rain had stopped, but clouds still dipped low, their fringes hanging like an old man's sooty-gray beard. Precisely the type of man Katharina did not want to marry.

On possibly the worst day of her life, she set out for the five-minute walk to the mining office. Thank God her children were in school and would have no knowledge about this. She marched along the road, puffs of her breath trailing behind her in the cold damp air.

The mining offices hummed with activity as clerks prepared the monthly payroll. One of them paused in his scribbling and asked what she needed. She replied that she needed a favor. The clerk smirked.

"I'm Mrs. Henry Messerschmidt."

"So?"

"My husband was one of the men killed in the accident two weeks ago."

With a blank look he said, "Yes. Sorry for your loss."

"I have this month's rent." She held out her open palm with the four one dollar bills. She paused, and then said, "I've heard there's a way I can pay for next month's rent, too."

The clerk's bloodshot eyes lit up. "If you go upstairs, someone will be with you shortly."

Katharina held her head high and walked up the wooden stairs, trying not to show any fear. Who would actually be meeting her, she had no idea.

At the top of the stairs she peered around at the rooms. One of them did not have a door, but only a dirty curtain partitioning it from the hallway. She shuddered, but walked in, surprised to discover the smallness of the space. She glanced at the stained cot and tried not to think of how many other women had been there before her. It really did not matter. She just had to get through the ordeal.

A moment later, a man parted the curtain and entered the room.

She knew exactly who he was, and what he expected of her. "I

can give you what you want, but I'll need a pass on next month's rent and a list of all the single or widowed miners who work for the CVC. I also want their ages listed."

Her soon-to-be cot partner stared at her with smugness. "We've never had someone brazen enough to try and negotiate conditions. What if I decide you aren't worth it?"

She remained stoic. "Then you'll never know what you could have had."

"All right. I'll play your game. Take off your clothes and then we'll see about the list of names you want—and a month's pass on your rent."

Determined not to show any fear or disgust, Katharina slowly took off her coat in an attempt to delay the inevitable, all the while whispering, "Survival."

Later, after he finished with her, she put her clothes back on and followed him downstairs. She found it difficult to walk and winced in pain. Without waiting for him, she shuffled into his office.

"My, my, anxious for that list, are we?"

"I gave you what you wanted."

"First, we trade. I want you to leave something here. Something I can hold to remind me of our little escapade just now." He looked her up and down. "Your scarf will do. Hand it to me."

Her eyes flashed, but she handed him the scarf.

He went out to the clerk and mumbled an order, then returned to the office. "Would you like to sit?"

"No thank you, I won't be staying."

"Suit yourself."

A few minutes later the clerk knocked. "Here's the list, sir."

Her tormentor took it and scanned the names. "I think I see where this is going. You're pretty smart."

Katharina took the list from him and left. Without looking back as she limped away from the mining office, she walked back through the dismal day to Miners Row.

Once home, she chewed a teaspoon of Queen Anne Lace seeds she had harvested in the fall. Hopefully, this would prevent any preg-

nancy. Then she forced ice-cold water from the pump in the yard into several tin pails. Then she brought them into the kitchen where she proceeded to light her small stove and set the pails one at a time to heat.

When the water was suitably warm she poured it into an old wooden tub, stripped off all her clothes, grabbed some Lava soap, and climbed into the tub. Then she vigorously scrubbed every inch of her body. She did not want any residue of his sex-smell lingering on her when her children returned home.

After the bath, she dressed, threw out the dirty water, and then sat down with the list. She saw twelve names. She crossed off anyone still in his early twenties; no one that young would be interested in a married woman with children. She read the remaining names and eliminated those that seemed to be from countries where they might only speak a bit of fragmented English. That left half a dozen men to consider.

Her next step would be locating these men and then making the best choice possible.

*

Back at the mining office another woman, this one barely older than a girl, had timidly asked the clerk how she could get some shoe coupons for her children. He smirked and told her to go upstairs and wait.

Terrified, she climbed the stairs and then stood in the hallway.

"What's wrong with you? Are you stupid? You're supposed to go in there." A man pointed to the doorway leading to a small room.

He was dressed in a sharp wool suit, but she couldn't understand everything he said. She did understand about going into the room.

*

Hours later he left for his dinner, snapping his suspenders and

congratulating himself on this wonderful day where two women had been his in the Curtain Room. He decided that whoever the next woman might be, he wanted something different, something more demanding to satisfy his sexual needs.

Upstairs at the mining office, the dingy curtain hung limp.

*

The mining accident that had left Katharina a widow had also caused Annie to discuss her concerns with Frankie.

"I was so worried when I heard the coal whistle blow for another accident. All I could think of was that you might be trapped like Stephen."

"You shouldn't have worried. Part of the coal roof fell on two men, but I was nowhere near them."

"But, Frankie, don't you see? It could have been you! The mine is a dangerous place to work and the coal company is negligent with their safety precautions, if they even have precautions."

"I told you, Annie, I'm careful."

"Let me tell you this, then. I don't think I could be a wife who lives her days in fear of hearing that whistle and becoming a widow."

Frankie put his arms around her. "I give you my word of honor, I won't let you become a mining widow."

Annie knew his words were sincere, but incredibly idealistic.

CHAPTER 15

Henry Lemmert, killed by fall of top rock,
Eckhart Mine.

When the calendar turned to December, any remaining traces of late fall vanished and snow fell daily, turning the landscape into a vista of Arctic white. The freezing weather insured that the snow would stay.

It wouldn't be till early spring that a fresh layer of coal dust would reappear, mingle itself with any left-over snow, and blanket Porters Glen in slush the color of dirty ashes.

December also brought the painful memory of losing Stephen.

Annie's antidote to the seasonal sadness was to stay busy. She buried herself in studying for her exams during the week, and then saved Saturday nights for going out with Frankie.

Each time he came to call, he whispered to her about returning to the cabin. The memory of his touch on her bare skin and his gaze at her partially naked in the moonlight still caused her heart to race but she was afraid of what would happen if they returned to the cabin.

Surely other girls her age with a steady beau had already proven their relationships.

What was really holding her back? Or what was it that kept her with Frankie?

She longed to talk to someone about the issue, although confiding in Aunt Hulda or Marie was out of the question. That left Josie Canavan as her only plausible option. While the two of them had become quite close, Annie wasn't sure it would be appropriate to ask Josie about such a personal matter.

Perhaps she could start by asking Josie her opinion about love in general and then work up her courage to ask Josie how one knew when they had met the right person to marry.

That week after the lesson concluded, Annie broached the subject.

"Miss Canavan, can I ask you your opinion on a sensitive subject, one we aren't going to be studying."

"Of course you can."

Annie took a deep breath. "How does one know when they have found true love?"

"Ah, that is a sensitive subject. Your father has not talked about this with you?"

"Papa? No." She paused. "Have you ever been in love?"

Josie's lips curled into a faint smile. "First off, being in love and actually loving someone are two different matters. It is easy to fall in love, the feeling when you're swept off your feet and hang onto his every word. But that is not the same as truly loving someone. Loving someone is when you are willing to make sacrifices for the other person."

Annie hesitated. "Do you mean like letting him go…down there?" She looked down at her private area.

Josie shook her head. "No, that wasn't what I was referring to. That act should never be a sacrifice, but more of a sacrament between two willing people who love each other. Two people who would both sacrifice for each other."

"But how do you know when falling in love turns to real love?"

Josie looked down in her lap and smoothed a wrinkle from her hounds-toothed checked wool skirt. "I would say that occurs when you know that life without the other person would be meaningless."

Annie tilted her head to the side.

"The real trick, Annie, is finding someone who would find his world empty without you."

Annie looked at Josie. Surely any man would find her attractive. No wonder she has already been in love.

"Well, is there some kind of sign?"

Josie laughed gently. "Believe me when I tell you that when love comes and knocks at the door to your heart, you'll know."

But Annie didn't know. Was she in love with Frankie, or did she truly love him? What sacrifice would she be willing to make for him? And what would he sacrifice for her?

*

A few weeks into December, two miners' wives entered the bakery.

"Morning, Anne, Hulda. We need to buy a few onions and two heads of cabbage. We plan to make soup."

"Certainly," Annie replied. "The onions are three cents a pound and the cabbages are eight cents."

"But today, we're running a special," Hulda interjected. "Today, we're selling them for two cents a pound, and the cabbages are five cents each—did you forget, Annie?"

Annie stared at Hulda, but mumbled, "Yes, today we are running a special."

The women selected their produce and then dug out pennies. "Thank you." They directed the comment to Hulda.

"Our pleasure."

As soon as they left the shop, Annie turned to Hulda. "Really Aunt Hulda, you are too much of a soft touch."

"Have you ever had soup with nothing but onions and cabbage?"

"No, not really."

"Well, it's only a bit more nourishing than *Potage au Lait*."

"Milk soup?"

"*Oui*, you can make soup from almost any ingredients, and the miners' wives are desperate sometimes on how to feed their families. Be thankful you've never had to go hungry."

"Aunt Hulda, have you ever heard of a soup kitchen?"

"Mostly in cities, I think. Why?"

"When I studied for my history exam, I read how some of the English Protestants set up soup kitchens in Ireland during the Great Famine to help stave off starvation. They gave the soup out for free."

"Free?"

"Well, they told the Catholic Irish they would have to agree to convert before they could enter the soup kitchen."

"Ah. Always strings attached. Are you thinking of something like that here? The miners' wives wouldn't go to a soup kitchen. They have too much pride, and no Catholic in Porters Glen would renounce their faith."

"No, my idea has nothing to do with the church. I have to come up with a senior project as a graduation requirement. Miss Canavan said the new rules stipulate that the project has to benefit the community. I would love to expose the Curtain Room for my project, but I think it would be too dangerous."

"The Curtain Room? *Mon Dieu*, Annie. You must not even think that."

"Maybe I could help the miners' wives by assembling a soup cookbook with different recipes to help them stretch their food through winter."

Hulda cocked her head. "This is a change. You, thinking about the miners' wives. But this will have nothing to do with the Curtain Room?"

"No, not the Curtain Room. At least not yet. But I do keep thinking of Mama, and what she would do."

"Your mother gave what she could. You do know that many of the miners' wives can't read, so they don't use cookbooks. They rely on the memorized recipes their mothers and grandmothers handed down to them. But...what about a bread line? It could be here at the store, and you could give out your soup recipes to anyone who wanted them."

"What's a bread line—and how could I make it a part of my senior project?"

"Long ago, a baker in France gave away his day-old bread to the poor. Because they had to wait in line for the shop to close before they could get the free bread, the practice became known as a bread line."

"But how could that be my project?"

"You could write out the soup recipes and make the bread available. Anyone who receives bread also gets your recipes. You could do a different recipe each week, or combine them in a booklet."

"What about the women who don't read English? And would Papa agree to us handing out free day-old bread?"

"I think he would." Hulda became unusually quiet. "I know there are women here who cannot read English, but what they really need is shoes for their children."

"I thought you didn't want me to do anything about the Curtain Room."

"I don't. But that doesn't mean that I condone the evil that goes on up there."

"Maybe I can still do something to help those women."

"Whatever you do, you would have to be very careful. The CVC would be watching, even if it is part of a school project."

"I want my project to be worthwhile, and I'd like to help the miners' wives. But they make me feel…like an outsider."

"Because you are one. You have money and clothes and education—everything they would love to have. You're not a part of their struggles."

Annie turned and looked out the window. Snow had started falling again, adding to the inches already on the ground. Was this part of what was holding her back in her relationship with Frankie? If she married him, she would become a miner's wife, just like the women who shopped in the bakery. Just like the women whose presence bothered her.

"We're lucky, Annie, that all our customers aren't miners. Otherwise, we'd go under. But the miners' wives deserve to shop here, just like the other women of the village."

"Mama understood, didn't she?"

"*Oui, ma cherie*. Your mother had the gift of a true and open heart. Her way of helping was to offer what healing remedies she could, and the women respected her for that. Perhaps this school project will help you to realize what you can offer."

"But Aunt Hulda, I don't have the gift of healing like Mama did."

"God gives us our gifts. You just need to find out what yours is."

Annie gave Aunt Hulda a hug and went to find Louis to ask him about giving away some day-old bread for her senior project.

*

On Wednesday afternoon as Annie trudged through a path of snow, a strong wind whipped down from the mountain and made the snowflakes spin upward into a dancing spiral. Annie paused momentarily to watch the unusual spectacle. It lasted only a few moments and then the wind blew straight into her and buffeted her every step, making the trip longer than usual.

By the time she arrived at the high school, she should have been chilled to the bone, but the excitement about her senior project warmed her.

"Miss Canavan, I think I have an idea for my project, but I would need your help."

"All right, let's hear it."

"The beginning of the heavy snows and frigid weather is about to start, which means the mines will soon shut down for winter because they won't be able to ship coal again till the canal thaws in early spring."

"I didn't know that."

Annie nodded. "Winters are tough here. The mines shut down for three months, and mining families rely on the food the women were able to preserve from the harvest season. The wives are good at stretching what they can, but it's never enough. I'd like to combine the idea of a bread line with free English lessons."

"A bread line? Tell me more."

"Very few of the immigrant women here can read or write En-

glish." Annie paused.

"All right, go on."

"I read about soup kitchens in Ireland and England, but Aunt Hulda said the miners' wives here would be too proud to accept charity. So, if you and I would offer free night class to the miners' wives and give out day-old bread from our bakery with a cup of dried lentils and a soup recipe to take home after each class, the women would have food to take back to their families, and they would be learning English at the same time."

"All right. But wouldn't they still think of it as charity?"

"Not if they must attend the class in order to get the bread and lentils." Annie took a deep breath. "In addition, they would get a two-dollar coupon for shoes they could use for their children."

"And the coupons wouldn't be charity either?"

"No, because the women would have to study to earn it. I might never get the CVC to admit their responsibility in Stephen's death, but at least this way we can stand strong against the CVC and help the immigrant wives."

Josie Canavan leaned forward. "Why lentils, where would the class be held, and more importantly—where will you get two dollars per family?"

"You can ask your brother about using one of his schoolrooms on Sunday evenings. Lentils can be bought wholesale at twenty pounds for a dollar. They're supposed to be really nutritious according to Aunt Hulda, and my father would be willing to give any leftover bread that didn't sell. I can ask Mr. Meyers to advance me money for tutoring Robby again. I won't have classes with you anymore, so I would be able to work with Robby all spring."

"How did you come up with this idea?"

Annie swallowed the painful memory of her mother's death. "My mother was a healer. She tended to the poorer families who couldn't afford to send for the doctor. She wanted me to follow in her footsteps, but…that didn't happen. Aunt Hulda told me I should search for my own gift. This is the best way I think I can help."

"I think it's a terrific idea. But let's slow down and think it through. We should probably limit this to fifteen women, and if they

each get a two-dollar coupon that will amount to thirty dollars. Let me approach Mr. Meyers. We've become…friends, and I think I can convince him to help."

Annie did not comment on Randall Meyers, but wondered if Josie Canavan was another of his just-talking-friends?

Josie became more animated with the lure of the idea. "I know! Let's get Jonathan to host a Family Soup Night the evening after New Year's. The school could provide free soup to all the families who attend. Each family will have one of their children stand on stage and recite a poem. Then we can send home a note with each family explaining that we are going to offer a free English class on Sunday nights for the first sixteen women who sign up." Her eyes sparkled in contrast to her usual serious nature.

"But how will we pay for the lentils? I don't have any saved cash right now."

"You leave that to me and Jonathan. And another thing, if we are going to be in this project together, then you must start calling me Josie."

"But I'm still your student."

"I graded all of your exams. You passed with flying colors. There's no reason you won't be getting your diploma in June. If we're in town, you can address me as Miss Canavan. But outside of Mount Pleasant, I will be simply Josie. Agreed?"

"Yes, agreed…Josie." Annie smiled.

"One more thing. By giving the women shoe coupons, that means they will no longer have to obtain them from the CVC. We need to be prepared for some possible type of back lash. I doubt the company will just sit back and not react."

Annie thought back to Hulda's attack in Riverton.

"I understand your concern. But if we do not go ahead with our plan, the CVC will only continue with their injustices. It's time someone does something. I know my mama would approve of the idea."

"All right, Annie. Then it's full steam ahead. I just hope we don't incur the wrath of the coal company."

Annie nodded in agreement, and saw in her mind the image of the hawk circling.

CHAPTER 16

Edward Smith, run over by coal hoppers,
Midlothian Mine.

Young Sophie Petrova stood alone in her kitchen trying to mop the coal-dusted pine floor, but unable to concentrate on the task. Outside, a cold wind rattled the windows of her small cottage, making it sound like the heathens of hell battling on her front porch.

She missed her family back in Poland and how they would be celebrating Christmas. Here in America, she and her husband did not have enough money for even one gift for their two small children.

Tears slid down her cheeks. Most of all, her children needed winter shoes.

She glanced in the chipped oval mirror and saw the reflection of a young girl who was aging before her time.

Her husband's shift at the mine would end later in the day. Propping the mop up against the wall and grabbing her hand-me-down mackintosh with its mismatched buttons, she yanked on an old woolen scarf brought from the old country and tied it tightly. Wrapping up her two little girls, she took them next door to her trusted neighbor Mrs. Lipinski, and asked her to watch them while she ran an errand.

Once on the road, new snow assailed her, but she plunged head first into the coming storm. She had to visit the mining offices.

Her clumsy shoes sent up plumes of snow as she plodded along under the mean clouds. A few minutes later she arrived in front of the CVC. She hesitated only a moment then held her head up high, swallowed her pride, and climbed up the four steps to the wide wooden porch where the sign read: Cumberland Valley Coal Company.

Walking in, she clutched a piece of paper indicating the two small shoe sizes needed for her children. Her hands shook from the icy weather and from fear. She knew the ropes because she had been here before. Go upstairs and wait. Once inside the Curtain Room, his lingering scent of cheap aftershave would make her gag.

Then he appeared—a nightmare of a weasel-man—and he advanced on her.

She closed her eyes for just a moment and then felt his revolting hands on her face. Trying not to cry, she took off her coat and began to unbutton her dress. He laughed with a wickedness that sent shivers down her spine. Sometimes she found it hard to believe he was human. Then he shoved her down on the stained cot pushed up against the wall and straddled her.

She turned her face to the wall so she would not have to look at him.

"Don't you be getting any stupid ideas of not cooperating. You complain, and I'll make sure your husband gets sent down into one of the old tunnels in the mine. We've gotten rid of other trouble-makers that way."

Her faced turned ashen.

Later, after he had finished, she had two shoe coupons clutched in her trembling hands. She wiped the blood from her split lip and silently cursed him in Polish.

Behind her, the curtain swayed for a moment, then returned to its original lifeless position.

CHAPTER 17

Archie Tennant, died from a saw cut,
Engine Side Mine.

Jonathan Canavan dipped his head as he left the warmth of the school to venture out into the cold afternoon. He flipped up his collar and shoved his gloved hands into his coat pockets. Thank goodness it was only a short distance to the bakery, less than a Philadelphia block.

"Why, Mr. Canavan! How nice to see you. Did your sister tell you about our idea for the Soup Night, or are you here to shop?"

He took a minute to appreciate how attractive Annie was, and how he felt drawn to her.

"Josie told me, and I must say it is a bold venture for both of you—courageous, too. I'm in total agreement that you can use one of my classrooms for the lessons. But I think the three of us should sit down together to plan for the Soup Night, and for the class. You'll need supplies."

"Yes, of course."

"How about Saturday afternoon? Can your father spare you from the shop? Say, about three o'clock? We can meet at the school.

Unless of course you need to do some Christmas shopping." He smiled.

"No. I'll come to the school at three."

"Till tomorrow then." He tipped his hat to her as he left.

Not fifteen minutes later, Frankie walked into the bakery, and as usual tracked in a trail of coal dusted footprints on the floor. At the same time, Jonathan returned to the bakery and opened the door. When he saw Annie and Frankie in conversation, Jonathan stepped behind a shelf of canned goods.

"Frankie, did you wipe your feet on the outside mat? I just swept."

"Somewhat. No matter how much I try and stomp off the coal dirt, it still clings to my boots."

"Don't come any further, I'll come over to you."

"Sorry about the dirt, but I heard there's to be a party Saturday night in Mount Pleasant. How about I pick you up at seven o'clock?"

Jonathan's mouth turned into a slight grimace as he realized that Annie and Frankie might be a regular couple.

"Can you come at eight o'clock instead? My family is having a late supper that night." She cast her eyes down.

Frankie tilted his head. "Sure, I can come at eight." He leaned toward her with his lips parted.

Annie gave him a quick kiss. "I need to straighten up some things here in the shop."

"See you Saturday." He whistled as he left the shop without noticing Jonathan poised behind the canned goods.

As soon as new customers walked into the shop and Annie offered to help them, Jonathan slipped out unnoticed.

*

On Saturday Annie walked up the hill to the Porters Glen School and found Josie and Jonathan ensconced in his office, both of them making lists.

"Anne, come in. We are just getting started. I'm making the list of things we'll need for Soup Night, and Josie is starting a list for class

supplies. I applaud you for this idea. It shows that you'll make a great teacher one day."

She felt herself blush. "I'm not sure you know enough about me to say that."

"Well, this idea shows that you not only have creativity, but you are a caring soul as well."

She lowered her eyes a moment to enjoy the compliment, and smiled inwardly to think of the comparison to her mother. "Is there a way, then, to fund both the Soup Night and the supplies?"

"Josie and I have a discretionary fund from our trust that we are allowed to tap into for special situations. We both agree that your senior project qualifies as a special situation. Josie, go ahead and tell Anne."

"Remember when I said that Mr. Meyers might be able to help us? He located a gentleman in Pittsburgh who has agreed to fund the shoe coupons as a mitzvah. A one-time gift."

Annie's face went blank.

"A mitzvah is a good deed that someone does as a way of helping others."

"I've never heard the word before."

"It's a Hebrew term."

Annie sat silent. "Are you Jewish?" she turned and asked Josie.

"Our mother was Jewish, so yes, we're Jewish, and she taught us everything we know about Judaism. But, our father's family was Catholic, so we went to Catholic Mass with our grandmother. When Grandmother Canavan died, we stopped going to Mass. Actually, Jonathan stopped going to church of any kind, but I still go to temple."

"But there isn't a Jewish church in Mount Pleasant."

"It's called a synagogue, and there is one in Riverton." Josie smiled. "That's where I met Mr. Meyers."

"I had no idea that he was Jewish. Of course, it makes no difference to me what church you attend, or where the money comes from. If a mitzvah provides shoe coupons for the women, then I'll gratefully accept it."

Jonathan lowered his voice. "Josie also explained to me about

the Curtain Room, and I will help you in any way that I can. You're brave, Anne." He leaned over and put his hand on hers.

Caught off guard, she felt a tingling run up the length of her arm with his touch.

"On a lighter note, are you ready for Christmas?"

"Almost." She smiled.

"Tell me, what is your favorite holiday memory from when you were young?"

She thought a moment. "I think the tradition our family has of going up on Piney Ridge to search for evergreen boughs. When we were little, we would come back home loaded with pine boughs and spend an hour carefully decorating the entire downstairs. Mama made *chocolat chaud* and Madeleine cookies."

"Sounds like you have a close-knit family."

"We do, but my mother died when I was eight. Christmas has never really been the same without her."

"I'm sorry for that, Anne. Someone as nice as you should have only happy memories of childhood." He gave her a tender smile, and she felt like they were the only two people in the room.

A warm glow washed over her.

Once the meeting was over, Annie gathered up her dark-brown wool cloak and matching felt hat and left for home. Gobbling her supper, she dashed upstairs to change her clothes for the date with Frankie.

As usual, he was late.

"Frankie, are you ever on time for anything?"

"Come on, Annie, I'm, what…twenty minutes late? We're only going to a party."

"But…"

"But, what?"

"When you don't arrive on time, it makes me feel like I'm not special enough for you to make the effort."

"You're making a big deal out of nothing."

"Are you late for your shift at the mines?"

"Of course not. That's different. Now, come on, let's go. He grabbed her hand, and she was struck by how rough his touch felt in

comparison with Jonathan's.

*

Two days before Christmas, Annie had shut down the pot-bellied stove and was cleaning up when the shop door blew open and she found herself face to face with Herman Schumn.

"I'm sorry, Mr. Schumn, we're about to close."

"I ain't here to buy nothing. Came to deliver a message."

Annie felt her throat go dry.

"The message is for Hulda Kirby." He stopped talking and pinned his gaze on Annie's face.

Her mouth felt like it was full of marbles. "I'm sorry, but Mrs. Kirby has left for the day."

"Of course she has. I know that."

"Then perhaps you should leave, Mr. Schumn." Annie walked toward the door, then turned back to see if he had moved.

"As I said, I have a message for her. We know that Mrs. Kirby and a certain Molly S. of Riverton have been mailing letters to the editor of the *Mount Pleasant Journal.* Letters intended to make the CVC look responsible for mining accidents."

Annie felt the color drain from her face.

"Here's the message. Tell Mrs. Kirby if she ever becomes involved with slander against the CVC again, we would have to recommend she be placed in Scriveners' Asylum for evaluation."

Bile rose in Annie's throat. Her voice came out in a low throaty whisper. "How dare you come in here and make threats against Hulda Kirby. Powerful man like you, you can't be scared of an old woman."

Schumn's eyes turned into slits. "You're right; she is an old woman with no family to take her in. So unless you want to see her go before the Asylum Committee for charges of slander and senility, I suggest you talk to her about keeping silent."

Annie stared at him with all the hatred she could muster.

"I also suggest you watch your own steps. The company's been aware of your interfering attitude for quite some time."

"Get out of our shop."

"Why, I was just about to leave. Merry Christmas, Anne… or is it Molly?" He snickered when he saw Annie recoil at the name being directed to her.

*

Christmas Eve descended with a hush over the valley and only the sound of crunching boots on snow broke the stillness. Annie wanted to enjoy the Christmas Mass, but she still felt unsettled by Schumn's visit to the bakery yesterday. Thank goodness he did not attend St. Bridget's.

Once inside the crowded church, Annie sat with Louis, Marie, and Aunt Hulda. She scanned the rows looking for the Hennessey family, and found them up front. Each member of the family appeared to be wearing new winter outfits, and she saw that Frankie was sitting at the opposite end of the pew from his father.

Annie let out a deep sigh. If Frankie stayed with the mines, would he be able to protect her if Schumn ever came after her family? Here it was Christmas Eve, and Schumn was still an ugly presence in her thoughts. She shook her head as if to shake him from her mind.

The entrance hymn started, and the musical strains of "Oh Come All Ye Faithful" plunged Annie back into the holiday spirit. The familiar story of The Nativity soothed her unease about Schumn. Walking past Frankie on her way back from Holy Communion, she gave him a big smile. He acknowledged her with a wink.

At the end of the service as the congregation left the church, each child received a small piece of peppermint candy, courtesy of the CVC. Annie saw with distaste, Herman Schumn doling out the treat.

Dear God, I can't believe he's here. Annie filed out along other parishioners and came face to face with Schumn.

"No thank you."

"What's a matter, Anne? Too good for a free piece of candy?"

"Does the mining company really give away anything for free?" She rebutted.

"Molly S. would take candy, I'm sure," he snipped.

"I don't know why you keep mentioning that person's name to me, whoever she is." Her smile was dripping with honey.

"Annie!"

She turned around to see Frankie calling to her as he and his family came out of the church. She turned on her heel and left Schumn's presence. "Hello, Mr. and Mrs. Hennessey. Merry Christmas."

"Merry Christmas to you too, Anne. Tell your father we still buy his Madeleines for our Christmas Eve treat, even though most of our children are full grown now."

"I'll tell him, Mrs. Hennessey. He'll like to hear that."

Frankie maneuvered Annie out of earshot from his family. "I'm hoping part of my Christmas gift is spending more time together."

"Then, can you come and join our family for Christmas tomorrow?"

"Yes. But, I'm hoping for a lot more time together—not just on Christmas."

Should I tell him about the night class? Not yet, it isn't the right moment.

"Ah, Frank, Merry Christmas." Louis came over to wish holiday greetings.

"Merry Christmas, Mr. Charbonneau."

"Are we going to see you tomorrow for Christmas?"

Frankie looked at Annie. "Yes. How about three o'clock? I need to have dinner with my family first."

"All right. We'll see you around three."

Louis turned to walk home and Frankie gave Annie a quick kiss on the cheek. "I'll see you tomorrow."

As the foursome of Louis, Annie, Marie, and Hulda walked back from the church, their cheeks turned rosy from the cold. The lingering smell of peppermint candy in the air made Annie remember Schumn's threat to Aunt Hulda. It had to be the CVC's way of retaliating against her letters to the editor.

Marie spoke up. "Annie, did you notice that the Morelli girls each had a new pair of shoes under their rubber snow boots? I bet their mother has been saving to buy those."

"Yes, I saw, but that won't keep on happening."

"What do you mean?"
"I'll explain it later."

*

On Christmas afternoon Frankie arrived with a wrapped present for Annie, and she could tell by the paper it had come from his father's store. He also carried a bone wrapped in butcher paper for Bon.

"Oh, Frankie, you brought a gift for Bon!"

"Of course I did. He's part of your family, isn't he?"

"Thank you. Did you bring gifts for us humans, too?" She playfully grinned at him.

Teasing, he held her gift behind his back. "First things first." Reaching into his jacket pocket he pulled out a sprig of mistletoe and held it over her head. Before she could even react, he leaned in and kissed her fully on her lips. The kiss hinted to obvious passion waiting to ignite.

As always when he kissed her, Annie felt the delicious emotion of love mixed with budding sexual awakenings.

"Frankie, where did you find mistletoe?"

"My father had some in the store. Want to try its magic again?" He grinned.

"Why, hello Frank. Merry Christmas." Aunt Hulda came out from the kitchen.

"Merry Christmas, Mrs. Kirby. Here, I brought something for you to hang in the kitchen for good luck." He gave her the sprig of mistletoe.

"Thank you. I see that you and Annie have gifts for each other. Why don't you go sit in the parlor? Have you had dessert? I made a special almond torte."

"Thanks, I'd love a piece."

Hulda went back to the kitchen and for a few minutes the parlor was empty, and private.

"Where are your father and sister?"

"Out for a walk; they'll be home soon. Let's go ahead and ex-

change our gifts."

"First, let me kiss you again."

They embraced, locking their arms around each other's body, and causing both of them to flush with excitement. When the kiss was over, Annie nestled her head up against his shoulder.

Frankie took a deep breath to regain his composure. "I should've asked for two kisses."

Annie grinned and went to the sofa. "Here's your gift." She flashed him a wide smile, knowing he needed heavy leather gloves in the mines.

He opened the box. "Thank you. I'll really be able to use these. Now, you open yours." His gift to her was a wool scarf in sky blue, the kind she could wrap around her neck to keep out the cold when she walked.

If the gifts lacked in romance, they excelled in practicality.

Just then Louis and Marie returned from their walk as Hulda brought out plates with warm fragrant slices of her sugar-dusted almond cake.

"Wait. I'll get the wine." Louis went to retrieve his homemade elderberry wine. "Here you go, Frankie. Guest of honor gets the first drink." Then Louis poured a glass for Hulda, Annie, and Marie. "To our health. *Santé*."

Toasts were given all around.

"So, how has working in the mines been?"

"Not too bad. As soon as the heavy snows come, the mines will shut down for winter."

"Do you think you want to stay a miner?"

"Papa, stop asking such personal questions."

"That's all right. I think so, Mr. Charbonneau. At least for now."

The conversation stalled and each person finished sipping their wine.

Hulda stood up and collected the glasses. "I'm on my way home, then. Merry Christmas everyone!"

"Merry Christmas, Aunt Hulda."

Frankie glanced at Annie. "Annie, how about we take a walk?"

"All right, but it's awfully cold out."

"I'll keep you warm."

Annie turned so that no one would see her blush.

Outside they held hands and walked down Coal Bank Lane.

"I'd like to take you back to the cabin."

"It's the middle of winter, Frankie. Besides, I told you before that I don't want to seal our love in that place."

Frankie's expression went blank. "Well, when will you be ready? I hope you don't mean wait for spring?"

Annie hesitated. "I don't know when I'll be ready. I just want it to be right."

His holiday mood crashed. Irritability clouded his face. "Not yet, then. Well, I guess there's no reason to keep walking in the cold air. I'll go on home. Merry Christmas."

"No, Frankie, wait."

"For what?"

"I don't want you leaving like this, it's Christmas."

"Then think about making me happy."

A chill that had nothing to do with the cold night air descended on Annie.

Frankie stalked off uphill toward Mt. Pleasant. Annie chewed her thumbnail. Had she pushed him too far on the issue? She wasn't sure.

Annie came back into the kitchen and heard a scratching at the back door, Bon's signal that he wanted to come inside. When Annie opened the door, her face brightened with the ever-present love she felt for this creature. Bending down, she placed his Christmas bone right in front of him. His tail beat a rhythm of joy as he lay down, moved the bone between his paws, and gnawed on it.

If only my life could be that simple.

Her stomach still churned with thoughts about Frankie. There had been other girls in the village she knew, like Stella Warner who had gotten pregnant and shipped off to an aunt somewhere in Pennsylvania as soon as her stomach had begun to show. Stella never came back. Annie did not want that to ever happen to her, but she did not want to lose Frankie either.

This was not how she wanted Christmas Day to end.

CHAPTER 18

John Keirs, age 30, killed by fall of roof,
Bowery Mine, leaves four dependents.

Annie looked at the list of supplies that Jonathan and Josie Canavan had compiled for Soup Night. Smiling, Annie couldn't help but think how her mother would have loved this project.

She wondered if Frankie might be interested in coming to the Soup Night event—probably not; it wasn't really his cup of tea. Each time they talked, it seemed more likely that he wouldn't give up the mines. Even with his irritating habit of tracking in coal dirt to the shop, her heart still fluttered every time she saw him. She just hoped she hadn't ruined things between them.

The day before New Year's Eve, a knock sounded at the Charbonneau's front door.

Annie opened the door with a happy surprise to see Frankie. She bit her lips with relief that he had returned.

"Hi, Annie. I wanted to come over and wish you Happy New Year. Perhaps we could talk?"

"Of course, come in."

"I don't like it when we have cross words with each other." He smiled at her.

"Me neither, Frankie. But I want you to understand that I really don't want to go back to the cabin on Piney Ridge."

"Do you know of a better place?" He folded his arms somewhat playfully across his chest and waited for her response.

*He must be joking, or he's not really taking me serio*usly. "Frankie, please stop pressuring me on this. I love you, but I don't want to fight every time we see each other."

"So, is this a game you're playing with me?" His river gray-green eyes darkened.

"Of course not." She looked up at him. "Couldn't you just come over tomorrow night and we celebrate New Year's here? I'd like to tell you about the night class I'm going to teach starting in January."

"Night class? So one more thing added to your schedule? Don't think so, Annie. It looks like you're planning your life without thinking about my needs. I'll celebrate up in Beer Alley with my friends. Happy New Year, I guess. Don't bother getting up, I know my way out." He strode out of the room and a moment later she heard the front door open and close.

Annie sat on the chair. Why was their relationship hitting such a rocky point? If she agreed to consummate it, would that smooth everything over? Then she thought about Josie Canavan's talk about real love makes sacrifices for each other. If she sacrificed this for him, what would he sacrifice for her?

She thought about her mother and Aunt Hulda. They both had married young with no plans for their future, other than becoming housewives. Had they been content with their decisions? Or did they even have a decision in the matter?

And certainly there must be other girls who dreamed of more than just getting married and starting families. Annie wanted to get married eventually, and of course she loved children…but she and Frankie had never even talked about children.

Something was wrong with their relationship, and she wasn't sure she could fix it.

*

"Wonderful meal, Hulda."

"Thank you, Louis."

Annie looked at her father with new eyes. Ever since she fell for Frankie, she had become more aware of her father's role as a widower. He missed her mother, she knew. But he must also miss the companionship they had shared, and the warmth of sleeping in a bed next to the one you love.

Before, Annie would let herself daydream of sleeping next to Frankie, as his wife. Maybe that was her problem, she equated sleeping together only with marriage. How long had her parents courted before they married?

Would her father ever want to remarry? If so, where would he find a new wife? On impulse she stood up and crossed over behind him.

"Here, Papa, let me rub your shoulders. You always work too hard during the holidays."

He smiled. "Ah, that feels wonderful. *Merci*. I work harder during the holidays because I know the season will bring extra customers into the shop. Your mama taught me that."

"You still miss her, don't you?" she said in a soft voice.

"More than you can know, and hopefully will never find out in your lifetime." He stared down at his hands. "Enough sad thoughts. This is the New Year and calls for new beginnings, eh?"

"Yes, Papa, new beginnings."

"Thank you for the rub. I think I'll go upstairs and put on my slippers."

Marie was already upstairs getting ready to go out with Giselle to another friend's house. Annie decided to approach Hulda. "Aunt Hulda, I have something I need to talk to you about. Something serious."

Hulda stopped fussing at the kitchen counter. "Now?"

"Yes, now."

Hulda dried her hands and walked back over to the table and sat down.

"Did you, have you…told anyone about mailing the letters in

Riverton?"

"No, of course not."

"Are you absolutely sure?"

"I did mention it in confession to Father Kelley, but he would never break the vow of the confessional."

"Could someone have overheard you speaking to Father Kelley?"

"I don't think so."

Annie remained silent for a moment. "Well, Herman Schumn came to the shop right before Christmas, saying that the CVC knows you mailed the letters for Molly S."

"Oh, God."

"I think for your safety you should not speak of the letters to anyone, not even a priest."

Hulda's eyes darted side to side. "Am I in danger? Has my assailant been spotted here in the village?"

"They don't have any real proof and I'm sure Schumn is just trying to scare me. But I want you to be extra cautious and trust no one. Just let this lie, for now."

Hulda's eyes widened in alarm and surprise from this dictate.

At the same time, Annie realized that instead of being the child, she had reversed the role and taken hold of the situation. They were actually speaking together as woman-to-woman, almost like her conversations with Josie Canavan.

"There won't be any more letters, and since I typed them on Stephen's old second-hand typewriter, no one can prove anything." Annie got up and went over to Hulda, who had begun wringing her hands. "Don't worry. This is the start to a new year and nothing bad is going to happen."

*

Both Annie and Marie got up early on New Year's Day in anticipation of who might be the first to visit the Charbonneau's for first-footing. Started by the Scots, the belief held that if the first visitor on New Year's Day should be a young dark-haired man, then the family would have good luck in the year to come, and any unmarried daughters would find husbands.

For the moment, Annie put the Curtain Room, the Soup Event, and the threats from Schumn out of her mind. But she couldn't get Frankie out of her thoughts since he had stormed away from her. She wondered if he had gone to Beer Alley after all, and gotten drunk with his friends. She reminded herself that she had chosen her words carefully and honestly and if he preferred the other miners' company to her—then he wasn't making much of a sacrifice.

Secretly though, she hoped Frankie would be the first caller on New Year's Day.

From breakfast on, everyone kept a watchful ear out for sounds of a guest. Even Bon seemed to sense the excitement hanging in the air. Then at eleven o'clock, a knock sounded at the front door. Marie and Annie giggled. Bon raced to the door in anticipation and the girls ran to the parlor room where they could greet the visitor. When Louis opened the door, there stood not one, but two people: Josie and Jonathan Canavan.

"Wait!" Marie shrieked, and while Louis tried to explain first-footing, Marie returned with a dark brown hat and tossed it on Jonathan's head.

"What in the world?"

Marie and Annie dissolved in laughter. "Your hair! It's too light! We fixed it so you look like a dark-haired man. After all, you are the first person to enter our house on New Year's morning."

"All right. Do I have to wear the hat all day?"

A new round of laughter ensued.

"You can take it off now." Louis grinned. "Can we offer you a sip of New Year's wine?"

"This early in the day?"

"Just a sip, so the luck is guaranteed."

Jonathan turned and looked at Josie, who nodded with a silly smile.

Presently the Charbonneau and Canavan families sipped wine and toasted to a profitable new year. Everyone still giggled over Jona-

than's role in the first-footing tradition.

"All right, now we do need to get to work. Annie, Josie and I came to pick you up on our way to the school. We figure it will take us a couple of hours to prepare for Soup Night."

Annie gave Marie and Louis a quick kiss. "I'm off, then."

The recipe for Lentil Soup indicated it would take an hour for the lentils to soak and two hours for the soup to simmer properly, so getting an early start made sense. They arrived at the school and started the preparations. Annie had gone to school here as a child, but had never been in the kitchen area. It made her feel like a real adult to be involved with this event.

"Annie, let's start with you and Jonathan chopping the onions."

"All right." Annie opened some drawers.

"What are you looking for?"

"Matches. If you hold an unlit match in your mouth, your eyes won't water from chopping the onions."

"Whoa! Where did you learn that?"

"I'm French, Mr. Canavan. Every French housewife learns that trick."

Jonathan laughed. "You're not a housewife, though."

Annie grinned. "I should have said every French cook learns the trick."

"I don't think I'll need the match."

"Oh, no? We'll see."

As they chopped onions to sauté in cast iron skillets, Jonathan's eyes teared up. "I surrender! Give me a match!"

"Is this where I get to say, 'Told you so'?"

"I admit defeat in this round, and must tell the truth that I have never cooked a meal in my life."

"Obviously," she grinned.

"This *Potage aux Lentilles*[1] that we are making is one of the first recipes a young French girl is taught to master. You can start peeling the potatoes next."

He groaned. "Do I need a match for that, too?"

---

1 Recipe included at end of book.

"No, but our family adds small chunks of potato to make the soup more filling. Here, let me help you. If you hold the potato peeler this way, then the peelings fall away from the soup—not into it." She stifled a giggle.

"Good thing I never had to survive on my own cooking." He chuckled. "I'll have to take some lessons from you."

Annie blushed with a touch of giddiness.

Within the hour, Jonathan insisted that Annie stop calling him Mr. Canavan and use his first name instead.

"I'm not sure if that would be appropriate."

"Well, you're calling my sister by her first name and all three of us are cooks in the kitchen here together, so I think my request is fair."

"Then you can stop calling me Anne. My friends and family call me Annie."

"Agreed, Annie."

That evening, almost half the families in the village attended Family Soup Night, and each one brought along the requested tin cups. Parents beamed as children took center stage in the auditorium and recited a few verses from the poems of Henry Wadsworth Longfellow, a poet studied by most of the classes.

After the program, Annie and Josie ladled out soup. Last month's mining accident had claimed four more men from the village, and their widows had attended the program bound in the solidarity of loss. Their grief was a poignant reminder of Stephen's death.

As Annie ladled, she listened to their conversation.

"Staying on?" One woman spoke in a hushed whisper.

"Trying to." Answered another woman.

"CVC helping you out?"

The other woman lowered her eyes to the floor. None of the others responded.

Were these widows staying on in their homes because they've submitted to the Curtain Room? Annie felt her first real stab of empathy.

At the conclusion of the meal, Annie and Josie passed out notes explaining that a free English class would be offered on Sunday evenings from five to six o'clock at the school. They would accept the

first fifteen women who signed up, and each woman would be asked to bring an empty can with a lid.

When the last family left and Marie started out the door for home with Louis, Annie told her father she needed to go back to the kitchen to help Josie and Jonathan clean up. She would come home soon.

"How do you feel about your big success?" Jonathan asked.

"Great, actually. But, I saw the newest widows here with their children. They need more than just a handout of lentil soup."

"Slow down and take this project one step at a time. You alone cannot change how the mining company operates."

"Their husbands died in some of the old tunnels. Just like Stephen."

"It was a tragedy, I agree. Let me walk you home and we can talk about it, if that would help."

Just as she was about to say it wasn't necessary, she found herself accepting his offer. "How will Josie get back to Mount Pleasant?"

"We've convinced my landlady to rent out a small room to Josie tonight and every Sunday night during winter while the English class is in session. Mrs. Eisner's husband will drive Josie back up to Mount Pleasant in his wagon early each Monday morning."

"My, I'm impressed you have this all figured out."

"I'm a great planner; you'll soon find that out about me, Annie."

She felt a rush of heat to her cheeks as he used her nickname. It felt intimate somehow and she was surprised by how her heart skipped a beat.

CHAPTER 19

George Jones, age 19, killed by fall of roof,
Carlos Mine.

Olga Dewitt had loved her husband from the first day they met, and this January was their thirtieth anniversary.

He had stolen her heart with his laughing brown eyes, muscular arms, and fearless attitude toward life. She married him at sixteen, and children came quickly. Even though they had both aged through the years, neither had ever strayed from one another's arms.

But now, thirty winters after their wedding, she knew he was dying.

Frederick Dewitt had worked the Porter Mine since the age of fifteen, quitting school to take place alongside his father. The early years had honed his body into a solid working machine and he paid little attention to the coal dust he inhaled ten hours a day.

Recently, his coughing had become more virulent, and he spit up gobs of gray-tinged phlegm. By the time Olga had insisted that the doctor come, Frederick had full-blown miners' asthma, and nothing could be done to help him.

Dr. Tanner shook his head, knowing that the insidious disease wormed its way into a man's lungs and then took up residence without any chance of being evicted. Silent and steady, the coal tar penetrated the lining of the lungs and slowly filled in the cavity with a toxic layer of carbon, much like a coat of black varnish. An agonizing death was always the final result; the only variant was how long it would take before the victim could no longer breathe.

Olga watched as a violent spasm wracked his body. She tried to comfort him, holding his frail chest as he writhed in pain and then spit a bloody mess of phlegm into the bucket next to his bed. Dr. Tanner told her it would not be long now.

She had forced herself to appear strong, but inwardly the fear of life without her husband tore at her heart.

The CVC would give no compensation for his death. Their hollow words of "sorry for your loss" would not help to pay any of the extra medical bills, either. In every fiber of her being, she resented the callousness of the CVC.

Thankfully she had a grown daughter living nearby, so that when the end came, she would have somewhere to live. Other women her same age, grandmothers like herself, had been forced to visit the mining office.

The Curtain Room took them at any age.

CHAPTER 20

Anthony Clupp, age 62, killed by fall of roof,
Pine Hill Mine.

Annie hardly noticed the brittle taste of January, because her anticipation of the Sunday night class now took precedence over everything else. When the women showed up for the first night of class with lines of uncertainty etched in their foreheads, Annie realized she was as nervous as they were. Perhaps, even more so.

One by one, they entered the classroom, removed their heavy capes, untied their head scarves, and whispered to one another.

She looked over the group and recognized a few of them. The four women who had come into the store to get ingredients for a miner's pie arrived first. Then Rosa Morelli, the miner's wife who rarely bought anything from the store, walked in alone. Bridget Schooley came in with another Irish woman, and then the room began to fill. The last woman to get there was Sophie Petrova, the girl who barely spoke any English.

Annie took a deep breath and looked to Josie for a clue on how they would start.

"Ladies, welcome!" Josie beamed. "Please take a seat and get comfortable." She waited. "Let me start by introducing myself. I am Josie Canavan and I teach English at Mount Pleasant High School." Then she beckoned Annie to step forward. "And this is Annie Charbonneau, whom most of you know because you shop in her family's bakery here in Porters Glen."

None of the women made any comment, although Annie saw one woman raise her eyebrows.

"We are both very excited to have this opportunity to work with you. We'll start tonight by having Annie help you introduce yourselves and I will pull you aside one by one to read a sentence or two. Don't worry if you cannot read at all, we just need to see who knows what. So, let's start."

Annie gave the women her most warm-hearted smile and took a deep breath. "I know many of you know me from my father's store, but I do want to say that I feel honored to be teaching with Miss Canavan, and I hope to get to know each of you better."

Bridget Schooley nudged her neighbor and whispered loud enough that Annie heard her say, "We'll see how sincere she really is."

It made Annie wince. "All right. So we'll introduce ourselves. You know my name, but you may not know that my parents came here from France. Who'd like to go next?" Annie smiled at a shy looking woman in the second row.

"My name is Bianca Dinelli. My husband and I grew up in Italy."

One by the one, the other women followed by introducing themselves and telling where they had lived before coming to Porters Glen. Even Sophie Petrova stuttered out a brief introduction.

Josie explained the program—how the women would come on Sunday nights for the three months of winter. Their goal would be learning to read and write English on a beginner's basis. The added bonus of attendance would be a pound of lentils each week to take home along with some day-old rolls from the Charbonneau Bakery.

"So, let's begin. Here on the front board I have written out the English alphabet. We will sing it, just like children do, because it is easier to learn that way. Ready?"

As the women nodded, Josie pointed to each letter and the

group began to chant the letters in a sing-song melody. After three rounds, Josie clapped. "Bravo! Very good!" Then she turned to Annie. "Let's help them learn the letters of their first names."

Annie walked over to the third row and stopped in front of Bridget Schooley.

"Bridget, do you know the letters in your first name?"

"I do."

"Please tell us." She waited while Bridget spelled out her first name. "Now, let's see if anyone else in the room has a name that also begins with the letter B. The letter B makes a b-b-b sound."

The shy woman from the second row tentatively raised her hand. "I think my name, Bianca, does."

"Well, of course it does," laughed the woman next to her. "The beginning of your name says B, right away!"

Nervous giggles broke out among the women.

"I'm glad to see we have such bright students." Josie smiled. "So I hope you see that learning to read and write English depends on knowing both the alphabet and what sounds each letter makes. I'd like you to move now and sit with the study partner I assigned you. That way you can all help each other."

The women got up, shyly at first, and found their study partners.

"Good. The assignment for next week is to ask your study partner to help you learn to spell your first name. If you already know how to spell it, don't worry, we will find other ways to help your English improve."

The women talked with one another and then in childlike handwriting wrote on their slates, practicing how to spell their first names.

When the class concluded, Annie handed out small parcels of lentils, rolls, and a simple recipe for Lentil Soup. She could tell by their smiles that the women were appreciative of the food. As they filed out the door, each woman thanked both Josie and Annie.

"Whew! The time went fast," exclaimed Annie. "I was afraid the women wouldn't like having me as a teacher assistant."

"Why not?"

"Because I'm never the one to give away free samples in the shop. Aunt Hulda does that."

"Don't sell yourself short, Annie. This project started with you."

A heady feeling of accomplishment wrapped itself around Annie like the aroma of a tray of freshly baked bread.

*

By the end of two weeks each woman could write both her first and last name almost completely by memory—a rare feat for many who had never learned to read or write in their own native tongue.

Annie and Josie made the accomplishment a celebration by handing out the shoe coupons. Each coupon entitled the bearer to two dollars' worth of children's shoes from any local store. The coupons had been drawn up by the Citizens Bank, and the miners' wives radiated with joy at this golden opportunity.

At the end of the evening, as the women got up to leave, Rosa Morelli handed her coupon back to Annie.

"No, Rosa, this is yours to keep."

"I can't."

"Why not?"

"Because my husband doesn't want me to continue with the class. He says I have shamed him learning to write my name, when he cannot write his."

"Rosa, please keep the coupon and reconsider coming back to class next week."

"I'm sorry, but I cannot." With silent tears staining her cheeks, Rosa walked out of the school.

Annie stood still, a feeling of empty success forming a lump in her throat.

Tying on her winter hat, she walked down the stairs thinking about Rosa. Seeing Jonathan standing at the front door made Rosa's decision feel more heartbreaking. It wasn't fair that men could discourage women from bettering themselves. Annie intended to help these women, not causing them discord at home with their husbands.

"What's wrong, Annie? You look like you lost a friend."

"I did, in a way. Rose Morelli is quitting the class because her husband doesn't want her to be more educated than he is. It's so unfair."

"Don't go blaming yourself. You're offering those women a gift, but you can't change their families. Besides, Rosa's husband might change his mind when he sees the other mining wives helping their husbands with correspondence from the CVC."

"I hope so."

"Let's start walking home; perhaps the brilliance of the starry winter sky will cheer you." He led both Josie and Annie down to Store Hill and then they turned north onto Porters Road and headed toward Lower Porters Glen.

They dropped Josie off at the Eisner's boarding house and then Annie and Jonathan began the slight ascent that would lead them to Coal Bank Lane. "Annie you need to concentrate on the women who are staying in the class. Those are the women you'll help the most."

"You're probably right, but I still feel badly about Rosa leaving."

As they crossed over Squirrel Creek, Jonathan stopped. "Look." He pointed up to the night sky. "That's the constellation Cassiopeia. Can you see it?"

Annie only saw billions of stars lighting the sky. "I'm not sure. There're so many stars."

"Here, let me help you." Gently, but with his hands solidly supporting her shoulders, he tipped her back so she could look directly up at the sky. "Follow where I'm pointing. It almost looks like the outline of the letter M."

It took Annie a few moments to adjust her sights. "Yes. I think I see it. But how did it get named Cassiopeia?"

"After a beautiful queen in Greek mythology, and it does brighten the winter sky, don't you think?"

She nodded.

"When you smile, your face brightens."

Annie felt her face glow. Instead of paying attention to the stars, she noticed the warmth of his hands on her shoulders and how secure it felt to be held by him.

*

Winter descended on Porters Glen with January snowdrifts that could almost bury a mule, let alone dogs and cats.

When the snow lessened for a day, two miners' wives trudged up the road to Hennessey's Store in Mount Pleasant to redeem their shoe coupons. They walked into the grand shop with a feeling of pride they had not experienced before. But a few minutes later their happy moods burst when the store clerk returned and handed them back the coupons—explaining that they were not valid in this shop.

Embarrassed and not knowing what else to do, they retreated back down the Pike to Porters Glen and went directly to Charbonneau's Bakery.

"Good morning, Miss Annie. We just attempted to exchange our shoe coupons at Hennessey's Store, but we were refused."

"For what reason?"

"The clerk didn't really give us a reason. Just said the coupons were not honored there."

"Thank you for coming to tell me. Please hand them to me."

The two women stood back and watched Annie tie on her hat, and wrap a blue scarf over her wool cape, and stomp out the door.

*

With anger blazing in her eyes, Annie tramped along the snowy road up to Union Street and Hennessey's Store.

"May I help you, Miss?"

"Yes, I would like to speak to Mr. Hennessey about these!"

The clerk almost recoiled when he saw Annie holding up the exact same coupons he had refused the miners' wives an hour or so earlier.

"I want to speak to Mr. Hennessey himself and I won't leave until I do."

The clerk scurried to the back of the store and knocked at the office door where Annie assumed Mr. Hennessey would be sitting in his large mahogany captain's chair, studying the morning's receipts.

While the clerk talked with Mr. Hennessey, Annie glanced over at the display tables holding the newest shipments. The shelves appeared to be divided based on the quality of the merchandise. One side of the room displayed bleached cotton sheets with plain hems, while across the room the opposite shelf contained the newest in fine lace bedding.

Then Annie turned and saw the new shirtwaists. A lovely dove-gray one with a pointy flat Robespierre collar caught her eye. She reprimanded herself that she was not here to shop, but to rectify a mistake.

A moment later, Mr. Hennessey lumbered to the front of the store. Like Frankie, he had an impish Irish smile that spread across his broad face and made him appear years younger than his actual age.

"Anne, how nice to see you. My clerk seems to think you have a problem? I would rather think you've come to check out some of the new shirtwaists that have recently arrived. Or perhaps I could help you with borrowing a book? We have a small circulating library now. Ten cents gives you two weeks of reading. Would you like a copy of *Little Women*? I hear the book is quite popular with girls your age."

"I am here, Mr. Hennessey, because I want to know why the shoe coupons from Porters Glen are not being honored. They are guaranteed by a bank in Mount Pleasant." Her eyes smoldered.

Mr. Hennessey appeared to be a bit taken aback. "And might I ask what business is it of yours about the shoe coupons?"

"I teach a night class in Porters Glen. The women who came to your store are our students. We issued the shoe coupons to them."

"You! I had no idea. But the only shoe coupons I'm able to accept come from the Cumberland Valley Coal Company."

Annie's eyes hardened. "Are you aware, Mr. Hennessey, what some of the women in Porters Glen must do in order to get those coupons from the CVC?"

"It's none of my business how they get the coupons, and might I say that this is a bit out of your league, too."

Annie felt the heat of anger crawl up her neck. "Do you accept cash in your store?"

"Of course we do."

"Fine. Then I will be coming back with cash."

"Thank you for stopping in, Anne."

She didn't really care if she had acted with a lack of manners. She stormed out of the store.

God, it's bad enough that Frankie hasn't called in over two weeks now, this altercation with his father won't win me any points in my favor. I have to be more careful with my words.

Turning east she tromped back down the road to Porters Glen and realized she was heading straight for the school.

Pushing open the school door, she ran into Jonathan.

"Annie, what are you doing here? Is something wrong?"

"Jonathan, something is terribly wrong and I think we'll have to rely on you to get it fixed."

"What?"

"Hennessey's Store is refusing to accept the shoe coupons we gave out."

"Why?"

"Mr. Hennessey said he could only accept shoe coupons issued by the CVC."

"Didn't you tell him that the shoe coupons are guaranteed by the Citizens Bank?"

"The coupons have the name of the bank printed on them, so he knows."

"How can I help, then?"

"You and Josie put the mitzvah money in the bank. I want you to go back to the bank and explain that you want to take the money out; all of it. Then we will accompany the women to Hennessey's Store with the cash equivalent of the coupons. Mr. Hennessey can't refuse taking cash for shoes."

He smiled at her. "You've got chutzpah, Annie. I love seeing flashes of your courage. I'll go uptown tomorrow and tell Josie. Then we'll withdraw the money. How I'd love to see the mining company's reaction."

*

The following week Annie and Josie marched into Hennessey's store with all twelve of the women from the class.

"We are here to purchases shoes," Annie announced.

"All of you?" the astounded clerk asked.

"Yes, all of us, and we will each be paying in cash."

As the timid clerk shuffled back and forth from the stock room with various children's shoe sizes written down, Mr. Hennessey witnessed the activity from his open office window; a scowl hardened his face. He could tell by the fierce look of determination on Annie's face that she was in his store on some sort of mission, one that would probably cause him frustration. A part of him admired her spirit and more than once he had thought that she had more balls than Frankie did. However, that was not always an asset for a husband.

*

On the second Sunday in February, Jonathan met Annie as she arrived at school an hour early, as usual, to set up for the class. He looked forward to these evenings, but when they reached the second floor, the door to the classroom hung at a strange angle, as if ready to fall off the hinges.

"Wait." He approached the doorway and saw that a hinge was missing. Cautiously, he stepped inside. "Dear God!"

Annie followed him and almost dropped her supplies. "Oh, Jonathan! Who would do this?"

The desks and chairs had all been overturned, and several chairs had their legs sawed off. All the books lie on the floor, most with huge chunks of pages torn out, and all the slates had been broken in half. Then her eyes focused on the front board. In a large scrawl, someone had written in large chalk letters, *Go Home Bitch*.

Annie's shoulders trembled as a few tears spilled down her face. With quivering lips, Annie tried to regain her composure. "Jonathan, someone got in here and did all this. But who, and why? Do you think it could have been the CVC's thugs?" All the color drained from her face. "Maybe I shouldn't have pushed so hard on the shoe coupons."

Jonathan went over to her and tenderly put his hand under her chin. "This isn't your fault. We'll go to the police."

"Oh dear God, what happened?" Now Josie had arrived.

"Looks like someone is trying to discourage the two of you from teaching."

Josie stood tall. "Well, that's not going to happen. Come on, Annie; let's clean up this mess before the women arrive."

The task was monumental, even with three of them working together. Jonathan turned the usable furniture back upright, and moved the broken chairs to the back of the room. Josie erased the message from the board as Annie moved among the books, seeing if any could be salvaged.

Women started trickling in for class, each one shocked at the sight in front of them.

"No reason to be alarmed, ladies, we'll all pitch in to help."

Jonathan realized that the night could have been a total loss, but the very act of the women working together molded them into a cohesive, supportive group. He wrote down an inventory of what had been destroyed.

At the end of the evening, Bridget Schooley spoke up.

"I think we should approach Father Kelley and ask him to announce at church that he will accept any contributions that could be used to put the classroom back together."

"But, Bridget, we're not all Catholics," said another woman.

"What if I," interjected Jonathan, "made a plea to all the area churches? As the principal, I could ask for contributions to help recover the supplies that were destroyed."

The women talked among themselves and agreed that Mr. Canavan carried more weight in the community than they did, and perhaps the various pastors and priests would be more agreeable to a petition from the school's principal.

"Good. That's settled. Ladies, thank you for your help here tonight. Please know that my sister and I, and of course Anne, are indebted to you."

Josie spoke up. "Yes, and please collect your lentils and bread

from Annie, and we'll meet again next Sunday, as usual." Josie went to each woman and shook her hand in a gesture of thanks.

After the miners' wives left, Annie turned to Jonathan.

"That was noble of you, to agree to go to the different churches."

"I did it because I did not want either you or Josie to suffer any repercussions from the CVC, or whoever ordered this heinous act. Come on. Let me lock up for the night and walk you home."

As the trio walked back down the snowy road toward Coal Bank Lane, they kept their voices hushed in the sharp night air. Jonathan bid Annie good-night at the edge of her property and watched her as she trudged the final steps to the house. He admired how she cared about the miners' wives and how dedicated she was about her teaching. In truth, she was like no other girl he had ever met and he found himself always looking forward to spending time with her.

*

Annie climbed the stairs and headed to bed. On the landing, she remembered the hawk she had seen circling the sky in summer.

Today the destruction had just been aimed at the school, but when would the hawk come back? She sat on the edge of her bed and realized her mother must have taken risks to help the women on Miners Row. A feeling of remorse descended.

How could I have been so selfish? Always looking to how we could make money when the miners' wives were desperately trying to survive. I was so judgmental, and for what reason? Because they made me feel uncomfortable? Mama understood the power of kindness, and I always turned away.

Annie got out of bed and knelt down on her knees. *Holy Saint Anne, bring me courage that hawk or no hawk, I will help these poor women in the best way I can. Amen.*

CHAPTER 21

William Bevans, age 21,
run over by coal cars.

To Frankie, February dragged on with its gray skies, sullen snow storms, and frigid weather.

During the winter hiatus from the mines, Frankie felt trapped in the store, working for his demanding father. He passed the days waiting on repeat customers he had no interest in, and hoping in vain that Annie might appear.

It's her that should be apologizing to me. She's caused the distance between us, and I refuse to be the one who breaks our standoff.

A week later when some friends were giving a barn party, Frankie decided on a whim to invite Becky Kidwell, a buxom beauty from further up the mountain. He drank more beer than usual at the party and soon found himself in a back room where Becky pulled him to her and began to passionately kiss him. He did not stop her brazen advances.

As the winter weeks continued, snow piled around the village with drifts that turned Porters Glen into a ghostly landscape, and made social travel almost impassable. When the roads opened, Frankie worked as a teamster—driving a pair of mules to make deliveries, anything rather than be stuck in the store under his father's thumb.

This was the first winter where he could not wait for spring to arrive.

Frankie had hoped that his involvement with Becky Kidwell would rouse jealousy in Annie, but he still heard nothing from her. On the other hand, Becky provided other pleasures, and he continued to see her.

*

On the last day in February, the weather cleared. As the first group of men approached the mining offices to see when the mines might reopen, they saw an announcement tacked to the front board.

BECAUSE OF THE DEPRESSED NATIONAL ECONOMY AND THE DROP IN COAL PRICES, THE CUMBERLAND VALLEY COAL COMPANY IS FORCED TO LOWER THE WORKING WAGE FROM 50 CENTS PER TON TO 40 CENTS PER TON LOADED. THIS CHANGE GOES INTO EFFECT AS SOON AS THE MINES REOPEN AND WILL LAST UNTIL THE CUMBERLAND VALLEY COAL COMPANY HAS REGAINED LOST PROFITS; BRINGING THE COMPANY BACK TO INDUSTRY STANDARDS.

Alberto Morelli stood silent while another miner read the edict. Some men jammed their fists in their coat pockets while other miners stalked off; everyone seethed with anger. The loss of ten cents per ton would have a disastrous effect on the take-home pay, but no one wanted to strike and get blacklisted. The brutal winter had left the miners with hungry families. Alberto looked down at his hand with missing fingers. No longer being able to swing the pick-axe like he could before meant less tonnage—and now at inferior pay.

The group, including Frankie, drifted back to Beer Alley and headed into Murphy's Saloon. Frankie spoke. "We've got to join together and fight them on this."

"Hell, yes," piped up one of the other miners.

"Yeah, well how you gonna do that?" asked another.

"We contact the UMW, that's how," replied Frankie.

"That organization, way off in Ohio? They won't care about us."

"That's where you're wrong. I've heard they're helping miners in many states. We can draft a letter to them, make it anonymous, or hell, I'll sign my name to it. We let them know just what the CVC is doing. Lowering wages might be legal, but the UMW will see the injustice of it all."

They raised their glasses with a faint glimmer of hope stitched on every man's face.

The men drafted a letter, and it was read aloud in secret meetings the next week to all the miners in Porters Glen. Frankie Hennessey mailed it himself from the post office in Mount Pleasant.

Now they only had to wait for a reply. The UMW's help could not come soon enough.

CHAPTER 22

Thomas Hunter, age 21, killed from fall of breast coal, Koontz Mine.

Winter had not yet released its grip on Porters Glen, and strong March winds swept down from the surrounding mountains, adding more physical discomfort to the cold enveloping the village.

Annie rubbed her hands together in front of the shop's potbellied stove and looked up when she saw Josie enter the shop.

"Hello. Are you here for some of Aunt Hulda's milk bread rolls? Or I could make us a cup of *café au lait*."

"No, I'm here to invite you to go on a trip." Josie's eyes sparkled.

"A trip?"

"Yes, a trip to Philadelphia for a few days during the Easter break when school's out on holiday. Jonathan and I both think you would enjoy it. Plus, the weather should be warmer in the city."

"Philadelphia?"

"I'll be visiting some old friends, and Jonathan has business with Mr. Barrow, our family lawyer. It would be the perfect opportunity for you to try to find a sponsor for next year's shoe coupons. Philadelphia is known for its charity."

"Then you *are* planning to teach the English class with me again next year?"

"Let's not worry about my schedule for next year. The important thing is for you to find a sponsor."

"I'm flattered, but I'd have to ask my father, and he would want to know where we'd stay, and how much the trip would cost."

"We'll set out early the day after Easter, and we'll travel by train. Once we're in the city, we'll stay at the Stratford Hotel. It's only pricey if you choose the American plan, so we'll use the cheaper European plan at $2.00 a night."

"You stay in a hotel when you go home?"

Josie laughed. "We still own a home in the city, but we rented it out this year while we're in Maryland. And don't worry about cost; our trust fund is paying for the hotel since we need to meet with Mr. Barrow. You can share a room with me. By leaving on Monday it will give you four full days in the city to try and find a sponsor. Plus, it will be fun to show you around the city."

Annie did not want to admit she had never stayed in a hotel and consequently had no idea of what an American or European plan meant, nor did she really understand what a trust fund was. "Sounds like an adventure," she nervously replied.

"It will be. Let me know what your father says. Should Jonathan be the one to ask your father for permission?"

"No, that won't be necessary. I'll ask Papa today."

*

"Tell me again why you want to go on this trip."

"Because with the Canavan's contacts in Philadelphia, I should be able to find a sponsor for next year's English class. It's the shoe coupons, Papa; we still need funding for next year." She chewed her thumbnail while waiting for his reply.

"I've told you before, those shoe coupons shouldn't have to be your concern."

"Papa, the miners' wives are being subjected to horrible atroci-

ties in order to get shoes for their children. Someone has to help those women."

"It's not that I'm not proud of your idea, I just…can't help you with the trip."

Annie leaned over and kissed him. "You don't have to help me, Josie and Jonathan Canavan will be with me."

Louis took a deep breath. "No, I mean I can't give you any money for the trip. I'm short on cash right now."

"I only need money for the round-trip train ticket. I've saved some from the extra tutoring I did for Mr. Meyers at the end of summer, so I can use that for spending money."

"I don't have any cash for train tickets."

"Why not? The loan is paid off."

Louis averted his eyes.

"Isn't it?"

A rush of silence descended on the room.

"No, it isn't."

"But, I don't understand. It should have been paid in full by now."

"I've never wanted to burden you and Marie with the financial details about the shop. In most years, we have been able to hold our own, especially when we had Stephen's mining wages to help.

"The loan for the new oven was due the first of February, and I fully intended to pay it. But, Hulda received a letter from her cousin in New York who couldn't afford a doctor she needed. I gave Hulda the money for the doctor's fees, in the belief that the bank would extend my loan.

"However, since I couldn't make good on the original terms of the loan, the bank insisted I make a double final payment. There simply is not one penny left for anything extra."

"Oh. Papa."

"I'm sorry, Annie. I would not have given Hulda the money if I had known about this trip."

"That's all right. Hulda's cousin needed the money. You did the right thing. Where will you get the money for the double loan payment?"

"I'm going back to the bank on Monday morning and ask if I

can renegotiate the payment, even if it means added interest onto the original loan."

Annie swallowed hard. "I hope you're not thinking of asking Herman Schumn for help."

"No, I'll only deal with the bank." Louis paused for a moment and looked at her. "Have you given any thought of how Frank Hennessey will react to this trip?"

Annie took a deep breath. "We had a falling out on New Year's, and he hasn't called since. He didn't even send a valentine, so I guess we're not really a couple anymore."

"It seems to me he was very interested in you last summer and fall."

"Things have changed."

Louis arched an eyebrow. Annie knew he could usually tell whenever she or Marie fibbed, so he would be able to discern something was truly amiss between her and Frankie.

*

Once the shop closed, Annie walked up to Mount Pleasant to leave a note for Josie at the Quinn's boarding house. The familiar trip Annie had taken five days a week for the last several years seemed now to stretch forever. Finally, she arrived at Mrs. Quinn's on Water Street.

Josie was out, but Mrs. Quinn invited Annie inside where she could write the note. Annie made the message as short and pleasant as possible, thanking Josie and Jonathan for the invitation but because of financial circumstances at home, the cost of the train ticket would prohibit her from taking the trip.

She fought the waves of disappointment. Then with heavy steps, she trekked back down the mountain to Porters Glen before dusk settled over the valley.

*

"Jonathan, look at this note from Annie."

He peered up from the newspaper in the drawing room of

Josie's boarding house.

"They can't afford an eight-dollar train ticket?"

"Apparently not. How can we help her?"

"She wouldn't want charity; it would dampen her pride."

"I thought you supported this idea of searching for a shoe coupon sponsor, and, I thought you really liked Annie."

"I do support the reason behind the trip, and yes, I do like Annie, very much."

"What's your suggestion then?"

"Why don't we ask her to put whatever she can toward the train ticket and then we can think of ways for her to earn the rest of the money."

"Jonathan, she already works—at the family bakery; remember? No, we need to think of a way to help Annie's independence and still get her to Philadelphia. I think I have an idea. Leave this one to me."

*

On Sunday night after the English class finished, Josie said good-night to each woman by giving her the small paper bag of lentils and some day-old rolls. Inside each bag she had tucked a note:

> *Miss Annie and I want to take a trip to Philadelphia to try and find a shoe coupon sponsor for next winter. Annie needs money for the train. Can you spare 5 cents from your bread money to help her?*
>
> *Sincerely,*
> *Miss Josie Canavan*

*

The following Sunday night, as the women entered the classroom they each wore wide grins. When Josie asked for everyone to take their seats, Bridget Schooley remained standing.

"We, I mean the other women and me, want to give Miss Annie

a gift. It is a thank you for our shoe coupons."

Annie blushed and stood up in front of the class. "You don't need to give me anything. Those shoe coupons are your reward for your hard work of learning to read and write English."

The class clapped and Bridget held out a small sack.

Annie was perplexed, but also touched that they wanted to give her a gift. When she looked inside the small brown cloth bag she saw it filled with pennies.

"We have saved from our bread money, to help with your train ticket to Philadelphia."

Annie's hand flew to cover her mouth. "Oh, my goodness! Thank you, but how did you know?"

"Words fly fast in Porters Glen." The women all nodded in agreement.

"All right, I accept your gift, knowing it will help me find a shoe sponsor for next winter. I want you to know how much I am touched by your generosity." Annie wiped a tear out of the corner of her eye.

"Ladies." Josie beamed. "Let's start tonight's lesson."

After class, Jonathan offered to walk Annie home. His polite offer had become their weekly tradition.

"Jonathan, did you know?"

"I knew money was tight at your house and Josie had concocted an idea. But I honestly didn't know it would involve the miners' wives. How much money is in the bag?"

"Sixty-five cents and a note. Here, let me read it to you."

In our countries bakers sometimes give a baker's dozen. That means 13 treats for the price of 12. The 13th treat is for good luck. We are 12 women and we each gave 5 cents, but this gift is baker's dozen, so you have 65 cents to help toward the cost of your ticket. We thank you, Miss Annie, for your kindness to us.

"Jonathan, I'm speechless. I know they had to sacrifice to give me even one penny." Her lips quivered.

"Let me see the note."

Annie handed it to him.

"My, most of the spelling is correct, too."

"Really, Jonathan, the spelling is not as important as the message."

He grinned at her. "You're right. I guess the teacher in me never dies."

"I can't wait to get home and count the total of what I've saved. The 65 cents may not seem like a lot to you, but it is probably one of the most thoughtful gifts I've ever received."

*

"Papa, you will never guess what happened at class tonight!"

As Louis sat at the kitchen table and listened to the tale, his eyes glistened and he choked back tears. "I'm so proud of you. To think the women you are teaching, hold such affection for you! Your mama must be smiling in heaven." He went over and hugged Annie.

Marie clapped with congratulations as she walked into the room.

"I already heard about the gift! Now you'll need to spruce up some of your outfits and get a new spring hat. The girls in Philadelphia will certainly dress in a finer style than here in Porters Glen."

"I can't afford a new hat. I still need three more dollars for the train ticket."

"Oh, come on, Annie. I know you have money saved."

"I do, but I still need a few more dollars for the train, so no new hat!"

Marie said nothing but looked over at Hulda, and then brushed past Annie to walk into the pantry room. Aunt Hulda stopped what she was doing and followed Marie.

A few minutes later both of them emerged together, giggling like school girls, and went into the parlor.

Annie looked at her father with a puzzled expression. "What are they doing?"

Hushed whispers drifted from the other room. Then Annie and

Louis watched Marie climb the stairs while Hulda waited at the bottom.

A few moments later Marie came back to the kitchen with a Cheshire cat grin. Marie opened her closed hands and let dimes, nickels, and pennies tumble onto the cherry table. "I have an extra dollar!"

"And I have the other two at home. Together we will be able to give you the three dollars you need." Aunt Hulda glowed.

"No. I'm not taking money from you. But thank you both for the gesture."

"This is a present from me and Aunt Hulda. Of course you'll take it. When might you ever get another chance to visit an exciting place like Philadelphia?"

Annie hesitated. "All right, then I accept. But only because I need to find a sponsor for next year's shoe coupons. I'll pay both of you back, I promise."

"You'll want to impress any potential sponsor and show that you are current with the latest fashion. So, listen to me your little sister when I say...you need a new hat! Please let me make you one and it can be your new Easter bonnet as well."

"If it makes you feel better, then I'd be delighted with a new spring hat." A tender smile graced Annie's answer.

"Will your plans for teaching next year change if you get admitted to Mount Pleasant?"

"I'll still teach the English class on Sunday nights and give out the shoe coupons. But what I really want...is to shut down the Curtain Room."

Marie looked at Louis and then Hulda. "Annie, I hope you're not setting your goals too high. I would hate to see the CVC beat you down."

Annie stood up tall. "I won't let them."

*

Out of the blue, Frankie appeared at the shop a few days later.

"Frankie! What are you doing here?" She stopped arranging the pastries.

"My mother wanted some of your milk bread rolls. But, I really came to see you."

"You haven't come near me since New Year's."

"I know." An uncomfortable silence hung between them like a barricade. "I'm kind of seeing someone else now, Becky Kidwell. It's not the same, though, as it was with us. Becky's more of a party girl."

Annie felt a prick of surprise, but not true jealousy.

"A guy needs a girl. And I got tired of waiting for you to show more interest in me than you did with your studies and your night class."

"My studies were important, and the Sunday night English class is, too."

"You're never going to change on that. Am I right?"

"I don't want to change who I am."

"Not even for me?"

Frankie twirled his hat.

"You're not being fair, asking me to give up my goals."

He stared at her for a moment, then leaned forward, resting his elbows on the front counter. "Don't think I've just been sitting around mooning over you. I've found my important goal."

She glanced at his hands and forced herself not to stare at his black cuticles. "What do you mean?"

He stood back up and looked around, then lowered his voice. "We've written to the UMW about the pay cut at the mine, and I've become somewhat of a spokesperson for our group."

"Frankie, I hope you aren't getting involved in something dangerous. What is this UMW?"

"United Mine Workers. It's a union with headquarters in Cleveland, Ohio. Me and the other miners talk down at Murphy's about the unfairness of the new pay cut. We've decided to ask UMW to help us. The big fear is that the coal company will try to reduce our wages even further. If that happens, then we'll have to stand up for our rights."

"You don't mean go on strike? Not after the stories you told me of '82 when the men were out of work for six months."

"We don't want to go on strike, but we'll fight if we have to."

"So, does this union oppose a strike, or be for it?"

"They'd sanction a strike if necessary."

"Be careful, Frankie, it could be dangerous to associate with those people."

"I won't do anything stupid." He looked at her directly. "I miss being with you, Annie."

"That's nice to hear, Frankie. But I think our lives are taking different paths right now."

"They don't have to."

"I'm going to go on to college, Frankie, one way or another. Then I plan to teach somewhere, maybe even leave Porters Glen."

"Leave Porters Glen? Why would you want to do that?"

"I want to go where I could make a difference in other women's lives."

A new customer came up to the counter with her purchases and cleared her throat. The conversation between Frankie and Annie stalled.

"But, honestly, Frankie, I do still care about you."

"Yeah, but it'll never be like before, right?"

Annie bit her lips, but did not answer him.

"Good-bye, then." He left the shop without purchasing anything. There was no whistling as he went out the door.

Annie finished waiting on the current customer, then walked over to the window and looked out. Frankie had already disappeared down the road. She was a bit surprised at his nerve, and she admired him for trying to help the other miners. But she prayed he would stay safe. Even though their relationship had changed, Annie still felt a soft spot for him in her heart.

After all, he had been her first love.

CHAPTER 23

John Ayer, age 40,
died in the Potomac Mine, four dependents.

Rosa Morelli had lost weight during the winter. The days dragged on, one after another; each day like the one before. Her young daughters had lost weight, too, as the food supplies from summer had dwindled and Rosa rationed each jar of tomatoes, corn, or peas.

She could hardly wait for April when the hens would start laying again. Even at the steep price of 15 cents per dozen eggs, at least she would be able to cook them in several ways. Their winter diet of rabbit and squirrel still made her queasy, although Alberto's hunting is what had kept them alive.

Alberto had done his best to stay employed, but his meager pay had dwindled. He had tried to get hired on as an itinerant carpenter, but so had many other miners—men who weren't missing any fingers. She saw her husband's rough face become more deeply creased with worry lines as each new week of winter dragged on.

She wasn't bitter. He was better than a lot of husbands, even with his old-fashioned ways. Her one harbor of resentment was his refusal to allow her to attend the English class.

Two days ago she awoke to icy fingers of snow sliding down the sides of their cottage and drifts beginning to sweep across the road. She had hoped it would only be a light spring snow, but it wasn't. As the winds howled and the temperatures swiftly dropped to freezing, she realized this snowstorm was coming from the northeast, and would be formidable. It would mean all of them barricaded like prisoners, and everyone looking to her for something to eat.

*

The March blizzard raged on for two more days. In the small house, tempers flared with everyone on top of each other. Rosa worried that Alberto would explode if the girls continued to bicker.

On day three the snow stopped. Alberto left to shovel out a path to the neighbors, and the children bundled up and went outside with him, walking in his path to the family next door. Left alone, Rosa sat at the kitchen table with her head in her hands. She couldn't go on like this, hunger gnawing at her stomach every day and no money for food. Their daughters slept three to a bed, curtained off from Rosa and Alberto so the family could rent out the top room, but they'd had no boarder for months. Their savings were just about gone.

In despair, Rosa thought that Alberto would be better off without her. Perhaps a different wife who would not feel trapped in poverty like she did. Maybe he wished he had a wife who could bear him a son.

She sat up and blew on her hands, swollen with red blisters from scrubbing out laundry on harsh washboards in the cold. The kindling for the stove had to be saved for cooking.

Feeling a bit weak, she thought if only she could just lie down and sleep. She glanced over to the chipped linoleum floor mat where the girls put their shoes when they came in from outside. Their new rubber boots were lined up together neatly in a row. Instantly her hands flew to her face as she covered her eyes. *Dear God, don't ever let my babies become curtain women.*

An image of the man in the Curtain Room loomed in her mind. His disgusting scent always lingered on her after he left, and his

hideous laughter gave her nightmares. On her last visit, he had been unbearably rough. She could not face going back there, ever again.

A moment later she walked over to the battered hanging shelf and rummaged along the top, finally finding a particular medicine bottle. It was Paregoric; used for stopping diarrhea in the children when they got the runs. She knew it was so strong that the girls could only take a tiny amount. If anyone swallowed a big dose, it brought on a deep sleep. The entire bottle would…

Almost in a trance, she opened the full bottle and smelled. Then she got up and trundled over to where Alberto kept his bottle of elderberry wine from last summer.

Carrying both bottles, she pulled aside the curtain of their bedroom area. Before her resolve might fail, she uncorked the Paregoric and tipped the bottle to her lips and drank the entire contents. Then she quickly opened the wine and drank liberally from that bottle too. The combination of the opiate and the alcohol soon made her drowsy. *God forgive me. No more Curtain Room. Alberto, I love you.*

She lay back on the bed and soon breathed her last.

*

Alberto found her later, near noon. Opening the back door, he called out her name. When she didn't answer, he went to their bedroom area and pulled the privacy curtain aside. Her face was pale and a strange color stained her lips. He bent down to rouse her and felt her body cold to his touch. Tenderly he reached for her wrist and held it. No pulse beat beneath her skin.

He pulled her into his arms and wept his soul dry.

The mining whistle always blew three sharp blasts whenever a fatal accident occurred. But there would be no whistle for his Rosa. He covered her body with their wedding quilt and left the house locked so the children would not find her. Then he trudged through the snow to his neighbor, Renata Costa, and knocked on her door. The tears streaming down his cheeks were evidence of the recent tragedy.

*

The women of Miners Row washed and dressed Rosa's body, and combed her hair. Rosa's corpse was laid out on an old door placed over the backs of two kitchen chairs. One by one the families of Porters Glen plunged through the deep snow, under a leaden sky, to come pay their tearful respects.

*

Father Kelley wrestled with his conscience. After all, Rosa Morelli had committed a grave sin by taking her own life. A mortal sin in the eyes of the Church—she was not allowed to be buried in consecrated ground. But, in an unexpected decision, Father Kelley broke canon law and told Alberto he would allow Rosa to be buried in St. Bridget's Cemetery. A funeral mass would be offered right away, but Rosa's corpse would be given to the undertaker to keep on ice till the ground thawed.

*

All the mining families from Porters Glen attended Rosa's funeral. The women from the night class all sat together in a group with their husbands and children. Annie sat in an adjacent pew, crying silent tears.

"Annie." Louis tried to comfort his daughter.

"Papa, if only I had tried harder to get Mrs. Morelli back into the English class, perhaps I could have given her the gift of hope and she wouldn't have taken her own life."

"Annie, you are not responsible. Even your mother would tell you that." He put his arm around her shoulders.

When the service was over Louis and Marie walked out with Annie.

Then Jonathan stepped forward. "Annie, I am so sorry."

Her red-rimmed eyes looked up at him, but then Frankie

emerged from the crowd. "Annie. Are you crying? I didn't think you knew the Morellis."

Louis rescued her from answering either of them. "Frank, Mr. Canavan. We need to go home. This has been such a sad day. If you will excuse us." Without looking back at either Jonathan or Frankie, Annie let her father lead her to the borrowed wagon and she climbed in.

Annie held onto Marie as Louis cracked the reins and the horse pulled out into the snow packed street, snorting in the frigid air.

*

Ten days later, Easter Sunday started chilly, but by the time the Charbonneau's entered St. Bridget's, the sun was peeking through the clouds. Snow still carpeted the ground, but it was melting.

Marie had designed new Easter hats for both her and Annie, modified from a design called "The Florence" from *McDowell's Fashion Journal.* Each hat was constructed from a rough straw turban with folded ribbon and velvet around the crown. Rosettes of ribbons had been added, and knots of velvet graced one side of the hat, with two bunches of silk violets sewn on top.

As the Charbonneau's entered the church, all the women turned their heads to scrutinize the new hats.

For once, Annie found some small comfort in being fashionable, although the pall from Rosa Morelli's death still infiltrated Annie's thoughts. Finding a sponsor in Philadelphia became even more important after the Morelli tragedy.

Later, after the holiday meal of lamb chops, mashed potatoes, canned peas, and stewed tomatoes, Aunt Hulda served a delicious applesauce cake for dessert. She asked Annie to come back to the kitchen while Marie and Louis went into the front room to read. "Annie, I want to give you something special for the trip."

"Thanks, Aunt Hulda, but that's not necessary. You already gave me money."

Hulda smiled. "Your Papa made a sacrifice helping my cousin Margaret. And you need a lady's handbag suitable for a fancy city like

Philadelphia. Here." She turned around and then presented Annie with a tapestry drawstring bag the size of a small melon.

Annie held it softly in her hands. The slightly worn material with its hues of cerulean blue, deep purple, and moss green supported a lovely design of muted violet flowers against an ebony background. Annie peered closer and saw that the pouch bag had been stitched together with strong thread and glossy black cording made up the drawstring.

"Aunt Hulda, this is a special bag. I can't take this."

"Yes, you can. This is my decision."

"It's so beautiful. I've never seen you with it."

"It was a gift from my cousin Margaret. She's a milliner in New York City, and I think this is a perfect swap. Your Papa helped her, now her bag will help you."

"I never knew you had a cousin in New York. And she's a milliner? Does Marie know you have a cousin who designs hats?"

Aunt Hulda winked with a bit of a mischievous smile. "I keep some secrets to myself. I visited with her a long time ago and this bag was her gift to me." Hulda closed Annie's fingers over the bag in a final gesture of new ownership.

"Thank you. I'll take good care of it."

*

That evening, Marie and Annie took all of Annie's clothes out from the wardrobe and laid the pieces on the double bed. They stepped back to scrutinize the choices available, although Marie took the initiative of what to combine.

Bon had followed them up the stairs and into the room. He lie down on the floor, watching their activity as if he might be a fashion critic.

"All right, you have a hat with violets, which will go perfectly with the bag that Aunt Hulda gave you, so let's see if your short cape would complement that."

Annie brought out her dark brown winter cape.

"No, that won't do. Here, you'll need to take my beige cape. It's

lined so it should keep you warm if Philadelphia is chilly, and it will fit over the leg-o-mutton sleeves on any of your shirtwaists." Marie stood back and looked at the outfit. "No, you still need a piece of jewelry." She pulled out her treasure box from under the bed and rummaged through it. "Here, this will be perfect."

"No, absolutely not. That's your special bar pin. I won't feel comfortable taking it."

"It's not real silver."

"It doesn't matter what it's made of, I'm not going to take the chance of losing it on the trip."

"All right. But I still think you need a piece of jewelry."

They spent the next half hour categorizing pieces for traveling. First, Marie put Annie's white Garibaldi shirtwaist next to the hickory brown gored skirt. Then, Annie's cream colored linen top with puffed leg-o-mutton sleeves and tiny marmalade colored rosebuds paired easily with the same skirt. That made two outfits.

The ensemble for the train would be the sensible gray-colored serge skirt with the organ pipe pleats in back, paired with a white-on-white checkered shirtwaist. It would do for both legs of the journey.

"Will you remember to pack a button hook?"

Annie grinned. "I bought myself a new pair of shoes! And they do not need to be buttoned up over my ankles!"

"My, quite the fashion plate you've turned out to be." Both girls laughed. "Show me the shoes!"

Finally, Marie selected Annie's Easter outfit of a pink-striped shirtwaist accompanied by a deep violet flared skirt and matching belt. The beige cape would work with all four outfits and Hulda's bag would be the crowning touch.

"I think Jonathan Canavan will be pleased with your outfits," said Marie.

"Jonathan? He won't be interested in my clothes. I don't think he ever notices what I'm wearing."

"Oh, I doubt that, Annie. I doubt that very much. How about you, Bon? What do you think?"

Although only sixteen, Marie Charbonneau was sometimes wise beyond her years.

CHAPTER 24

Charles Mussetter, age 16, crushed between coal cars, New Hope Mine.

As the rooster crowed, Annie finished dressing while Louis waited for her downstairs in the kitchen. When she stopped at the bottom of the stairs, Louis awkwardly held out a bulging handkerchief.

Annie opened it and saw her mother's starburst pin with amethyst center. "Papa?"

"This was to be your graduation gift, but I want you to have it for the trip. I want my daughter to be as stylish as any other girl in Philadelphia." His eyes gleamed.

Annie stifled a sob, with this unexpected outburst of sentimentality from her father.

She attempted to give it back to him. "Thank you, Papa. But I'm too afraid I would lose it."

Louis smiled. "Pretty gifts, like pretty girls, are not meant to be stashed away at home. And I know Mama would agree." He tucked it back into her palm. "Consider it a good luck gift from both of us."

His large hand covering her small palm made Annie feel loved.

"I'll wear it with pride, Papa."

"Now let's go get the wagon and pick up the Canavans."

"Is there room for Bon to ride with us to Riverton? He'll keep you company on the return trip."

"That's a good idea. Toss his old blanket in the back for him to lie on."

Bursts of a late March wind forced them all to secure their hats as Louis drove Annie, Jonathan, and Josie in a buckboard he had borrowed from Mr. Eisner. The metal wheels of the wooden wagon clacked along the hard-packed roadbed of trodden rock and dirt. The sturdy draft horse clopped out a rhythm as he pulled the wagon along the Pike, and the sun's rays glistened off small bits of embedded coal in the road. Bon sat in the back, wedged among the bags and nestled on his old blanket.

They passed swatches of mountain laurels, red maples, and tulip poplars growing on the slopes of the mountains. Soon their buds would appear in preparation for their summer colors. As Piney Ridge receded in the background Annie stole a glance at Jonathan, and smiled with anticipation about the trip.

As the four passengers chatted, the horse continued his even pace toward Riverton, eleven miles away.

They arrived at the Queen City Train Depot and saw the platform crammed with waiting passengers. The ornate complex at the other end of the station caught Annie's gaze. A large, magnificent red brick hotel built in the Italianate style and capable of seating over 400 people for dinner sat in its glory like a queen on her throne.

Jonathan and Josie didn't even glance twice at the structure.

Annie had seen the hotel many times before, but she had never been inside.

"Here, Annie, let me help with your travel bags." Jonathan turned toward Louis. "Just to ease any concerns you might have, I promise to watch over Annie throughout the entire trip."

"This is her first time away from home; she's not used to a big city."

"Papa! Please, I'll be able to take care of myself." A scarlet blush crept across her face.

Jonathan grinned. "Annie will be fine, Mr. Charbonneau. Don't

worry." He turned and winked at her.

A shrill whistle split the air and set the bustling crowd climbing up the steep steps into the rail cars.

"All aboard." The conductor yelled.

Louis hugged Annie in a tight embrace. "Have a wonderful time."

Jonathan helped both Josie and Annie manage the steps of the train while a porter hoisted their suitcases, allowing the trio to maneuver through to the second car. Annie saw Jonathan tip the porter and then she took a window seat and looked out to see her father still watching from the platform.

Jonathan sat down next to her. "You might as well relax, because this is going to be a long day. It will take us about twelve hours to get to Philadelphia."

"That's all right; I'm used to long days."

With multiple lurches, the locomotive belched a great cloud of steam, and the wheels whirled into motion with a tell-tale clickety-clack. In no time at all, the train was underway.

*

Frankie knew nothing of Annie's trip to Philadelphia. He had been busy corresponding with the United Mine Workers, hedging his bets they'd become defenders of the miners in Porters Glen.

He had no knowledge that the UMW had already planned their first massive strike, intending to cripple the coal industry from Indiana to eastern Pennsylvania and from Georgia to the Great Lakes.

What he had read in secret pamphlets being passed around in the village were the long term goals of the union to establish an eight-hour workday, secure collective bargaining rights, introduce health and retirement benefits, and guarantee safety measures. What the pamphlets did not mention, was the immediate plan: every miner across multiple states would be asked to support the strike, slated to start on April 21st, barely a month away.

Unaware of the magnitude of their plan, Frankie hoped the

miners would not have to go on strike. He had heard the gruesome tales about the strike of 1882 that had lasted six months. Almost every family involved lost someone due to illness or hunger when the men went without pay for so long.

He had only been a small boy then, and his father's store had more than adequately provided for their family. Now, as a full-fledged miner, he wanted his comrades to get honest day's wages for the work they completed. Was it so much to ask?

One of the older miners cautioned Frankie not to be swayed by any union group promising that in the end the fight will be worth it. "Tell that to the women of Porters Glen who still tend the graves of '82. They'll tell you to go to hell with that idea."

But Frankie knew he would not sit idle if the UMW sent help to Allegany County. He would become involved, because it was the right thing to do.

*

As Annie and her group descended from the mountains of Western Maryland, she took a moment to look around the train car. Her only other train rides had been on the local out of Mount Pleasant. This time she wanted to remember every detail of the train ride.

Their car was fashioned with two leather seats to a side. Josie had placed all three of their day bags on the seat next to her, which had afforded Jonathan the opportunity to sit next to Annie on the opposite side.

The brown leather made the seats comfortably soft, and Annie appreciated the ample amount of leg room. As the train chugged along, she watched from the large window as they skimmed the rocky shores of the Potomac River and then rolled due east through bucolic farmlands to Baltimore, Maryland.

"We'll pick up more passengers in Baltimore, as well as some supplies, I think. Then, straight through to Philadelphia. It's a good thing we're on an express, else we wouldn't reach the city until tomorrow. Josie and I noticed that you brought a food basket. Did you bring

food for all of us? If not, we can always get something quick at the Baltimore station."

"Aunt Hulda packed us ham sandwiches, pickles, and some slices of pie. She told me not to expect good food on the train."

"Has she made this trip before?"

"Years ago, she went to New York to visit a cousin."

The train rolled on for another hour and Annie's stomach rumbled. Josie produced three bottles of cider as a surprise from her canvas travel bag. They moved their day bags to spots under the seats and spread Aunt Hulda's "train picnic" on the seat next to Josie.

"I don't think it's dinner time yet, but I am starved," claimed Annie.

"Train travel always makes me hungry," quipped Jonathan. "I think it has to do with the constant rhythmic movement of the rail cars, and the scenery flashing by."

The three of them dove into their meal, and finished with no left-overs.

Back in her own seat once again, Annie decided to be bold and ask Jonathan about Philadelphia and his childhood there.

"You really want to hear this?"

She nodded.

"All right. Josie and I were born in the section called Kensington, that's in northeast Philadelphia where all the textile mills are located. I think Josie told you our father died before our birth. That was in August, 1861, while saving his sister who had become trapped in the Nolan factory fire."

"Josie didn't mention the fire, or your father's sister."

"Her name was Ellen. Ellen Canavan Nolan. We loved her and her husband, Uncle James. Growing up, they lived near us—only a few blocks away. We spent a lot of time playing there with our cousin Daniel.

"But after Aunt Ellen died, Uncle James remarried a year later. His new wife, Sarah, didn't want us underfoot, so Daniel came to play at our house. The following year, Uncle James and Sarah had a little girl, Catherine. But we call her Katie."

"I envy you having cousins to play with. That's something we never had," Annie said.

"You'll meet them on this trip."

"Is your uncle still alive?"

"No, Uncle James died just last year. Unfortunately, the factory passed out of the family over a decade ago when he lost it in a bank seizure."

Annie felt a lump of fear rise in her throat. "A bank seizure?"

"He offered the factory as collateral in a bank loan for a friend. When the friend filed for bankruptcy, the bank took the factory. It was sold a few months later in a sheriff's sale."

Annie steeled herself not to overreact, and she certainly did not want Jonathan or Josie knowing about the overdue bank loan her father was dealing with.

If a bank could repossess an entire factory in Philadelphia, then a bank could easily take away the family bakery in Porters Glen.

Annie felt a bit nervous now about leaving her father without the final determination of how the new loan would get paid. She felt out of place going to Philadelphia. Jonathan and Josie had more worldly experiences than she did. Her world revolved around a small coal village. How would she deal with a big city? As the train sped along, her bravado about going to Philadelphia started to thin.

"Why don't you close your eyes and try to nap?" Jonathan said.

Within minutes she dozed off in a fitful sleep.

*

The twelve-hour trip took them east and then north, up through Maryland, Delaware, and into Pennsylvania. The mostly rural scenery showed naked trees recuperating from winter, but with the verdant hope of spring lurking in their branches. The train followed major rivers like the Potomac and traversed over others like the Susquehanna, before crossing the Schuylkill and into Philadelphia proper.

Night had fallen by the time they pulled into the Reading Terminal. Annie peered out the train window and saw the large depot

bathed in the soft glow of electric lights. It looked like it belonged in a fairy tale.

The trio disembarked, and Annie was glad she had brought along Marie's cape. The night air was cold. What she hadn't been prepared for, was the noise level. Although it was dark, people still jostled on the streets, going into restaurants and other buildings. What a contrast to Porters Glen!

Jonathan hailed a hack to take them to Broad and Walnut Streets, the address of the Stratford Hotel. In the dark, it was hard to appreciate the building taking up an entire city block. Multiple stories tall, its stone façade faced Broad Street. Among the Philadelphia hotels, it was considered to be one of the jewels.

They walked into the ornate lobby and Jonathan went to the front desk to pay for the rooms. Annie stood in awe at the luxurious crimson and gold carpeting stretching from wall to wall, and the electric chandeliers hanging in the lobby. She tilted her head and glanced up at the punched-tin ceiling with intricate designs that led her gaze over to large columns that appeared to be supporting the ceiling.

She felt like she had been dropped into a foreign land.

A bell hop dressed in a crisp navy blue uniform came to collect their bags and accompanied them onto the elevator. Annie stepped inside and smiled at the operator, who promptly wheeled a lever to close the gate. When the elevator started to rise, Annie felt her stomach flip-flop. She had never ridden in one before, and she marveled to see how quickly it ascended to the third floor.

Once the bell hop opened their rooms, Annie saw Jonathan give him a tip. Josie kissed Jonathan good-night and entered the room she and Annie would share.

Dead tired, Annie tried to appreciate the accommodations. Papered with a design of tiny flowers covering the walls, the room was far more decorative than anywhere she had ever been. Lovely mahogany furniture, including a chest of drawers, two sitting chairs, a large bed with night side tables, and a single daybed were positioned throughout the room. She unpacked her bag, changed into her night dress, quickly brushed her teeth, and crawled onto the single day bed in the room.

The larger bed she left for Josie. Within moments, Annie fell asleep under a lovely cream-colored chenille coverlet.

*

The next morning when Annie woke, she sat up and stretched her arms. Yesterday's reservation about the trip had vanished with the light of a new day.

Not sure which outfit to wear, she pulled out her clothes and held them up in front of the full-length gilded mirror, then chose the white-on-white checkered shirtwaist with the brown skirt. Once they left the hotel she would wear Marie's tan cape with her own spring bonnet. She slipped on her new pair of shoes with the black-patent leather tip at the front, and lastly pinned on the amethyst pin. She tapped the pin. *Wish me luck, Mama.*

Twisting her hair in a loose chignon, she then accompanied Josie down to the hotel dining room. As soon as they entered, Annie was delighted to see all the small intimate tables covered with white damask tablecloths. The walls of the dining room were also covered in a matching damask type pattern of oyster-colored wallpaper. She wished she could paint Marie a picture.

They found Jonathan seated with a cup of tea, a plate with some sort of buns, and a copy of *The Philadelphia Inquirer*. He lowered the paper when he saw them.

"Come sit here with me. I already ordered for myself, but I'm sure you'll want to choose your own breakfast."

Annie decided to be adventurous and eat what Jonathan did. "I'll order what you're having, Jonathan."

"Not me, I intend on treating myself to some good Pennsylvania waffles." Josie ran her tongue over her lips.

The waiter arrived dressed in black trousers, a gray vest, and starched white shirt. He asked Annie for her order, but she did not know what the buns were called. Jonathan realized her dilemma and came to her aid. "I believe the young lady would like an order of the raisin cinnamon buns, and could you please warm them for her? Thank you."

Raisin cinnamon buns?

He saw her inquisitive look. "They're a Philadelphia specialty and date back to when the British occupied Philadelphia during the Revolution."

"And to drink?" The server waited politely.

"Can I order a cup of coffee with steamed milk in a separate cup?"

The waiter nodded. When he returned with the beverages, Annie saw with satisfaction that her coffee was just how she wanted it. Not quite the same as her favorite *café au lait*, but a reasonable alternative.

The two raisin cinnamon buns on the other hand, were much better than she anticipated. They arrived on a delicate cream-colored plate; each split open with a hefty pat of butter melting into the sweet cinnamon-swirled dough. As soon as she bit into one, she knew she had the perfect gift for Papa. The recipe for the buns would allow him to create a new innovative treat at the store.

"Good, aren't they?" quizzed Jonathan. "Bet you've never had anything like it before."

"They are good, and I bet I can duplicate them once we get back to Porters Glen."

"But they won't be Philadelphia cinnamon buns, then."

"Of course not. They'll be Charbonneau cinnamon buns," she said with a smug smile. She just needed to convince the waiter to give her the recipe.

After the meal, Josie left the hotel for a meeting with a friend, and Jonathan walked with Annie two blocks north to Chestnut and the streetcar stop. Annie carried her cape over her arm with the pleasantly warm morning being a significant change from the cold air of last night. Her spring bonnet sat snugly perched atop her head.

As they walked, Annie reminded herself not to gape as they passed all the intriguing sights. Multiple buildings, five stories tall, lined both sides of the street and men dressed in impeccably tailored walking suits and derbies, emerged from the banks. Hansom cabs drove by, shuttling passengers to and fro. But it was the women, dressed in exquisitely embroidered two-piece outfits with lavish hats that drew Annie's gaze. No one back in Porters Glen would ever believe that Philadelphia had so much to offer.

No sooner had they arrived at the streetcar stop, when a vehicle of mustard-colored paneled wood pulled up and the driver reined in the two white horses. Jonathan held Annie's arm to help her into the car and paid for both of them. Her arm radiated from his touch, coaxing a glow to her face.

"What do you think of the streetcar?"

"It's almost like a short railroad car, isn't it; only pulled by horses?"

He laughed. "I guess so. I never really thought of it like that before."

"Are you excited to be home?"

"I think I'm more excited to be showing you the city." His smile relaxed her and at the same time made her feel somewhat special; she wasn't really sure why.

"Jonathan, where is the Catholic church I'm supposed to go to?"

"It's St. Michael's in Kensington on North Second Street. The priest there is an old friend of my grandmother's. Father Reilly is his name. I'm hoping he'll be able to help you find a sponsor. I can introduce you, if you'd like."

"No, thank you. Obtaining a sponsor for the shoe coupons is my goal. I need to do it by myself."

"All right. If you change your mind once we get there, just say so."

She took a deep breath and let it out slowly; the nervous apprehension of meeting with the priest began to fade. After all, he couldn't be that different from Father Kelley back home.

The driver signaled to the horses they needed to turn left, and the car proceeded over the worn bricks in the road for well over a mile on Fifth Street until it reached Kensington. The tall factory smoke stacks belched plumes of erupting gray-tinged smoke and the relentless sounds of machines spilling from the textile mills filled Annie with an energy she never anticipated. Kensington was almost a living, breathing creature.

Jonathan's eyes sparkled as he leaned toward the window, looking at the houses. "Wait a minute, there it is, 1225 N. Fifth Street!" He pointed to a row house that looked to Annie similar to all the other

houses on the street. "That's where I spent my childhood. That was Grandmother Canavan's house." The streetcar continued to the end of the next block and Jonathan pulled the cord. Once the car stopped, they both got off.

"It's only a few blocks east and we'll come to St. Michael's. I'll walk with you to the church, but I promise to let you go in on your own, if that is still your wish."

"It is." She waited a moment. "Jonathan, does all this make you homesick? Being back, I mean."

"I guess there will always be a part of Philadelphia in me. Josie probably misses the city more than I do."

As they continued walking, Annie pressed him to continue. "Why do you say that?"

"Josie needed a change. A certain man here broke her heart, so I suggested we teach somewhere else. Get away from Philadelphia for a year or two. The Canavan family motto is 'family sticks together, no matter what.'"

"Oh, I had no idea. What about you, Jonathan? Did you leave someone behind?" She stopped. "I'm sorry, that was too personal a question to ask."

"It's all right. I did have a lady friend back here, but no more. She decided not to wait for me while I went out teaching in the wilderness."

"The wilderness? Oh, you mean Porters Glen? It's not exactly wilderness."

"Compared to Philadelphia, it does seem like a different world. Look. I can see the Second Street intersection coming up. No time to bore you with any more of our family stories."

"They weren't boring at all."

Within moments they arrived at the corner of Second Street.

Annie felt relieved that the edifice of St. Michael's Church was similar to St. Bridget's red brick front. The familiar architecture put her at ease.

"You go on, Jonathan. I'll meet you back at the hotel. I saw how to take the streetcar, so I'll find the right one to bring me back to Wal-

nut and Broad. I have my own money, so I should be fine."

"Ask Father Reilly to write down which streetcar to take. I'll feel better about leaving you here, if I know you have written directions."

"I'll be fine, Jonathan. Thank you."

She walked to the rectory door, knocked, and turned back to wave at Jonathan. He grinned and started off walking south, presumably toward the returning streetcar stop.

*

Father Reilly shuffled a bit as he got up to answer the ring at the rectory door. The years had been kind to him, but he now needed a cane for support when he walked.

Unlocking the front door, he encountered Annie on the front steps.

"May I help you?"

"Yes, Father. I have traveled a great distance and would like to speak to Father Reilly about an important matter."

The girl was attractive; even in his advanced years he could clearly tell that. "I'm Father Reilly, so come in and we'll see if I can help you."

He led Annie down the hall toward his study. "Don't mind the mess, please, I'm in between housekeepers, so several things are strewn about." They entered his study and he motioned for her to sit down. "Now, tell me who you are and why you came here."

"My name is Annie Charbonneau, and I live in a small coal mining community in Western Maryland. I'm here in Philadelphia with friends: Josie and Jonathan Canavan. Perhaps you remember their family?"

His face broke into a wide grin. "Do you mean Cecilia Canavan's grandchildren?"

"Yes, I suppose so, although they have only referred to her as Grandmother Canavan."

He leaned forward. "Of course I remember the family! But, what can I do for you?"

"I help teach the miners' wives, mostly immigrant women, how to read and write English. In addition, I—I mean we—have been able to provide them with shoe coupons for their children. But the shoe coupons cost money, and I need to find a sponsor to help us."

Father Reilly shook his head. "It sounds like a noble cause, but St. Michael's is a poor parish. I'm afraid we have no benefactors that could help you. Any charity we get is earmarked for the unfortunate of our own parish."

"But Josie and Jonathan Canavan were born and raised here."

"Aye, but they are neither poor, nor residents of Philadelphia now. I'm sorry."

"Father Reilly, if you knew the plight of these miners' wives and how they have been subjected to humiliation in order to get shoes for their children, you would understand why I need to find a sponsor."

"What about your local parish? Aren't there any charity groups?"

"Not really. The big coal companies own everything in our area. Unless they have cash, the miners' wives are forced to...to bargain with the coal company for shoe coupons."

"What do you mean, bargain?"

"They use the only commodity they have to trade: themselves."

Father Reilly's cheeks flamed. "What of your parish priest?"

"As I said, Father, the coal company is very powerful. Nothing is sacred. I don't feel I can trust anyone in Porters Glen."

Father Reilly put his fingers together, almost in prayer. "There is a chance that one of the wealthy Episcopal churches here in Philadelphia might be able to help you find a sponsor."

Annie grew quiet. "All right. Where might I find one of those Episcopal Churches?"

"There is a well-to-do congregation near Rittenhouse Square."

"Is that close by here?"

Father Reilly smiled. "No, 'tis down in Center City. But I could draw you a quick map."

"Are there any other churches near here where I might go today and talk with someone?"

“The Quakers have a meeting house down on Arch Street, at the corner of Arch and Fourth. They have a reputation for supporting worthy causes. You could take the streetcar south on Second Street until you reach Arch. The streetcar stop is just down the block from here. I can point the way.”

“That won’t be necessary, I’ll find it. Thank you, Father. I did not know about the Quakers.”

As Annie retreated down the hallway with her head held high and opened the door to leave, Father Reilly mused out loud, “She reminds me so much of Ellen Canavan. Can thirty years have passed so quickly since Ellen was here? Perhaps ‘tis no coincidence Ellen’s nephew and niece have met this Annie Charbonneau.”

*

I really don’t need written directions. And if I walk, I can save the nickel fare. It can’t be that far.

As Annie strolled along looking at the houses on Second Street, she realized this section of Philadelphia was not so different from Porters Glen. No coal dust roadways, but factory soot had settled on the tops of the houses and in the streets, making the area appear gray and a bit forlorn.

Forty-five minutes later her feet ached from walking in the new shoes, and her cape felt heavy on her arm from carrying it all day. Finally, she saw a sign that read, *Arch Street*. Not sure which direction to turn, she stopped a woman walking by, who merely pointed to the right.

Annie spied a solid red brick wall, some six feet high that extended for an entire block. She smoothed her skirt, tucked back some errant strands of hair, and crossed her fingers for good luck. Taking a deep breath, she marched across the street and went through the open doorway of the imposing wall. A plain brick building now in front of her matched the design of the outside wall, each in symmetry with one another.

She knocked on the door and smiled as it opened. A woman with snow-white hair, dressed from head to toe in a lovely dove-gray

dress, smiled back at her.

"Hello. May I help thee?"

"I hope so. May I come in?"

The woman took a moment to scrutinize Annie up and down and then opened the door further to allow entrance.

Stepping inside, Annie followed the woman further into the lobby. Ahead of her appeared to be a long hallway.

"How may I help thee?"

"I have just come from a meeting with Father Reilly at St. Michael's Church on Second Street, and he suggested your church might be able to help me. So I walked here."

"Thee walked from St. Michaels? But that is almost two miles."

"I walk a lot at home and am accustomed to exercise." Annie smiled. "The reason I have come to Philadelphia is to find a sponsor for a worthy cause back home."

The Quaker woman nodded. "I think perhaps thee might like some refreshment first. I can offer thee a glass of cooled tea or water."

"Thank you. The tea would be nice."

As the Quaker woman left to get the tea, Annie stepped into the long corridor. She turned left to look down the hallway and saw a large room at the end. Turning the other way, she was surprised to see another large room at the opposite end of the hallway.

Intrigued by the woman's strange way of talking and this meeting house, Annie wondered if these Quakers could help her.

The woman soon returned with the tea. "Now, please follow me and we can sit in the West Room."

Annie trailed after her and noticed that there were no paintings or pictures on the walls. Once inside the large room, Annie lowered herself onto a nearby wooden bench and took a long sip of the refreshing beverage. Then she glanced around the room. No evidence of a pulpit or a choir loft existed. Of course, she had not expected to see a crucifix, but the absence of any church-like furnishings bewildered her.

"My name is Evalyn Paxson, and I come here on Tuesdays to straighten up the library. Sometimes we get visitors, but not often."

"Well, my name is Annie Charbonneau, and I live many hours

west of here in a small coal community in Western Maryland called Porters Glen. I am pleased to meet you, Evalyn Paxson."

"Now tell me why thee has come here. I know thee is not a Quaker."

"How could you tell so quickly?"

Evalyn pointed to Annie's brooch. "Quakers are plain people and we do not wear jewelry."

"Oh. I hope that will not affect the outcome of our conversation?"

"Certainly not," the older woman's eyes crinkled at the edges with kindness.

"I teach an English class in Porters Glen to the newly arrived immigrant women who are married to coal miners. A lot of the men cannot read or write, and the coal company often takes advantage by having the men sign papers of legal contract that affect their families. By teaching their wives to read and write, at least one person in the family can be armed to deal with the company."

"Thee is participating in a worthy cause."

"Thank you. But the other goal I have is to provide free shoes to the women's children. You see…when money is scarce, the children go without shoes. We live in the mountains, and winters are very cold with long lasting snows. The children all need shoes."

She paused.

"Go on, Annie Charbonneau, I am listening."

"These women are poor. Sometimes they cannot afford shoes of any kind for their children. There is a room at the company's office… it's called the Curtain Room because, I have been told, it does not have a door, but only a curtain setting it apart. The women go there to…offer themselves in exchange for shoe coupons for their children."

Annie sat back in the chair. She felt her cheeks getting hot. She watched Evalyn Paxson's face to see what type of reaction might occur.

The sparkle disappeared from Evalyn's eyes. "Well, I do see why thee is here, Annie Charbonneau, but I am afraid I am not the person who can offer you a solution."

A wave of disappointment rolled over Annie.

"But, I can bring this to the attention of the Elders. How long will thee be in Philadelphia?"

"Only until Friday afternoon. I'll be on the train early Saturday morning heading back home. My father will be expecting me to help open the shop on Monday morning."

"What type of shop?"

"My family owns a store that is part bakery, part grocery. We are an independent store, which means the miner's families do not have to use the coal company script to purchase food items."

"And what is script?"

"Instead of receiving cash for their pay, the miners are given mostly coins imprinted with the name of the Cumberland Valley Coal Company. The men have to use the script to buy their goods at the company affiliated stores. And of course the prices are always higher there. Any cash they receive goes toward the rent."

"Then the mining company is taking unfair advantage of the miners, too. I will not only present the situation to the Elder's committee, I will plead thy cause. Your miners' wives deserve to be able to give their children shoes for winter. Can you come back here Thursday afternoon at three o'clock? I will make sure the Elders are here to meet you."

"Thank you, Evalyn. Thank you so much. I would be delighted to come back. But right now I need to return to my hotel at Walnut and Broad. Is it much farther from here?"

"Thee only has to walk two blocks west to Sixth Street to pick up the streetcar. Make sure thee tells the driver thou is going to Walnut and Broad. If thee gets lost or confused, ask anyone on the street. Philadelphia is the city of brotherly love and most residents are quite willing to help strangers."

Annie impulsively went over and gave Evalyn a hug. "Thank you, Evalyn. I don't know the outcome yet, but I feel as if I was meant to meet you."

"We will have to wait and see what God has planned for us."

CHAPTER 25

John Yates, fell under mine cars,
Ocean Mine.

The afternoon had turned quite warm, so Annie continued to carry her cape. She found her way to the streetcar stop and waited. Big fluffy white clouds drifted in a soft blue sky, and Annie found herself quite content to just watch the people walking by. When a double bicycle pedaled by two people passed her on the street, she managed not to appear surprised. Philadelphia was loaded with discoveries, and she was enjoying each and every one.

The only disappointing fact was that she hadn't yet managed to procure a sponsor. But, at least she had a group who might be interested.

The streetcar ride brought her back to the hotel. Entering the lobby, she found Jonathan and Josie sitting in the day lounge chatting with two other people, a man and a young woman. Jonathan saw Annie and waved her over.

"Annie," Jonathan stood up. "We want you to meet our cousins, Daniel and Katie."

"Hello."

The man stood up and leaned over to shake hands. "Josie and Jonathan have been telling us all about you. You have a fascinating story."

"Oh." Annie smiled and sat down, noticing his tall slender frame and eyes the color of walnuts. His coloring differed from both Jonathan and Josie.

"Would you like a Coca Cola?" Daniel asked her.

"What is a Coca Cola?"

"It's a wonderful new drink. Think of it like a root beer, but sweeter and less tangy."

"Yes, thanks. Another new discovery."

"Did Father Reilly have a surprise?" asked Jonathan.

"No, Evalyn Paxson did at the Quaker Meeting House."

"Quakers? You need to tell us everything that happened this afternoon."

Annie regaled them with her tale of how she met Father Reilly, and how he had recommended she visit the Quakers.

"So, I'm hopeful," Annie said to the group.

"Why don't we have an early meal, all five of us?" asked Jonathan. "Daniel? Katie? How does that sound?"

"How about the Sansom Street Oyster House?" Daniel answered for both he and Katie.

After the group finished their Coca Colas, they walked to the restaurant, and Jonathan signaled to a waiter who found them a table. "This place is known for their oysters, but I know the menu has other choices, too." He directed the comment to Annie.

"Oysters are good with me."

"Well, practicing Jews don't eat them, so Josie will order something else."

Once the meal and drinks arrived, the group settled into a lively discussion about family traditions and food.

"Josie, so, you're still going to temple?" Katie asked.

"Yes. And I can still cook a good brisket."

"But you're half Irish!" This came from Daniel. "So can you also make shepherd's pie?"

"Only if she's forced to," Jonathan joked.

"Annie, how about you? What's your family background?"

"My parents both came from the Alsace region of France, which means I can bake."

"So, we have Jewish, Irish, and French at the table—all eating together!" Daniel laughed. "Annie, you should come next year and visit our fair city for St. Patrick's. It's a day when the entire city turns Irish for the day and celebrates with a huge parade."

"Sounds grand," Annie smiled.

"How old are you, Annie?" Katie inquired with an inquisitive look.

"I'll be turning nineteen this summer."

"Me too! Are you employed already?"

"Yes and no. I hope to enroll in college in September and take a two-year course to become a teacher. In the meantime, I help my father run our family store. It's a combination bakery and grocery."

"Oh, that sounds nobler than me. I just work in a department store." Katie's eyes danced with mischief. "But I work in the most fabulous store in all of Philadelphia, Wanamaker's!"

"What do you do there?"

"I work in ladies' hosiery. Come to the store tomorrow and I'll show you around the different departments."

"Daniel, do you work at Wanamaker's too?"

"No, I'm in the purchasing department of a coal yard."

Annie's eyebrows shot up, but no one seemed to notice. She had not expected coal to follow her on this trip.

After supper, Daniel and Katie left to catch the streetcar home, while Jonathan, Josie, and Annie walked back to the hotel. Josie announced her fatigue and the intention to go straight to bed. Before Annie could concur, Jonathan asked her to sit with him in the lounge and elaborate on her independent afternoon.

She found the time with Jonathan slip away with their easy banter, and his genuine interest in what she had to say.

*

Annie and Josie agreed to meet Katie the next morning at

Wanamaker's. They would spend time in the store looking at the new spring displays, and Annie wanted to buy some presents for Marie and Aunt Hulda.

As Josie pushed open the tall, heavily etched glass front door to Wanamaker's, Annie tried not to gawk. She followed Josie to the center of the first floor. When Josie pointed upwards, Annie saw multiple floors above, each showcased by marble columns that matched marble designs embedded on the walls. Her eyes opened wider when she spied a figure dressed like a woman, but obviously not real. Not wanting to appear naive, she looked over at Josie.

"Yes, isn't it wonderful? It's called a mannequin. This is how Wanamaker's is showing off the latest in fashion. She almost looks real, doesn't she?"

Annie nodded in amazement. She had never in her wildest dreams expected a fake woman to be wearing clothes as a display in a store. Would any of the miners' wives ever believe this, when all Hennessey did was display clothing folded on tables?

"Come on, let's shop, and then we can join Katie for lunch."

After perusing a lot of merchandise, Annie finally bought two new sets of black cotton hosiery for Aunt Hulda and some Valenciennes lace with a delicate scalloped bottom for Marie. All together her purchases added up to a grand total of 30 cents, which would have cost double that at Hennessey's Store for any of the miners' wives.

At the noon hour the three girls met in the Wanamaker restaurant. The lunch prices were surprisingly affordable, and they dined on a meal starting with chicken-rice soup, followed by eggs chimay served with asparagus tips and warm dinner rolls, and finished off with individual portions of Charlotte Russe. This new experience of eating in a department store tea room delighted her, although the Charlotte Russe was nowhere as good as Aunt Hulda's.

They left the restaurant and walked around a new floor. Annie couldn't help but admire the smart new two-piece outfits on display. Each one contained lined bodices with high necks, and fancy crocheted covered buttons on turn-back cuffs.

Since Katie had gone back to work, Josie offered to take Annie

on a streetcar ride around the city. Annie wondered if Jonathan would be accompanying them, but when he did not show, she assumed he had other plans.

The ride through the city was overwhelming with all the sights and sounds, but also a bit hollow without Jonathan there to share in the experience with them.

That evening Josie received a message from Jonathan that he had reservations to dine with the family lawyer and that she and Annie should not wait up for him. Annie tried to hide her disappointment and concentrated instead on how she could cajole the waiter to give her the cinnamon bun recipe[1].

*

The next morning Annie chose her tan linen skirt and white-on-white shirtwaist and she waited till Josie was dressed before going down to breakfast.

"I've got a surprise for you." Jonathan plopped himself down next to Annie in the Stratford's dining room.

"This early in the day? We haven't even eaten."

"How about going to the Philadelphia Zoo?"

"The zoo? Why, yes, that would be fun. I've never been to one before. But, I have to return to the Arch Street Meeting at three o'clock to meet with the Elders. Would I still be able to make that?"

"Of course. We can stop in plenty of time to get you to Arch Street." He turned to Josie. "How about it, Josie? Are you up for a trip to the zoo?"

"No, thanks. I've been invited to a luncheon."

"It'll just be you and me then, Annie. All right?"

"Of course." She looked directly at him with a look of anticipation that would be hard to ignore.

They ate breakfast in more of a rush than usual.

*

1 Recipe appears at the end of the book.

"Jonathan, I need to step outside and see how warm it might be."

"I already did, and it's supposed to be a delightful spring day, so you won't need anything heavy."

"I'll go upstairs and get my short cape. I'll be right back down." She walked to the elevator and told the operator she wanted to go to the third floor, please. Once inside the room, however, she faced a dilemma. Would her outfit do for a morning at the zoo and an afternoon with a group of religious men?

Jonathan could say he would get her to Arch Street, but what if the streetcar ran late, or she spilled something on her skirt, or the time slipped away from them? There might not be time to change outfits.

No, she would have to wear something that could be transformed from zoo to meeting house, and she would have to be extremely careful not to soil her outfit in any way. She went over to the wall peg and retrieved Marie's short beige cape and the spring bonnet. Then she slipped out of the tan linen skirt she had on, and pulled out the light gray wool skirt from the mahogany wardrobe. It would still look good with the white-on-white checkered shirtwaist. She would carry the cape over her arm at the zoo and then add it for the meeting later, where she hoped it would lend a touch of suitable decor to her appearance.

She purposely did not wear the brooch because of Evalyn Paxson's comment on Quaker's not displaying jewelry.

Back downstairs, Jonathan stood twirling a new tan fedora hat, which made him look older; but his boyish smile charmed Annie to the bone.

"Come, on. We need to catch the streetcar at Broad." They walked sided by side, chatting about the lovely warm spring weather.

"Tell me about your shopping trip yesterday to Wanamaker's."

"Oh, it was wonderful. I've never seen so much merchandise in one store! I found the perfect gifts for both Marie and Aunt Hulda."

"No gift for your father?"

"I'm giving him the cinnamon bun recipe from the Stratford." Annie grinned.

"What did you buy for yourself as a remembrance?"

"Nothing. The trip is my gift."

The streetcar arrived, and they climbed in. A moment later the vehicle lurched out into the street and the sudden movement caused Jonathan's body to careen into her. They both laughed and he moved, but only a fraction of a space away. A silly smile formed on Jonathan's face as he acted as a tour director.

"May I tell you about the zoo, Miss?" he declared in a formal voice.

Annie grinned at his antics, and nodded an enthusiastic yes.

"The Philadelphia Zoo opened in 1874 and lies beyond the west bank of the Schuylkill River. The current collection holds an amazing assortment of over 1,000 animals, all housed in accommodations approximating their own natural habitats. You probably don't know the Philadelphia Zoo was the first zoo to open in America."

Annie clapped. "Bravo! I had no idea you knew so much about zoos."

He reverted to his normal voice. "I don't actually, but Josie and I got to attend its opening the year we turned thirteen. We came back often because it's a grand place to spend a day. And, believe it or not, the admission price is still the same: 25 cents for adults and 10 cents for children."

Annie thought how far 25 cents could stretch for a miner's wife.

The streetcar soon reached the Girard Street intersection and they disembarked, waited a bit, and then boarded the next streetcar heading west on Girard.

They soon arrived at the Schuylkill River and crossed over the wide Girard Avenue Bridge.

She pointed down. "Jonathan, is that the Schuylkill?"

"It is."

"What does 'Schuylkill' mean?"

He laughed. "No one has ever asked me that before. *Kill* is the Dutch word for river. Schuylkill means 'hidden river.'"

"Dutch? I thought Quakers settled Philadelphia."

"Actually, Philadelphia was settled by a group of Dutch and Swedes before William Penn and his Quakers arrived. The Dutch gave the Schuylkill its name."

The streetcar came to a stop in front of the Philadelphia Zoo.

"Here we are." He held her elbow as she descended from the vehicle and once again she felt his touch to be warm and comforting, but also a bit delightful as a mild shiver ran up her arm.

Jonathan paid their admission, and they walked through the ornate Victorian iron trellis gate and into the zoo proper. Annie saw that it was actually called the Zoological Park.

"Morning is my favorite time to visit here, before the crowds, and while the animals are still active and not in need of a nap."

While Jonathan took Annie to some of his favorite exhibits, like the snakes, she found that the monkeys fascinated her the most. It was hard to believe she was actually standing in front of animals that usually live in a jungle.

They stopped to eat at a vendor's cart where the man dressed in dark trousers and a red shirt offered them sausages in a bread roll, washed down by a glass of Coca Cola.

"Save room for dessert, I want to buy you some famous Philadelphia ice cream."

"Why famous?"

"Because, Philadelphia had the first ice cream shop in America too."

"Oh, Jonathan, Philadelphia couldn't have been first in everything!" She laughed.

"Here's the ice cream place." They walked into a small building where the heavy scent of sugar wafted in the air and made Annie's mouth water in anticipation.

"Seems like you've been here before," she teased.

"I've been here many times. Now, what is your favorite flavor?"

"Chocolate, I guess. At home we call it *crême glacée au chocolat*."

"You guess? Have you tried a lot of flavors?"

"In the summer we usually churn chocolate, vanilla, and either strawberry or raspberry to sell in the shop."

"Well, you're in Philadelphia, so you can experiment with several new flavors. Bet you can't guess George Washington's favorite?"

"Something tells me that you know the answer and I won't be

able to guess it anyway."

"You won't, because the answer is tomato!"

"Tomato ice cream? Oh, my goodness!"

They both dissolved into peals of laughter. Annie finally chose cherry vanilla ice cream and allowed the cold treat to dissolve on her tongue before she took further bites. It was the sweetest ice cream she had ever tasted, and she wondered if that was Philadelphia, or perhaps the playful nature of their excursion?

After the ice cream, they continued walking with their arms nudging up against each other. They looked at a few more exhibits and laughed when the animals seemed to act out for the audience. Any passerby could have mistaken them for a couple.

All too soon two o'clock loomed on the horizon and they needed to leave.

"I hope I didn't keep you here too long."

"It was one of the best times I've ever had. Thank you."

"I don't think you'll have time to go back to the hotel, so we'll have to take a streetcar that goes directly to Arch Street. I'll go with you. Unless of course, you don't want me to."

Her face flushed a bit and she lowered her eyes for a moment. "No, I'd love to have you there. I'm hoping the Elders will agree to my petition."

"If they decline, you can always look for a different sponsor."

"There isn't enough time to do everything I want here in the city."

He spoke softly. "We can always come back on another trip. And you'll do fine today when you meet with the Elders. I can't imagine anyone not wanting you to succeed."

A loud screech from the hawk cage made Annie immediately think of Herman Schumn. "Oh, I can think of someone."

Out on the street they picked up their pace and soon spied the streetcar up ahead. "Come on!"

Jonathan grabbed her hand and she picked up her skirt, and they ran together. The unique emotion of feeling cared for enveloped her, and she blushed again in spite of herself. Thankfully, Jonathan kept

looking ahead, and did not see her face. When they reached the transit stop, they jumped into the streetcar and fell down into the seat almost on top of each other as the car pulled with a jerk out into the road.

Rather than be unsettled, she found the impact of his body to be stimulating.

*

They arrived at Arch and Fourth Street precisely at quarter to three. Moving closer to the brick wall, Annie put on her cape, smoothed the errant locks of her hair as best she could, and took a deep breath. Then she readjusted her spring bonnet so she appeared more modest.

"How do I look?"

"You're not wearing the pin you had on when you met with Father Reilly."

"Quakers don't wear jewelry, so I didn't want to look pretentious." *And I'm surprised you noticed what I was wearing.*

"Just be yourself and you'll be great." His words gave her a feeling of confidence.

They walked up to the front door and knocked. Annie felt a bit of relief when Evalyn Paxson greeted them.

"Welcome back, Annie Charbonneau." Evalyn leaned forward and gave Annie a kiss on the cheek.

"Evalyn, this is my friend, Jonathan Canavan, who is helping me on this trip. Jonathan, this is Evalyn Paxson."

"How do you do?"

"Welcome to thee, too, Jonathan Canavan. Please come in." Inside the foyer, Evalyn turned and led them left, down the corridor to the East Room. "Thee will be meeting with Elder William and Elder Charles. They are in a position to make a decision about thy request." Evalyn looked directly at Annie. "Do not feel embarrassed; remember, thee is pursuing a noble cause."

As the trio entered the room, Annie saw once again how plain their rooms were, devoid of even paint. Pegs on the wall accommo-

dated hats, coats and capes, and the wooden benches in methodical rows offered seating. She reminded herself to hold her head erect and smile directly at the two older men, who stood to greet her. Both were dressed somberly in outfits of dark gray trousers, vests, and black jackets. Each man also had a full length beard, not the current style in Porters Glen.

"Elder William, Elder Charles, this is Annie Charbonneau and her friend Jonathan Canavan. They have come to speak about a charity project."

"Please sit down here. Jonathan Canavan, please take a seat as well."

Evalyn nodded to Annie.

Mon Dieu. Aidez-moi. "Thank you for agreeing to meet with me, I mean, us." She took another deep breath and began. "We live in a very small mining community called Porters Glen, in the mountains of Western Maryland. Half of our village is comprised of mining families, many of whom cannot read or write. I help to teach an English class to the miners' wives."

Annie paused as one man nodded his head.

"We also provide our students with shoe coupons, as an incentive. The coupons enable the women to buy winter shoes for their children."

"Shoe coupons?" Elder William seemed perplexed.

"Yes. Winters are brutal. The mines usually shut down for three months and the men become unemployed."

"Go on." This time it was Elder Charles who had spoken.

"The mining company controls everything in Porters Glen. If a miner's wife does not have money to get her children shoes for winter, the company has a system where she can get free shoe coupons by visiting the Curtain Room."

Annie stopped. She felt awkward now having to explain further.

"Annie, continue." Evalyn smiled at her with encouragement.

"The women who go to the Curtain Room offer themselves in exchange for the shoe coupons."

There, she had said it. The silence deepened.

"Why hasn't anyone gone to the authorities on this?"

"Because the authorities are under the thumb of the mining company."

"And you, Jonathan Canavan. What part do you play in this?"

"I am the local school principal. Annie holds her English class on Sunday nights in one of my classrooms, and my sister teaches with her. They currently have twelve women enrolled."

"How do you see us helping thee?" Elder William addressed Annie.

"I came to Philadelphia hoping to find a sponsor who would enable us to dispense our own shoe coupons for next winter."

"How much money do you need?"

"Each woman gets a coupon that is worth two dollars toward shoes for her children."

"And two dollars is sufficient for all the children in each family to obtain shoes for winter?"

"No, but it is usually enough for three children per family. We simply did not have enough money to provide for more. We are hoping to increase our class to 20 women next year, so I would be asking you for forty dollars in sponsorship."

"Thank you, Annie Charbonneau. We will confer on the matter and let you know."

"I am returning to Porters Glen on Saturday morning. When will you reach your decision?"

"It will be necessary for us to discuss this idea at Meeting. Then we will write thee a letter with the decision. Before you leave, please give us your address."

Evalyn got up and went back to the foyer and soon returned with a piece of paper and a pencil.

"I'll give you the address to our family store. That is where I work with my father, and the post office is directly across the street."

The two Elders smiled and stood up. "Thank you for coming to see us, Annie Charbonneau. We will send the decision of the Meeting as soon as possible. Good day to thee."

"Thank you for listening to my cause."

Evalyn led Annie and Jonathan back to the entrance. "Take heart, Annie Charbonneau. The Elders will be fair in their discussion, and once it is brought up at Meeting, the women will have a chance to voice their thoughts as well. Have a safe journey back home."

Annie and Evalyn embraced, and Jonathan escorted Annie outside.

"I know you are disappointed, but they did not dismiss the idea."

"Jonathan, I had so hoped they would agree to be our sponsor."

"They might do so yet. Let's get you back to the hotel so you can rest before supper. Daniel and Katie are joining us again."

Annie nodded, trying to swallow her disappointment.

As soon as they stepped into the lobby of the Stratford, a bell boy approached them.

"Miss Charbonneau?"

"Yes."

"A telegram was delivered for you while you were out."

"A telegram? Jonathan, who could possibly have sent it?"

Annie tore open the telegram and quickly scanned it.

MISS ANNIE CHARBONNEAU
C/O STRATFORD HOTEL

MARIE HURT IN ACCIDENT (STOP)
DO NOT DELAY COMING HOME (STOP)

PAPA

"Oh, my God!" Annie passed the telegram to Jonathan.

He read it. "Don't worry. We'll leave for home first thing tomorrow."

CHAPTER 26

James Hannan, age 22, killed,
Potomac Mine. Newly married.

Annie clutched her travel bag the next morning as they stood on the corner and waited for the hack driver. Jonathan had already sent a telegram alerting Louis that they would be returning today. She hardly even noticed the blue sky and rose-streaked clouds of early morning. The good parts of the trip were now overshadowed by her fear of what had happened to Marie. Why hadn't Papa explained it in the telegram?

The ride to the Reading Terminal went without any incidents, and once inside the rail car Annie sat down, grateful that Jonathan was with her. Josie took a seat across from them. The train pulled away from the station and Annie peered out the window for one last look at the city. Her former delight in sight-seeing with Jonathan now felt frivolous.

Minutes later when they were passing close by the vicinity of the zoo, Jonathan spoke quietly to her. "I know you are worried about Marie. But until we get home, all the worrying in the world is not going to help."

"I'm just scared, that's all."

"I know you are. But whatever has happened, I promise to stay by you and help you deal with it." He reached down and clasped her hand. "I bought you something so you would have a memento from this trip. It was meant to celebrate a happy memory, but now perhaps it should be a talisman for good luck."

"Jonathan, that's thoughtful but not necessary."

He retrieved a small box from his jacket pocket. "Here."

Annie's hand shook as she took the small square blue box with the silhouette of a white unicorn's head on it. Opening it, she found a single delicate silver-tone bangle bracelet with a scroll design around the rim. "Jonathan, it's beautiful, but I don't think I can accept it."

"Why not?"

"In our family, jewelry is only given as a gift by family members."

"Consider me a family member, then, at least in spirit. I want the bracelet to be a reminder to you of never giving up on your goals."

"Thank you, but until we find out about Marie, I won't feel comfortable wearing it. I hope you understand. But I will put it in my bag and take it home."

"Of course I do. And, Annie…I plan to be around for a long time to help you with any problems you incur."

Annie felt the universe tilt in a new direction; one where she wanted to stay.

*

By the time they arrived at Riverton they had been traveling for twelve hours. In an exhaustion-induced stupor they climbed down from the train car. Annie scanned the platform for Louis. It was already dark and hard to find him.

"Papa! Over here!"

As soon as Louis walked over, she saw the tell-tale lines of extreme fatigue ingrained across his craggy face.

He looked like he had trouble keeping tears at bay. "Annie, I'm so glad you're home, and home safe." Then he turned his head aside.

Jonathan reached for the three suitcases and walked to the wagon.

"Papa. Tell me what happened to Marie."

"We'll talk at home."

The ride back was completely silent.

As the horse pulled them up the steep Pike, Jonathan finally announced, "Why don't we drive directly to Coal Bank Lane? You and Annie can get out there. I'll take Josie over to the Eisner's and stable the horse and wagon. Then I'll come back tomorrow to see if there is anything I can do to help."

Louis nodded a sign of relief. When they reached the bottom of Coal Bank Lane, Louis pulled on the reins for the horse to stop. Jonathan leaned forward and whispered to Annie, "I'll see you tomorrow." Then Louis helped Annie down, grabbed her bag, and they walked the path to the house. The old draft horse blew snorts of steamy air and then with Jonathan's coaxing, lurched his large body forward, pulling the wagon behind him.

Annie did not even turn to look back. "Tell me now, Papa, how bad is it with Marie?"

"She's alive, but with a badly broken ankle, and…there is more, but right now we both need to sleep. Thank you for coming home right away. I didn't realize how much your presence means to me. With your mama gone, I guess I look to you for reassurance that we can solve our problems. Just having you home is calming me down. But I do think we both need to sleep. Aunt Hulda is in the room with Marie, sleeping on a borrowed cot. Why don't you take Stephen's old room?"

Annie climbed the stairs and peeked into the bedroom she shared with Marie. Both figures were sound asleep. She crossed the hall to the bedroom that had been Stephen's, undressed, and climbed under the bedspread without even stopping to brush her teeth. Sleep took over as she said a prayer of thanks for Marie's life.

*

The noise of early-rising robins woke Annie, and she went down into the kitchen to start the coffee. A few left-over rolls sat on a plate and she felt hunger pangs. Popping a bite from one of the rolls

into her mouth, an unexpected memory-taste of the Philadelphia cinnamon raisin buns came to mind. Her excitement over the Philadelphia buns seemed silly now because of what had happened to Marie.

Twenty minutes later she heard Louis moving around upstairs and then he came down to the kitchen. Circles under his eyes indicated he had not slept well.

She walked over to him and caressed his forehead. "Papa, tell me everything now."

Louis lowered himself into a chair at the kitchen table. "On Thursday, she and Giselle were going over to the Porter Mine and wait for the men to come off the shift. I think they were really waiting for that boy, Anton Sivic, you said Giselle likes. Anyway, they had stopped by the gob pile and were watching boys picking up small chunks of coal and loading their pockets."

Annie could picture this because she'd seen that activity numerous times. There would be young boys with unkempt hair, and dirty suspenders holding patched pants rolled up at the knees for quicker momentum. They would try and capture any free coal that had fallen off the carts before the mining company thugs chased them away. For many families, this was the main way of obtaining enough fuel to warm their houses.

Louis went on. "Suddenly, a runaway coal car careened down the mine track. Giselle jumped away in time, but Marie twisted her leg in the attempt to get clear. She fell backward and her ankle snapped. The coal car missed her by only a few inches." He wiped his eyes as a new stream of tears trickled down his chin.

"Thank, God, Papa, she's all right, but do you think that it might not have been an accident?"

"What do you mean?"

"What if she was singled out for an attack?"

His shoulders slumped. "God, I hope not, because Herman Schumn announced he is charging Marie with trespassing and intends to take her to court."

"What? I don't believe you." But the look on Louis's face told her the opposite. "Papa, the court levies fines for trespassers, and how

will Marie even be physically strong enough to stand up in court? Why would Schumn be doing this to us?"

"Don't interfere, Annie. I told you long ago he was not a man you wanted as any enemy."

It's me he's trying to get even with. Annie drank a long draught of her *café au lait,* hoping the hot drink would give her sustenance. *Schumn is my enemy, and I'll be damned if I let him do this to Marie.*

*

Hulda opened the shop for Louis because they could not afford to miss the lucrative Saturday shopping.

An hour later, Annie convinced Louis that she could stay with Marie while he went and checked on the store. "But first, Papa, I want to give you my gift from Philadelphia." She held out the piece of paper on which she had copied the cinnamon buns recipe.

"Annie, that was so thoughtful of you." Louis looked it over. "I can see how they are made. Were they tasty?"

"They were, Papa, and I think they'd be popular at our bakery. Now, you go to the shop while I stay with Marie."

Once they had the house to themselves, Annie brought Marie a cup of *café au lait* and a warmed roll. She bent down to hug Marie.

"I am so glad you are all right. But, listen to me. I'm going to see Mr. Hennessey first thing Monday morning and ask for his help with this trespassing charge."

"How can Mr. Hennessey help?"

"He and Herman Schumn do business together. I'm going to appeal to Mr. Hennessey's sense of reason and ask him to intervene with Schumn."

"Do you think he would do that?"

"I'll do everything I can in order for Mr. Hennessey to understand that forcing you to appear in court in your condition is unfair."

Annie took a moment to look at her sister, with her one leg wrapped in a soft cast. Marie's normal healthy complexion had paled and was touched by obvious pain.

"Here, let me brush your hair. I know you can't really stand and do it easily for yourself."

"Thanks, Annie."

*

On Monday morning she walked up the Pike wondering why Jonathan had not stopped over on Sunday like he had promised. But, right now she had bigger problems. The sky opened and let loose a relentless downpour, which combined with the early spring breeze, managed to completely soak the lower part of Annie's skirt. At least her top half managed to stay dry under her umbrella.

She tromped, wet and sodden, into Hennessey's Store, which was already filling up with Monday morning shoppers. Drops of water formed small puddles at her feet. Seeing Mr. Hennessey in his office, she closed her wet umbrella and marched directly toward his door. Biting her nail for a moment, she knocked on the office door and then opened it.

"Mr. Hennessey, might I have a moment to talk with you? It is of an important nature."

Hennessey stood impassive behind his desk and straightened the lapels of his jacket. He was stocky and solid, like Frankie, and a reminder of their ancestors who had fought their way out of poverty in Ireland.

"This is a busy morning for me, Anne. Can't it wait?"

"No, I'm afraid not."

"Very well, a few minutes are all I can spare. I hope this has nothing to do with shoe coupons." He arched an eyebrow. "You can put your wet umbrella down over there, rather than make a mess in my office. What is it you need from me?"

Annie ignored the barb about the umbrella. "I'm sure you heard of the accident that occurred Thursday down in Porters Glen? My sister Marie was injured."

"Yes. I also heard she was trespassing."

Annie stared at him for a moment, forcing herself to remain in

control.

"That is why I am here. Dragging Marie to court will only cost our family money we don't have in order to pay the fines. We are still trying to pay off the new loan to the bank. And I fear the humiliation of having to appear in court will interfere with Marie's healing from the accident. I know you are associated with Herman Schumn, and I want you to ask him to reconsider."

"And why would I be doing that?"

"As a favor to me and my family."

"A favor to you? You're the one who brought down the entire shoe coupon mess on my shoulders."

"Mr. Hennessey, those women were entitled to buy shoes from your store, and you know it."

"What I know is that there is an unwritten code in this town, and you violated it. You put me in an unfortunate position having to explain to Mr. Schumn about the shoe coupons. But… there might be a way I can help you. Provided of course, that you reciprocate."

"What do you mean?"

"Why are you no longer seeing my son?"

"What does Frankie have to do with any of this?"

"He mopes around the house whenever he's not in the mines or in the saloons. We've asked him why the two of you are no longer a couple, but he just shrugs."

Annie could not believe he was bringing Frankie into the discussion.

"We know how much he still cares about you. If you agree to start seeing Frankie again, without mentioning this conversation, then I will speak to Mr. Schumn and have him keep Marie out of court."

"That's blackmail, Mr. Hennessey."

"Call it what you want. I thought you and my son had talked about marriage?"

"What we talked about was personal." Annie realized this was not the time to antagonize him. She gritted her teeth, aware that she was caught in a tight situation. "All right. I'll start seeing Frankie again, but only if you hold up your end of the bargain first."

Hennessey said nothing for a moment, but fingered the tips of his waxed moustache, as his lips morphed into the crooked grin of victory.

"Perhaps you could also convince my son to leave the mines and return here to work in the store."

Annie refused to answer. She turned on her heels and walked out of the store. She passed several women looking in the large glass windows, but she never even glanced at them. Life had turned on her once again. How could she explain this to Jonathan? Then she remembered what he had told her back in Philadelphia—the Canavan family motto. *Family sticks together, no matter what.* But would he understand the sacrifice she was about to make? She had to protect Marie, but could she really give up Jonathan as part of the bargain?

*

Later that afternoon Annie heard a knock at the front door. When she opened it, her face flushed at the sight of Jonathan, and her heart pounded.

"Annie, I came back to see how Marie was doing. Both of you were napping yesterday when I came to call."

She smiled at him, but turned her head aside. The sadness in her eyes would betray her. She would soon be seeing Frankie again, and how could she ever explain it to Jonathan?

"Thank you, come in. Marie is resting, but we're expecting Dr. Tanner to stop by and check on her."

"Your father told me some of what happened."

Annie heaved a heavy sigh.

Jonathan picked up her hand. "I'm so sorry, but with Dr. Tanner taking care of her, she should mend well."

"We're all hoping for that." Annie turned her face away from Jonathan, because she did not want him to see the longing in her eyes.

"Annie? What else? There's more. I can tell."

"I guess I'm just tired from the trip and then coming home to this situation. Please, Jonathan, I think I need to go lie down. Thank

you for coming over."

He tilted his head. "All right, but I will call on you again tomorrow."

"That won't be necessary, really."

"I didn't say it would be necessary. I'll come because I want to be here with you. Surely you must know by now how much I care about you."

Annie fought to suppress the tears that were forming at the corners of her eyes. Unable to check them, they spilled in delicate streaks down her cheeks.

"I didn't mean to make you cry. We can talk tomorrow, or even next week when things settle down. Would that help?"

She only nodded, because she knew if she spoke, she would fall into his open arms.

*

When Dr. Tanner arrived later in the day, he apologized that he had been detained with another patient, a young boy with a broken leg. Adjusting his spectacles and giving his long curly beard a stroke, he leaned over the foot of Marie's bed to check on her damaged ankle.

Dr. Tanner was somewhat of an anomaly in the village because he was hired by the CVC to provide minimal care for the miners, but he also saw patients from the outside. Throughout the past three decades, he had treated hundreds of families from all levels of society. Unfortunately, the poorer mining families often called him only as a last resort, when it was usually too late.

Marie had been dozing, but now awoke when Dr. Tanner lightly touched the soft cast he had fit on her foot. "Hello, Dr. Tanner, how do I look?"

"Mighty pretty, if you ask me." He winked.

"I meant my ankle."

"Well, let's unwind the bandage and remove the soft cast to give the ankle some breathing room before I wrap it up again. Some of the swelling has gone down, which is good. And I do not see any glaring red marks that would indicate infection. So, if you follow my orders and do as I say, you'll be able to order a new pair of shoes and go dancing at graduation. You are graduating in June, aren't you?"

Marie blushed. "No, Dr. Tanner. I graduate next year. Annie graduates this year."

"Too many patients." He grinned at Louis. "I simply cannot keep track of everyone's ages. Marie, how about the pain? Is the ankle still hurting?"

"Yes, but Aunt Hulda brewed some of the tea that our mother used to make when Papa had a tooth-ache."

"What's it made from?"

Marie looked over at Annie. "Do you remember the ingredients?"

"Mostly dried oregano, rosemary, and thyme."

"All right. If you need something stronger, let me know. Otherwise, keep the foot elevated at all times, but I do want you to walk around the house once every hour. Use the crutch I left, but do not put any weight on that foot for several days. This is important for your leg muscles. No climbing stairs yet, either."

"When will I go back to school?"

"School? I think you should stay home at least a week, maybe even two, and after that you'll still need a ride up to Mount Pleasant. Your ankle will heal, but not if you put too much strain on it."

"We'll figure something out. Thank you, Dr. Tanner," said Louis. "Let me see you to the door."

Louis returned and asked Annie to help him move some wood on the back porch. Once outside, he touched her elbow. "I don't need any wood. I need you to tell me why you went to speak with Mr. Hennessey."

"I asked him to intervene on our behalf about Marie. He and Schumn are like associates."

"You shouldn't have done that, Annie. Hennessey will hold that over you."

He already has. "He agreed because of my relationship with Frankie."

"Your relationship? I thought you and Frank Hennessey were

on the outs?"

"We were, but that has changed again." She fought tears.

"Annie, I hope you know what you are doing. I had the distinct impression you did not want to become a miner's wife. Have you told Frank your feelings?"

"It's more complicated than that. Family should stick together, Papa, no matter what."

*

The next Sunday Annie went to Mass alone. She sat down and was surprised to see Jonathan in a pew a few rows ahead of her. It was the first time she had ever seen him at St. Bridget's. She felt her pulse quicken.

Oh, God, please do not have the Hennessey's attend this Mass. Annie turned her head and saw with dismay that the Hennessey family had seated themselves in the row directly behind her.

When the service concluded Annie hoped to say a quick greeting to Frankie and then leave for home with the excuse that Marie would be waiting for her.

"Annie." Mr. Hennessey's voice stopped her in her tracks. Without looking around for Jonathan, she addressed the Hennessey clan.

"Hello, Mr. Hennessey, Mrs. Hennessey."

Mr. Hennessey's eyes shifted to where Frankie was standing at the middle of the row.

"Hi Frankie, it's good to see you." Annie forced a smile, but not one laced with love.

Frankie turned his head. "Really? That's about the last thing I thought I would hear from you. How's Marie doing?"

Annie saw this as a good chance to begin talking with him, even though in her heart she wanted to be with Jonathan. "She's beginning to mend, although Dr. Tanner has told her to limit her activity. I suspect she'll get bored pretty quick. Aunt Hulda sits with her during the day, which means I'm the main clerk at the shop. Papa's chores around the house are getting neglected."

"Like what?"

"He usually hauls wood from the back woodpile and chops it into kindling pieces. Then he brings in enough coal from the coal shed so we don't need to get any for a few days. That hasn't happened, so I guess I'll have to help with that too."

"I could come over and help him. Unless of course, you object to me being around."

"No, Frankie. That would be nice. My father and I would both welcome the extra help."

Out of the corner of her eye she saw Mr. Hennessey begin to grin. She said her farewells and quickly slipped out of the church and hurried down the street when she saw Jonathan run to catch up with her.

"Annie, wait. I need to speak to you."

Just looking up at the concern showing in his vivid blue eyes made her wish they were back at the Philadelphia Zoo, when everything had seemed so perfect.

"Please tell me what's wrong. Besides Marie, I mean. We need to talk."

"There's nothing wrong, Jonathan. I'm just preoccupied, worrying about Marie."

"You're not telling me the truth, and we both know it. When we were together in Philadelphia I got the distinct impression that you cared about me in the same way that I care about you."

"I do care about you." She saw in his eyes the look of genuine care and concern and she felt her heart break.

"Then why am I getting the idea that you are suddenly shutting me out? Does it have to do with Frank Hennessey? I saw you talking with him just now."

"The Hennessey's are family friends." She averted looking at him directly. "I really must be getting home."

"No." He gently tugged on her chin to face him. "Tell me now if what I thought was developing between us in Philadelphia was real, or not?"

"Please, Jonathan. I...I can't explain things right now."

"What do you mean, you can't?" His eyes pleaded for the truth.

She tore herself from him and ran down the road before he could see her dissolve into a flood of tears.

CHAPTER 27

Robert Hadda, killed from fall of slate,
Hampshire Mine.

As soon as Aunt Hulda stopped at the Charbonneau's house, she could hear muffled sobs coming from upstairs. With Marie on the porch chatting with a neighbor, Hulda knew the cries must be Annie's. "Annie? Are you all right?"

When there was no answer, Hulda pulled her girth up the steps one leg at a time, panting with each breath.

She found Annie curled in a ball on Stephen's old bed, her eyes red from crying. "*Ma cherie*, what could be causing such tears this early in the day?"

Annie reached out and Hulda lowered herself onto the bed and pulled Annie into her arms, rocking her in much the same way as she had done when Annie was a child. "Now, tell me."

"I can't."

"Yes, you can. There isn't a problem on earth I haven't encountered."

Annie hesitated. "What if I told you I love someone who can never be mine?"

Now it was Hulda's turn to hesitate. "Is it because he's married, or is there a different complication?"

"A different complication."

"Tell me, and we'll see what can be done."

"Nothing can be done."

"Something always can be done."

"I can't tell you because I gave my word on an obligation, and this obligation means that I cannot have him in my life."

"We're not talking about Frank Hennessey, are we?"

"No."

Hulda nodded. "I see. And this someone, does he love you?"

"I think so."

"Well, if you can't tell me, your only option is to talk to St. Anne."

"St. Anne?"

"Yes, the patron saint of families. Remember, she was the mother of our Virgin Mary. You are named after St. Anne, so she is your protector, too. Do not discount the power of prayer, Annie." Hulda knew that in many ways, Annie was still an innocent young woman, and needed the support of prayer. With a tender glance at Annie's tear-stained cheeks, Hulda turned around and started to pad back downstairs. But a hunch made her stop. She peeked back and saw that Annie had moved to her knees with her head bowed.

Then Hulda felt Bon brush silently past her and enter the room with Annie. Hulda watched as the dog cocked his head, staring at Annie on her knees. Much to Hulda's surprise she saw him lie down next to Annie and fold his paws in what looked like canine prayer.

"Ah, even the dog understands."

*

A large beefy man wearing a smart black bowler folded his newspaper with the date Saturday, April 14, 1894, and disembarked from the train in Mount Pleasant. Employed by the United Mine Workers Union (UMW) in Cleveland, Ohio, he was on a mission to agitate. His goal was to whip up fervor among the miners of the western Al-

leghenies in preparation for the soon-to-be-called national strike, only one week away.

He stepped off the train in Mount Pleasant carrying his brown canvas traveling bag in one hand and smoothing the ends of his handlebar moustache with the other hand. He'd grown up in the anthracite coal fields of Pennsylvania where the land was hilly, but not overly steep. A groan of surprise escaped his lips at the sharp incline he saw he would have to negotiate to climb up Depot Hill.

Young and healthy, he began the ascent. Part way up the hill he was huffing and puffing, and by the mid-way mark he had to stop and catch his breath. When he finally reached the top, he discovered that the main business district was located on yet another steep hill. He checked himself into the nearby St. Cloud Hotel, put his bag in an unremarkable but adequate room, and started out to explore the town. The information he sought would be found in one of the local saloons. He just wasn't prepared for the fact that Mount Pleasant had twenty-nine of them. The first one he encountered happened to be McAllister's, located directly across from St. Bridget's.

He walked straight up to the bar and rested his foot on the scuffed brass rail while he eyed the bartender wiping down the polished wooden surface slick with spilled beer. Spittoons were located conveniently nearby on the floor.

The bartender met his gaze. "Can I help you?"

"A pint." He threw down some coins. Glancing off to the side, he saw how the other men in the bar were dressed; this was a working man's place. He'd grown up in bars like this, but now preferred to drink in establishments where the bars were built from mahogany and sweat-stained odors did not soak the air.

"You come on the train?" a fellow next to him asked.

He nodded.

"Where from?"

"Cleveland."

"Is that so? You have kin here?"

"No. I'm here to meet with some of the miners. When does the Saturday shift end?"

"Ended at noon. You ain't been a miner yourself, or you'd know that."

The newcomer held up both hands, where every finger displayed hard calluses.

"Sorry, didn't realize. Where'd you mine?"

"Carbondale, Pennsylvania."

"And you ain't there no more?"

"No, not anymore."

"What do you do now?"

"I help fellow miners."

"How's that?"

"I help them get better pay. Now, can you tell me which saloon the miners here frequent?"

"Hell, they go to all of them!" another man piped up. Laughter rippled around the bar.

The UMW man smiled. Then he caught the bartender's eye and slowly pushed a coin halfway toward his reach.

"Another pint?"

The UMW man lowered his voice. "No. I'm trying to locate a miner, name of Frank Hennessey. Do you know him?"

"I know him."

"Any suggestion where I might find him?"

"What do you want him for?"

"He wrote, asking for help."

The bartender nodded. "Go down the Pike about one mile to the next village. He works in the Porter Mine." He pointed east.

"Thanks." The organizer turned back to the man sitting next to him. "My name is Williams; in case anyone needs to know." He left the bar and walked outside. Turning right, he walked down the street's steep slope.

When he reached the bottom of the hill the land stretched out onto a small flat open plain and he assumed he'd left Mount Pleasant behind. Ahead, the dirt road turned south and became a bit narrower. He walked along as it dipped sharply. At the turn he noticed a large stately home situated off to the left. Probably belongs to the mining su-

perintendent. As he continued walking, he wondered what kind of man this Frank Hennessey would turn out to be.

Williams spied the tall wooden building called the tipple and knew he'd found the coal town. Like all coal villages, the tipple was an essential part of the coal operation where coal was pulled in, weighed, and then tipped over into waiting railroad cars below. This tipple had weathered with age.

Turning off the main road, he headed down the dirt-packed street into the village. First there was a wooden building on the left with a sign that declared, Cumberland Valley Coal Company, but he knew the miners' saloons would not be near the company offices.

He'd been in many coal towns. They all had that same desperate look of wanting to be more than they were, but forever dependent on the slick black rock. Here, buildings wore a dusting of coal grit like a mantle, surrounded by air that groaned with the sounds of loaded coal cars shuttling back and forth from the hoppers.

A barber shop and another storefront that appeared to be a butchers came next in the store line-up, then as he continued on the street passing a few saloons, he noticed an unusual sight—one not normally seen in coal communities. It was a sign for a bakery, and he decided someone inside would know which tavern he needed to find.

Opening the door, he noticed the attractive girl behind the counter. What a shame that such a pretty young woman should spend her life stuck here.

"Good day, sir. May I help you?"

He took in her young figure and her hair style casually piled up on her head. Such pretty skin, too.

"Yes. I'm looking for the most popular saloon here in town that the miners favor."

"You're new, then." She pointed out the window, slightly to the right. "You'll want Murphy's. Up there on Beer Alley."

Beer Alley? They always invented such quaint, no nonsense names in coal towns.

He gestured in the right direction, but she came around the counter to help.

"Here, I'll show you. We actually have eleven saloons."

He followed her out the door and watched as she pointed out his destination.

"Make sure you turn right."

"Why?"

"Because if you go left, you'll soon smell the mule barn up ahead, and it's not a pretty odor."

"Mules don't bother me."

"You looking for work?"

"Not really, just looking for an acquaintance. Thank you."

He tugged on his jacket and walked away with an authoritarian gait.

It took him less than five minutes to locate Murphy's.

The saloon was dim inside and the air was heavy with halos of pipe smoke and the smell of warm beer. The place was crowded with miners who had recently finished their shift, and they all seemed to be talking at once. Some were standing at the bar while others sat at small tables scattered throughout the room. Williams made his way to the bar and leaned in, tossing down some coins and asking the bartender for a pint. Then he simply stood there drinking and listening.

A few minutes later the door opened and a young miner sauntered in. The whole place nodded at the miner and someone yelled, "Over here, Frankie. We saved you a spot."

Williams focused his attention on the Frankie guy.

"Did you hear anything today?"

Frankie Hennessey looked around the bar and spotted the stranger.

"Not really. Nothing to report." Then he looked away from the stranger and made small talk with the men standing around him.

Williams continued to drink, but paced himself. Finally, a few of the miners started to leave. The stranger made his move.

"Mr. Hennessey. Can I buy you a drink?"

"How is it that a stranger knows my name and is offering me a drink?"

"Just being friendly. Bartender at McAllister's gave me your

name."

"Oh, did he?"

"Let's have a drink together. How about in the back corner where we can talk privately?"

Frankie picked up the free drink and moved to the back of the room.

The stranger lowered his voice. "We received the letter."

"You from the UMW?"

The stranger nodded and Frankie let out a long slow whistle.

"You wrote, and I'm here. What we need now from you is a willingness to help."

Frankie lowered his voice. "What do you mean?"

"We're looking to sign up all the miners from the Cumberland Valley Coal Company to agree to support a big strike set for a week from now. We'd like you to get the word out."

Frankie leaned in closer. "The miners here don't want a strike; they just want to negotiate with the mining company to reinstate the pay to fifty cents a ton."

The stranger snorted. "They're not about to give you back the fifty cent ton rate. That's why the strike's been called. Men from Indiana to Pennsylvania are set to strike against their coal companies so the rich fat cats who own the mines will see that the men who dig their coal are not to be toyed with."

"There're bad memories here from the strike of '82."

"That's because it failed. This time, the strike will succeed, but only if we have every miner join in the fight."

"I can get to the men and tell them about the strike, but I can't guarantee that they'll support it."

"We already have men from the mines west of here agreeing to go on strike. Your men need to show solidarity with their fellow miners."

Frankie looked around the room. "We shouldn't really be talking here; too many ears. Give me a couple of days. I'll meet you at half past five on Tuesday, in front of Hennessey's Store in Mount Pleasant, and tell you how the men reacted to your idea."

Williams put his bowler hat back on and tapped the crown.

Then with a satisfied smile he uttered, "Much obliged."

Frankie continued to drink his beer, but kept lifting his head to look around at the bar.

By now Herman Schumn, Randall Meyers, and every other official from the CVC would know a stranger had come to Porters Glen.

*

There was no turning back now; Frankie had already tossed his hat into the ring. For the next few days he spoke to as many miners as he could, passing on the message about the national strike to be called on April 21st, and how the UMW wanted every miner to support the cause.

As predicted, the topic was not taken lightly.

"Kid, you're too young to remember the strike of '82. With the men out of work for over six months, many a family lost children too frail to survive without enough food and elderly who gave up, and gave in to death. Strike is a bitter word to many in Porters Glen."

"Yes, but the UMW organizer told me this strike would be successful if every miner joins in."

Another old-timer spoke up. "And what if it ain't? Any man who strikes not only loses his pay, but stands to be black-listed, and once you're on that list, you ain't never gonna work in these parts again."

"Look, I think the UMW really wants to help us," Frankie insisted.

"And what if we refuse to strike? What then?"

"I dunno. But if all the other mines shut down, I'm betting we could become targets from the striking miners."

A young miner piped up, "But wouldn't the Cumberland Valley protect us?"

"The CVC? Hell, they don't care if we all die, they'd just hire new immigrants to take our place. No, the Cumberland Valley ain't going to back us at all," chided an older miner.

Later, in hushed voices either on the mantrip, in the heading of the mine, or as they walked home at the end of the day, the only topic

discussed was the upcoming strike.

*

On Tuesday evening, as soon as the men spilled out of the mine, Frankie hurried over to Charbonneau's Bakery.

"Annie, I'm on my way up to Mount Pleasant. There's going to be a big meeting with miners from all over the Cumberland Valley area."

Annie pointed at the coal dirt he had tracked into the shop. "Frankie, I've asked you before to wipe your feet before coming inside."

"Sorry, I guess I'm in a hurry. The UMW has sent a man, an organizer from Cleveland, Ohio, asking all the miners to support a big strike that's slated to start on Saturday. I'm meeting with him first, and then the big meeting starts half an hour later."

"I thought we'd talked about this before, and that you were going to be careful."

"I will be careful, but I can't sit by and watch the other miners make the decision without me. I have to be there. Listen, Annie, whether they, we, decide to strike or not, I'm going to be busy working out details with the men."

"Just be careful, Frankie."

"Of course." He was delighted that she was worrying about his safety, and now that they were seeing each other again, Frankie felt happy. He looked at her with a longing in his eyes, but then reminded himself he needed to concentrate on the current situation with the UMW representative. Then he turned and hurried back to the Pike.

Once he arrived on Union Street near Moats' Opera house, he came face to face with a crowd of 300 miners representing the various surrounding mines, all waiting to hear what the UMW organizer had to say. There was no time for Frankie to talk with the union organizer alone.

Mr. Williams stood tall with his bowler hat perched snug on his head as he climbed onto a makeshift platform and addressed the crowd. The silence from the miners was eerie. After his hour-long talk he asked the men to cast their votes in support of the UMW, and not show up for work after Saturday, April 21st.

Immediately a heated discussion ensued where men from various mines spoke out.

"I say we all join together, and show them sons-of-bitches that we refuse to work for lower pay," said one of the miners from the Elk Garden group.

"Hell, yes!" shouted a man from Klondike.

"Not all of youse remembers the strike of '82 when the mines shut down for half a year and people literally starved. I ain't so sure that this here man with the UMW can actually deliver on what he promises." This comment came from the oldest miner in the group, Mr. Lewis from Porters Glen.

"I can promise you this—if you continue to work for reduced pay, you'll never get back the decent wages you deserve." Williams eyed the crowd for emphasis. "We take the vote, now."

Of the forty mines represented, only the men from Ocean, Hoffman, and Porters Glen held out and decided not to strike.

Frankie realized there was no turning back. A burst of adrenalin shot through his veins. His mine wasn't going to back down and kowtow to the union; they were going to stay strong and work. He just prayed it was the right decision.

Not sure about what the next step would be, he headed over to McAllister's for a beer.

*

On Wednesday, as Louis was about to close up shop, he turned to Annie. "Aunt Hulda asked me to get a small smoked ham from Engle's. I think she wants to cook your favorite meal."

Annie smiled. Aunt Hulda was doing that to lift her spirits. If only *jambon en croute* could really solve problems.

"All right, I can go over and pick it up." As Annie walked out of the shop and turned left down Store Hill, she saw miners coming out from Big Vein Street. Annie almost expected to see Stephen's ghost

among them and wondered if this group would strike or not. Mr. Watson practically bumped into her, squinting as his eyes adjusted to the bright daylight. He was walking from the mine with his son John.

"Good day, Miss Anne." The older gentleman took two fingers and gave her a small mock salute.

"Good day, Mr. Watson. And, is this John? My, you've grown."

Mr. Watson nodded in agreement. "He ain't a trapper no more. Today he did his first half turn. Strike or no strike, he earned himself his first pair of hobnail boots."

Annie smiled at the young teen. "Congratulations." She went to extend her hand to shake, but then withdrew when she saw his black cuticles and fingers covered with coal grit and grime—just like his coveralls, and just like his father. "Congratulations anyway." She grinned.

As the father and son passed by, Annie couldn't help but wonder if John Watson would make it through life without any crippling accident in the mines. If he had started as a trapper boy, opening and closing the ventilation doors when he was nine and earning 85 cents a day, he probably had quit school then. He must be at least thirteen by now and could probably dig half what an adult miner did. Even though the legal age for a boy to become a miner was fourteen, no one in the valley adhered to the supposed regulation.

Digging two tons a day instead of four or five, John Watson would be a "half turner" until the age of fifteen, when he would earn the designation of full-fledged miner. How many strikes could he endure in his lifetime?

Once a miner, always a miner.

She turned and watched the coal-covered duo saunter up the hill and knew the boy would follow the legacy of his father. With a slight shake of her head, she turned and walked in the butcher shop.

"Hello, Miss Anne. What can I do for you?"

"Hello, Mr. Engle. Papa said Aunt Hulda would like a small smoked ham. About 8 pounds, I think."

"Your aunt making one of them ham pies?"

"Yes, sir, we call them *jambon en croute*," Annie smiled. "That means ham in crust."

"So it is ham pie, then." He grinned. "It'll be 90 cents for the ham. Expensive, I know. But she'll be able to stretch it into several meals. Do you want me to put it on the book, so your father can settle up later?"

"Yes, thank you."

It occurred to Annie that the courtesy of credit she had always taken for granted was no different from what the miners' wives had wanted from her. She winced in recognition of her former callousness.

CHAPTER 28

James Edwards, age 23, caught in the hoisting engine, Ocean Mine.

As Frankie was planning how to negotiate with the UMW, one of the miners' wives was planning a negotiation of a different nature.

Sophie Petrova had to visit the CVC Office. Her cheeks flamed as she visualized the humiliation he would make her go through again. She needed money in order to visit a doctor in Riverton. She didn't want Dr. Tanner, because everyone knew him.

Glancing at the shadows on the wall, she calculated she had to move quickly before the men would be coming home from the shift.

Wrapping herself in the hand-me-down spring coat she had received from the church, she walked out of the small cottage and left her two small children, once again, with Mrs. Lipinski next door. Then she headed for the weathered clapboard building of the mining offices.

She hadn't expected him to be standing in the entrance room, but she managed a weak smile and told him she needed some money. He stared at her in a rage-filled silence.

"We don't give cash; I've told you that before."

"I need to get to a doctor." She swallowed the nausea that was climbing up her throat and put a hand on her stomach.

"There's ways of solving that."

"I can't, I'm Catholic. Can I clean the offices in exchange for cash?"

He stroked his chin. "We don't need no cleaning lady, but if you come here to me, every day for two weeks, I'll consider helping you. Just this one time."

"Every day?"

"Do you want the cash, or not?"

"Of course. I can come every afternoon, or in the morning if you like."

"Good. Then I want you to start right now."

She did not respond because she hadn't anticipated this possibility.

"Did you hear what I said?"

"Yes."

"I'll meet you upstairs."

She closed her eyes for a brief second and told herself this was the only way. She touched her hand to her stomach as she climbed the stairs.

Later, as she walked home with her body sore from his invasions, she let the tears flow unabated. God damn him, he had better hold up his end of the bargain.

*

The strike was called on Saturday, April 21st, but life appeared to be normal in Porters Glen; at least on the surface. The women came into the village to do their shopping, and children peered in the windows of Charbonneau's Bakery hoping for a treat. Being Saturday, Louis always baked a tray of pigtails; sweet dough rolled in the shape of pigs' curly tails sprinkled with cinnamon and sugar. He sold them two for a penny.

At noon, when the half day shift ended, the miners left the Porter Mine together in solidarity. Instead of going home, they trooped in unison to Murphy's pub where the conversation zinged back and forth.

"I say we stand strong. No sons-of-bitches are going to force me to strike."

"Yeah, but we've all heard rumors of possible retaliation against

us because we didn't strike. We'll be called scabs, even though we've worked the mine for years."

"So what? Names ain't nothin'. But if they stir up real trouble, we'll meet 'em head on. Come Monday morning when all them other miners are walking around with their hands in their pockets and no work, we'll still be diggin'."

Frankie spoke up. "But we'll have to look out for one another. Not everyone lives in Porters Glen. Some of you walk two or three miles to get here for your shift. That means you could be targets for any striking gangs."

Heads nodded all around the bar.

"So what are you suggesting?"

"I say we start walking in groups. You men from Barton, can you walk as a unit?"

"Yeah."

"Good. How many miners do we have from Clarysville?"

Several men raise their hands.

"I think you men should all meet at Kelly's Pump and then walk up the Pike together."

"Those of us coming from Mount Pleasant will meet each morning on the flats. The men from Porters Glen should stick together as well. There'll be safety in numbers."

"You don't think them bastards would actually attack any of us?"

"I heard the Connellsville miners are set for violence against any men who aren't on strike. So we need to look out for each other. As I said, there'll be safety in numbers."

*

As Joe Haines sat with his wife in church on Sunday, he noticed it was standing room only. The minister gave a sermon on the evils of disobedience, but Joe hoped that even a man of the cloth would realize the Porters Glen miners needed to provide for their families.

Tomorrow would be the first day of true reckoning, and Joe prayed that no blood would be shed as the mining strike began in earnest.

Early Monday morning as Joe Haines and his fellow miners, including Frankie Hennessey, showed up at the entrance to the Porter Mine, they were greeted by a crowd of about thirty striking men calling the non-strikers scabs and blacklegs.

The Porters Glen miners pushed through the crowd and climbed on the mantrip.

That night, they met in a room over Drum's Store to discuss their plan of action if violence did occur.

Joe voiced that he was worried striking miners might come into the village while the other miners were at work. If so, then the women and children of Porters Glen would be vulnerable.

None of the miners wanted to give up a day's pay to stay home, but if violence started, they voted to rotate—one man per day would go off shift and walk about Porters Glen checking on the miners' homes. If the CVC docked him a day's pay, it was the sacrifice they would all make in order to ensure their families would be safe.

Every night for the rest of the work week, Joe Haines and the other miners met in groups in various locations throughout the area. Meetings took place in halls, or out in the woods, or even in fields. Joe was surprised that sometimes the meetings were attended by only a handful of miners and at other times the meetings were as large as 300, with the UMW agent holding court.

By Friday, when Joe and the other working miners came off their shift, they heard that Sheriff King had gone up to Mount Pleasant to see how many strikers were now sitting idle in front of the businesses of Mount Pleasant.

One barkeep, Tom Layman, said he heard the count was 1,800 men on strike throughout the area.

Joe Haines let out a long slow whistle. That's a whole lot of men with time on their hands.

*

Schumn had reluctantly agreed to Hennessey's request of dropping the trespassing charges against Marie Charbonneau, although he couldn't imagine why Old Man Hennessey had capitulated. Meyers rarely interfered with Schumn's actions in the company, but this time he agreed with Hennessey and told Schumn to forget the charges; they had bigger concerns with the strike.

Actually, Schumn thought, the CVC could benefit from the strike. While the men were out on strike, the CVC had hired blacklegs, men from Pennsylvania to come in and work the mines, still at the 40 cent per ton pay. If the Georges Creek area miners won the strike, the CVC would blacklist every striking miner in retaliation. Either way, the coal company would come out on top. He made sure they always did.

But Anne Charbonneau stuck in Schumn's craw. Her attitude against the coal company infuriated him, and he often dreamed at night of bringing her to her knees, both figuratively and literally. She was a whore, just like his mother.

His father had abandoned Herman and his mother as soon as they arrived in America. Herman had been only nine years old, but he clearly understood why other men sought his mother out. When she took Herman to Appalachia, he realized that his mother had simply traded the destitution of Germany for a different type of hell in Appalachia.

Prostitution became the pathway to her survival.

They moved from one coal camp to another, and his mother took in laundry to earn some money. Later, he listened to the grunts and groans when she entertained the local men, lying behind a curtain in the rented shacks she shared with Herman. Always, she demanded a new pair of shoes from the men, in addition to the financial bargain. The shacks were pitifully bare, but his mother's shoes were lined up along each wall almost like a tally of conquests. When money ran out, she sold off a pair or two.

He grew up filled with contempt for her, and her damn shoes.

It was the same contempt he felt for Anne Charbonneau.

In his dreams he shamed her in front of the entire village, exposing her to be the whore he thought she was. Other nights he dreamed he evicted the entire family and she came to him begging for mercy. On those nights he experienced wet dreams and it was only in

the mornings when the top sheet carried stains, did he realize the hold she had on him. Then he would strip the bed and demand that Widow Thompson, who owned the boarding house, wash his sheets even if it was not wash day.

Long ago he had established a bargain with the widow. He would pay extra if she gave him the large room on the main floor as his own, and allow him to take his meals in the kitchen so he would not have to socialize with the other boarders. In addition, she would wash his sheets whenever he asked.

Once, she had made a vague allusion to him about the miners' wives. That day he had one of his thugs dig up a sizeable pile of rat droppings from the mine. When everyone had gone to sleep for the night, Schumn slinked to her kitchen and placed the rat shit in a prominent corner.

At breakfast the next morning he never said a word, just ate his meal in silence like always. But that evening he returned to the house and went to the kitchen and began looking in the corners. Widow Thompson asked him what he was looking for. He said there had been talk down at the mining offices that her boarding house was rat infested. If that was so, he would need to move elsewhere and condemn the premises.

The widow trembled. He waited for a few moments, then suggested he could help her. He would give her some lethal powder to sprinkle along her floor boards in the kitchen. She would leave the powder down for a full week, after which no rats would invade. In exchange, she would defend him in all circumstances.

She agreed, not realizing the powder was simple baking soda mixed with Borax; she never mentioned the miners' wives to him again.

Schumn wondered if Randall Meyers harbored any sexual fantasies about Anne Charbonneau, but since the two men never shared anything personal with each other, Schumn could only assume that Meyers had his own dreams about the bitch.

*

Nineteen days into the strike, on May 9th, Josie Canavan hurried as she walked up Coal Bank Lane to the Charbonneau house and rapped hard at the front door.

"Why, Josie, how nice to see you. Is something wrong? You don't usually come here on a Wednesday evening." Annie's face turned pale.

Josie darted inside. "Annie, I need to talk to you, but not here. Can we take a walk?"

"Of course. Going out, Papa," she called.

The two women started walking briskly down the lane. "Josie, what's wrong? Does this have something to do with Jonathan?"

"Jonathan? No. Let's go to the schoolhouse. It's after hours and I have the key. We can talk once we're inside."

Josie opened the school door and peered around, almost as if she were expecting an intruder. "Annie, I have something important to tell you, and I need your complete confidence."

Annie suppressed a nervous shudder. "All right, of course. Go ahead."

Josie took a deep breath. "I think trouble is coming."

"What kind of trouble?"

Josie grabbed Annie's hands. "I've heard a rumor that a significant retribution is being planned against the non-striking miners of Porters Glen."

"Oh, Josie, you know how people talk."

"This is different; you need to be on your guard. Even the saloons in Connellsville are closing early tonight so the men won't congregate there."

Josie's face was pale with fright, and Annie felt anxious.

*

The next day Sophie Petrova walked into the bakery with her willow shopping basket on her arm. After a few minutes of wandering around in the shop, she approached the front counter and stood silent

until Annie could wait on her.

"Good morning, Sophie. What would you like?"

In halting English, Sophie said, "Good morning. Four milk bread rolls please."

Annie wrapped up the rolls and as she began to place them in Sophie's basket, Sophie lifted the checkered cloth. A small folded note lay tucked underneath. Sophie took the note and added it to the coins in her palm. Then she placed both the note and the coins in Annie's open palm and closed her fingers over it.

Annie looked perplexed but said nothing. Sophie murmured, "Thank you," and left the shop.

Several other customers came forward to pay for their selections and Annie hastily stuffed the note in the back of the store's register. Once there was a lull in the shop Annie retrieved the note and went to the back of the shop to read it in private.

Urgent!
Meet me at 7:00 pm tonight
behind the school.
Many people are going to get hurt.

Annie was perplexed. How could Sophie have written this note, when she still only spoke fragmented English? Who really wrote the note and why? Did this have anything to do with Josie's warning?

Annie was silent through supper with her thoughts about the note. "Papa, I'd like to take a walk with Bon. There is still a lot of daylight and I need the exercise. Marie, can you do the dishes alone? I'll do them tomorrow night."

Marie looked skeptical, but shrugged her shoulders and agreed.

Precisely at seven o'clock Annie approached the back door to Jonathan's school, with Bon on a leash.

A silent lone figure stepped out of the shadows and Sophie beckoned Annie to come into the doorway. Bon whimpered as if he detected trouble.

"Shh, Bon. Everything's all right." She turned toward the girl.

"Sophie, what is the meaning of the note, and who wrote it for you?"

"Miss Annie, there is much you do not know about me. I wrote the note."

"You? I've never even heard you speak English this well!"

"I speak it quite clearly, but no one knows that."

"What's going on here?"

Sophie took a deep breath. "I work for the CVC. In exchange for information, they give me food and shoe coupons so I don't always have to visit the Curtain Room. It was me who listened to Hulda Kirby's confession to Father Kelly about mailing the letters to the editor. I then reported her to the CVC. It was also me that let the vandals into our classroom."

Annie's cheeks flamed. "You're a traitor."

"Traitor? No, Miss Annie. I'm just trying to survive. Don't judge me until you've been forced to make difficult decisions yourself. You've never had to go to the Curtain Room."

Annie choked. "So what does this note mean?"

"A vigilante mob formed last night in Wrights Crossing. On Saturday morning they've been instructed to go to the Porter Mine between 6:30 and 7:00 am. They will be armed, perhaps with guns. Their goal is to stop the Porters Glen miners from going into the mine. This isn't to just scare them; any miner who resists could get both his legs broken, or worse."

"Why are you telling me?"

"Because you need to warn them."

"The miners? I doubt they would listen to me."

"Not the men. You need to warn their wives, so they can keep their men home from work. I don't know anything more." Sophie turned to leave.

"Wait! This has to be dangerous for you too. Why are you doing it?"

"I'm pregnant because of the Curtain Room. He laughed when I told him, and handed me a pair of knitting needles."

Annie recoiled. "He? Who?"

"It is better for both of us that you do not know." Then Sophie slipped off into the dusk, leaving Annie speechless.

She walked back with Bon toward Coal Bank Lane, trying to match Josie's warning with this new information. Annie knew that involving the miners' wives would put them in danger as well. Their husbands would never stay home from work, not when they had voted against the strike. She tried to think how the women could actually help the men. Then a daring idea struck her. She would only have twenty-four hours to implement her plan.

*

During Friday, the hours seemed to drag by endlessly. Annie needed to talk with Josie as soon as possible, and she would need to leave work early.

"Papa, can you get by without me for the rest of the afternoon? I have some business with Josie Canavan."

"All right. Hulda and I can manage."

Annie dashed out of the bakery, only to see Josie walking briskly toward Store Hill.

"Josie, shouldn't you be in school?"

"I got another teacher to cover for me. Let's walk up Beechers Avenue. We need to talk."

Once they arrived at the top of the hill and had turned left, Josie blurted out, "Have you acted on my information?"

"I'm about to. Thankfully I was also warned by Sophie Petrova."

"Sophie?"

"Yes, it's a sad story, but she filled me in with specific details."

"What did she tell you?"

"A vigilante mob has formed and will descend on Porters Glen early tomorrow morning, using violence to prevent the miners from going into the mine."

"Oh, God. Annie, this is worse than I thought. You should stay out of it."

"I can't just sit on this information and do nothing." Annie could feel blood rushing to her head. "Men could get killed." Frankie would be going to work tomorrow morning.

"Annie, don't get involved!"

"Josie, what if the wives went to the Pike early tomorrow morning, and formed a human chain? They could slow the mob from advancing onto the village."

"Are you crazy, Annie? That would be too dangerous."

"Not any more than what the miners would be facing. Besides, a mob wouldn't be expecting a group of women, and they certainly wouldn't attack us. Our presence might give them pause for thought. We won't fight them, just block their way."

"We? You would be a part of this?"

"Of course I would. Won't you?"

Josie turned her face aside. "I don't think I can be involved."

"Why not?"

"Because it would jeopardize my contract with the school board. I signed a statement that I would not participate in any unladylike behavior."

"What? I didn't realize that."

"If you become a teacher here, you'll be asked to sign a similar agreement."

Annie nodded silently.

"Annie, in order for this to work, you would need to get word to the miners' wives by tonight."

"I can do that. But, do you think that we could ask Randall Meyers for help?"

"I don't think so. He's the superintendent and has company rules that he has to adhere to. I think that we, I mean you, should not trust anyone but ourselves in this matter."

"Can you at least help me by talking to Aunt Hulda? Ask her to get a few older women to come to Miners Row by six o'clock in the morning and act as babysitters for an hour. Just till the miners' wives come back. Tell her I sent you."

"All right. I'll go talk with her right now."

"You'll also have to make up an excuse to Aunt Hulda as to why I won't be home for supper tonight."

"Leave that to me."

By the supper hour, Annie knocked on the first door on Miners Row. In all the years she had lived in Porters Glen, she had never been inside any miner's home and wondered which ones her mother had visited. "Good evening, Mr. Schooley, may I speak with your wife?"

Once invited in, she was surprised by the small living space, it was almost like stepping into a doll house. With a low ceiling and only two windows in front, and one on the side, the house was dimly lit. In spite of the ever present smell of coal dust, the front room was remarkably clean.

She realized this room was actually the main room of the house. The left side appeared to be a kitchen area, and the right side had a tick mattress, possibly the sleeping section? Ahead, she spied the opening to a narrow staircase leading, she assumed, to a loft upstairs where the children slept. Beyond that on the main floor she thought she saw a small storage area.

Rather than stare at the sparse furnishings, she riveted her eyes on Mrs. Schooley. "Good evening, Bridget. Is there somewhere we could talk in private?"

One by one she knocked on all twelve doors of the women who had been in the English class, and one by one she whispered the reality of the situation. Then she waited as a deathly silence hung in each home, until the miner's wife nodded.

"Here's what we have planned. Tomorrow, you will accompany your husband to the mine for his half-day Saturday shift. Arrangements will be made for older women in the village to watch your children and keep them safe at home. If your husband asks any questions, tell him you are marching to support his choice not to strike.

"Once the men are safely inside the mine, we women will march in force to the edge of the Pike. Locking ourselves together, we should deter the mob."

Each miner's wife eyed Annie with a bit of fear in her eyes.

"I know you're thinking we could be putting ourselves in danger, but no mob is going to hurt women. If we stay strong, show no fear, and link our arms one-to-one across the road, we can slow the mob's advance. If you have a sister, or sister-in-law, or even a trusted neighbor, you can ask them to join us. But no one can ever admit to being a part of our group."

Annie sighed with a breath of relief when each woman agreed to help.

"We'll assemble with the men in front of Murphy's Saloon at six o'clock in the morning. Remember, this will only work if we all stick together and don't tell anyone about our plans. Not even your husband. We'll also march together in support of Rosa's memory."

Then Annie walked home to Coal Bank Lane. "I'm back, Papa."

"Did you have a nice time with Josie Canavan?"

"I did, but I am very tired and think I'll retire early. *Bon Nuit.*" Annie quickly climbed the stairs before her face could betray her lie.

CHAPTER 29

Charles McGrogan, died from fall in deep shaft,
Hyndman Mine.

Very early the next morning Annie quietly slid out of the bed. Tiptoeing across the room, she stepped into the hall. Her father had already left for the bakery, and Annie had stowed her clothes in Stephen's old room. Treading softly, she opened his door and inhaled deeply, even though she knew his scent was long gone. She still remembered him coming home from the mine and washing off the smell of the coal dust.

She left the house before the May morning awoke, and had to reassure Bon that he needed to stay in the yard and not follow her. Annie wondered how many women would be meeting at Murphy's Saloon, and prayed that none of the husbands were forbidding their wives to walk with them.

She picked up her pace. Nervous energy flooded her body as she walked down Coal Bank Lane and crossed onto Porter Road. Eight minutes later, she could see a sizeable group forming in front of Murphy's. *Stephen, I'm marching for you, too.*

Frankie was talking to some of the miners in the middle of the group. He saw her and immediately walked over.

"Annie, what are you doing here?"

"I'm going to walk with the miners in support of them opposing the strike."

Frankie's eyes took on the glint of anger. "I'm not stupid, Annie. Something else must be going on. The wives never walk with the men."

"Some of the women were talking yesterday and we decided that it would be a good show of faith if we stand by the miners in their resolution not to strike. As soon as we reach the mine, the men will go to work and we'll head home."

Frankie narrowed his eyes. "And?"

"And, nothing."

"Who's watching the miners' children, if the women are here?"

"I guess the wives made arrangements." She continued to stand under his scrutiny, her face a mask of hidden emotion, but her mind a whirlwind of worry about real violence. Wasn't it in the strike of '82 that several protesters were shot?

Within moments the large group was ready to move. Annie counted twenty women and about seventy-five men. The crowd started off, with the women walking alongside their men. Once they reached the intersection of Store Hill and Charbonneau's Bakery, they turned left onto the main thoroughfare. Annie made sure she was in the middle of the pack, just in case her father might be looking out the shop window.

When the group reached Big Vein Street, the miners kissed their wives and then veered off toward the Porter Mine.

Frankie lingered a moment. "Make sure you go straight home, Annie, and for God's sake don't do anything foolish."

She averted her eyes slightly and nodded her head. He kissed her lightly on the cheek and went to join the men heading for the mine. Within minutes the men were on the mantrip and rumbling out of sight.

The women turned in unison and continued walking toward the Pike, instead of home.

They heard the mob before they saw the dust cloud from its tramping. The vigilante men were grunting and calling out to one an-

other as they marched down the road. When the mob approached the turn-off for Porters Glen, they stopped momentarily.

"What the hell?" One of the men in the front of the mob quipped as he spied the line of twenty women strung across the Pike, arms linked together. Two women were carrying babies on their hips, but all of them were silent.

The mob continued at an unfettered pace. The front leader stopped just in front of the women's line. "Get out of our way!" he bellowed, as the others swung their baseball bats in the air. Annie nervously scanned the mob to see if they had guns.

Other men started snarling at the women. "Back off!"

However, the women stood their ground. Annie could feel sweat running in rivulets from her armpits to her waist. By now, all the miners would be safely inside the mine and unaware of what was happening out on the Pike.

"I said, step aside!" The veins in the leader's neck bulged, and his eyes looked wild. When none of the women made any movement his eyes narrowed to slits. "So, which one of youse is Frankie Hennessey's whore?"

None of the women flinched, although Annie's eyebrows shot up in surprise.

It was enough of a facial movement that the leader singled in on her. She was positioned in the middle of the line, but he walked right up to her and slapped her hard across her cheek. Her face stung and she fought the urge to crumple in front of him, as several of the other women let out audible gasps.

"I hear you ain't nothin' but trouble. I'll say this once more—get out of our way, or so help me God I'll knock you down where you stand."

He raised his hand to strike her again, but one of the other men at the front of the mob pushed forward and grabbed his upraised arm. "They never said there'd be women. We ain't hitting no women."

One woman in the line yelled, "If you prevent our men from working, we'll go down in the pits and dig the coal ourselves."

Her words stopped the mob, but only for a moment, then the

men began to pound the ground rhythmically with their baseball bats. The noise sounded like war drums.

A murmur occurred along the women's line. At first the noise was guttural, but then grew as woman by woman took up the chant, louder and louder. "Rosa, Rosa, Rosa." Annie leveled her gaze at the ring leader and parroted, "Rosa, Rosa, Rosa."

The baseball bats fell still. "Who the hell they talkin' about?" one man said to the mob at large. Other men lowered their weapons and muttered among themselves. "Crazy bitches, they shouldn't be here." Then one man said, "God damn it, he never said women would be involved. I ain't taking part in no violence against women."

Annie's ears perked up. Who was 'he'? Could it be Schumn?

"Shut yer traps!" the leader admonished the men. Then he turned to Annie. "I won't forget this. And you best be watchin' yourself whenever you're alone, 'cause I'll come back."

The mob began to disperse, turning and walking back up the Pike toward Mount Pleasant. The women did not break rank, but stayed linked together until the last menacing figure had retreated around the bend. Then some of the women fell against each other.

Annie's legs shook, and she had to hold onto the woman next to her. In a clear voice she called out, "Go home. No gloating over this, because this is not the end. You heard the leader, those men will be back. We may have stopped them this morning, but the strike is still in effect. Go home and do not admit you were ever here. That way none of us can get into trouble with the CVC."

As the women scattered, Annie touched the side of her face where the leader had hit her. The imprint of his open palm still stung. It would be hard to pretend she had not been involved. For now, she needed to get back home, splash her face with cold water, and use some of Aunt Hulda's pancake make-up to hide the red mark. She still wasn't sure what she would tell her father. Admitting she had been part of the women's group was out of the question. For now, she had to bide her time.

*

By Monday morning, Frankie, like everyone else in Porters Glen, had heard the story of the group of women who faced the vigilante mob on Saturday, May 12th. No one was admitting they had been there, but Frankie knew Annie had been with the group early that morning. *What in the hell was she trying to prove?*

That afternoon, a dozen striking miners came to Porters Glen. Frankie was on his way home when he saw the strangers walking up Porter Road, and he decided to watch them.

The group entered Murphy's Saloon, and Frankie heard the leader announce that they were from Elk Garden, and here on quiet terms. They wanted to talk with as many miners as possible about the ramifications of the strike.

Charlie Lancaster stood up. "I'll pass the word and get more of the men to come here." Soon, there was not a spot of empty space left in Murphy's.

"The UMW has assured us they will help any miner who goes out on strike." One of the Elk Garden men resumed talking.

"Where's that UMW man that's been around? How come he's not here?" asked Charlie Lancaster, a miner from Porters Glen.

"He went to Cleveland on Friday to prepare for the big union meeting on Tuesday."

"At least that's what we've been told," another of the Elk Garden men commented.

"Yeah, well, we heard he was afraid of tangling with our women." Snickers were heard throughout the room.

"We heard what happened Saturday, but none of us were involved."

An older miner spoke up. "Just what will the UMW do for us, if we strike?"

"They'll ask you to join their union. In exchange for a modest membership fee, they'll work to get you back your old pay and better working conditions for all the miners."

"I'm too old to be joining any so-called union. We don't even know for sure that they'll help us." A wizened miner spat some tobacco juice on the floor.

Frankie listened. "The union is going to bargain for more than just your restored pay. We've been told they're going to fight for an eight-hour work day and medical benefits, to boot.

The meeting continued for an hour, when Frankie spoke up.

"We'll talk among ourselves and consider what you've said. If we agree to join the strike, we'll get word to you. But, if any violence comes to Porters Glen, don't be thinking we'll just sit and take it. We'll fight back."

Frankie watched as the Elk Garden men left as a group and turned up the road, back toward Mount Pleasant. He stayed in the saloon, listening to the men discuss whether or not the union might really help them.

The debate lasted another hour. Then, Murphy's cleared out, with no decision made about joining the strike.

*

The following Monday, in the middle of the night, Henry Eisner woke with a start as his bedroom window was shattered by a barrage of rocks. His wife ran from their bed, but was hit by a large piece of airborne glass, and it cut her arm as she attempted to shield her face.

Henry was livid. He and his wife had grown up in the village. He had worked the mines for a few years, but quit to open a small dry goods store. His wife had turned their home into a small rooming house and took in boarders. They had never expected to be the targets of any strike.

The next morning Henry did not go to work. He stayed home to protect his wife and to repair the window. He passed word to the miners that they should be starting safety patrols in order to protect their families.

Henry Eisner was paid a visit by Sheriff King.

"Henry, what the hell happened?"

"We were asleep when some son-of-a-bitch threw rocks at our bedroom window. Susan got hit by some flying glass. I tell you, Sheriff, I ain't going to just stand by and let it happen again."

"All right, Henry, we're checking into this. Your wife wasn't in that group of women last week that faced the vigilante group, was she?"

"Hell, no. And even if she was, she'd never admit to it. None of them women are talking."

"I wish to Christ they would just call off the strike. Make my job a lot easier."

*

Four days later, on Saturday night, the violence returned in full force when Charlie Lancaster and his wife were sound asleep. A roar like a locomotive awakened them at two in the morning as an explosion tore off their front door and shattered the front wall of their home. The Lancaster house had been dynamited.

For the next several nights, three more houses on Miners Row were stoned sometime after midnight. Fortunately, no one was reported hurt.

The village slept with anxiety for several days.

Everyone in Porters Glen sighed with relief when the postmaster announced that Sherriff King had telegraphed Governor Frank Brown, and demanded that soldiers be sent to western Allegany County to help quell any further violence.

*

Ever since the mob incident, Annie tried to keep a low profile. She wanted to talk about her fears of possible retaliation for the women's group, but she was too afraid to admit her involvement, even to Frankie. A stab of unexpected loneliness shot through her when she realized it was Jonathan she really wanted to confide in.

To cover her feelings about Jonathan, she concentrated on her next goal—to attend graduation and then prepare her essay application for college. Somehow, she would find the means to pay the tuition, if she got in. Right now, she tried to busy herself with the normal work of the bakery.

On Friday, June 1st, the Porters Glen postmaster walked across the street to Charbonneau's Bakery. Mail addressed to Annie Charbonneau from Philadelphia was in his hand.

"Hello, Anne. Looks like a special day. I've got two letters for you, both from Philadelphia."

Annie flew around the counter and took the letters in her hands. She tried to quell the trembling of her fingers. "Thank you, Mr. Martin." Shaking with nervous excitement she saw that both letters had come from the Arch Street Meeting House. She said a quick silent prayer that the Quakers were going to become her shoe sponsors.

Tearing open the first letter she scanned the lines and felt the immediate sting of disappointment.

Dear Annie Charbonneau,

We trust this letter finds thee well. After a lengthy discussion at Meeting, we regret to inform you that we have voted against giving you a monetary sponsorship. However, we were impressed with thy mission and decided to help in a different way. Our Meeting will conduct a shoe collection, whereby we will ask for donations of slightly used children's shoes and then send the collection to you to disburse next winter.

Respectfully,
Elder Charles
Elder William

Annie's initial disappointment turned to elation when she got to the end of the letter. There would be shoes for the children after all! Then she tore open the second letter, which she found was from Evalyn Paxson.

Dear Annie Charbonneau,

I pray this letter finds both thee and Jonathan Canavan in good health. If thee hast read the letter from the Elders, then thee knows that we Quakers will be helping thy cause after all. It warms my heart to think of so many children with solid shoes next winter,

and more importantly no more Curtain Room for your women. I trust thee and Jonathan Canavan are progressing in thy relationship with one another. Am I correct?

Sincerely,
Evalyn Paxson

Annie sighed with wistfulness at Evalyn's perceptive insight. It seemed as if the Philadelphia trip was years ago, not just seven weeks' past. She would write back to both the Elders and to Evalyn, but she would not mention anything about her forced decision to separate from Jonathan.

She stared at the two letters and tucked Evalyn's in her purse. Even though they had not seen each other for several weeks, Jonathan deserved to read the letter from the Elders. On impulse she turned to her father. "Papa, I need to go to the school for a bit. I won't be long." She saw Aunt Hulda grinning from the other side of the bakery, but Annie didn't smile back.

A few moments later she was walking up Store Hill to Beechers Avenue and the school. Being late in the afternoon, all the children had been dismissed, which meant Jonathan would be in his office.

Without giving any thought as to what she would actually say, Annie knocked on the door frame.

Jonathan looked up in surprise and his eyes shone with delight. Instantly, the light evaporated and was replaced with a thin icy stare. He rose to standing.

"Hello, Annie. I didn't expect to be seeing you."

"Hello, Jonathan. I just got the most wonderful news and wanted to share it with you."

"News?"

"Yes, from Philadelphia."

"Oh, I see. Did you get your sponsor?"

"Not exactly. But the Quakers are going to hold a shoe collection for slightly used children's shoes and then send us what they get for next winter. Isn't that grand?"

He stared at her for a moment. "Yes. I'm happy for you. But now

if you'll excuse me, I have work to finish."

His dismissal stung.

"Jonathan, there's another reason I came here today."

"Is that so? I can't imagine any reason for you being here."

"Jonathan, don't sound so cold. It isn't like you."

"Isn't like me? How would you know? You never gave me the chance of getting to know me better."

Annie became silent, her lips trembling. "Jonathan, you don't really know the whole story."

"Oh, I think I do. Let's see. You went to Philadelphia with me, but planned all along to come back to Frank Hennessey. Yes, I think I know the story."

"But that isn't the way it happened."

"Are you back with Frank Hennessey, or not?"

"Yes, in a way."

"In what way?"

"In a way I can't really discuss with you, except to remind you of the Canavan family motto: family sticks together, no matter what."

"That's my family motto, not yours." He crossed his arms against his chest.

"I know, but it relates to my family, too."

"You sound like you're talking in riddles, and honestly, Annie, I don't want to be involved. You made it very clear that I was not the person you wanted to share your life with."

Tears started to slide down Annie's cheeks.

"You don't have to resort to tears. For God's sake, go marry Frank Hennessey. I'm not returning to Porters Glen in the fall, anyway. My only request is that you take care of yourself." He turned his head aside.

She tried unsuccessfully to wipe away the tears. "Not returning to Porters Glen? Where would you go?"

"Any place where I would not have to watch you become another man's bride. There, now you know the truth. Please leave." His blue eyes had turned frigid.

For once in her life Annie did not immediately react. She stood frozen and sobbed. Then she reached out for him.

But Jonathan picked up his papers and strode out of the room.

Deep down, Annie knew she couldn't blame him for reacting the way he did. The cold hard reality of knowing he would never forgive her was unbearable.

The tears continued to run down her face. Everything was such a mess right now. She still worried about repercussions for the women's actions against the mob. She knew Schumn would never let the incident go without punishment. She wanted Frankie kept safe, but she ached for Jonathan, even though he had just made it perfectly clear their relationship was completely over.

Her only bright thought was that Marie was safe and Jonathan was not involved with the strike.

If anything bad were to ever happen to him, she would blame herself, and then her sacrificial bargain with Mr. Hennessey would be a cruel joke. Taking a deep breath, she reminded herself to be grateful that at least she was graduating from high school.

*

By Monday, June 4th, the Governor of Maryland had dispatched the Maryland National Guard to western Allegany County.

Charlie Lancaster stood by the depot in Mount Pleasant the very next day and watched as one thousand soldiers arrived by train. His face lit up with satisfaction that surely now, the residents of Porters Glen would get protection.

"Where you boys headed?" He asked one of the soldiers.

"Some place called Stoney Meadow."

Charlie nodded. The location was perfect with its clear sight down the valley into the village of Porters Glen.

Within twenty-four hours, journalists from the Baltimore Sun were quickly dispatched to Mount Pleasant to cover the news. One of the journalist's, Mr. Duffy, found Charlie Lancaster talking with another man. The journalist commented he heard the army was in town to keep the peace, and protect the women. Would Charlie like to comment on that?

"Our women can take care of themselves."

*

The soldiers who were camped above town held little interest for Annie, even though Marie had hinted that several of the school girls were asking for some of their brass buttons as souvenirs.

With the mob incident behind her, and Jonathan's abrupt dismissal, Annie turned her focus to the immediate future. It was only another week until she would receive her high school diploma, and then she would have to come to terms about her relationship with Frankie.

She did care about him, but it would never be what she felt for Jonathan. A deep, sorrowful sigh escaped her lips.

Annie knew that both Louis and Marie understood that Annie had negotiated with Mr. Hennessey to keep Marie out of court. They just didn't know the depth of the sacrifice. No one did.

*

Friday afternoon, the shop bell rang, and Annie looked up to see a tall, good-looking stranger walk in. Annie noted how he carried the jacket of his gray summer suit over his right shoulder and sported a gold pocket watch hanging from a chain attached to his vest button. He glanced briefly around the store and then headed straight for the counter.

"Good afternoon, sir. Can I help you?"

The lines at the corner of his eyes stretched a bit as he smiled. "Well, I hope so. I was told that this store has what I'm looking for—the best local rolls, and perhaps some information."

Annie's antennae buzzed a warning. "We do have the best rolls, but I doubt we have any information different from any other shop."

His mouth turned up at the corners as his smile grew into a slight grin. "Let me introduce myself and then perhaps we can talk further. I'm Dennis Ackerman, an assistant attorney general, which means I'm a lawyer for the state. I'm not involved with either the mining com-

panies or the UMW. I represent the Maryland Governor's Office."

He waited for this information to sink in. "I don't suppose you would have any knowledge about the group of women who faced a vigilante mob a few weeks back?"

Her fingers gripped the edge of the bakery counter and she felt her breath stop. "I only know what I heard: some women formed a barricade on the Pike as their husbands reported for work in the Porter Mine." She smiled sweetly.

"Nothing else?"

She shook her head, but leveled her gaze to meet his.

"You know, those women were heroes, but they took a big chance—they could have easily become the victims of violence themselves." His deep blue eyes pierced her with sincerity.

"Yes, I suppose so."

"No names you could give me, then?"

"No. I'm sorry. I wish I could."

"They could be put in jeopardy if they tried anything like that again. My job is to offer them protection. But of course, I cannot do that if I don't know who they are." He leaned closer.

Annie held her ground. "If I hear anything, Mr. Ackerman, I will get in contact with you."

He took out his business card and wrote his address on it, then slid it over to her. "If I can help in any way, don't hesitate to contact me. I'm staying at the St. Cloud Hotel in Mount Pleasant. I've learned that sometimes women know more about what's going on than people realize. As I said, if there is anything I can help with, please contact me." With nothing left to say, he tipped his boater hat and turned to leave the shop.

"Wait, Mr. Ackerman. You forgot your rolls. Remember these are the best in town." She wrapped up two rolls in paper.

As he came back to the counter, she turned his card over. On the back side she wrote:

Cumberland Valley Coal Company. Curtain Room.

Then she slid it back to him, but did not move her fingers off it.

He glanced down and read what she had written.

"Are you good at memorizing, Mr. Ackerman?"

"Actually, yes I am."

"Good." She whisked the card back and took it to a crockery mixing bowl. She found a box of matches, lit one and held the card over it. They both watched the paper stock ignite. Annie then dumped the burning debris and ashes into a waste bucket half filled with water. The gray bits of paper swam around on the surface, but no letters were visible.

"Enjoy your rolls." She smiled at him.

"They will be memorable, I'm sure." He left the bakery and scanned down the street.

*

Dennis Ackerman easily found the Cumberland Valley Coal Office located at the end of the main street, near the large tipple. Removing his hat, he walked in.

A sour-faced looking man was seated at the front desk. "Can I help you?"

"Yes, I'm looking for whoever is in charge here."

Schumn peered back at him, squinting. "Who are you?"

"My name is Dennis Ackerman; I am a lawyer for Governor Brown's office in Annapolis. I'm here with the National Guard to ensure that no further violence breaks out."

"Is that so? What are you doing here, then? There's been no violence at the mining office."

"Part of my job is to inspect the various properties of the mining companies, to make sure that none of the buildings are in jeopardy of collapse. Just routine. I'll be inspecting your other buildings as well. Then I can report back to the governor that your company is in compliance."

"All right. I'll take you through the building myself, but we need to be quick. I'm a busy man." Schumn rubbed the back of his neck.

"I'm sure you are."

They started on the main floor with Mr. Ackerman poking his

head into each room, looking intently around, and making notes. Once they were finished with the main room, Schumn walked back toward the front door.

"I noticed you have a second floor. I'll have to inspect that as well."

"Second floor ain't nothin' but some storage rooms."

"I'll still have to include those in the report."

Schumn made an unpleasant gurgle in his throat like he was ready to spit tobacco, but walked to the staircase and up to the upper floor. Once there, he merely pointed at the doorways of several rooms.

"What about this one with a curtain instead of a door?" Mr. Ackerman asked.

"Nothing, just another storage room." Schumn stood with his arms on his hips.

Then before Schumn could stop him, Ackerman walked over and pulled aside the curtain. He saw that the room only contained one item—a cot.

"What do you store here?"

"It's an extra room."

"Why the cot?"

Schumn stammered. "In case someone has to work late, they can sleep here."

"Without a pillow or a blanket?"

"I think you're done," Schumn barked as a snarl twisted his lips. "If you need more information you can contact Mr. Randall Meyers, he's the mining superintendent. As I said, I have work to do, so you'll need to leave and write your report somewhere else."

"Of course, Mr.?"

"Name's Schumn."

"Thank you, Mr. Schumn, for your cooperation."

Outside Dennis Ackerman shook his head slightly from side to side, and then walked off toward the Pike.

Schumn watched from the window. He'd noticed that Ackerman took notes in every room he had ventured in, except the Curtain Room. Schumn had also seen Ackerman's eyes betray instant recognition to the Curtain Room's real purpose.

"Pinkerton's hiring. Maybe it's time for me to leave here and seek my future elsewhere," Schumn mumbled to the air. Then he sat back at his desk and began to tap his pencil up and down, up and down, like an angry woodpecker drilling into a tree.

With a loud crunch, he snapped the pencil beneath his hands.

CHAPTER 30

Noah Skidmore, age 56, crushed by fall of roof coal,
Union Mine.

The following Tuesday, June 12th, speculation flew through Porters Glen with the news that Mr. Williams of the UMW and two other organizers had been arrested on conspiracy charges by Sheriff King.

The miners didn't quite know what to make of this information, nor could they figure out what type of conspiracy had occurred. Mr. Williams had been living in the area on and off since April 14th, but no one expected him to get arrested. Would this be the death-knell for the strike?

Annie heard the news but only with a mild interest. She wanted the strike to end so everyone could get back to normal living. Right now she was waiting for graduation, only three days away.

She spent time with Marie planning which outfit to wear for graduation, and exactly how she should fix her hair for the big event. There were only twelve students graduating, and Annie wanted the evening to be perfect. She assumed Frankie would attend, although she had not asked him outright because they had talked about how excited she was to finally get her diploma. Who she really wanted to celebrate this milestone with, was Jonathan. Shaking her head to rid her heart of emotions that would only tear her apart, she concentrated instead on vigorously sweeping the floor of the bakery.

*

Finally, graduation day arrived on Friday, June 15th. Barely able to sleep the night before, Annie had tossed for hours while dreaming of walking up on stage to receive her diploma.

The high school was closing at noon for students to get ready for graduation at six o'clock. Annie worked through the morning at the bakery, and at the end of the lunch hour Louis turned to her. "I am going to be the proudest father there tonight."

"Thank you, Papa. I know you realize the importance of this for me."

"Go home and rest. You have a big night ahead of you."

Without a moment's hesitation, she agreed. Taking off her shop apron, she waltzed out the door on feet that barely seemed to touch the ground. Along the way she stooped to pick some tall stems of orange hawkweed when she heard the ominous cawing of a flock of crows. She stopped and made the sign of the cross, then chided herself for believing in silly superstitions.

Minutes later when she reached home, she was surprised that Bon did not race out from his lean-to area to greet her. Since Marie only had half a day of school, Annie wondered if Marie had taken Bon for a walk.

She opened the door and stepped inside, then spied the dirty breakfast dishes Marie had left on the sideboard. Even dirty dishes could not dampen Annie's enthusiasm today.

With a slight sigh, she stuck the hawkweed in a glass jar from the shelf and poured in some water for the stems to drink. She walked over to the hook by the back door, grabbed her full-length apron, and slid it over her head—wrapping the sturdy strings around her slim body and tying them in back. Once the dishes were washed and left to dry, she turned around to see if any other plates were left on the kitchen table.

She saw a note propped on the table instead.

Your dog is hurt. I put him in the hunting cabin up on Piney Ridge and left to go get help.

Bon hurt? The note was written in a scrawl, similar to that of a young child. Had Bon gotten loose and found his way up Piney Ridge? Who found him and how did they know to come here?

Without a moment's hesitation she stuffed the note in her apron pocket and dashed out the door. Within minutes she reached the old abandoned tram road that would take her near the foot of the mountain. Frantic with worry, she did not even notice the brambles reaching out to cling to her skirt.

Running up the bottom slope, she came to the fork way up the mountain and veered left. Within several minutes the cabin was in sight.

"Bon!" Annie yelled, but there was no responding bark.

She ran to the cabin and pulled open the door. Bon's body lie completely motionless at the back of the room.

"Oh, God, no!"

She ran to the dog's crumpled form and reached out to him.

In the next instant, she was grabbed from behind. Her assailant was stronger than she and quickly clamped a damp rag over her nose and mouth. She fought back, but his strength intensified with the struggle. Several minutes later she fell limp to the floor.

*

The assailant sneered at the image of her being completely helpless. He hoisted her up over his shoulder and left the cabin.

The lifeless body of the dog did not concern him.

*

Her eyes fluttered as the numbing effects of the inhaled drug began to ebb.

Open. Shut. Open. Shut. Finally—open. Mon Dieu, where

am I? Something is terribly wrong; everything is completely dark. Is it night? Where's Bon?

Annie slowly sat up, groggy. She had a throbbing headache and nausea threatened to overtake her. Her first instinct was to flail her arms into the air around her, because in the stygian darkness she felt blind. A sob broke from her throat with the sudden terror that she might be buried alive. Her heart pounded with fear. Very carefully she moved her arms around, in an attempt to better understand her space. Cautiously, she tried to move to her knees and stand. But without being able to see, she lacked balance and fell back to the ground.

Petrified by the all-consuming darkness, she sucked in giant gulps of air in an effort to quell her terror.

Rubbing both her arms, she realized her shirtwaist was wet; no, that wasn't completely correct. One sleeve felt dry, but the other sleeve was wet. She reached down to touch her apron bottom and skirt. They were both wet as well, but only on one side. Had she been lying sideways on wet ground?

She took a few more reasonable breaths to try and calm herself. Where could she be? There seemed to be sufficient air, but she could also smell the unmistakable odor of rotten eggs. She struggled to remain clearheaded.

An image of Stephen came to her. What would he tell her to do, trapped in this darkness? Then tears flowed as she thought of how horrible his last moments in the mine cave-in must have been, alone in the dark.

The mine.

Could she be in a mine? She squeezed the wet part of her skirt and smelled her fingers. The strong rotten egg smell could be from sulfur run-off. Oh, *mon dieu*! Was she in the underbelly of a mine?

She tried to remember what had happened. Cleaning up the kitchen. The note about Bon.
The mountain path. The hunting cabin. Bon on the floor—and then… what? Had she been knocked to the ground? She couldn't remember anything except seeing Bon lying on the floor. She cried for him and prayed somehow he might still be alive.

Someone had brought her here. But who? How much time had passed? She wasn't sure. Then with a stifled sob, she realized she had most likely missed her graduation. Tears streamed down her face at the unfairness of it all: Stephen's death, her leaving school, being tutored by Josie Canavan…Jonathan. All for naught.

By not arriving for graduation, several people would know something was wrong including Papa. Then the image of Jonathan joking with her at the Philadelphia Zoo came into her mind and a new sob caught in her throat.

Her mouth felt terribly dry and her stomach lurched with queasiness. Who would have done this? Herman Schumn? She didn't think he would be that bold.

Dennis Ackerman. God, could Schumn have associated Ackerman with her? Maybe suggesting he go investigate the Curtain Room had been far more dangerous than she had realized.

And the cabin? Who else would know about it? Randall Meyers would. God, could he be that angry with her for refusing his attentions last summer? Was he the hawk, then, after all?

She tried to collect her galloping thoughts. Her father would organize a search party, but how would they ever be able to find her?

Her first instinct was to get out of the darkness. But in which direction should she move? If she was in a mine and not careful, she could actually push herself deeper into the earth. Not knowing what else to do, she prayed. "Holy Mary, Mother of God. Help me. Saint Anne, patron of families, come to my aid." Exhausted from the ordeal, she lowered herself prone on the damp ground. She needed to rest and conserve her strength. The wet ground, combined with the cool temperature of fifty-seven degrees and her soggy clothes, made her shiver.

Perhaps she should use her apron as a cover. Sitting up and then kneeling, she untied the apron. When she brought the cloth up to cover her shoulders, she nudged a lump of something in the deep pocket. Digging inside, her fingers closed over the note she had found on the table at home, and below that was a small box of kitchen matches!

Saint Anne!

Carefully, she slid the box open and counted eight matches with

her fingers. She almost wept with delight. Hoping there might be more matches in the other pocket she stuck her hand in that one, too. This time she discovered the thin leather strap of bear bells. She had forgotten they were there.

Her two new discoveries gave her hope and bolstered her courage. She realized the eight matches would not last long, so they would have to be used carefully. What she needed was to figure out her surroundings. Carefully, she struck one match. The light did not go out, which indicated sufficient oxygen in the immediate area.

She held the match up and saw the slick walls of black coal all around her, so she was in a mine. Just before the match went out she spied a ledge with some object lying on it. Groping up in the darkness she ran her hand along the ledge until she felt the item. It was metal and by running her fingers over it she realized it was an old miners' lamp.

Shaking it in desperation and hoping that it still held oil, she did not hear any sound of liquid. Sitting back down with the lamp in her lap, she twisted the top off and stuck her fingers down in the compartment where the oil should be.

No oil in the lamp, but there was some greasy substance there. She dug into the grease and then brought her fingers to her nose. Bacon grease! This would be her salvation because bacon grease was flammable.

Thank God Aunt Hulda taught me that.

She would smear the grease on the dry top part of her apron and then use one of the matches to set it on fire. The material would burn, hopefully at a slow pace. Then she would have a torch.

Pulling off her apron she set to work, smearing the grease. The apron however, would need to be attached to something; she could not hold a burning apron in her hands for long.

Using match number two, she held up the light and looked along the ledge. As the match was about to burn out, her eyes detected a piece of wood. She reached the wall and moved forward, groping along the ledge until she found the wood. It felt like the handle to a pick-axe, although it seemed to be broken.

Merci, Ste. Anne.

Kneeling down, she wrapped the cloth around the pick-axe handle, tying it tight with the apron strings. She was about to light the torch when she heard an unusual sound. There was movement near her. Something alive ran over her foot. She screamed. Then it happened again. Whatever it was, it came back and jumped onto her thigh and off again. In a panic she struck out her hand and felt…hair.

A primeval scream tore from her lungs and bellowed into the darkness as hundreds of creatures stampeded over her body. She was being besieged by an army of rats. Desperately she dropped the apron and flailed her arms, striking several of them; but they were quickly replaced by new hordes. Dozens ran up her body and jumped onto her shoulders and then some climbed onto her head. In her panic, she tore out pieces of her hair in the process of striking them down. For the next several minutes she fought desperately for her life.

Then the numbers of rats crawling over her seemed to lessen a bit.

With a sudden clarity she realized the rats were not attacking her, but running over her in a frenzied attempt to escape their present location.

A remembered horror swept over her as she recalled Stephen saying that rats can sense a cave-in or unusually high levels of gas sooner than a miner could. These rats were on the run! She tried to crawl after them, but her skirt and petticoat hampered her movement. She unhooked the skirt and tore both garments off.

From the waist down she now wore only her knickers, stockings and shoes. She knelt and lit the apron-torch and holding it up in the air she began a slow hobbled gait, hunched over, trying to propel herself forward to follow the rats.

Stephen had told her that mines usually have three separate openings, so she could only hope that the rats were heading toward one of those, and not further into the bowels of the mountain.

The rats turned left and she moved after them, holding her apron-torch aloft.

She glanced off to her side and was surprised to see an old rope attached to the ribs of the mine. Frankie had told her that the tunnels had ropes attached to the walls in case a fire broke out. With smoke

so thick that men could not see, the rope would guide them out of the mine.

As long as she followed the rope and the rats, she would hopefully be going toward safety. She had been following the rats for almost ten minutes when her torch started to dim with its remaining fabric. Charred threads dropped to the floor of the mine and the fire went out.

"Dear God, don't leave me in darkness again!" she sobbed.

She grabbed hold of the rope and moved along its slick, worn fibers. Although she could not see the rats, she could hear the colony begin to slow their pace. At the same time, the rope twisted into a new tunnel and in the far distance she saw a small shaft of light. *Mon Dieu*! She scrambled toward the light, even as the rats disappeared into other parts of the mine.

When she reached the beam of light and looked up high, she saw multiple fractured beams of light. Her heart pounded with hope. Fresh air! She wanted to call out for help, but her throat was too dry. Squinting upwards she saw that the daylight was partially blocked by what looked like black strips laid across a hole. She sank to the ground and sobbed in relief.

The modest amount of light allowed her to see that she was in an old mining room. The walls were slick with the oily black sheen from coal residue and the ground had been tramped smooth over the years by the miners who had worked in this space. The pervasive smell of sulphur still hung in the air, but less than where she had started from. At least, thank God, she could stand in this space and not be cramped.

Then she noticed a few old wooden boards lying on the ground not far from her. She crawled over to them and brought them back to the shaft of light. At least this way she could lie down on the wood and not the cold damp mine floor.

Hours later the light slowly disappeared into night as the mountain prepared for sleep. Deep below in the abandoned mine, exhaustion claimed Annie and she too, fell asleep.

*

Louis had been perplexed when he returned home and found Annie gone. Marie pointed out that Annie must have been there because the dishes were done, but Bon was also gone.

By half past five, panic set in. Louis and Marie knew the graduation ceremony meant everything to Annie, and she would never miss it. Louis walked over to Henry Eisner's house and asked if he could borrow the horse and wagon. He, Marie, and Aunt Hulda rode to Mount Pleasant, hoping that Annie might already be at the school.

She wasn't.

Josie Canavan must have seen the look of worry on Louis' face. "Mr. Charbonneau, where's Annie?" she asked.

"We don't know. She would never miss this. I'm worried."

Mr. Conner, the Principal of Mount Pleasant High, motioned for Josie to join him on stage.

"Don't worry. As soon as we give out the diplomas, I'll help you look for her."

The ceremony began, and Louis spied Jonathan Canavan sitting at the back of the auditorium. He was craning his neck and looking around the room. A look of concern spread across his face.

*

As soon as the graduation ended, Josie left the stage and went to the back row to alert her brother. "Jonathan, Annie's missing."

"What do you mean, missing?

Louis and Marie trooped over. "Jonathan, have you seen Annie?"

He shook his head. "She'd never miss graduation. We still have plenty of daylight to search for her. Let's go back to Coal Bank Lane and fan out from there."

While Aunt Hulda stayed at the Charbonneau's house with the hope that Annie might return, the small search party of Jonathan and Josie, Louis and Marie combed the lanes of Lower Porters Glen.

After an hour of an unfruitful search they realized they would need help. The small group ran up Porter Road until they reached Beer

Alley and Murphy's Saloon.

"Mr. Charbonneau, let's ask in here."

Louis and Jonathan entered the saloon filled with miners celebrating another week of working while the strike continued. A dense smoke cloud hung in the air and raucous laughter erupted around the room.

Frank Hennessey stood at the bar and showed genuine surprise at seeing Jonathan walk in, but Louis approached him before he could speak.

"Frank, Annie is missing."

A little into the drink, Frank grinned. "You mean she's missing me!"

A few guffaws sounded from his cronies.

"No, she's missing—gone!"

"We think Annie's in trouble. Have you seen her?" This was from Jonathan.

Frankie turned to face Louis. "Her and me were supposed to see each other tomorrow night. Tonight's the night she's graduating."

"Well, she never showed. Can you help us organize a search for her?"

Frankie quickly sobered. "'Course I can help." He stood up and put two fingers in his mouth and gave a shrill whistle. "Listen up. Annie Charbonneau's missing. We need to start a search party and help look for her. Every man who's available, meet us outside."

The surprised miners put down their unfinished beers and filed out of Murphy's. Marie and Josie were speechless.

"Josie, would you take Marie home? The men will continue searching until we've looked in every corner of Porters Glen." Louis seemed to be aging right in front of their eyes.

As darkness of night took over, there was still no trace of Annie or Bon. The search had to be called off until the next day.

*

She woke sometime early on Saturday morning, stiff and cold. Moving away from the spot where a draft of chilly air descended on her, she rubbed her arms in a futile attempt to get warm. An overwhelming thirst parched her entire system; she needed water.

The light shaft meant she had fresh air, but she needed to attract attention to her location. A bit unsteady, she stood up and retrieved the bear-bells strap in her hand. Methodically she began to swing the leather back and forth, until her arm got weary from the effort. Then she switched hands, summoning a strength that only comes from the drive for survival, and continued to shake the bells until her fingers grew numb.

Weak from lack of food, and disoriented from a lack of hydration, she lay back down to rest. Her body instinctively moved into the fetal position and trembled in despair.

Hours passed and night found her again, still a captive of the mine.

*

By Sunday, Jonathan was almost delirious with worry. They had searched all day Saturday to no avail. Annie had been missing now for over thirty-six hours. He headed over to the Charbonneau's to start searching again.

Jonathan arrived to find Louis drawing up a list of all the possible places Annie might be.

"We'll find her, Mr. Charbonneau. Don't worry."

A scratching noise sounded at the back door. Louis went to investigate.

"*Mon Dieu*! Look, it's Bon!"

Jonathan saw Bon, bedraggled, but very much alive. Louis dropped to the ground and hugged the dog while tears streamed down his face.

"If Bon's still alive, there's strong hope that we'll find Annie."

"Come on Mr. Canavan, we need to tell the searchers that the dog has returned."

"Mr. Charbonneau, under the circumstances, please call me Jonathan."

Louis nodded in accordance.

Jonathan and Louis took Bon with them as they met the search-

ers and talked about which direction to take. Bon began to bark repeatedly and turn his head toward Piney Ridge.

"I'm not sure why, but it looks like he wants to go to Piney Ridge."

"You're right. Let's head there." Louis paused. "Thank you, Jonathan, for caring about Annie."

Men and women from Miners Row joined to help, along with a few representatives from the CVC. Frankie Hennessey was leading the search group from Mount Pleasant as the searchers fanned out over Piney Ridge. Louis joined that group.

Bon loped up the trail ahead of everyone and struck out to the left, so Jonathan followed. Jonathan was breathless as he ran to catch up to Bon, who was now standing in front of a hunting cabin. The door of the hunting cabin hung ajar. Jonathan ran in, but there was no evidence of Annie having been here.

Robby Meyers arrived on his own. "Can I help, Mr. Canavan? I know this mountain cause me and Bon played tag up here."

Jonathan gave the go-ahead sign to the boy. "All right, let's see where Bon goes."

About a quarter of a mile from the old abandoned Sands Mine, Jonathan saw Bon stop in his tracks. A faint tinkling of bells sounded deep in the earth, but the noise was too dim for Jonathan to hear.

Bon's ears stood up on full alert.

No one in the search party noticed, except for Robby Meyers.

"What is it, Bon?"

The dog cocked his head and then bolted through the forest with Robby Meyers running behind.

"Robby!" Jonathan yelled.

"I think Bon's picked up her trail." Robby yelled back.

Jonathan took off through the woods after them.

"Robby, why would she be up here?" Jonathan gasped.

Robby didn't respond, but neither did he falter. He kept breaking through the bushes following Bon, and so did Jonathan.

When the dog stopped, he pawed the earth near some old earthen timbers, and then he tipped his head and let out a series of

howls.

Robby and Jonathan reached the old timber planks and looked around, but saw nothing.

"Annie!" Jonathan shouted with all his might. A moment later he heard the weak tinkling of a bell. He yelled out her name again. "Annie!" But there was no response.

At this point, Bon let out a howl that raised the hairs on Jonathan's neck.

"She's gotta be down there, Mister Canavan." Robby pointed to some openings between the timbers.

"What do you mean? You think she's down there?"

"Dogs howl to communicate. I read it in a book Miss Annie gave me. So she must be down there." The boy pointed again to the timbers.

Jonathan got down on his hands and knees and cupped his hands around his mouth. "Annie!" he shouted through one of the openings and heard his voice echo in the space below. "Annie, can you hear me?"

A faint but dim response of bells sounded, and his heart beat wild with hope.

Jonathan stood up and blew three short blasts on a whistle. From far, two blast answers were given. In a matter of minutes, the forest was swarming with women and men running through the trees toward the three blast signal.

Louis Charbonneau was the first to reach Jonathan, closely followed by Frankie.

"Have you found her?"

"We think she's down there." He pointed to the opening. "I don't know how, but I think she's got a bell with her. When I yelled her name, the tinkling of a bell sounded."

Louis sank to his knees, looking like he might vomit. "What is this?" Shaking, he pointed to the opening.

"It's a narrow air shaft," responded Frankie. "Some of the old abandoned mines never had their shafts closed up. This must be one of them."

"How can we get her out?"

Frankie turned toward Jonathan, but said nothing.

"Listen, Frank. This isn't the time for us to be on opposite sides. The only thing that matters is that we save her." Jonathan's voice was firm.

Frankie nodded. "We can pull up the timbers and enlarge the opening to bring her out. But she's been missing for two days, so she must need water."

"Can we drop a canteen down to her?"

"If she's too weak to talk, Mr. Charbonneau, she might be close to unconscious and not able to reach a canteen."

No one spoke as fear squeezed itself into the group.

"If you make the hole a little bigger and tie a rope around me, I can be lowered into the shaft." The group turned to the speaker. It was Robby Meyers.

"It would be dangerous and we couldn't do that without your Pa's permission." Charlie Lancaster shook his head.

"My dad's searching up here, too, and I know he'd give his permission. If Miss Annie needs water like you say, then you gotta lower me down right now. We can't wait."

As more members of the rescue party came upon the scene, some had rope, others had shovels, and some of the women were carrying canteens. A team of men set to work digging a larger opening and scooping dirt from the upper sides of the shaft. From time to time shovelfuls of dirt dropped into the mine, but there was no response from below. Finally, the digging team used a substantial tree branch to scrape off dirt from the walls of the narrow shaft.

"Even if we get Robby down there, how can we get Annie out?"

"There are three entrances, Mr. Charbonneau. I think I can find one of them. Maybe some of the older miners know the closest one."

"Thank God, Frank, you're here." The long lines of worry across Louis's face had deepened over the course of the two days.

Working together, the men tied a rope under Robby Meyers' armpits and secured a water canteen to his belt and lowered him down into the hole.

"I can see Miss Annie," the boy shouted. "But she's not moving and she looks like she's asleep."

"Robby," Frankie called down into the opening. "Get down close to her ear and whisper-talk to her. Tell her she's safe. Tell her who you are and that you have water. Then open the canteen, pour just a bit on your fingers, and gently rub your wet fingers over her lips."

"All right." The shout echoed back.

*

Robby touched solid ground and bent down next to Annie's ear. "Miss Annie, it's me— Robby Meyers. I'm here and Bon's up above on the ground and you're safe now. Everyone says you need water, and I'm gonna open this canteen and put a few drops on your lips. I'm gonna have to get real close to your face because I don't have my glasses on, but don't be scared 'cause I would never hurt you."

Her eyelids fluttered. Robby shook out a few drops of water and gently caressed her lips with the moisture. He repeated the task again and again.

"What's happening down there?" Louis shouted.

"I'm giving her the water, but she's not really opening her eyes."

Then Robby crawled behind her and gently lifted her shoulders. He slowly squeezed in the space and let her head and shoulders rest against him. "I'm not gonna leave you, Miss Annie, so don't worry. I'm going to give you a few more drops of water, this time on your tongue."

*

Two hours later Frankie, Jonathan, and three miners finally broke through a closed-up opening to the abandoned mine, carrying a blanket to use as a stretcher. Self-made torches helped them see their way through the tunnels. All the while they kept shouting to Robby, and he yelled back.

When they found him, he was still sitting on the mine floor, bracing Annie in his arms. Her arms and legs were bloodied, and she

appeared to be going into shock.

The men lifted Annie onto the blanket and Robby whispered in her ear, “I love you Miss Annie, and you’re goin’ be all right.”

The procession threaded their way back out of the mine with Robby Meyers following them. Almost unconscious, Annie mumbled only one word—“Jonathan.”

CHAPTER 31

Andrew Walker, age 9, fall of top coal,
Lord Mine.

Herman Schumn watched the rescue unfold. He was positioned high on Piney Ridge and could see the search teams, but they couldn't see him.

When he spied the boy being lowered into the air shaft, he stomped his foot like Rumpelstiltskin. "Damn it! She didn't deserve to be rescued!"

His eyes smoldered with remembered anger from his past.

Betty Sue Henderson. She'd had eyes the color of mountain pine and long, loose black hair. He had fallen in love with her at the age of fifteen. Her sordid reputation did nothing to prevent that folly, and he invited Betty Sue to the shack he shared with his mother.

As they walked in, Betty Sue asked him what all the shoes lined up against the wall were for. He hemmed and hawed but could not think of a polite answer. Then she laughed, telling him she already knew. She pointed at the shoes and said, "You'll have to offer me more than just a pair of shoes to get what you want." When he didn't respond, she turned and walked out the door, leaving Herman to nurse a bruised ego.

The sound of her humiliating laughter still rang in his ears, even now, and he had vowed never again to allow any female to disgrace him.

Schumn looked down on the scene. At least the Charbonneau girl would not be able to accuse him of abduction. He'd made sure she hadn't seen him hiding behind the door. It had been easy. He darted over and covered her mouth and nose with a chloroform-soaked rag. He held her in a vise grip until she became unconscious.

Furious now, he turned away from the scene of her rescue and stormed off into the woods. Leaving Porters Glen, was now a necessity. Thank God he didn't trust banks; all his money had been hidden in an innocent looking miners' lunch pail back at the boarding house. With the commotion surrounding Anne's disappearance, he'd brought the pail with him today—just in case his landlady got it in her mind to snoop in his room.

By tomorrow morning the CVC would realize he was gone, but by then, no one would be able to trace him.

Climbing through the woods, with the miner's pail tucked under his arm, he came across an old path. Stepping out onto it, he found the trail blocked by a small bear cub.

"Scram," he snarled. The cub blinked its dark eyes, but stayed put. "I said, scram, you dumb shit." Still the cub did not move. Schumn picked up a rock and threw it with perfect aim and hit the cub on its muzzle. The unmistakable sound of an animal whimpering in pain echoed off the trees.

Within seconds Schumn heard a crashing sound. He looked up to see a female black bear thundering toward the cub.

It took the she-bear only a moment to see that her cub had been hurt. Even if he had been armed, Schumn was no match for the massive animal. Rearing up to a height of five feet, she let out a bellow that was the last audible sound Schumn heard. She crashed down and in a few steps swiped her huge right paw against his shoulder. He fell. Instinctively she went for his throat, ripping open his jugular vein. Not stopping there, she clawed open his abdomen—exposing his intestines. By the time she finished, his mauled body lay crumpled on the ground. The smell of fresh blood saturated the air.

The mother-bear went over and nosed her cub, then licked his

face. She nudged him, and lumbering by his side, the two moved off the path and back into the safety of the deep woods.

Schumn was now one with the forest.

*

Due to Annie's youth and good health she recovered quickly, although she remembered little about her rescue. Having been nearly unconsciousness as they carried her out of the mine, her memory was vague.

Everyone told Annie how lucky she had been, and no one mentioned the graduation ceremony that had gone on without her. A week after the rescue, Josie brought her the coveted document proclaiming that Anne Thérese Charbonneau had been awarded a high school diploma from Mt. Pleasant High School. It was dated June 15, 1894.

Dr. Tanner checked on Annie every few days and declared with complete assurance that after a week of rest she could resume her normal activities. Thankfully, no lasting damage had occurred, and her hair would grow back where the pieces had been torn out by the episode with the rats.

*

The Fourth of July started with heat so heavy that no one even felt like eating. Annie pulled the kitchen curtain aside to coax any possible puff of breeze to enter the house. Looking into the yard, she took a moment to think about all the events of the past few weeks. The strike had ended last week with the coal companies not budging on the lower pay and the union organizers had gone back to Ohio. Her letter from the Philadelphia Quakers meant she would be able to continue teaching and give out free shoes next winter. Come fall, she still hoped to enroll in college.

Then, Frankie unexpectedly showed up at the front door.

"Hi, Frankie. I wasn't expecting you."

He stood twirling his baseball cap. "I'm playing a game this afternoon at the Fourth of July Fair."

"Of course. I remember from last summer."

There was a strained silence that hung in the air between them.

"You know the strike is over."

"Yes, I heard that."

"We didn't get our pay rate re-instated after all."

"I'm sorry about that, Frankie, but at least no one was hurt."

The conversation stalled, until Annie continued it. "Which team are you playing against this time?"

"The Borden Boys."

"I don't feel much like going to watch. I hope you understand."

"No, I kinda figured that. Annie…"

"Frankie, wait. You deserve the truth from me. It's not just the baseball game. You're a wonderful person. And it's not that I don't care about you, because I do. It's just…I don't see us spending the rest of our lives together."

There, she had come clean.

"I've been expecting you to say something like this." He drew in a sharp breath. "I think I've known it for some time, but I guess I was holding out hope." Frankie swallowed. "You'll always be special to me, Annie. I hope you know that."

She nodded.

He bent down and lightly kissed her cheek, then slowly walked out the door and away from her life.

Annie felt hot tears trickling down her face. She wiped them away with her fingers, wondering if she was crying for something lost, or something gained.

Jonathan had not come by, and although it stung, she had to honor his decision. The last time they had seen each other, he had stalked off away from her. His message had been clear. But when she'd been trapped in the mine, clearly aware that she might die, her only regret was the possibility of never seeing Jonathan again.

On impulse, she walked out the door and through the hilly meadow shortcut to Mount Pleasant. The summer sun and even the heat made her feel alive again, and her legs craved the exercise. Without planning it, she soon appeared at the Fourth of July grounds.

The fields were crowded with people celebrating the holiday.

Annie scanned the area and saw the gypsy woman's table. She walked over and sat down in front of her. The gypsy smiled and shuffled the cards. "Pretty lady want to see me again?"

"I do. I want you to read the cards for me one more time. There is an important decision I have to make."

The gypsy woman smiled a crescent moon. "The two men, am I right?"

Annie just shrugged her shoulders and dug in her pocket for two pennies.

The woman leaned across the table and gently folded Annie's fingers into a closed fist. "You do not need the cards. You already know which one holds your heart and will give you the child you will love. Go home, pretty girl. You do not need me. The answer you seek is in here." She placed a closed fist over Annie's heart.

Annie let out a deep breath. "Thank you. Will you be here again next year?"

"I go where the cards lead me."

Annie's mouth twisted into a wistful smile, suspecting she would never see the gypsy again.

But then, she really didn't need to.

She walked back down the Pike to Porters Glen and boldly went to the Eisner's boarding house, and asked if Mr. Canavan was in. Mrs. Eisner asked Annie to sit while she summoned him.

Annie turned as Jonathan walked into the parlor.

"Jonathan. There's something you need to hear from me."

He crossed the room and without hesitation gathered her into his arms. "I heard the words I needed when we brought you out of the mine. The only word you spoke was my name."

"It was? I didn't know that."

"I've been waiting for you to come back to me. So I would know for sure." He kissed her long and hard and Annie tasted the sweetness of love reborn.

*

A week later Annie sat in the audience of the Mount Pleasant Town Hall. Louis had accompanied her with the explanation that the town council had announcements about the fall class of Mount Pleasant College. After a short business session conducted by the mayor, Annie was completely surprised to see Jonathan climb on stage. She hadn't realized he was in the back of the room.

"It is my extreme pleasure, on behalf of the School Board, to present a gift of thanks to Miss Annie Charbonneau for her valiant efforts in establishing an English class in Porters Glen." Then he beckoned for Annie to come forward.

Not sure what to do, and blushing from the attention, Annie got up from her seat and joined him on stage as the audience clapped. "This certificate from the school board is awarding you the first ever scholarship to attend Mount Pleasant College, tuition free, for a two-year program to pursue certification in teaching."

The crowd erupted into thunderous applause, and the twenty miners' wives with whom Annie had faced the mob, all gave her a standing ovation.

Annie wanted to throw her arms around Jonathan but restrained herself and grinned at him instead. From the back of the hall, Frankie Hennessey quietly slipped outside and headed in the direction of McAllister's Saloon.

Jonathan's face beamed with pride. "Annie, let me drive you home."

"Drive? Jonathan, you have a wagon now?"

"I have a wagon for tonight. And if we don't use it, then I bet that Josie and Randall Meyers will."

"Randall Meyers?"

He grinned.

Annie tried not to show her surprise and only hoped that Randall Meyers would turn out to be the right man for Josie.

Jonathan helped Annie up into the borrowed farm wagon and they drove down the Pike heading to Porters Glen. They passed the bakery and the horse turned right into Beer Alley and eventually onto Porter Road. Jonathan slowed the horse to a stop next to Squirrel Creek where the orange hawkweed had grown profuse around the fences.

"Jonathan, we're not home yet."

"I know. Let's get out here for a moment; I have a surprise for you."

He helped her down from the wagon. "Remember back in January we stopped here, and I held your back so you could look up into the winter sky and find the constellation Cassiopeia?"

"Yes."

"I want you to look and see if you can find it again. I'll still hold your back."

"It's like an M, right? Will it be in the same spot?"

"I'll point you in the right direction."

As Annie strained to find the star pattern in the early night sky, she heard the horse whinny and she could feel Jonathan's strong arms supporting her. "There it is, Jonathan, I found her." She pointed up to the constellation.

"And look what I found." He turned her around to face him and held out a small parcel wrapped in brown paper. "It's a package from Philadelphia."

"From whom?"

"Daniel."

"Well, it's addressed to you, Jonathan, so open it."

Jonathan peeled off the paper to reveal a palm-sized plain box. "Now you open the box."

As Annie opened it, Jonathan bent down on one knee.

Her eyes darted from the contents of the box to his bent form. "Oh, Jonathan!"

"Annie Charbonneau, there should be a piece of jewelry in there, and this question goes with it. *Veus-tu m'ëpousseter*?"

Her hand flew to cover her mouth, and she burst out laughing.

"Whoa! What's so funny?"

"You just asked me to dust you!" She flew to him, knocking him to the ground. "I think, I hope, you meant something else!"

He stood up laughing and shook the dirt off his trousers. "Now I do have to be dusted. I wanted to impress you and ask you in French. But I should have just said it in English. Annie Charbonneau, will you

marry me?"

"Yes, yes, and *oui*!"

They kissed a long soulful kiss with the promise of the future together.

A few moments later Annie peeked in the box. "Oh, Jonathan. They're beautiful, too."

He looked puzzled. "It should only be my mother's wedding band. I had Daniel retrieve it from our safety deposit box so I could give it to you."

"Yes, it's here, but so are these." She held up a pair of amethyst cuff links.

"I don't understand. Is there a note?" She took a slim piece of paper from under the jewelry and handed it to Jonathan.

Dear Jonathan,

Your mother's ring is in here, just like you asked. I wish I could see Annie's face when you propose. The cuff links were my father's, and I believe he wore them at his wedding when he married my mother, Ellen Canavan. I do know they're real amethysts. You are the first of our generation to be married, so I want you to wear them at your wedding. Katie and I send our love.

Your Cousin,

Daniel

"Oh, Jonathan, I can't believe that Daniel thought ahead to our wedding day."

"And that day can't come soon enough." He swept her into his arms and kissed her under the moonlight.

Then she stepped back and shouted up to the sky, "Hey, Cassiopeia: I'm going to college, I'm getting shoes for the children on Miners' Row, and I'm marrying the man I love!"

Cassiopeia and her army of stars winked down on them.

*

A few weeks later, Alberto Morelli was hunting on Piney Ridge, hoping to shoot a deer. He had invited the widow, Katharina Messerschmidt, to come for dinner with his family. Shouldering his rifle, he found the old animal path and followed it up the mountain. Turning a corner, he stumbled upon some human remains with pieces of clothing sticking out from the skeleton. Bending down he noticed what looked like a handkerchief, now soiled with dried blood. Peering closer he discerned three poorly stitched initials, *HES*, and nodded his head. "So this is where you disappeared to, Schumn."

As he straightened up, a shaft of sunlight glistened off a piece of metal partially hidden nearby. Alberto went to investigate. He knelt down and found the metal was an old miners' lunch pail. "What the hell is this doing up here?" he thought. Opening the pail, he was amazed to find a substantial amount of cash laid inside.

My God! He looked back at the skeleton and then at the pail once more.

"There's no name on this, so who knows who it really belongs to." He took the cash out and stuffed it in his overall pockets. "If I am careful, and dole this out bit by bit, no one will ever know. My children will never go hungry again. Neither will Katharina Messerschmidt."

Then Alberto unbuttoned his fly and proceeded to urinate on the bones. When he was finished, he closed his fly and picked up his rifle.

"That was for Rosa."

*

The disappearance of Herman Schumn was talked about for months, as well as the memorable scene of twenty women advancing on the Cumberland Valley Coal Office, all armed with scissors.

Led by Annie Charbonneau, soon to become Mrs. Jonathan Canavan, they marched inside the building and went directly upstairs to the Curtain Room. As a group, they began to hack away at the curtain until nothing remained but ragged threads.

Annie climbed on a chair and slashed the last bits from the

supporting rod. She watched as the shredded strips fell to the floor. The women scooped up every last bit of the fabric debris and walked outside. In full view of everyone on the street, they set fire to the thread pile until nothing remained but ashes.

A hawk sliced through the sky overhead, and the wind tore down into the valley. In one decisive gust, the air current changed direction and blew the ashes off toward Piney Ridge.

It was the last curtain call.

THE END

Linda Harris Sittig
April 2016
Purcellville, Virginia

AUTHOR'S NOTES

The question always asked is, "Which parts of this story were true?"

I based the novel on the actual 1894 coal mining strike of western Allegany County, Maryland.

While all of the facts concerning the mines and the mining strike were accurate, I added additional characters and detailed events to bring the tale to life.

The village of Porters Glen is a fictitious composite drawn from numerous coal communities in Pennsylvania, Maryland, and West Virginia, but mostly based upon the real village of Eckhart Mines, in Western Maryland—one of the three communities that refused to participate in the 1894 strike. It was the women of Eckhart Mines who did face a vigilante mob and whose bravery was detailed in stirring accounts by the journalists of the *Baltimore Sun*.

Western Allegany County residents will most likely recognize that the town of Mount Pleasant is based upon Frostburg, and Riverton is based on Cumberland. The college of Mount Pleasant, though, was my invention because Frostburg's State Normal School was not built until the late 1890s.

To insure authenticity, I spent time in former and contemporary coal areas from eastern Pennsylvania to the hollows of Appalachia. I even descended into a coal mine so I could understand both Stephen's claustrophobia and Annie's near death experience.

In my research I discovered that the sport of baseball was actually written as base ball until the mid-1890s. However, I decided to stay with the modern version of the name, so as not to confuse readers. I also discovered that disposable aluminum pie tins did not exist until after 1900. So what would a rural baker do if a customer wanted the whole pie? He took a deposit for the tin until the customer returned it!

Both the Charbonneau family and the Hennessey family were real, as was Hennessey's Store and Charbonneau's Bakery. I was fortunate enough to be able to interview several of the family descendants for colorful snippets of life in Frostburg and Eckhart when coal had dominated the economy. However, I changed the actual family names to protect the privacy of existing family members today.

Even though the incident of the women and the vigilante mob was well documented by the *Baltimore Sun*, none of the women involved were ever identified in print. I chose to create Annie Charbonneau as my protagonist and have the story told through her eyes. I modeled her after a real girl from Eckhart Mines.

I felt Annie would have been a natural choice to marry into the Canavan family. In real life, Magdalena Canavan gave birth to two daughters, not boy-girl twins as in this novel. By inventing a Canavan son instead, I was able to have him meet Annie Charbonneau from Eckhart Mines and thus continue the Canavan legacy.

The real Canavan family members of Philadelphia, as we met them in the first book of this series (*Cut From Strong Cloth*), began to die in the decade after the Civil War. Patrick Canavan died first, then Cecilia Canavan, and Ellen Canavan Nolan in 1873. Magdalena Canavan died in the early 1880s and James Nolan in the early 1890s. Other than Magdalena's children, the second generation included Daniel Nolan (son of Ellen Canavan and James Nolan) and Catherine "Katie" Nolan (daughter of James Nolan and his second wife, Sarah Jane Brady).

The character of Herman Schumn was invented, but represented the real misuse of power through The Curtain Room. While there was no actual Curtain Room in Eckhart Mines, rooms like that did exist in many coal mining communities—usually where the superin-

tendent forced the miners and their families to shop exclusively in the company store for all their needs.

I visited an intact, but non-functioning, company store in Appalachia where a Curtain Room had actually been located on the second level.

When I heard the story of that Curtain Room and the degradations of the women who had been forced to visit it, I knew I had to include it in my novel. I was determined that the miners' wives in my story would triumph over its evil.

My research indicated that Curtain Rooms existed in the coal mining villages of France, before the custom ever came to America. Unfortunately, the concept of a Curtain Room still exists today in various forms around the world wherever women are sexually exploited.

Lastly, the amethyst cuff links that Daniel Nolan loaned to Jonathan Canavan were actually worn by Daniel on his wedding day, June 30, 1909, to Mary Alice Quinn of Philadelphia. Because Daniel and Mary Alice never had any children, Daniel showered his affections on his sister Katie's only child, Mildred—my mother.

My mother inherited the cuff links along with the Nolan factory chest and many other family items. When I became engaged, my mother took the cuff links to a jeweler and had them made into earrings for me to wear at my wedding. Thirty years later I had the earrings made into two identical rings, so that each of our twin daughters could wear them at their weddings.

It is my hope that our granddaughters, Chambers and Avery, will continue the tradition when they inherit the amethysts, and be the sixth generation to wear them.

We leave Book Two here and look ahead to Book Three which will tell the story of Annie and Jonathan's daughter, Maggie, and bring the series, "Threads of Courage", full circle.

ACKNOWLEDGEMENTS

I am indebted to my Beta Readers, who read the first early draft and gave valuable input: Katie Conaway, Holly Day, Kathy Marsh, Mary Jo Price, and Pam Williams.

Thank you to independent editor, Ramona De Felice Long, and David Hazard, my writing coach. Both of you made the story stronger.

Feelings of pure gratitude go to my publisher, Eric Egger of Freedom Forge Press, and my awesome editor, Val Muller.

Thank you to my two wonderful writing groups, The Round Hill Writers and The St. Simon Island Writers, who have provided professional and moral support for years.

MARYLAND

Allegany County: Thank you to the staffs of Allegany College of Maryland Library, Cumberland Public Library, Frostburg Public Library, Lonaconing Public Library, and the Land Records Office of the Allegany County Courthouse.

Eckhart Mines: Thank you to the following people who grew up in Eckhart Mines and allowed me to interview them: Erma Jean Baker, Tom Chabot, Eileen Cumiskey, Mary Louise Sittig, Ed Tippen, and Robert Wright. A second thank you goes to Maria Cosner who allowed me inside her original home on Miners Row.

Frostburg: The Frostburg Museum was invaluable—especially

Liz Eshelman and Ralph Bender. Mary Jo Price and Pam Williams from the Ort Library, and Jeff Snyder, Bureau of Mines provided various maps and schematics of the mines in the area. Matt McMorran and the Frostburg Fire Department helped me with the history of the Fourth of July parades. Polla Horn from the Adopt-a-Miner Project provided all the miners' obituaries at the beginning of each chapter.

Kitzmiller: Debbie Brady of the Kitzmiller Coal Museum and her father, former coal miner George Brady, shared their memories and walked with us through the streets so I would have a visual connection to living in a coal village.

Mt. Savage: Dennis Lashley provided me with first hand narratives of coal miners. Janice Keene of Evergreen allowed me to walk the old coal tram road on the Evergreen property.

A big thank you goes to Dr. Anthony Crosby, Sandra Pantall, and all the folks of the Council of the Alleghenies who have diligently published *The Journal of the Alleghenies*, chronicling life in Western Maryland throughout the centuries.

Thank you, Liz McDowell of the Maryland Native Plant Society, for your help in determining which plants would have actually been in existence in the area around Eckhart, and up on Piney Ridge.

Many thanks go to the following writers who penned their stories about coal mining in Western Allegany County: Lilian Boughton, Nanci Bross, Francis S. Decker, Joseph P. Drum, Harry E. Eckhart, Al Feldstein, Walter Festerman, Paul L. Footen, Curtis B. Haines, Juanita Isiminger, Mary Meyers, Joe Martarano, Olive Patton, Jim Race, James Rada, Margie Grim Runion, Bucky Shriver, Pat Stakem, and Betty Van Newkirk. I read every single article or book you wrote.

But most especially I am indebted to the late Katherine Harvey whose book, *The Best-Dressed Miners*, started me on my novel journey researching the women of Eckhart who had faced an angry mob of strikers in 1894.

PENNSYLVANIA

Eckley: This living museum coal town was where the *The Molly Maguires* was filmed. Each building housed so many authentic artifacts

that I felt myself going back in time with Annie Charbonneau.

Philadelphia: Lynn Calamia who showed me around the Arch Street Meeting House and pointed out so many wonderful details about Quaker worship. Greg Barnes of the Arch Street Meeting House who read through my manuscript to make sure my details of Annie with the Quakers would be realistic and correct.

A delicious thanks to the Alexander Inn of Philadelphia where I ate the Philadelphia raisin buns!

WEST VIRGINIA

Beckley: LeRoy White took me down into a coal mine and Joy Lynn took me on a tour of the former Whipple Store.

WASHINGTON, D.C. AREA

I am indebted to Mike Copperthite of the Connecticut-Copperthite Pie Baking Company for helping me authenticate behind the scenes workings of a bakery at the turn of the century.

Thank you to Anthony and Barbara Chavez, owners of Layered Cake Patisserie, who gave me invaluable details about the life of a French baker.

REFERENCE MATERIALS

This is a partial list of the many books I read while researching. Each one contributed to my understanding of coal mining, and/or French food.

A Coal Miner's Bride, Susan Campbell Bartoletti, 2000, Scholastic.

All That Mattered, Barbara Angle, 1994, Crown.

An Ethnic Mosaic Cookbook, Jacqueline Berger, Eckley Miners' Association.

Coal, A Human Story, Barbara Freese, 2003, Penguin.

Coal Mining and Railroads, Al Feldstein, 1999, Commercial Press.

Cooking the Coalwood Way, 2002, Coalwood Community United Methodist Church.

Green Glades and Sooty Gob Piles, Donna M. Ware, 1991, Maryland Historical Trust.

Growing Up in Coal Country, Susan Campbell Bartoletti, 1996, Houghton Mifflin.

Our Story, Jeff Goodell, 2002, Hyperion.

Patchtown, Jolene Busher, 2011, Sunbury Press.

Rocket Boys, Homer H. Hickam, Jr. 1998, Dell Publishing.

Saving Shalimar, James Rada, Jr. 2012, Legacy Publishing.

The Best-Dressed Miners, Katherine A. Harvey, 1969, Cornell University Press.

The Cuisine of Alsace, Pierre Gaertner and Robert Frédérick, 1981, Barron's, Inc.

The Little French Bakery Cookbook, Susan M. Holding, 2014, Skyhorse Publishing.

The Molly Maguires, James O'Neill, 1969, Fawcett Publishing.

The Philadelphia Cookbook, Anna Wetherill Reed, 1963, Clarkson M. Potter.

Wanamaker's, Michael J. Lisicky, 2010, The History Press.

Whisper Hollow, Chris Cander, 2015, Other Press.

Wish You Well, David Baldacci, 2000, Warner Books.

In conclusion, a huge thank you to the anonymous woman in an Appalachian store who whispered to me, "Please tell them about the Curtain Room." Those words launched Annie's quest.

As always, I am continually grateful to my husband, Jim Sittig, for his assistance and unwavering support of my writing. Many, many years ago, he brought me to the mountains of Western Maryland and pointed out where his great-grandfather's bakery had once stood in the small coal village of Eckhart Mines. Little did I know; I was standing in the setting of a future novel.

GLOSSARY

Advent – the four weeks preceding Christmas
Aidez-moi – French for help me
Bastille Day – French Independence Day
Blackdamp – mixture of carbon dioxide and nitrogen
Blackleg – a miner who works in spite of a strike
Bowler – man's hard felt hat with dome shaped crown
Brioche – rich, buttery, yeast bun
Bonjour – French for good morning
Bon Nuit – French for good night
Café au lait – French morning coffee laced with steamed milk.
Cassoulet – a slow cooked stew of white beans and various forms of pork
Charlotte Russe – a cake made of ladyfingers filled with custard and topped with fruit
Chien miserable – French for miserable dog
Chocolate chaud – French for hot chocolate
Crème glacée au chocolat – French for chocolate ice cream
Croissant – a crescent shaped flaky pastry
Diebinnen – German for thieves.
Fedora – wool hat with a dented crown
Gob pile – a pile of coal mine refuse
Half turn – when a young miner picks half of a full load

Hopper – railroad car to transport coal
Jambon en croûte – French for ham pie
Kirsch – cherry flavored liquor
Kugelhopf – sweet, raisin filled Bundt cake
Ma petite chou – French term of endearment
Madeleines – small French butter cakes thought of as cookies
Mantrip – car carrying the men into the mine
Masticot – French for maggot
Merci – French for thank you
Milk bread rolls – traditional dinner rolls made with milk
Mon Dieu – French for my God
On the book – paying by extended credit
Oui – French for yes
Pâte Brissée – a pie dough
Petit-four – a very small cake made as one serving
Peut-être – French for perhaps
Ponhaus – German type of fried, meat flavored mush
Potage aux Champignons – French for mushroom soup
Potage au Lait – French for milk soup
Potage aux Lentilles – French for lentil soup
Santé – French for to your health
Scabs – men who continue to work during a strike
Shirtwaist - blouse
Tarte à la Rhubarbe – French for rhubarb pie
Teapot light – a type of coal lantern fixed to the front of the miner's cap and fueled by grease
Tipple – the building used to load the coal for transport
Tram road – a flat pathway leading from the coal mine to the tipple
Trapper – young boys employed to open and close ventilation doors in the mines
Un jour sans pain – French, literally a day without bread, or a very long day

*

Rhubarb Tart with American and French Measurements:

1 pound (500 g) of rhubarb stalks
2/3 cup (150 g) superfine sugar
½ cup (113 g) sliced strawberries
1 cup (1/4 L) heavy cream
Pâte Brisée = 1 recipe of pie dough
2 large eggs

Weigh all ingredients and set aside. Wash rhubarb and cut into small slender strips. Toss the rhubarb with 2 tablespoons of sugar and let sit. Wash, hull, and slice the strawberries, then mix in with the rhubarb. Let the fruit rest as you prepare a Pâte *Brisée* and line a tarte pan with the pie dough. Using a slotted spoon, spoon out the fruit mixture over the dough. Bake in hot oven for 20 minutes. Beat the eggs, add cream, remaining sugar, and a spoonful of kirsch. Remove pie from oven and pour the cream mixture over the fruit. Bake for an additional 15 to 20 minutes.

*

Pâte Brisée

2 cups (250 g) all-purpose flour
½ teaspoon (5 g) salt
½ cup (125 g) butter, cut into small pieces
1 egg yolk
1/3 cup water

Mix flour and salt. Cut butter into the flour until the mixture resembles small pebbles. Add egg yolk and water. Mix well with fork. Knead the dough until it forms into a small ball. Wrap in wax paper and chill until ready to use, usually about 2 hours. When ready, roll out the dough on a floured surface to about ¾ inch thick. Transfer to pie pan.

*

Potage aux Lentilles or Lentil Soup

1 ½ cup (300 g) lentils
1 onion
1 large potato
2 ½ quarts of water
Salt and pepper

Soak the lentils for 1 hour while chopping the onion and peeling potato. Once the lentils have soaked and have been drained, add chopped onion with small chunks of peeled potato, and the water. Bring the soup to a boil, then reduce heat to a simmer and cook for 90 minutes to 2 hours.

*

Philadelphia Cinnamon Buns

1 cake of yeast
¼ cup warm water
1 cup scalded milk
2 cups of flour, sifted
½ cup sugar
¼ cup melted butter
½ teaspoon salt
2 egg yolks
6 tablespoons brown sugar
2 teaspons cinnamon
½ cup raisins
1 pound brown sugar and ¾ cup of Karo syrup

Dissolve yeast in warm water and add to the cooled, scalded milk. Stir in the flour and set mixture aside till it bubbles (approximately half an hour). Then add sugar, melted butter, salt and yolks. Mix well, adding a slight amount more of flour to make a light batter. Turn out onto floured pastry board and knead well for 10 minutes. Place in a bowl, lightly brush some melted butter on top. Cover the bowl and let rise in a warm place for 90 minutes, or until doubled in size. Divide the dough in half, working with one half at a time. Roll dough on floured board into a rectangle ¼ inch thick and approximately 15 inches long. Brush with melted butter. Stir together the brown sugar, cinnamon, and raisins. Spread evenly over the batter. Roll up in jelly-roll fashion and cut into 1 and ½ inch slices. Butter a deep baking tin and sprinkle in the 1 pound of brown sugar. Pour the Karo evenly over the sugar. Place the buns flat side down in the pan with all the buns close together. Brush with melted butter and let rise in a warm space for another 30 – 45 minutes. Bake at 325 heat for 45 minutes. Turn out immediately when finished baking.

About the Author

Born in Greenwich Village, New York City, and raised in Northern New Jersey, Linda was lured into reading by *Lad, a Dog* and *Nancy Drew, Girl Detective*. Later her attraction to history and a bit of wanderlust led her to study in Switzerland, before returning stateside to earn a B.A. in History and a M.Ed. in Reading. Linda eventually chose to live in Loudoun County, Virginia, where the beauty of the Blue Ridge Mountains inspires her to write.

Combining her passion for history, stories, and the need for literacy, she began publishing commentaries on how parents could encourage the love of reading with their children. That led to a twenty-year weekly newspaper column, "KinderBooks" (*Loudoun Times-Mirror*); a non-fiction text, *New Kid in School* (Teachers College Press); and writing for a nationally syndicated educational newsletter, *The Connection* (PSK Associates).

Linda has been twice recognized by the Virginia Press Association with Certificates of Merit for her journalism. Her articles have appeared in *The Washington Post*, *The Reston Connection*, and *The Purcellville Gazette*, in addition to numerous professional journals and short story anthologies. Passionate about lesser known women in history who led extraordinary lives, Linda blogs monthly at www.strongwomeninhistory.wordpress.com, and has followers in over 64 countries.

From 1982 – 1994 Linda received three separate distinguished

educator awards from metropolitan, state, and international organizations. She continues to teach at Shenandoah University in Winchester, VA, where she works with educators on how to immerse literature into children's lives.

Contact email: Linda@LindaSittig.com
Website: www.LindaSittig.com
Blog: www.strongwomeninhistory.wordpress.com
Twitter: @lhsittig

"Every woman deserves to have her story told."

Freedom Forge Press

About Us

Freedom Forge Press, LLC, was founded to celebrate freedom and the spirit of the individual. The founders of the press believe that when people are given freedom—of expression, of speech, of thought, of action—creativity and achievement will flourish.

Freedom Forge Press publishes general fiction, historical fiction, nonfiction, and genres like science fiction and fantasy. Freedom Forge Press's two imprints, Bellows Books and Apprentice Books, publish works for younger readers.

Find out more at www.FreedomForgePress.com.

Also Available Featuring Linda Harris Sittig

At nineteen, Ellen Canavan lives for the dream of her late father: to succeed in business. But being a woman in 1861, she finds the path to entrepreneurship blocked many times over. The threat of war, her mother's disapproval, and even a malicious arsonist threaten to limit the aspiring textile merchant to the status of impoverished Irish immigrant. As she travels from the factories of Philadelphia to the riverfront wharves of Savannah with her business mentor, James Nolan, the Civil War explodes amidst their blossoming love, and the two are separated. Can Ellen's undaunted, fiery strength guide her through a divided nation, or must she abandon her dream in order to save her own life?

Whether we struggle against an external oppressor or battle our mind for control, humans desire freedom. In Forging Freedom Volume 2, nineteen authors examine freedom--and the situations that threaten it. Some of the stories are true, based on experience or history handed down through the generations. Others are imagined--mere stretches of reality and the ways it might be pulled away from freedom. This eclectic mix of freedom-themed stories covers the spectrum, including such ideas as longing for one's native land, earning communal grading, being forced to donate an organ, battling mental illness, and fighting for the right to give birth to a child regardless of its genetics.

Also Available From Freedom Forge Press

Freedom is not the natural state of man. There are always those who would exert power over others. Too often people are willing to trade their individual freedoms for the fleeting promise of security or for "the greater good." But freedom should never be sacrificed. Thirty-five authors living in seven countries tackle this issue in Forging Freedom—a collection of stories from our contributors' personal and family histories; stories as people pictured today's headlines and imagined how freedom tomorrow may be impacted; stories imagining freedom from a world suspending reality or far into a hopeful future. Our contributors hail from across the globe, united in the idea that freedom is the right state of man. It is something that must be preserved, fought for, and won. And when it lost, freedom is something that must be forged once again.

This anthology is for those who appreciate the freedom in our lives. For those who have seen their freedoms stolen and those who see freedom at risk. For those who have sacrificed their time and energies and risked their lives to preserve freedom. Those who believe that humanity has not yet reached its peak, that there is more to the world than we can currently imagine. This anthology is for those who gaze at the stars and wonder.

CPSIA information can be obtained
at www.ICGtesting.com
Printed in the USA
LVHW012009021219
639196LV00003B/207